DAMIEN

BOOK THREE OF THE PERFECTLY INDEPENDENT SERIES

AMANDA SHELLEY

Editor: Renita McKinney
A Book A Day
www.abookaday.biz
Editor: Sue Soares
SJS Editorial Services
https://www.facebook.com/sue.soares71
Proof Reader: Julie Deaton
Deaton Author Services
http://jdproofs.wixsite.com/jddeaton
Cover Design: Amy Queau
Q Design Covers and
https://www.qcoverdesign.com

Visit my website at
www.amandashelley.com

CONNECT WITH AMANDA SHELLEY

Want to be the first to know about upcoming sales and new releases? Make sure you sign up for my newsletter as well as connect with me on social media and your favorite retail store.

Website:
www.amandashelley.com
Newsletter:
https://bit.ly/3iyENe6
Facebook:
https://www.facebook.com/authoramandashelley/
Instagram:
https://www.instagram.com/authoramandashelley/
Twitter:
https://twitter.com/AmandShelley
Reader's Group:
https://www.facebook.com/groups/AmandasArmyofReaders/
Tik Tok:
https://www.tiktok.com/@authoramandashelley
Amazon:
https://www.amazon.com/author/amandashelley
Goodreads:

https://www.goodreads.com/author/show/
19713563.Amanda_Shelley
Book Bub:
https://www.bookbub.com/profile/amanda-shelley

ABOUT THE BOOK

When I walk into the diner, all I'm looking for is a decent meal. As a civil engineer for the largest project on campus, I just want to eat in peace. I'm happy to find this hidden gem since students are scarce. Don't get me wrong, coeds on campus are beautiful, but I was over that scene when I graduated three years ago. I need to finish this job and move onto the next one by the end of the year.

Then Vanessa walks up with a simple smile and takes my breath away. The next thing I know, I'm making every excuse imaginable to dine with this intriguing woman. She's not only smart and sexy, but she's also completely focused on reaching the goals she set for herself.

The more I get to know her, the more I know she's the one. I just have to find a way to make her deviate from her perfectly laid plans and take a chance on me.

1

DAMIEN

KNOWING I have time before my first meeting, I pop into the diner to grab some breakfast. I've become a regular here over the past month or so, since taking the job as the site engineer for Columbia River University's newest housing project. At first, I had chosen this place for its convenience, but the amazing food and friendly waitress has me coming back for more each week.

Taking my usual spot at the counter so I can leave the booths for other patrons, I reach for the menu and stop as my phone buzzes with an incoming text.

Mal: Meeting got changed to 9 to meet with CRU.

Well, that just freed up my morning as it's only a little after six now. Sure, I've got plenty to do but knowing I'm no longer on a time constriction, I relax further into my seat and quickly tap out a response to thank her. Then I flag down the waitress rushing by to signal for a cup of coffee.

"Coming right up." She places her last order then grabs a cup for me. As she sets it in front of me, she offers, "If you're in a rush, I'll put in an order for your usual."

Already knowing the menu, I don't bother to pick it up. "My meeting was just cancelled, so let's change it up. I'll order a stack of pancakes with a side of bacon."

"Ohh... living dangerously." Her hazel eyes dance, and her bright smile has my heart picking up the pace. "Are you sure you can handle it?"

"I think I can manage," I say, patting my belly. "I might be getting soft in my old age... but I'm still able to pack it away, trust me."

Is it bad that I absolutely love the way she blatantly checks me out?

As her eyes peruse me, I take this moment to do the same to her. Her dark-blond hair is pulled into a long ponytail, and it swishes behind her back as her brows furrow, and her perfectly pink lips purse, taking her new task seriously. Damn, she's breathtaking. Sure, I'm only a few years older, but I don't think at twenty-six, I'd be considered an old man by any means, but I'll take this scrutiny any day if it means I have her full attention.

"Uh... I'd hardly say you're old."

"Well, I feel old in this town, now that I'm around college students again," I admit.

Raising a perfectly sculpted eyebrow, Vanessa, as I learned

from my first trip into the diner, punches a hip with her fist. "And just how long ago did you graduate, *old man*?"

Yep. It's conversations like this that have me coming back each morning. She never fails to entertain. Even with her face free of makeup, she's devastatingly gorgeous. But the thing is, from what little I've gotten to know about her, I'm not so sure she even knows.

But as those glorious hazel eyes continue to stare at me, I'm not able to contemplate this further. "Oh, just three years ago, but I didn't graduate from here. I went to the University of Washington."

"Oh... well, since you're such an old man, maybe I should get you the senior menu instead next time you come in."

"Well, I wouldn't go that far," I tease in return. "I'm not ready for the early bird specials or anything like that. But as I'm typically at work by seven, I do have an early bedtime these days... you know... adulting and all."

"Yeah, adulting and all... I'm here before six every morning as you know, so I hardly stay up late myself. But I'll admit I'm still a spring chicken compared to the likes of you. I get to attend classes so I can still work on that pesky degree so I can be a nurse when I grow up."

A nurse, that's interesting. She's never divulged much personal information, so I'll take what I can get.

Unfortunately, another customer comes in and grabs her attention, so I'm left to my own devices for the time being. She smiles apologetically, and I nod in understanding. She has a job to do, and I won't get in her way. I watch her quickly grab two menus and greet the other customers without missing a beat. Her genuine kindness for people will take her far in nursing.

Instead of staring at her like a fool, I distract myself by taking a drink from my coffee. Lifting the mug to my lips, I distinctly remember my first encounter with Vanessa.

I'd stopped in the diner that first week I'd come to town. I'd willingly moved when my company offered me a promotion. As a civil engineer, I'd taken the lead on this project and became the onsite engineer for the entire project. I had nothing tying me down and saw this as the opportunity of a lifetime.

I'd heard from my personal assistant Malorie, or as she prefers to be called Mal, that this diner was the best in town. Apparently, the college students usually stick to their side of town, near campus. The place was busy with their early morning rush, and I literally took one of the last places at the counter.

I remember watching in awe as this woman carefully stacked more plates than I thought anyone could hold onto her arm and carried it to a party of five patrons, without missing a beat. I watched her greet each guest with a smile on her face and made them feel as if they were home or a part of her family. When I was lucky enough to have her wait on me, her dazzling smile and beautiful hazel eyes lured me in from her simple words. "Hi! I'm Vanessa. Are you new in town? I don't think I've seen you around here before."

Of course I told her my name, and she handed me a menu before excusing herself to give me time to look it over. But as she walked away, I couldn't help but watch and notice her every move. She was busy that morning, so we didn't get much of a chance to talk. She waited on me like any other patron, and I left eager to be on my way to work. But as I look back on the last few weeks, I'd be lying if I didn't say she's a reason I've quickly become a regular.

No. I'm not a pervert or a creepy stalker. There's just something about Vanessa that's intriguing. She's wise beyond her years, yet is completely unaware of the attention she draws from the male customers in particular. Every once in a while, our eyes meet and linger a bit longer than usual, but then she shakes it off or is distracted with something, and I'm left wondering if it's all in my head.

"Everything okay, Damien?" Vanessa's sexy voice brings me out of my thoughts as she sets my pancakes and bacon in front of me.

"Uh... sure." I shake my head to regain my thoughts. But my eyes linger on hers longer than necessary as I wonder if I'm the only one affected in this situation.

"Need more coffee?" she offers, holding up the carafe as she awaits my answer.

What the hell is wrong with me? She's young, probably has a boyfriend, and is likely having the time of her life in college. There's no way she'd be interested in the likes of me. Besides, I've got the biggest project of my career to focus on and don't need any distractions.

Fuck. She said something. What is it?

Noticing the carafe in her hands, I nod. "Sure, I'd love some more."

She tops off my mug, and I'm blessed with another heart-stopping smile. "What's on the agenda for conquering the world today?"

Somehow, she's managed to get me to talk more about myself than she'll ever divulge about hers. She knows I've moved to town to work on the new housing project for CRU but not a lot of the specifics. When it's been slower, I've even talked with a few other older patrons who are regulars; the old men seem to be busy bodies and like to know what's brought a stranger like me into the diner on such a regular basis.

I'm young. I'd rather not cook if I'm only cooking for me, and the food here is great. The fact that I enjoy the company of the beautiful woman before me, well... I've kept that part to myself.

Trying not to sound too cocky, I shrug my shoulders and respond to Vanessa's question. "Well... you know... making sure everything runs smoothly and no major hiccups is considered a win."

Rolling her eyes, she swats with her free hand at the air between us. "Oh, I'm sure you'll do much more than that. I happened to drive by that site, and it's quite the undertaking your company's doing. It'll be great to see affordable student housing help families in the future."

"It sure is. I just hope we can keep meeting our deadlines and complete it under budget. So far so good. But I don't want to jinx anything," I tease as I knock on the wood counter.

"I'm sure you'll do just fine." She reaches out and pats my shoulder across the counter as if she's done it a million times. Electricity zings through my spine, and I try like hell not to show my reaction to her. Holy shit, what is she doing to me? I'm not some preteen experiencing his first crush.

Not being able to find words to exit my mouth, I just nod in agreement as I stare into her eyes. Damn. They've got flecks of gold and a darker ring around the exterior. I've never noticed that before.

"Van, your order's up," someone calls from the kitchen, and we both break whatever spell she's cast on me in that instant.

Impishly, she grins. "I'd better get back to work. Let me know if you need anything."

As I finish my meal, I force my eyes not to follow her as she works. It's damn hard, but somehow, I manage with only a few glances when she's directly in front of me.

When a couple in a booth to my left make Vanessa laugh, I can't help but turn to appreciate the sound. In the short time I've known her, I've seen her laugh a handful of times, but this is a genuine, almost doubled-over laugh. Whatever was said must be something because as I look closer, I see unshed tears about to roll down her cheek.

What could they have said to get a reaction like that?

I recognize the couple Vanessa's talking with as the ones that got engaged the morning of the championship game. I'd come in wanting to beat the crowd for the morning rush and got something my sister would write in one of her books. The dude planned his proposal to perfection and clearly, she didn't see it coming.

Don't get me wrong. I think it's fantastic for someone to

proclaim their love publicly. But I'm not so sure I'd want to draw so much attention to myself.

My sister Dani would flip her shit to see something of that epic proportion go down like it did. Being a romance writer, she'd likely pull out her nearest notebook and jot it all down so she could use it in a book. But I'm not so sure I'd want to draw so much attention to myself.

I watch as Vanessa swipes a finger under each eye as she shakes her head and says something I can't quite catch. Then she bats the air as if she wants the guy to stop saying what he's saying, so she can catch her breath, but she continues to laugh as he explains.

When another customer draws her attention, she excuses herself to move on to help them. I hear the girl call out, "Go. We can catch up later. Tell Syd we'll meet at eight." Then she looks to the guy in the booth beside her and giggles some more.

Vanessa nods in agreement but soon gets busy with the customer and their needs. She briskly walks past me, but I catch her smile in my direction as she says, "Be right with you." Within a minute, she returns with a container of powdered sugar, and I'm blessed with another brilliant smile as she makes her delivery.

When she returns, I'm mid-bite.

"Need anything else, Damien?"

The way she says my name sends a shiver up my spine.

"Uh..." *Stop being such a blubbering idiot.* I inwardly scold but manage, "I'm good," even though it sounds way too gravelly to sound natural.

Of course, this gives her reason to pause with scrutiny.

Oh, geez! What the fuck is wrong with me?

"Are you sure?" When I don't say anything, she asks, "Ready for the check?"

"Sounds good." I go through the motions of pulling out my wallet and handing her my card before she can return.

As she runs the card, my phone buzzes in my pocket.

My good mood disperses in an instant when I read the words, and my blood turns to ice.

Mal: There's been an accident at the site. Called 911. Waiting on their arrival now.

Fuck, I need to be there.

Without another thought, I'm on my feet and rushing out the door.

2

VANESSA

AS I TURN from running Damien's card, I see his face morph from jovial to downright dread. His fork clanks against his plate as he jumps to his feet. Before my mind can register to return his card, he's already out the door.

I rush to the door to follow him, but he's already dashed across the parking lot and jumping in his truck. When I step out onto the stoop, he's backing out and long gone before I can flag him down.

This isn't the first time a customer has left their card, but clearly something's wrong. Immediately, I'm paralyzed with fear as I'm brought back to the day I lost my parents. No one deserves a tragedy like that.

"Everything okay?" Tara asks as she meets me at the door. "Did he skip out on the bill?"

Shaking my head, I sigh. "No. There must be some emergency because he left his card in my hands. I couldn't even flag him down in the parking lot."

"I'm sure there's some explanation. Though the good news is he'll be back."

"Yeah," I slowly say as I stare in the direction he fled.

"Do you know where to find him?" Tara asks, raising her eyebrows, as if I should know what's going on in that crazy head of hers.

"Uh... I know where he works," I admit but still don't get why she's staring at me as if I should be following her train of thought. Tara's notorious for doing this. Half the time, I don't have a freaking clue what she's thinking.

This only earns me an eye roll. "Well... you could leave the card here and wait for his return or..." she trails off, and her eyes widen, expecting me to finish her thought for her.

"Or?" I prompt, clearly not following.

"Or..." she exaggerates for my benefit as if I'm slow on the uptake this morning. When I don't respond, she shakes her head exasperatedly. "Or... you could deliver it to him."

"Uh... why would I do that?" My words come out almost defensive.

"Oh, I don't know..." she practically singsongs. "Maybe because he's been coming here and flirting with you for the past month or so."

I scoff, "He does not."

"Uh... have you ever noticed he only sits in your section? He doesn't talk to me the way he does you, and his eyes certainly don't follow anyone else around the way he does with you."

Rolling my eyes, I can't help but laugh. "Tara, I've always known you've had a wild imagination, but I think you've lost it this time. Damien doesn't do any of those things."

"Oh, but he does." She smirks. "Just ask Jeff. He gets a front row show from the kitchen."

Walking back to the coffee maker, I shake my head. "You're delusional." But before she can prove her point and make this a public spectacle, I change the subject. "What's going on with you and that guy you met in here a few weeks ago? I've seen you on campus together. Did something come of it?"

"Oh, Keaton?" She waggles her brows as a huge grin splits her face. "Things are going good. I'm so glad I took him up on his offer of a date. We hit it off that first night and have been seeing each other since. Maybe you should try it some time, Van."

"Date Keaton?" I say obtusely. "I'm pretty sure he's taken by the look on that face of yours."

Tara sighs heavily. "It wouldn't hurt you to date, you know."

"I've got plenty going on in my life with Jules. I don't need anything more."

"You're a single mom, Van. Not dead. Besides, it might do you some good to live on the wild side and do something for yourself for a change."

She has a point, but I ignore it.

"Let's get back to work before Jeff lets us have it," I encourage as I slip Damien's card into my back pocket for safe-keeping. The jury's still out on whether or not I'll deliver the card myself. In the meantime, I'll hang on to it until the end of my shift in case he returns. Then I'll decide.

By the end of my shift, I've run through Tara's words at least a million times. Each time the bell rang signaling a new customer, my eyes darted to the door in hopes of catching sight of Damien. But no such luck.

Should I deliver his card to him? Or wait until he returns?

Hmmm... decisions... decisions.

As I pull out his card to place it in the register, my mind replays the events of this morning, and I make the snap decision to try to deliver it in person. There was something wrong, and I know I'll worry if I don't find out for myself what's going on. Besides, if I can't find him, I'll come back to the diner and put it in the safe.

Since his job site isn't too far out of my way, I head there after changing into a fresh shirt. I can easily head to class on time afterward. Typically, I use this time to study on campus, but a good deed won't put me too far behind. Besides, I'll feel better knowing everything's okay.

Pulling up to the site, I find Damien's truck parked haphazardly along the road as if he didn't have the time to properly park. The front end is closer to the curb, and it stands out as it's not quite parallel to the road, even though it's the only one parked there at the moment. Other construction vehicles are parked appropriately in the lot, but nothing else seems out of sorts.

Shoot. Should I have come?

I know I'd want my debit card, but maybe he doesn't need his as bad. Parking behind his truck, I take a moment to look for Damien before hopping out of my SUV. Across the parking lot is a construction trailer. I'm sure if I went in, I'd find where he is. But am I even allowed to be here?

In for a penny, in for a pound. I didn't come all this way for nothing.

Taking a fortifying breath, I calm my nerves and open the door to my SUV. Straightening my stance as I walk across the lot, I act as if I've been here a million times. When I get to the door of the trailer, I freeze, causing my newfound confidence to dwindle for a moment.

Do I knock or do I just walk in? I swear the last person who went in this building just walked in. It looks more like a school portable than a trailer as I get closer. My high school had one in much older condition where I was forced to take my foreign language.

Before I'm forced to decide, my decision is made for me. The door opens, and Damien walks out, startling me. I wasn't prepared to come face-to-face with him so quickly.

Shock covers his face as he clearly wasn't expecting me. Slowly, a grin forms, and his dark-brown eyes crinkle as he takes me in. "To what do I owe the pleasure of seeing you again this morning?"

"Uh..." I fumble for the words but eventually, they come to me. "You left in such a hurry. Is everything okay?"

With that, Damien grimaces. "Sorry about that. We had an accident onsite. I may have overreacted as it wasn't critical, but we had an ambulance on its way, and I felt I needed to be here."

"Oh, my. I hope everyone's all right."

He winces at some memory. "I had a member of my crew trip down some stairs and clearly break his leg." Damien sucks in a deep breath and shakes his head. "Bones clearly aren't meant to go that way. It's company policy to take an ambulance, but I'm sure he'll recover."

"I'm sorry to hear that," I whisper as I get lost in his eyes, so I don't miss when his expression turns to concern.

"Did you come all this way just to check on me?"

"Uh... you also left your debit card, and I thought you could use it," I admit in a shrug, then I reach into my back pocket to retrieve it.

"I guess I was distracted. I'm sure I would've figured it out eventually when I went to eat my next meal," he replies sheepishly. "I'm sure I would've remembered... eventually."

"I'm glad I could save you one less worry," I admit, remembering the forlorn look on his face with his abrupt departure. "You didn't need to worry about cancelling your card or anything for it being lost. We all know how much it sucks replacing them."

"True." His deep voice carries as he nods in agreement. "I appreciate this."

Rocking awkwardly from my heels to my toes, I'm not sure what to say or do next. I should just walk away and head to campus, but I'm not ready to leave yet either. I manage a quiet, "You're welcome," in response, but I'm still unsure what to do.

"Have you had lunch yet?" Damien grins.

"I ate at the diner while on my last break. I have class in an hour, but I thought I'd drop this by first."

"Another time then." He shrugs.

Is he just being polite or is he saddened by my response?

I'm sure he's just being polite, right? Why would he be sad? That makes no sense.

"Well, then…" I rock forward again, trying to rid myself of the awkwardness I'm suddenly feeling. Obviously, there's no reason to stay, and I have class soon. "I'll let you get back to work."

Damien's eyes lock onto mine, and I swear he tethers me in the spot. I can't walk away from him, yet standing here staring at him like a lost schoolgirl isn't an option either.

"Can I walk you to your car?" he suggests with the most beautiful lopsided smile. As if on instinct, my lips turn to mirror his. Before I can make an even bigger fool of myself, thankfully, someone walks toward us and stops me.

"Oh," I play off my craziness. "There's no need. I'm just parked there on the street." I point to my SUV and will myself to move away from him.

A playful smile teases at his lips as if he can see through my antics. "Well, then, I guess I'll see you in the morning. Be sure to save me a seat at the counter."

"You got it," I say as I turn in the direction of my car.

But I stop when he says, "Thanks again, Vanessa. I'm looking forward to tomorrow."

My hand moves as if it has a mind of its own to wave at him as I say, "See ya then." Realizing how silly I must look, I force myself to remain calm as I walk to my vehicle, get in, and drive away without looking back. God, did I want to look back, but what good would come of it?

LATER THAT EVENING as I put Julia to bed, that look on his face before I walked away replays on a loop. Was Damien asking me out? No. That's crazy. I'm sure he's just being friendly since I brought his card.

"Can you read me another bedtime story, Momma?" Julia asks in the sweetest voice, trying to get a third story for the night out of me. I'll admit my nearly five-year-old has some game, but I'm a pro at reading her—so her cuteness won't work on me—tonight anyway.

God, I still can't believe she'll be five in just a little over a week.

"Jules, I've already read two. I think that's plenty. Before long, you're going to be reading to me." She stifles a big yawn, and I know I'm right. "I'll tell you what. You sleep now, and if you're up for it tomorrow, I'll read the next story to you."

"Okay, Momma. Goodnight," she yawns heavily. But of course, if I call her on it, she'll claim she isn't tired until she's blue in the face. As much as I hate to admit it, she's so much like me, it's crazy.

As I exit her room, I leave her door open a crack, so she can see the light on from the hall. I honestly doubt she'll last another two minutes, but I've learned by keeping it open, she's less likely to get out of bed.

When I make it to the living room, I find my twin Vince, sprawled across the couch.

"You get her down?" he asks as I settle into my cozy chair and prop my feet on the leather ottoman in front of me.

"She tried her best to go for three stories tonight. I swear when she starts reading herself, she'll be sneaking books late into the night with a flashlight if we don't watch out."

Vince cocks his head in my direction, and I already know what he's thinking, but of course, the brat that he is, he feels the need to mention it aloud. "Uh, wasn't that your MO as a kid? If I recall... Mom and Dad actually took your flashlight a time or two to get you to sleep at a decent time. Thank God, we never had to share a room because your light would've annoyed the hell out of me."

Instead of dignifying a response, I change the subject and ask about his girlfriend as I look around the room. She should be here for dinner but is nowhere to be seen at the moment. "Where's Syd?"

"I'm right here," she answers for him as she brings two plates with cinnamon rolls. "If you want one, I'll go back and grab another," she says as she offers a plate to me. Her bright hazel eyes dance, knowing hardly anyone refuses her baked goods.

"You know I can't turn these down," I tease, reaching for the plate she offers. Then she hands the other to Vince before disappearing into the kitchen.

Sydney and Vince started dating a few months ago but knowing my brother doesn't do things halfway, I'm fairly certain these two will be in it for the long haul like my parents were.

God, I miss them, but I'm sure as they look down at us, they'd be proud of what we've become.

Just as I get my first mouthful, Vince asks, "Syd's been

keyed up about your girls' night tonight. I'm still kinda shocked she talked you into joining them."

"I won't be staying out too late, trust me. I still have to work in the morning, but as I don't have class after my shift for a change, I think I can manage a little less sleep for one night." I can't say I've ever been more thankful for a professor to cancel class for their daughter's wedding than I am tonight. "Are you sure you don't mind staying with Jules?"

"Vanny, you deserve a life. I'm glad you're finally taking Syd up on the offer to hang with her roommates. Abby's only going to be here for another month, and I know you and Chloe will hit it off."

I look to the kitchen to see where Sydney is before asking, "Has Syd mentioned anything about finding another place to live?"

Vince shakes his head. "No. She's starting to stress over it, too."

I lower my voice, so she won't overhear. "I was gonna mention this earlier... but have you considered asking her to move in with us? I don't want to put any pressure on you, but she's over here almost every night, and it's kinda pointless to spend the money on rent when she's already sharing your room as it is."

Vince's jaw drops.

Okay. Apparently, it's too soon for them, and I shouldn't have said anything.

When his face suddenly slits into a wide grin, I know I wasn't off track. "Were your Spidey senses going off? I was actually going to talk to you about this tomorrow."

Yeah, we have that weird twin connection people talk about. Not about everything mind you, but I'm sure it has more to do with the fact that we're best friends, beyond just being twins.

"Anyone need anything else while I'm up?" Sydney asks from the kitchen.

Vince looks to me, and I shake my head before he says, "We're good, Syd. Just come and join us." To me, he says in a lower voice, "Mind if we talk more about this tomorrow?"

Rolling my eyes as I'm not sure what there is to talk about, I shrug. "Sure."

When Sydney rejoins us, Vince puts his legs on the floor and sits up so she can join him on the couch. The room remains silent as we devour the rolls in front of us. I can bake, but I have nothing on Sydney. *Maybe if she lives here, I'll learn her recipe?*

When I finish chewing my next bite, I ask, "What time are we meeting your roommates?"

"As soon as we finish here, I'm ready to leave when you are." She's wearing a pair of jeans and a black form-fitting sweater. Her red hair is down, and she's only wearing mascara if anything at all. I wish I looked that good all the time.

Knowing I don't have anyone to impress, I look down at the dark skinny jeans and blue top I've worn all day. "I'll only be a few minutes. I just need to run a brush through my hair and brush my teeth after eating this."

"Are you sure Drew doesn't mind being our driver? I can easily take out Jules' car seat and be the DD for the night."

"Uh, no, you can't. This is a girls' night and trust me...

Drew is more than happy to make sure we're properly escort-ed." Then she looks to Vince. "He's hanging with his room-mate Grey tonight back at their apartment, while we get our groove on. Abby only has a few weeks left on campus, and he doesn't want to interfere with our girls' night—or so he claims. But I'll believe it when I see it."

"Are you sure I'm not intruding on your time with Abby?" I offer as an out.

"No way—You're not bailing on us." Syd sternly lets me know she's not listening to any excuse I come up with.

So, I sigh and shrug an explanation. "Just checking."

Syd raises a perfectly sculpted brow in my direction. "Besides your birthday, when was the last time you went out?"

Um... never.

Not really, but it's not like I frequent bars or anything. I've just turned twenty-one. Being a single mom makes my social life pretty limited and with everything Vince and I have gone through since graduation, it hasn't been on my list of priorities either.

Syd takes my silence as victory. "Okay, Missy, let's get this show on the road. I haven't been dancing in a while, and I'm ready to get my groove on."

"Is there something I should be worried about?" Vince teases.

Rolling her eyes, Sydney swats Vinny's shoulder. "I rarely get a night off from behind the bar on a night there's a decent band coming in to play. If we don't get a move on, we'll be stuck in a crowd at the door. I may have connections, but I'd rather snag a booth if we can."

The bar scene isn't my crowd—obviously. My baby girl is a constant reminder of my one and only wild night. But I have zero regrets—as she's one of the best things to ever happen to me. As a single mom, I rarely get a chance to just unwind and relax, let alone do something for myself. Besides, Vince is just as adamant I go, so if I stay home, I'll never hear the end of it.

Before leaving, I peek on Julia one last time to make sure she's down for the night. Vince is the best uncle there ever was, so I don't have to worry about leaving her with him, but as Mom, there are some things I just do.

Vince and Sydney chat at the door as they wait for me to be ready. After kissing Sydney goodbye, he turns to me. "Don't worry, Vanny. I've got this. If either of you need anything, I'm only a phone call away."

He pats me on the shoulder, which earns him a dramatic eye roll, and I can't help but remind him, "You know... baby brother, I'm sure I can handle myself. Besides, I've got Syd with me. If anyone gives us any shit, I'm sure she knows a bouncer or three that'll take care of them."

Vince chuckles at my antics. "Oh... I have no doubt the two of you can handle yourselves." He looks to Syd then back to me. "But big sister or not, I'm still your brother, and I love the hell out of you. I just want you to be happy, too, okay?"

"God, you make it sound as if I don't have any life... Come on, Syd. Let's go before he reminds me how boring I am."

Sydney kisses Vince one last time with a smile on her face at our sibling banter. Then she turns to me with a devilish grin. "Are you ready to go paint the town?"

Knowing she's only doing this to get a rise out of Vince, I add, "Sure. Let's do this."

IT FEELS amazing to just let loose and dance again. Knowing I have an early morning, I'm only on my second drink as we take a break from the dance floor. I used to love dancing for hours at high school, but since having Julia, I haven't had the opportunity.

"Uh... don't look now, Van." Chloe giggles as she not-so-discreetly looks in the direction behind me. "But I think you have a special admirer. That guy's been watching you since we arrived, but I'm not sure he'll be bold enough to make any moves."

Knowing she has to be out of her mind, I look in the direction she's trying not to point out. The only person I see is Vince's friend Ryan. "Oh, that's just Ryan. One of Vince's friends. I'm sure he just recognizes me."

Sydney speaks up over the crowd. "Oh, I've met him. He's a great guy." Then she looks closer in his direction. "But I'm sure Chloe's right. He's totally checking you out."

"I'm sure you're mistaken," I brush off. Ryan and I have known each other since freshman year. He's the only one Vince opened up to, and they're pretty close. "I'm sure he's just playing the protective brother role, since Vince isn't here."

"Maybe... but I swear... the way he's watching you isn't just being brotherly. The man seriously has the hots for you," Chloe states before taking another sip of her margarita.

"Uh... I have no idea what you're talking about," I dismiss. "Besides... I'm not sure he's my type," I qualify, hoping they'll drop the subject. I barely have time for myself, let alone throw someone else into the mix. Who on earth would want to hitch their ride to my crazy?

Sydney looks from Ryan to me, then boldly asks as only she can, "So, if you're not interested in him, what kind of guy *are* you interested in?"

Suddenly, I see beautiful dark-brown eyes and sandy-brown hair that's longer on the top and buzzed on the sides. Chiseled cheekbones that align perfectly with his square jaw. There's just the perfect amount of scruff on them. Not quite clean shaven, but at least a day or two worth of growth. I seriously don't know how he manages to uphold that look. Maybe he shaves on my day off?

"Van? Everything okay?" Sydney asks with concern, breaking me from my revelry.

Why the hell did Damien flash before my eyes?

I barely know the man. He's got a career to worry about and wouldn't want a built-in family at his age, I'm sure. He's become a regular customer. That's all. I'm sure he's just a friendly guy, and I'm reading too much into things.

But he might have been trying to ask you out earlier today?

"Van?" Sydney waves a hand in front of my face.

If that isn't embarrassing, I don't know what is. "I... uh... guess I don't have a type."

"Oh, sell that to someone who didn't just see you venture off into LaLa Land. I won't push you for details because if you're anything like Vince, I know you'll reveal it in your own time."

Shaking my head in denial, I use my go-to excuse when it comes to dating. "I've got school, Jules, and plenty to keep me busy. Why the heck would I want to throw dating into the mix?"

"Uh... because you're not dead yet?" Abby surprises me with her response. "Trust me, I thought there was no time for dating before I met Drew. I was one hundred percent focused on school. But little did I know how much I was missing."

"But Jules," I protest.

"I'm not saying you have to go out and marry the next guy you meet. But you're young and beautiful, and there are plenty of guys who won't care that you're a single mom." She pats me on the shoulder as she forces my eye contact to ensure I hear what she's saying.

I raise an eyebrow to prove my point. "When was the last time you met a college student who willingly dated a single mom? Uh... the last I checked, no one is lining up at my door. Hell, I haven't dated since I got pregnant with Jules."

As I look around my table of friends, I'm met with wide eyes and dropped mouths.

Okay. So, I may have overshared.

Sydney's the first to regain her composure. "That's all the more reason to put yourself out there, Van. You may not find Mr. Forever, but nothing's stopping you from enjoying yourself either. I'm not saying you need to even find a Mr. Right-Now, but you're young and deserve to put yourself first for once, too.

Anyone who isn't willing to get to know you *and* Julia is the one missing out."

I release a loud huff. "But my life is complicated," I protest.

"Not really," Chloe encourages. "I have a friend back home who's a single mom. She doesn't date often, but she will go out and have fun every once in a while. Anyone who doesn't understand her kids will always come first, doesn't get a second date. But she puts herself out there because she realizes she has more to offer than just being someone's mom."

Sydney pats my knee, so no one else will notice. "We're not saying you should hook up with some random guy. But after all you and Vince have gone through, just make sure you allow yourself some things for you, too."

She's right. But I'm not quite willing to admit it. Between Jules and losing my parents after graduation, Vince and I have been in survival mode. We've both put our personal lives on hold to keep from being the statistic my parents drilled into me the moment I found out I was pregnant. I *will* graduate from college on time, and I *will* raise an amazing daughter. But when is it okay for me to focus on my other needs, too?

The band starts a new song and Chloe gasps, "Ohmigod. This is one of my favorites. I have to dance to this." She grabs Abby's hand and doesn't spare us a second glance.

"You go right ahead!" Sydney hollers as they dash to the dance floor. "We'll be here when you get back."

When it's just the two of us, she turns to me. "Look, I'm not trying to pressure you. I just want you to be happy. I'll support you no matter what. *But if you ever need a babysitter*, I will volunteer any time I'm able. I'll even do my best to wrangle in Vince and his brotherly antics if he throws any BS your way."

"Oh, God." I laugh at the realization. "I can just imagine what it'll be like should I ever decide to date again. I thought my dad was bad. But even back in high school, Vince was protective. Did I ever tell you about the time I had a guy over one afternoon to watch a movie and he decided it was best to jump between us on the couch to 'watch' the movie with us?" Yes, I used air quotes because with him squeezed between us, none of us were comfortable watching the movie. Needless to say, I never heard from the poor guy after that day again.

"Oh, no, he didn't?" Sydney cringes.

When I nod, she rolls her eyes. "Though I can totally see him doing that. What a stinker."

"You can say that again," I agree. "But let's not remind him, or he's apt to do it again. I already have enough worries without his overprotectiveness getting in the way."

"If he becomes too much of an issue, you let me handle him," Sydney teases. "I'm sure I can think of something."

Knowing Sydney's reputation for putting people in their place, I have no doubts.

3

VANESSA

OKAY, I'm officially old. We barely stay out until midnight, but my alarm going off at five this morning is brutal. I make it to work with time to spare, but I may as well hook that carafe of coffee I'm passing out to customers into an IV for all the good my one cup this morning is doing for me.

I've mastered the chipper waitress act, so I'm sure no one else will notice how tired I am, but I'm counting down the minutes until the end of my shift. I plan to go home and nap before Julia needs to be picked up from daycare. Sure, I've managed many a sleepless night when she was an infant, but after getting used to a full night's sleep regularly, I'm out of practice, and a date with my bed sounds absolutely perfect.

My back is turned when the bell rings, signaling a new customer. But the electricity that zings up my spine leaves little doubt who has entered. Only one person has ever had this effect on me. I know it will only be a matter of seconds before I smell his mouthwatering aftershave that's subtle to most but almost toxic to me. It's like I can't get it out of my head. Not that I'm complaining. It's freaking delicious and makes me want to buy some of my own, just so I can sniff it without looking like a crazy stalker, anytime I choose.

When I turn, I do my best to greet Damien the way I would any other customer. "Good morning. Need a menu? Or will it be your usual?"

Damien glances at the bulky watch he wears and shrugs. "I've got time. So... I think I'll grab some waffles with strawberries and a side of sausage today... and if you don't mind, I'll take a cup of coffee while I wait."

Reaching for a cup, I say, "Coming right up," as I pour. Once it's full, I pass it across the counter to him. "Anything else?"

"No, thanks," he replies quickly but hesitates, which catches my attention.

"Everything okay?"

I'm surprised when he fumbles over his words. "I... uh... wanted to thank you for bringing my debit card to me yesterday. I'm sure I would've remembered eventually. But it was one less thing to think about yesterday."

"No worries," I quickly assure him as I brush a loose strand of hair behind my ear. "It was on my way to campus."

"I know, but it was still nice all the same." He smiles as he holds my gaze with his dark-brown eyes. I'm not sure I could look away if I tried.

Unfortunately, I have to because Jeff hollers from the kitchen. "Van! Order's up!"

"That's my cue," I stupidly say aloud as I unwillingly break my eye contact with Damien to deliver my next order.

Instead of returning to the counter to talk to Damien like I want to, I force myself to check on all my customers as well as the new ones who have walked in the door behind him. I refill a few drinks and place another order before returning to Damien to give him his.

As I approach, I ask my usual question of him since I learned he was the lead engineer for the campus housing project. "So, how are you conquering the world today?"

This earns me a full smile and a laugh that makes my spine tingle. "Well. I've got meetings today, but I'm conquering it one bit at a time. Maybe someday I'll manage to be done. But my to-do list never ends."

I can't help it. I laugh with him. "I can totally relate. I swear, just as I get mine to look relatively short, something is always added to it."

"When you're not working, or going to school, is there anything you like to do around here for fun?"

Hang out with my daughter. But I'm not ready for that conversation just yet. It's amazing how often people's opinion of me changes when they find out that tidbit. I swear they either judge me for being promiscuous or act as if I've lost my youth tragically... as if Julia's a burden. I know loss, trust me. But being Julia's mom is the biggest blessing I could ever ask for.

"Uh... I don't have much of a life," I admit. It's partially the truth. I don't have a social life outside of my family. "I guess I read and hang out with friends."

Damien scrutinizes my reaction. His eyes lock onto mine, and I swear they burrow deep into my soul. I'm not quite sure what he finds because I'm surprised by his response. "What's your favorite book?"

"Uh... that's like asking a mom to choose her favorite child. You just can't do that." Of course, I have it easy only having one but still, I wouldn't be able to choose if there were more. My mom used to cop out and say, "I love the one I'm with the most." To get us to snuggle her more.

Damien nods in agreement. "True. Being of four, my mom never chooses, either."

Four kids? That's a lot. "Are you the oldest?" I ask curiously.

"Nope. I'm third in line. Derek gets that spot, then Dani. Davis is the baby."

"Wait. Your mom had four boys? And each of you start with the letter D?"

"Nope. Dani's short for Danika." He chuckles. "Though growing up, she was just as feisty as us boys. I'm sure Mom had her hands full."

"I'm sure. It was just me and Vince growing up. But being twins, our parents were kept busy."

"I see we have something in common..." A smile pulls at Damien's lips. "Our moms like to keep our initials the same."

Rolling my eyes at how we were always called Vinnie and Vanny, I have to agree. But now, I'd give anything to be called that one more time by my parents. I guess that's why I've stuck with it when I'm alone with Vince, too. "Yeah. I guess you're right. But there are worse things."

"True. Is... uh... everything all right? You looked lost for a minute there."

I add perceptive to my growing list of traits for Damien.

"Yeah." I shrug. "I'm fine." But then I change the subject back to him. "Did your mom ever call you by the wrong name?"

"Always. But she made up for it by just listing us off, to make sure none were forgotten. It was always Derek, Dani, Dame, and Davis... Get in here. It didn't matter if some of us were gone or not. When she got out the list, you just came because she likely meant you."

"That's fantastic. I'll have to remember that. Were you the one most likely in trouble?" I tease.

"No. That would be Dani. She'd always be late to something because her nose was stuck in a book."

"I love your sister already," I tease, completely able to relate.

"She's still that way. I'm sure you'd get along fine." He seems to think about something for a moment, but then adds, "If you can't tell me what your favorite book is, can you at least tell me the genre?"

"Hmmm... let's see..." I tap my chin as I look to the ceiling for the answer. "I read a little of everything. I read romance, sci-fi, suspense. But when I get the chance to read anything other than a textbook lately, I've been into romance of some sort, though that's still a wide genre. It's got to be light and easy to follow, so I don't have to follow the plot so precisely, like I do when I read a Dan Brown novel or something like that. Don't get me wrong, I love having to figure things out, but I love my brain candy, too."

"Okay... note to self." Damien chuckles. "You and Dani would be the best of friends should you ever talk books."

Since that's my only social life, I can talk books all day long. "I'm sure I could handle that. There's nothing better than actually talking with someone who reads like I do," I agree.

"I'll keep that in mind," he says as he cuts a piece of his waffle off, dabs it in the whipped cream, and takes a bite.

Turning the tables, I decide it's time to learn more about him. "What about you? What do you do in your spare time?"

As he finishes his bite, he murmurs, "Hmmmm. I'm new around here, so I can't say I've done all that much. I love spending time in the snow, going kayaking on the Sound in the summer. I like being outdoors but am also fine with just hanging at my house and tinkering around there."

"Tinkering, eh? What does that entail?"

"It's not that exciting, trust me. As a kid, I always loved taking things apart and putting them back together. I guess that's how I ended up as an engineer. But as an adult, I have to say I've been remodeling the house I'm flipping when I finish this job."

"That sounds interesting. What made you take on that venture, alongside your huge job on campus?"

"Well, I didn't want to live in an apartment with a bunch of college kids—no offense. But they're loud. So, I started looking for a house to rent. But when I realized I could buy one for less than the cost of rent, I decided to use my downtime to flip the house when I'm done. I can either keep it as a rental myself or sell it when the time comes. Either way, I'm building equity and keeping myself busy."

Holy crap. That sounds like a lot of work, though Vince and I bought a house for the same reason. It's way cheaper to buy than rent in this town. And we needed a place to raise Julia. "You certainly are."

"Speaking of busy." Damien clears his throat and locks his eyes on mine. "Do you have any plans tomorrow?"

Did he just ask me out?

My heart rate spikes, and my hands sweat.

Was it just last night that I was having a conversation with Sydney about possibly dating again?

Just as I'm about to say no, I remember Julia's birthday party.

Shoot. There's no way I can make plans when I have a house full of people coming over tomorrow. Who knows when the party will end? And Vince and Sydney have plans tomorrow evening. I'm sure my face falls when I admit, "Uh, yeah. I have a family thing going on."

Damien shrugs it off. "I completely understand. Family first. Always."

If only he knew how true that is.

But I like this carefree and playful side of myself when I'm around him, so I'm not ready to spill my guts entirely to him. "Yep," I admit.

"I'd like to take you out as a way of thanking you for your help yesterday," he offers.

Shoot. Did I read this wrong?

Is this not a date?

God, this is what I get for even thinking about dating last night.

I shrug off my disappointment. "There's no need. We're all good."

Damien's face falls for a fraction of a second but then he regains his composure. "Okay, then."

Unfortunately, I can't question him about this further because Jeff hollers, "Van, order's up," and I'm forced back to my reality. By the time I get a chance to return to him, he's finished his meal and Tara has rung him up, so he doesn't have to wait for me.

But what if he was asking me out, and I was just too obtuse to do anything about it? Crap. I told him we're all good... Now, he probably thinks I'm not interested. What the heck do I do now?

4

DAMIEN

WELL, that went over like a lead balloon. I finally get her talking and feel comfortable enough to ask her out, and I make it sound like a pity date. No wonder she blew me off. I've been wanting to ask her out for some time but never felt the timing was right. But to make it sound like it was returning a favor? Could I be more of a jackass?

Unfortunately, my mind replays my mishap on a loop throughout the day. I'm so freaking distracted when OSHA shows up for a surprise inspection, it takes me a minute to figure out what's going on. Talk about getting caught with your pants down. I show the inspector where my employee tripped. Thankfully, he doesn't find negligence as far as safety is concerned. In the end, he basically deems the poor guy just had a case of dumb luck. Of course, with a labor and industries claim, I've spent more time than I had filling out paperwork, so even though I'm not behind—technically—I feel as if I am.

Thank God, Mal had most of it covered, and I just had to look a lot of it over to sign off on it.

When I'm finally able to call it a day, I'm still out of sorts. I've never had difficulty asking girls out before. I've never been what some would call a player, but I've had my share of interested girls. I've spent my early twenties young, single, and ready for fun. Now that I'm growing out of that scene, I'll admit substance is a great quality to look for in a relationship.

Hell, Vanessa might think I'm a dinosaur and not even be interested. For all I know, that was her way of letting me down easy.

But why did she seem disappointed when she had other plans if she isn't interested?

The better question is why am I still thinking about this?

As I make my way into my kitchen from parking my truck in the garage, I toe off my work shoes and realize I might be too keyed up to work on installing the baseboard in my master bathroom now that the tile is set. There's no doubt I'll mismeasure, and the entire night will turn into a cluster fuck.

Maybe I could use my pent-up frustration to demo the kitchen cabinets as new ones are set to arrive next week. Hopefully, one of the guys from my crew won't mind picking up a side job to help install them. Some things are just more efficient as a two-person job.

In my bedroom, I change into a pair of well-worn jeans I only use for construction and a loose black t-shirt. I grab my old work boots from my closet and sit at the end of my king-size bed to lace them up. I don't spend much on myself, but

I'm over college mismatched furniture. This bedroom set was one of my first purchases when I finally got my first real job in my career. Well, that and actual matching living room furniture.

I swear I had the world's ugliest couch in college. It was comfortable, but it was like a ninety-year-old picked it out. It was baby blue with pink flowers and ruffles on the arms. Everyone used to make fun of it—until they had the pleasure of sitting on it. Then they could overlook the design for its ability to pull you in and put you at ease in an instant they settled in, they never complained again. In my defense, it came with the apartment as it was heavy as fuck to move.

Making my way out to the kitchen, I'm proud of the accomplishments I've had with this house. I still need to finish the wood floors, but those will have to wait until I finish all the other projects. No sense in scratching them unnecessarily. Thankfully, I make fast work and get a few cabinets dismantled from the wall in no time. I've just finished putting them out of the way in the garage when my phone rings.

Seeing it's my brother Davis, I quickly answer it. Now that he's doing his internship at Oregon Health and Science University, he's always busy. I swear we may live closer now than we have since living with our parents but getting him to take a break is almost considered a miracle.

I can't help but smile into the phone. "What's up, man?"

"Just checking. Are you gonna be around this weekend? Dani wants to come down and visit the two of us but apparently, I'm the one who's better at returning her call. What the hell have you been up to? You know it's bad when she's calling me."

Yeah, he's right. He's lucky that he even looks at his phone for personal calls.

"Shit. She called yesterday morning when I'd just gotten to the job site after the accident, and I completely forgot to call her back."

"Wait... everything okay?" Davis asks with concern.

Shaking my head at the sheer luck of it, I sigh. "Yeah, a crew member fell down some stairs. It was a gnarly break, but the doctors say it was clean and should heal within a month or so. They were able to reset it without surgery. Though I'd want some serious drugs if I were him."

"But you weren't hurt?" he clarifies.

"No... I hadn't made it to the site. It was just a fluke accident." Thank God, it hadn't been more than that.

"Did Dani say when she was coming?" I ask, changing the subject because there's no need to jinx anything by talking about it further.

"She just said she's meeting someone about her books here in Portland. Since you live so close now, she requests our presence for dinner. Apparently, she and Luke are only coming down for the day."

"Wow... requests... huh... maybe they're finally going to set a date and tie the knot."

Davis laughs out a huff into the phone. "I doubt it. Between his schedule with the team and everyone being in their business, I'm sure it'll be a paparazzi nightmare attempting to plan something like that. Hell, Luke still gets flack for showing up at her book signings. Who knew an NFL coach supporting his best-selling girlfriend would be such a draw? I'll stay out of the limelight—thank you very much. His abs still circulate the Internet from time to time, according to one of the interns I work with. She was devastated that he's been taken off the market."

"Wow, I thought the hype would die down by now. It's been over two years since those women mistook him as a cover model for one of Dani's books. I get the hype—him being the youngest head coach in the league, but you'd think with the winning records the Rainier Renegades have undertaken since that debacle, his abs would no longer be a hot topic."

"Did you just hear yourself?" Davis asks. "I love Dani and will support her any way I can, but I don't think I would subject myself to those women at the book conventions she attends. I'd be running for the hills if they tried their antics with me."

"You just can't accept the fact you're a pretty boy, can you?" I tease. Davis has always had women interested in him, but he's been too busy to notice. He's laser focused on being an ER surgeon. "God knows what would happen if those women found out he had brains to go with the brawn."

"Oh, shut it," he spits out. "Listen, I've gotta run. I just got a call. Call Dani and work out the details, then text me the when and where."

"Sounds good," I offer, knowing his time is limited. "See you soon."

I hear something in the background, and the phone goes

dead. I admire the hell out of my baby brother and am so happy he's off saving lives, one incident at a time.

Knowing my conversation with Dani won't be short, I remove one more section of the cupboard before calling it quits. I take a quick shower, then settle into a comfortable chair before pulling her number up on my phone.

Of course, I'm greeted with, "What the hell took you so long?" by my loving sister.

Yep, I knew it. She'll give me shit for ignoring her. It's something I never do, but she wouldn't be my big sister if she didn't at least pretend to be offended.

I quickly apologize and explain my mishap yesterday, and all is forgiven. She catches me up on her adventures with Luke in the off season, and we make plans for next weekend. By the time we get off the phone, I'm exhausted and glad I'd crawled into bed before our conversation ended. Morning comes early, and I'm looking forward to setting things straight with Vanessa tomorrow.

WHEN I ROLL over to glance at my alarm, I bolt out of bed.

"Holy shit! It's after seven!"

I have to be in a meeting in less than thirty minutes. Thank God, I'd taken a shower last night because that's out of the question now.

I rush to my closet and grab the first button-down shirt I touch. Then I grab a pair of dark jeans and practically fall over as I jump into them with both feet as I make my way to the bathroom. Within a few minutes, I'm rushing out the door, on my way to the job site.

So much for seeing Vanessa this morning.

Fuck, I was looking forward to seeing her.

Just as I park my truck in front of the job shack, another thought hits me. *Maybe I'll be able to take an early lunch and catch her before her shift ends.*

As soon as I enter the job shack, Mal hands me the plans I need for the first meeting. Glancing at my watch, I realize I'm not as late as I could've been. I typically arrive closer to seven. I'm lucky I live close by. She doesn't give me a second glance for being late, either that or she's keeping her thoughts to herself.

As soon as I'm in the groove at work, the day flies by. I meet with the contractors, sub-contractors, and handle anything that needs my attention. The next thing I know, everyone's calling it quits for the lunch hour. Typically, I either bring lunch or grab something quick nearby, but knowing there's someone at the diner I'm hoping to bump into, my truck practically steers itself in that direction.

Of course, when I get seated at the counter, Vanessa is nowhere in sight. I keep a look out as the kitchen door opens frequently, hoping she might be on a break, but I'm left with nothing but disappointment.

With tomorrow being the day she's with her family, I doubt I'll even see her until Monday. A feeling of unease settles when I realize the more time she has to think I was just asking her out for returning my card, the more likely she'll never give me a chance again.

Why does it feel as if I've missed my chance?

I go through the motions of eating my French dip sand-wich and fries. But with the weight of my reality settling in my stomach, I hardly taste the food as it goes down. No. My mind is set on the intriguing blonde with the beautiful hazel eyes. I just hope like hell I haven't blown my chance with her.

5

VANESSA

"OKAY, Jules, are you ready to blow out the candles?" I ask as I bring her birthday cake from the counter to the kitchen table. She has four friends gathered around her, all eager to watch.

Their parents and our friends are gathered around our kitchen to help her celebrate. Her beautiful hazel eyes go as round as saucers when I place the red velvet cake in front of her. I'm sure the other parents won't like that it'll likely stain any clothes it lands on, but a girl only turns five once—and this is her favorite.

As soon as I've lit the candles, everyone begins the birthday tune. Her friends giggle and sing louder to be over-heard from one another. Just as we've finished the song, I remind her, "Make a wish," before she blows out her candles.

She's adorable when she takes in the biggest breath imagin-able, filling her cheeks with air, then exhales. The room goes darker and erupts with cheers and clapping when she's done.

A flash of the day she was born hits me out of nowhere.

She was so tiny, and I was so scared for our future. Thank God, my parents had done everything they could to help me realize it wasn't the end of the world to have a baby. People do it all the time. It was just the end of me being the center of my world. From the day I found out I was pregnant with Julia, I couldn't fathom living without her. I've never regretted my choice.

Believe it or not, Julia is the reason why I am where I am today. Failure hasn't been an option. I've had to do my best for her. Just months after her birth, when my parents' car crashed, she and Vince were the only things that got me through.

As if he senses my need for him, Vince slips an arm around my shoulder and squeezes as he whispers so only I can hear, "They would've been so proud of Jules. She's had us all wrapped around her finger from the day she was born. I love you so much, Vanny. You've got an amazing girl. You've come so far from that day I found you crying in your room with a pregnancy box in your hands—too afraid to find out the results. I'll tell you what. She's been the best thing that happened to both of us... God, I wouldn't miss moments like this for anything. I would've missed out on so much had I gone away to school as planned."

All I can do is nod in agreement; his words are the final straw on my mound of emotions at the moment. A tear slips down my cheek and catches on the smile I'm trying to hold in place. I love my baby girl so much, and there's nothing I won't do for her.

Vince squeezes me harder as I quickly wipe the evidence away.

Oblivious to my emotions, Julia squeals out, "Unks, are we cutting the cake?"

Looking to Vince who holds the serving knife in his hand, I can't help but laugh when he shrugs. "Coming right up, your highness." He bows exaggeratedly in her direction.

"Oh, Unks... I'm not a princess," Julia chastises. "I'm gonna be a bike racer when I grow up. You know dresses get caught in the wheels." This causes the entire room to break out in laughter.

Since she learned to ride her bike a few weeks ago, she's done nothing but race us. My girl is both a tomboy and a girly-girl when she wants to be, and I wouldn't have it any other way.

"Oh, I'm sure you're still a spoiled princess," Vince teases as he sets into cutting the cake. "Look at all your subjects who've come to celebrate with you."

Rolling her eyes, she sighs exasperatedly, "Oh, silly Unks." But she's distracted when he sets a slice of cake in front of her, and she runs a finger in the frosting and brings it to her mouth. "Yum!"

Laughter erupts at her goofiness from the room of watchers.

Once the kids are dished up, Vince and Sydney pass out cake to the adults in the room. The parents chat quietly among themselves. Having this free moment, I pull out my phone and snap a few photos to remember this occasion. Julia's wide smile melts my heart as she talks with her friends through a mouth-fulof cake.

To keep myself from getting emotional again, I distract

myself by chatting among our guests. Eventually, I grab a piece of cake for myself and am surprised when Ryan steps up beside me.

"Hey, Vanessa," he says with a nod in greeting.

"Hey, Ryan, thanks for coming," I say after finishing the bite of food in my mouth.

"I wouldn't miss it." He shrugs. "She's wormed her way into my heart since I've met her."

"True," I agree. "She has a way of doing that."

Most young college freshmen would be too busy to hang with a family, but I think the fact that we offered home-cooked meals on a regular basis that kept him out of the campus cafeterias might've had something to do with it. Though in all fairness, he's been an amazing friend to both Vince and me through the years.

"No kidding. You've got an amazing kid." He stops to watch her play with her friends before catching me off guard when he asks, "Did you have fun the other night?"

"Uh..." That look on his face makes me think there's more to this than a casual conversation. "It was great to hang out with the girls."

"I don't suppose you get out much, do you?"

He knows this. Why is he asking?

Oh, shit. He's not working up the courage or opportunity to ask me out, is he?

Immediately, my mind goes to Damien... Was he doing the same thing?

Shaking my head to both answer his question and stop myself from thinking about Damien, I remind him, "I'm pretty busy with Jules, but every once in a while, I need a night out with my friends. Though I paid for it in the morning with my lack of sleep." I laugh it off before changing the subject when Julia and her friends race out of the kitchen. "Do you wanna help me wrangle these girls, so we can start on presents?"

Ryan's almost a foot taller than me, so I have to strain my neck to see the shocked expression on his face. He may like Julia but has no clue how to handle her. I quickly put him out of his misery. "Don't worry, I've got this."

To the room, I announce, "Hey, Jules, ready for presents?" Then I announce to the small crowd still gathered in my kitchen. "Let's head to the living room."

Within a few minutes, everyone's gathered around to watch the birthday girl open her gifts. She squeals with delight as she opens each package. The look of pure joy is infectious as I glance around the room. Each person in some way or another smiles and laughs with her silliness. I can't believe how close Sydney's roommates Chloe and Abby have become to us in recent weeks. They've accepted me into their tribe as if I've been there all along.

Even my friend Margo has made the trip down from Seattle. She's been the one person who hasn't given up on me when my priorities changed from boys and makeup to diapers and bottles. She has declared herself Julia's adoptive aunt from day one. She could've blown me off or let our friendship drift apart, but no matter what's going on—she's always been there for me and my daughter.

As a mom, it's weird having Julia become so grown up and independent. This is the first year I've been able to sit back on the sidelines and watch her open her gifts with everyone else. Since Vince is closer, when she picks up a new gift, she asks him to read who it's from.

Margo slides up to my side and asks, "Hey, Momma, how are ya holding out? I still can't believe she's five already. Wasn't she just born... like yesterday?"

"Yeah..." I sigh. "Thanks again for coming down."

"Uh... nothing would keep me away. I know her official birthday isn't until the twenty-third, but I'm glad you opted for a weekend birthday party. I would've skipped class to be here, but now I get time with my bestie, too." She pulls me in for a side hug.

"Uggh.... It's been forever," I admit, hugging her back with one arm. "I can't wait to catch up." Margo had arrived at the same time as everyone else for the party, so we haven't had the chance to chat. I'm sure we'll stay up through the night talking... and I'll totally regret not being able to sleep in like we did in high school. Julia's up at the crack of dawn on a good day. But I'll take little sleep over my best friend any day.

By the time everyone leaves and only Vince, Margo, Julia, and I remain, I'm exhausted. Thankfully, there isn't much to clean up, and we have nothing planned for the rest of the afternoon.

As Margo and I settle in the living room while Julia plays with her new doll house in her bedroom, Vince walks in and plops on the couch beside Margo. "Whew. That was something."

"It sure was," I admit. "Thanks again for cleaning up the rest of the kitchen. Does Syd work tonight?"

"Yeah. She's meeting with someone in the morning to look at renting an apartment for next year."

Even though Margo's here, I ask, "Have you given any thought to asking her to move in?"

From the corner of my eyes, I see Margo's eyes raise, but she remains quiet.

Vince rests his head on the back of the couch as he sighs and stares at the ceiling. He's such a planner and overthinker. I'm sure he's been going round and round about this since our last conversation.

Knowing he'll let whatever is bugging him fester if he doesn't get it off his chest, I prompt, "What's the matter, Vinny?"

Sighing heavily, he rolls his head in my direction. "Are you okay with it?"

"Yeah, or I wouldn't have suggested it. But what's really bugging you?"

His carefree expression morphs to concern. "Is it too soon?"

"Only you can answer that," I admit honestly. "But you already spend practically every night with her. Don't even let me start on how I've never seen you connect to anyone the way you do with her."

"I love her like crazy and know she's the one for me... but isn't it crazy to live with a girl I've only been dating a few months? What do you think Mom and Dad would think?"

They'd want him to be happy.

But I keep that thought to myself.

Of course Margo doesn't. "They'd probably tell you that

life is short and make every moment count. You of all people should know that. They were the most supportive parents I knew."

True.

Vince continues to stare at the ceiling but doesn't say anything.

"Seriously, Vince, what's going on?"

"I don't know. I know Syd loves her independence and wants to do things on her own, so will she look at it as charity if I offer her a place to live?"

"Uh, I don't think she'd view it as charity."

"You don't know Sydney. She'd want to pay her way. But we don't even have a monthly mortgage to contribute to. I'm sure in her crazy, independent mind, she'd view it as charity."

"She can pitch in for groceries and utilities?" I offer as a suggestion, though it comes out as a question.

"How serious are you two?" Margo asks with curiosity.

"I'm planning to propose after graduation," Vince shockingly admits.

"Does she know this?" I blurt out before I can filter my thoughts. This is the first I've heard of his plan. But when I think about it, I'm not that surprised.

"She might have a clue I plan to marry her someday, but nothing specific." He shrugs as if it's not a big deal.

"Wow. This is huge," Margo draws out, then looks to me with a goofy grin on her face. "Our Vinnie is in love."

"Yes, he is," he deadpans.

"So, what's the problem? If you're planning on proposing, why wouldn't you ask her to live with you?"

"Like I said, Syd's stubbornly independent. She's managing to pay for school without taking out any loans until next year. She wants to do it on her own, ya know?"

"I wish I didn't have to take out loans," Margo moans. "At the rate I'm going, I'll likely be paying mine off until the day I die." Margo's attending a private school and majoring in pre-law. She still has to get into law school, so I'm sure the loans are astronomical. "Why don't you ask her in a way that will let her know you're not dishing out charity? From what I've seen, she's a great girl for you, Vince."

"She's the one for me... but now that I know you're okay with this, Van, when the time is right, I'll ask. Her lease runs through the end of July, so if she doesn't like my offer, she still has time to find another roommate." He shakes his head as he continues to stare at the ceiling as if he'll magically find the answers there.

"As happy as I am for Chloe graduating early, it's gotta be hard for Syd to consider moving in with a practical stranger."

"Don't even get me started on that," Vince grumbles.

"Maybe she's looking elsewhere because you haven't let her know she has other options," Margo suggests.

Vince's eyes dart to hers. "God, I'm so stupid. I haven't even thought of it that way. At first, I wasn't sure what to do. Then I didn't want to stand in her way once she started looking for the perfect place to live."

"Vince," I start but wait until his eyes find mine before continuing, "the only way you'll know what's going on in that head of hers is if you talk with her. Have an honest conversation and stop acting like you have to be the one to solve all the problems of the world. I love you, but you're totally over-thinking this."

Vince remains quiet for a moment, then doubt fills his features. "What if moving in together ruins everything?"

My brother is strong, fiercely protective, and usually confident, but the look of doubt on his face almost breaks my heart.

"Then it wasn't meant to be," Margo interjects before I can open my mouth to speak.

"She's right." I shrug in agreement. But my tone is sympathetic as I finish my thought, "You already spend practically every night together. Talk to her. I'm sure you'll work it out. Worst case—she has to get a roommate. Best case—for you—she'll move in. Time will tell what's meant to be."

Sighing heavily, Vince concedes, "When did you get to be so smart?"

"Uh... I've always been smarter than you—thank you very much." I feign in grievance, but everyone in the room knows I'm only joking.

Vince remains quiet for a moment, then slowly stands from the couch. "I think I'm just gonna take a shower and work on a paper I have due next week while Syd's at work, so I can spend time with her tomorrow." Then he turns to Margo. "I'm glad you could make it today. Thanks for coming down. I'll see you in the morning."

"I haven't missed a birthday yet," she acknowledges. "Besides, I'll use any excuse to hang with my bestie any chance I can get."

As soon as Vince is out of sight, Margo turns to look at me.

"Despite his worries about asking Sydney to move in, I swear... I've never seen him happier."

"You're right, he is. He still stubbornly tries to carry the weight of the world on his shoulders, but she's mellowed him out. I don't think I've seen him smile more since high school."

"That's amazing." Margo beams, then waggles her brows at me. "What about you? Are you happy?"

Taking a deep breath, I take a moment to think about her question. Knowing Margo, she won't be satisfied with a half-ass answer. She'll also be able to see through any BS I sling her way, too. Not that I'd try. With her, I've never needed to. She's seen me through my worst and still supported me every step of the way.

Chewing on my lower lip, I take stock of my life. Mentally, I'm in such a better place now. I still miss my parents every day, but it's manageable. Julia's happy and healthy, and I'm on track for graduating next year. I've got great friends. What else could I need?

"Yeah," I finally surmise. "I think I'm getting there."

Suddenly, Margo sits up on the edge of the couch, and her face lights up like the Cheshire cat. "Okay... don't shoot me... but what about *your* personal life?"

"Uh... what personal life?" I pull a WTF expression, I'm sure. "I've got Julia, Vince, and a few friends, but are those considered a personal life?"

"Have you even considered dating?" she huffs out as if I'm a toddler not understanding the words she's pouring from her lips.

God, what is it with my friends? I swear I've been asked

this more in the last week than in the last five years. When Margo just stares at me, I'm forced to find a response for her. "Uh... I don't have the time between work, school, and Julia. And the last I checked, most guys our age run screaming for the hills at the thought of a commitment... let alone to someone who already has a built-in-family option."

"Vanny, I swear you don't give yourself enough credit." She reaches out and pats my leg that's propped on the coffee table in front of us.

"Seriously, Margo, it's not like I can have a casual fling. That's not me, and you know that. But it's all I'd have time for."

Her brow arches high as she asks, "There hasn't been anyone who's even turned your head twice?"

Dark-brown eyes, a perfectly square chin, and perfectly sculpted lips come to mind, and I can't fight the smile that forms when I think of Damien. What is it about this man that has me squirming in my seat at the thought of him?

"Who have you not told me about?" Margo spits out. "I haven't seen that dopey look on your face since high school. Wait... is it that guy you were talking with in the kitchen during the party?"

Who is she talking about?

"What?" I start to ask, but she interrupts me instead.

"You know..." she exaggerates, though I clearly don't. "That tall one who was talking with Vince right before the cake?"

Wincing, I force myself to say his name aloud. "Ryan?"

What is it with everyone thinking I have anything going on with him? "Uh... we're just friends."

"Uh... he doesn't look at you like you're only friends," she protests. "Wait... have you even been paying attention?"

"I'm sure you're mistaken," I brush off. "Besides, he's never asked me out or given me any indication he's interested in anything besides being a friend to Vince and by correlation —me."

"When was the last time you even went on a date?"

I just stare at her—she knows this. She knows the last person I dated was in high school—before Julia. Sure, I went to senior prom and a few places with a group of friends, but those weren't real dates.

"You've got to be kidding me, Van.," Margo sighs as she shakes her head in disbelief. "Why not?"

"Uh... Julia?" I offer in explanation. But when her eyes narrow as if she's not buying it, I spit out, "Because no one's ever asked?" I shrug.

"You're telling me, in over five years, you've never been asked?"

I think about her words, then clarify, "Well, no one ever worth *actually* going on one has."

"How do you know if you haven't tried? Sure, you may end up with a few frogs, but how else are you supposed to find your prince?"

"I'm far from being a princess," I deadpan.

Margo's quiet for an unnecessarily long moment, but her mind is spinning. I've seen her calculating look a million times, so I know she's up to something. She's biting on her lower lip, and her eyes are so scrunched together, I swear she's going to need Botox at a young age to rectify her wrinkles.

Then suddenly, she smiles.

When she finally turns her attention to me, her face becomes unreadable and frankly, it makes me a little scared. What the hell is she plotting?

"You're seriously telling me that *no one* has asked you out worthy of dating?"

Yep—my thoughts drift back to Damien, and I'm sure my face gives something away. Her perfectly arched brow tells me not to feed her any more BS.

"Well... maybe..." I admit.

Confusion fills her features. "Maybe what? You've either been asked out, or you haven't?"

Cringing, I admit in a weak voice, "Maybe I was asked out this week... but I had to turn him down because of the party today." Maybe she can help me figure this out.

"Explain."

"Well, there's this guy who comes into the diner regularly..." Margo nods, encouraging me to continue. "He's in town for the next year or so, working on the new family housing complex for the university. I swear, Margo, when he even enters the diner, I can feel him before I see him," I start but realize I may have revealed too much. Quickly, I continue, hoping she might not notice, "But anyway... a few days ago, he abruptly left the diner and left his debit card. Thinking he might need it, I dropped it by his work site. Then when he came in next, he asked if I was busy today... of course I was... and I said so."

"Why didn't you suggest another day?"

I hadn't even thought of that.

Instead of revealing that, I add, "But he premised it with, 'I'd like to thank you for dropping off my debit card...' Isn't that... a pity date?"

"What the fuck is a pity date?" Margo hisses at me.

"Uggh..." I huff out exasperatedly. "I thought he was only being nice because I did him a favor. When he found out I was busy... so I told him no worries, we're all good because I didn't want him to feel obligated to do anything with me."

Margo holds up a hand to get me to stop my rambling. "Wait. Let's back up a step. First of all... how old is this guy if he's working for some construction company?"

"Uh, he's twenty-six, and he's the lead engineer on the project," I admit.

"You seem to know a lot about him—for just being a customer."

Well, I pay attention. If she knew what he looked like, she'd pay attention, too.

But I'm not telling her that. Though I do admit, "We've talked when he comes in and sits at the counter."

"Just how often does he come in?"

This question throws me, so I stop to think it over.

"Uh... he's there at almost every one of my shifts since he moved to town a month or so ago."

"Vanny... I love you, and you're one of the smartest people I know... but God, you're dense. The guy clearly likes you if he's showing up nearly every morning. Even if he's a bachelor who doesn't like to cook, I highly doubt he'd show up every day just for the food."

"You think so?"

The look I receive clearly screams, *duh.*

"And don't think I missed the fact that you feel him before you see him. You obviously like him, too. I've never heard you say that about anyone—though to be fair, you don't give yourself the chance. But think of it this way... what would you tell me to do if the roles were reversed?"

That brat. She knows exactly what advice I'd give.

"But my situation is different..."

"Different in that you're so out of practice with flirting, you don't know your ass from your elbow when it comes to your best asset."

What the fuck did she just say?

I burst out laughing. "Okay... Okay... I get it. I'll say yes if he asks me again. Or at least let him know I'm interested if I happen to be busy... Is that better? Ass from my elbow? Really?"

"Dude... you know you have sexy elbows," she teases.

Of course I take this opportunity to change the tables on her. "So, what about you... who have you been dating lately... oh, wise one?"

Margo's eyes practically roll into the back of her head, but she drops the subject about Damien, for now.

She tells me about her latest experience of being set up on a blind date. We chat into the wee hours of the morning about anything and everything, the way we do whenever we get together. Knowing I'll fully regret staying up this late but not caring at the same time. I hardly ever get time with my bestie, and I'm enjoying every minute of it that I can.

As I drift off to sleep that night, two things are clear on my mind.

One, I need to put myself out there more.

Two, how do I let Damien know he's the one I'm interested in?

6

DAMIEN

AS I WALK UP to the door of the diner, nerves I haven't felt in years hit me. Not seeing Vanessa since I royally fucked up has me on edge. *Why wasn't I clearer with my intentions?* I'll admit I came in both Saturday and Sunday morning, in hopes of finding her, but no such luck. God, how can I be such an idiot? I swear I used to have game. But maybe I'm out of practice? Who knows what the hell happened? Hopefully, I'll have the chance to rectify this.

The diner is bustling with its usual morning crowd but luckily, there's one open spot left at the counter.

"Morning, Jack, how's it going?" I say to the elderly man I've come to know. Jack loves to keep me on my toes. He's probably in his mid-seventies if I had to guess. He acts much younger, but when you get him going, he talks about his life before serving our country. He doesn't talk about the specifics, but I know he served in the Vietnam War, has a wife who passed away a few years ago, and two sons who have given him four grandkids who visit him often.

I'll never forget the time I finally got the courage to ask him his age. There was a twinkle in his eye as he looked around the room to see if anyone was watching. Then he slowly leaned in and whispered, "Can you keep a secret?"

"Of course," I replied and waited for his response.

Then he quickly pulled back and barked out a laugh. "So can I." The crowd around us laughed, and I have since learned that no one knows his age, and he plans to keep it that way until he dies.

I'm pulled out of my memory as Jack chuckles loud. "Oh, I'd say I'm doing all right. The heart's still tickin'."

"Well, that definitely beats the alternative." I laugh. Darn, this man. I never know what he'll say.

"You can say that again." He rolls his eyes and stuffs his mouth full of pancake. But his eyes get distracted from something behind me, so I turn to see what's suddenly captured his attention.

Vanessa's bright smile seriously stops all train of thought. All I can do is stare into her gorgeous hazel eyes. Her hair is pulled back into a braid showing off her high cheekbones. Without a stitch of makeup, she's the most beautiful woman I've ever laid eyes on. Her clear skin looks soft and inviting to touch, and I'd do anything to kiss those perfect lips.

I'm startled when Jack bumps me as he mumbles quietly, "You'd better close your mouth before you catch a fly."

And that's my reality check. "Morning," I say when I get my wits about me.

"Good morning, Damien. Can I get you some coffee?" she says, holding up the carafe expectantly.

Flipping the mug in front of me over, I nod. "Sounds great, thanks."

She wastes no time in filling my cup. "Want your usual?"

I think over the menu, then nod in agreement. "Yeah. Eggs and bacon sound great."

"Bacon goes with everything," Jack inserts.

Vanessa nods in agreement. "Bacon is always good." But then she turns her attention back to me. "Want anything else?"

Your phone number? Possibly a date with you?

Of course, I keep that part to myself.

"I'm good. Thanks," I say as I pull the mug of coffee to my lips.

She turns to walk away but hesitates, and I'm left staring at her to see what she's forgotten.

"I didn't see you in here Friday. Did something happen at work again?"

Why does my heart race at the realization she's noticed my absence?

But I stick to answering her question, "Oh, no. I was running late and wasn't able to stop in."

"Oh." Her expression morphs from concern to relaxed. "I'm glad to hear nothing was wrong."

"Nothing other than my alarm didn't go off," I admit. "Did you miss me?"

Jack mumbles something, but I swear he says, "Subtle."

Vanessa's eyes dance with delight as she punches her hip

and rolls her eyes. "I had a senior menu picked out and ready for you. Of course, I missed you."

God, I love that sass.

"Back with the old-man jokes, I see."

"Ha... you're a spring chick compared to the likes of me, son," Jack interjects.

Vanessa's attention turns from me. "Oh, you're not old, Jack. You've still got plenty of good years left in you."

"From your lips to God's ears," the feisty man beside me states, earning him a laugh from both of us. "I've got lots left to do on my bucket list. I'm not ready to meet my maker just yet."

"Good to know, I agree. Anything particular you've got in mind?"

"I want to see my grandkids graduate from school, so I've got a few years left in me," he assures us.

"What? No sky diving or getting another tattoo?" Vanessa teases.

"Oh, I've had my share of jumping out of planes. I'll leave that to the hotshots. As for tattoos, I think I've got plenty already." He rolls up his sleeve, and I find a Navy trident staring back at me.

"What about you, Damien? Do you have any tattoos I don't know about?" Vanessa shocks me by asking something so personal.

With the way she's looking, she's making me wish I had one, but of course I admit the truth. "Nope. Haven't found anything I'd want to permanently have on me just yet, though I haven't ruled it out."

"You?" I can't help myself now that she's got my mind

spinning about where a tattoo could be placed—I need to know.

"Uh..." she draws out as she looks to the floor momentarily, making me wonder if she's suddenly nervous. "Just one."

"Order's up, Van," someone calls from the kitchen, and she shrugs an apology for leaving as she tends to the food on the counter.

"Looks like you're the odd one out, kid," Jack says, patting me on the back.

"No kidding," I chortle. The man sure knows how to make me laugh daily. "Seriously, Jack, how are you doing today?"

"I'm good." He nods in assurance. "I've got an external door that's sticking in my garage. I'm gonna spend some time on that this week."

I have no doubt he can do it but knowing how heavy doors can be, I pull out a business card from my pocket and offer, "I'd be happy to help if you need some assistance. I'm off most evenings by six, and I'd be happy to see what I can do."

"I thought you were the boss of things and didn't get your hands dirty?" Jack teases.

"Well, I'm renovating the house I live in and don't mind getting my hands dirty from time to time. Besides, handling doors are much easier as a two-person job."

Realizing I'm right, he slips my card into his shirt pocket. "I think I might just take you up on the offer, son. That sucker's solid and bound to be heavy."

All the more reason to ask for help wants to slip off my tongue. But I hold back. Guys like Jack live on pride, and I'd never want him to think he isn't capable of completing the job himself. That man can likely still run circles around me.

Before I can say any more, Vanessa returns with my plate of food. "Here you go, Damien. Enjoy."

Why does it feel so good when she says my name?

"Thanks," I offer as I pick up my fork. "I appreciate it."

"No problem." Vanessa's smile shines bright. "Need anything else?"

This clearly isn't the time to tell her I want to ask her out—with no misinterpretations. So, I just shake my head. "I'm good. Thanks."

Vanessa leaves to wait on a few more people around the diner, and my eyes can't help but follow her. Though I'm brought back to awareness when Jack grunts beside me. He doesn't say anything but shakes his head and continues with his meal.

Yeah, I was caught staring. But I'm not ashamed. Without saying anything to Jack, I focus my attention on my food and wonder what's the right approach with her.

A few minutes later, Vanessa's back to check in with us. She chats up the crowd at the counter, but eventually, the couple next to me leaves, and it's just Jack and me.

Recalling our previous conversation, I probe about her weekend. "So... did you have a good time with your family this weekend?"

This seems to catch her off guard for a beat, but then she nods. "Yeah... I hosted a family gathering," she starts out slowly, but then her enthusiasm shows up. "My best friend from high school was in town, and we spent the weekend catching up." By the end, happiness radiates from her.

"Good for you," Jack says. "You need time for you, too, kiddo."

"Absolutely," Vanessa agrees. "I got to see her on my birthday in early March, but I'll never complain about my time with Margo—she's been there through everything and is the sister I've never had."

"I'm happy you have that." Jack nods. "Good friends are hard to come by."

Wanting to know more, I ask, "What did you end up doing?"

"Oh, we just hung out at home and chatted until the wee hours of the morning. I swear, every time she comes around, I forget I have to get up the next day."

"Ha." I chuckle. "I'm that way anytime I get around my siblings, now that we no longer live together."

"I lead a pretty simple life. I don't mind going out, but I'm just as happy being home and having great conversation."

Taking this opening, I force myself to confront our last conversation. "Speaking of going out..." I say, trying to switch the focus of our conversation.

This has her attention. Her eyes narrow on mine, and nerves creep up my spine. Knowing I won't be satisfied until I know, I meet that fear head on. "Would you be interested in having dinner with me sometime?"

Her long lashes rapidly blink, and her mouth drops open to form a perfect 'O.' "You... you want to go to dinner... with me?"

"Yes," I answer honestly, holding her attention with my eyes.

"Is this just because I brought your card to you?" she asks for clarification.

Shaking my head, I clarify, "No. I'd like the chance to get to know you better when you're not waiting on me. If you're interested, I'd love to take you out sometime."

Her mouth drops again and if I weren't hanging on by a thread for her answer, I might think it's comical. She's freaking adorable. She opens her mouth to speak but snaps it shut before words come out.

I swear this moment lasts a lifetime as I wait for her to find the words for me. I barely hear dishes clanking, customers chatting, or Jack cough near me as the blood gushes through my ears, thundering with each beat.

It's not like I haven't been rejected before, but I hope this isn't the case. Maybe I should've asked more privately. But this is all I've been thinking about since last week.

Finally, she nods. "When are you thinking?"

Well, this isn't a no.

"I'm free tonight," I answer honestly. But I then realize I'd better not come across too strong. "Or any night this week. Whichever works for you. I'm more than willing to work around your schedule."

Once again, I can visibly see the wheels spinning in her head. Her lips purse as her brows knit, contemplating my offer. Eventually, I'm put out of my misery. "Okay."

"Okay?" I ask, needing clarification.

"Okay. If you're serious about tonight, I think that might work best."

"About time," Jack grumbles at my side. "You two have been making eyes at each other since the day this poor fella came in."

"Jack." Vanessa swats a hand in the air in his direction.

"What?" He shrugs defensively. "I'm just saying what we're all feeling—aloud. Don't shoot the messenger."

I laugh. I can't help it. He's hit the nail on the head.

Thankfully, Vanessa does, too, and of course Jack joins— though I'm not sure he's laughing with us—or at us. Though does it matter?

Once we've regained our composure, I ask, "Does seven work for you?"

"I'm sure I can make that work... but there's something you should know."

Suddenly, my phone rings and when I look at the number, I know I have to take it.

Reaching into my pocket, I pull out my wallet and reach for a card and enough cash to cover my bill. "Look, I've gotta take this. Whatever it is, we can talk about it tonight over dinner. Text me your address, and I'll pick you up at seven. Wear something you're comfortable in, and we can decide what you'd like to do when I get there."

My phone rings for a third time, and I force myself to pick up the call, I keep my eyes on Vanessa as I answer, "Hey, Malik. I'm glad you called. Give me a second." Putting the phone to my chest, my eyes never leave sight of the stunned woman in front of me. "I'm sorry, this is my boss. I have to take this. Can what you have to say hold until this evening?"

Sighing, she shakes her head as she says, "Yes."

"I'm usually off around six. Please text me your address, and we'll work everything out. I can't wait to see you."

"Okay." She nods in agreement. "I'll text you when I get off my shift."

I smile and nod in agreement as I walk regretfully out the door of the diner to find out what brought Malik calling this early in the morning, hoping like hell my day hasn't just turned into a complete shit show.

7

VANESSA

AS SOON AS I finish my shift, instead of texting Damien, I pull up Syd's contact and call her. If I'm going on a date tonight, I need someone to watch Julia—and let's be real—I need reinforcements for my nerves.

She picks up on the third ring sounding out of breath. "Hey, Van, what's up?"

"Uh..." How do I even start? "Are you busy?"

"I just ran about seven miles. I'm actually about two blocks from your house. Everything okay?"

Not wanting to sound pathetic, I offer as I chew on the side of my lip, "Wanna wait for me there? I have something I'd like to run by you."

"Sure. I'll just let myself in through the garage if that's okay. I'm warning you though, I totally reek. How long will you be?"

"I'm just leaving the diner. But if you'd like a shower, I'm sure Vince won't mind you using his."

"I'm at the house now. You sure you're okay? I can tell something's bothering you." Syd's voice fills with concern at the end, almost as if she's contemplating letting me hang up.

Sighing heavily, I say, "It's nothing that can't wait. I'll explain when I get there."

"See you in a few," she says as she hangs up.

It doesn't take long before I'm parking in my garage and walking through the kitchen to my bedroom. Quickly, I discard my work clothes and change into a pair of dark skinny jeans and my favorite jade top. It's a few shades darker than my eyes, and I always feel confident when wearing it. Today of all days, I'll take all the reinforcements I can get.

By the time I return to the living room, Sydney's there fresh from the shower. She's dressed in jeans and one of my brother's CRU sweatshirts. Her hair is wrapped in a towel, and her eyes look me over with care.

"Everything okay?" she asks skeptically. "You look like a million bucks, but your tone earlier said otherwise."

Rocking back on my heels, I scramble for words. "I... Uh... you remember that guy I told you about the night at the bar?"

"Yesssss..." she draws out into four syllables as she waits for me to fill in the blanks.

"Well... he... uh... asked me out," I manage to spit out.

Realizing there isn't an emergency, she plops into the corner of the couch and tucks her feet under her. "This is a good thing, right?" she clarifies as she motions with her hand to continue.

"Yes," I admit too eagerly. Then the flood gates open, and I ramble out practically every thought in my brain. "But it's for tonight. I know you don't work tonight, but could you and Vince watch Julia tonight, here... he's picking me up at seven. I'm not even sure I want her to see that I'm going out... Crap... Maybe, I'll just meet him somewhere, so he doesn't come to the house. Maybe this is too much... or too soon. Maybe I should just cancel?"

"Whoa... Whoa..." She raises a hand and practically begs. "Slow down. Start from the beginning, and let's take it from there."

With her encouragement, I tell her every minute detail of the morning, including how I was about to tell him about Julia when he got a phone call. Even after rehashing the events of the morning, my nerves are back to hyper-alert, causing my fears from before to resurface.

"What happens if he doesn't want to date a single mom? Ohmigod, Syd! What if he thinks I've lied to him or..." I pause when another thought hits me like a ton of bricks. "What if he's just interested in a hook-up?"

Sydney stops me in my tracks with one perfectly arched brow and squinted eyes focused entirely on me. "Do you believe the shit you're spewing, or is this just a case of the nerves?"

When she puts it like that, I'm forced to admit, "Most likely—just nerves."

"Good. Now sit back and listen for a sec." She points at me, and I sink back into my favorite over-sized chair instead of bouncing on the edge. Then she gives me her two cents.

"First, you haven't lied about Jules. You've only seen him at work and the one time at his job site. You don't owe him your life story in that time. In fact—until you're good and ready, you don't owe him anything. *If...* and that's a big if," she exaggerates, "you decide to get serious with him, *then* you can tell him your life story. *Until then...* relax and enjoy getting to know him."

"You're right... I don't need to tell him every sordid detail, but I do feel like I need to be upfront about Julia in case that's a deal breaker for him. By knowing about her, he'll also understand why I can't be like every other carefree college student, making plans at the drop of a hat."

"If he's anything like you say he is, I honestly don't think it'll even faze him. This is the first guy you've been interested in, so he has to be something special. But you're right. If he can't handle the fact you have a kid, then he certainly doesn't deserve your time. You deserve a man who isn't intimidated or jealous of a five-year-old, and he certainly should understand Julia is your priority—no questions asked."

"You're right." I nod in agreement. "I'll tell him about Jules first thing—before we even leave the house." Then another thought hits me. "Though I'm not sure she needs to know I'm dating." If we still go out—that is.

How can I get out of the house without her knowing? She typically isn't in bed until almost eight, and anyone who comes to the door will certainly have her attention—whether I like it or not.

"That's probably a good plan," Sydney agrees.

Cringing because I need a favor, I slowly ask, "Would you..." I pause, wondering if I should scrap the whole idea and just stay home. But when Damien's face comes to mind, I think better of it. "I mean... could you... and Vince take Jules some-where tonight... before he arrives? I promise we'll be gone by seven thirty, so you can get her to bed with ease."

Sydney's face practically splits in two when she realizes I'm not chickening out of my date after all. "I'd be happy to help out. And for the record—if things work out between you and Damien, I'd be happy to babysit anytime you need."

When another thought hits me, I groan. "Oh, God, what do I tell Vince? He'd better not get all brotherly over-protective —even if it *is* my first date in over five years."

Syd shakes her head. "No. You let me worry about him. For tonight, let's tell him you're going out with a friend. If things get more serious, you'll have to cross that bridge when you get there. But seriously, Van—this is Vince we're talking about. As long as Damien's a good guy, I'm sure he'll be supportive. All he wants most in this world is to make sure you're living your best life."

"I know... I guess some habits die hard. He's not a fifteen-year-old punk anymore—not that he ever was, but one thing is certain. If I'm happy, he'll be happy for me."

"Why would I be happy for you?" Vince asks as he enters the living room from the kitchen.

Shit.

"Uh, when did you get home?" I blurt out, hoping he didn't hear our conversation.

Shrugging, Vince states, "I just walked in the door." To Sydney, he asks, "Well, isn't this a nice surprise. I thought you were going for a run, but you look fresh from the shower."

"I ran into Vanessa when she got home, and I used your

shower so I wouldn't smell like roadkill." I could kiss Sydney for not throwing me under the bus.

He leans in and kisses her quickly. "You never smell like roadkill, Syd. I'm glad you're here."

When he pulls back, Sydney looks at something on her phone as he asks, "How was your day, Van?"

Oh... you know... eventful, I want to say but shrug it off. "It was just a day at work."

God, I hate keeping things from my brother. But I'm not sure what I have to say would even be considered news just yet. Hell, I don't even know if I'll make it out the front door until I talk to Damien. So why waste time telling Vince about something that may never happen?

Syd interrupts my thoughts. "Hey, I have an idea. Let's take Julia to the new Pixar movie that just came out. We can hit the early show and be home before bedtime."

Vince turns to me. "What do you say? Wanna go?"

"I actually have plans with a friend." The words slip off my tongue easier than I could've imagined. "Syd's volunteered to hang with Jules tonight."

"Well..." he draws out as he snuggles next to Sydney, "it's settled. *You* get a night out, and *we're* going to the movies. Should I pick Jules up from daycare this afternoon so you can relax before you go?"

"Thanks, Vin, I'd love that." I smile in appreciation. God, I love my brother—even if I do feel guilty for not being forthcoming with my plans. It'll be nice to have some "me" time before heading out.

Now that my nerves have slightly settled, I glance at the

clock and realize there's plenty of time to get to class. "I've gotta run to class."

On my walk to campus, I dig out the card I've practically memorized from my purse to ensure I don't send a message to the wrong person. Knowing there's a good chance of chickening out if I don't just type the necessary message, I quickly tap out the basics.

Me: Hi, this is Vanessa Larson.

Before I finish sending him my address, I receive a text. I quickly press send before reading his response.

Damien: Hope the rest of your morning went well. Off to class?

Me: Yes. Walking there now. Still conquering the world?

Damien: One day at a time... Do you have many classes today?

Me: Only two. I'm done at four.

Damien: If I got off early, would you be opposed to starting our date early?

Crap. I'm not sure when the movie starts.

Pulling up the app, relief hits when it shows the movie starts at six. I'm sure I'll have plenty of time.

Of course, Damien mistakes my delay in response as denial.

Damien: Or not. We can stick to seven. No pressure.

Could he be sweeter?

My fingers fly across my keyboard.

The thought of seeing him sooner both thrills and scares the hell out of me. I'm so out of practice with dating, I just hope I don't make a fool of myself. But somehow, I manage to throw out a calm and collected response even if I feel anything but.

Me: Just let me know when you're on your way, so I can be ready.

Damien: Will do. My schedule is light today, so it might be closer to six than seven.

I arrive at the building to my first class as I tap out a response.

Me: I'll be ready, but I have to run. First class is starting.

Quickly stashing my phone into the pocket of my jeans, I pull open the door and dash to my class. Having a few minutes to spare, I quickly retrieve my phone when it buzzes in my pocket.

Damien: Looking forward to tonight.

Unfortunately, my professor chooses that moment to start class, so instead of responding, I stow my phone and do my best to focus on ethics in nursing. This class typically keeps my interest, but my mind drifts to Damien much more than I'd ever admit. I force myself to take copious notes as this professor often tests on the lecture, more than the required reading. For the first time this semester, I'm honestly glad to see this class end.

I will myself not to look at my phone burning a hole in my pocket as I walk to my next class. I'll find out soon enough if he said any more. My professor starts the lecture about our content for the day shortly after I find my seat. Though she may as well be speaking Greek; nothing of substance will be sticking in my brain in the near future with my current state of mind.

Since I'm usually on top of my studies. I allow my thoughts to drift off at will. Questions flit through my mind like raking leaves in a hurricane. The minute I catch hold of one to give it a serious thought, the next hurdles toward me at top speed, making my last thought disappear in the wind. The only common factor in all of it is Damien.

By the time class is over, I go through the motions of

packing my things and returning home. When I reach the house, I realize I have no idea how I even managed to get home. I could've been hit by a car and none the wiser.

Shaking my head, I force myself to do a few of my nightly chores that I won't want to do when I return home this evening. After popping some laundry in the wash and setting out Julia's clothes for the morning, I head to the kitchen to grab a light snack. My nerves are a bit frayed, but my stomach's rumbling from skipping lunch.

Careful not to fill up before dinner, I slice an apple and Tillamook cheese. Knowing Vince and Julia will be here within the next hour, I settle into my favorite chair and flip on the television. Typically, I'd use this opportunity to study, but knowing my concentration is total crap, I give up before I even begin.

Looking at my book on the end table, I see Charlotte Ann's latest release staring at me, waiting to be read. But I'm afraid even words from one of my favorite romance authors won't hold my interest. Or—knowing how obsessed I become with her books, I won't risk digging it out and getting lost in it either. I'll spend the evening thinking about my book rather than living in the moment with Damien.

So here I sit, flipping through the channels and not one holds my interest for more than a nanosecond. Vince had insisted on upgrading the cable when we moved in because he wanted all the sports channels, but out of the gazillion stations, I can't tell you what one of them features in this moment.

Eventually, I hear the garage door open, and the patter of little feet zips through the house. Vince reminds her to walk, but it's pointless. She's eager to see her momma, and I couldn't be happier.

Standing to greet her, she takes it as an invitation to launch herself into my arms. "Momma, I had the best day today!" she exclaims as I squeeze her tight. Like any five-year-old, she's oblivious when I hold on an extra moment, reveling in her child-like scent and octopus-like hug.

"You'll have to tell me all about it," I offer, setting her down before pulling her back to my chair with me.

Julia beams with delight as she prattles on about how much fun daycare was. It has a built-in preschool, and I'm proud to say Julia's enthusiasm for learning makes it easier to leave her each day, so I can focus on my own classes. It helps that she's been there since Vince and I started attending Columbia River University, and the staff has practically become a second family to us over the years.

Eventually, Vince interrupts her explanation of a science experiment with straws to say, "Hey, Jules, put your backpack in your room and go potty before Syd and I take you to the movie. We have to leave in a few minutes to pick up Syd, so we can grab dinner and watch our movie!"

"Yay!" Julia squeals as she jumps from the couch and rushes to her room. "I can't wait. Unks, did you know..." she gasps then continues, "Jonah was talking about it at circle time today? We *need* to see this movie." The way she exaggerates the word need has me covering my mouth with my hand to keep from laughing at her utter cuteness.

As serious as he can manage, my brother raises an eyebrow

in her direction. "Well, if you don't get moving, we'll be stuck here all night."

With that, she scoots to her room faster than most would consider walking.

Vince uses this time to check in. "How were classes?"

Not wanting to get into specifics, I shift the subject to him. "Have you talked to Sydney yet?" I arch a brow, wondering if he's asked her to move in.

When he shakes his head, I offer him a quick out. "Don't stress over it, Vin. Just ask. The worst that happens is she says no."

Shrugging, he agrees, "True."

Julia's feet pound down the hall as she enters the living room. She visibly slows to call, "You ready, Unks? Syd's waiting."

"That she is, squirt. The bigger question is—are you ready?"

Rolling her eyes, I'm quickly reminded of future conversations with a teenager. Please let her stay little for a long time.

"Give me a kiss, and you can go," I offer the room, though my intent's on Julia.

Vince beats her to me with a side-arm hug and says, "Have fun. You deserve a night to yourself." Before he can let go, Julia squeezes my waist eagerly.

"Have fun, Love Bug. Be good for Unks and Syd."

I don't tell her I'll be home later, because let's face it... I'll either be gone, or I'll be curled up with a book when she returns. Unfortunately, only Damien knows the answer to that one.

8

DAMIEN

THOUGH I'VE PHYSICALLY BEEN at work, my mind's been on Vanessa all day. I'm dying to know more about her. Our conversations from the diner simply aren't enough. Thankfully, Malik didn't have anything all that pressing when we spoke this morning. Today is a day filled with routines, and I fly through it on auto pilot.

Stopping at the local grocery store, I pick out a bouquet of flowers and hope like hell I'm not going overboard. I'm not sure what she's used to, but I want to leave a lasting impression. A part of me worries that she'll think I'm some fuddy-duddy and too old to be dating her. *Five years isn't that big of a difference, right?*

As I pull into her neighborhood, I'm surprised at how nice the homes are. This isn't the typical college neighborhood. It's more of a residential neighborhood for families. The streets are wide, and they appear to be single-family homes. When I pull up to her address, I find she lives in a large single-story modern home. It's a three-car garage with a large yard off to the side. It's much nicer than your typical college student home. *Maybe she lives with roommates?*

Parking on the street, I grab the flowers and head to the door. The ringing bell echoes through the house. When the door opens, my breath disappears. Instead of being up in her typical ponytail, Vanessa's hair is long and wavy and flows well past her shoulders. Gone is her uniform; in its place is a beautiful green top and a pair of skinny jeans. I'd be a fool not to take a moment to appreciate the sight before me. When my eyes reach her face, I notice mascara and her lips shining with gloss for the first time. If I thought she was beautiful at the diner, she's fuckin' stunning in this moment.

Pulling in her lower lip, she fumbles with the door. I have no fucking clue how long she stays there staring at me because I'm lost in her dark-hazel eyes and thick lashes. Eventually, she breaks the silence, "Hey," knocking me out of my revelry.

"Wow. You look amazing," pops off my tongue before I can give it permission.

Her cheeks pinken, and I'm blessed with a glorious smile as she mutters, "Thank you."

She hesitates at the door, so I ask, "Are you ready?"

"Yeah," she draws out almost shyly. "I'm ready..."

The way she says it makes me think there's more to it, and as much as I'd hate for my gut to be true, I clarify, "Do you still want to go?"

God, I've been dying to spend more time with her, but if she's not ready or is hesitant, I guess I'd rather know now, so I can cut my losses. Fuck, I hope she isn't backing out. She's all I've thought about the entire day.

Watching her every move, I notice her spine straighten and her shyness slip away. In its place is the confident woman I've been talking to for weeks at the diner. "Damien, I do want to go out with you..." she starts but trails off.

Shit. Don't let there be a *but*... please don't let there be a *but*!

"But..." She takes in a deep breath.

I knew it. Fuck. Fuckity-Fuck-Fuck.

"But there's something you should know. I tried to tell you at the diner, but we were interrupted. I think it's only fair that you know before we go."

"Okay..." So there's a chance we're still going. What the hell could be weighing on her so heavily?

"I... uh..." She looks to the frame above the door before looking me square in the eyes. "I guess there's no easy way to say this—but come straight out with it." She takes a fortifying breath and blurts out, "I have a five-year-old daughter." As if she can't look me in the eye, her eyes remain fixed on the door frame, waiting for my response.

"Okay..." I draw out as I take in what she's said.

A kid. That's unexpected. But nothing that would cause me to back out. Sure, I've never dated anyone with a kid. But from what I know about Vanessa, I'm fairly certain it's just another piece to the puzzle of how she's become the woman I've come to admire. What's the big deal?

As I look her over from head to toe, I notice she's wringing her hands at her waist. "What's wrong?" I ask, trying to get to the bottom of things.

"Well... I just wanted to be upfront with you. Let you know... so you could change your mind if you didn't want to be involved with me."

What. The. Fuck?

"Why wouldn't I want to be involved with you? We've been getting along fine at the diner since I moved to town. Why would I suddenly change my mind?" I blurt out and blink in disbelief. What the hell is she so worried about?

"Well... you know... being a single mom doesn't lend itself to much of a social life."

No, I suppose it doesn't. I agree. But I keep that thought to myself because I sure as hell don't want her getting the wrong impression. Instead, I drag out, "Okay..." prompting her to continue.

"Well, you might be used to dating women who can go out at the drop of a hat. I need you to know that won't likely be the case with me."

"Okay..." I draw out again, this time trying to formulate words to show I get what she's saying. "So... I'll need to give you advance warning if I want to see you... got it."

She pulls a face as if she didn't hear me correctly. "You... you want to give me advance warning... I mean, you... you still want to go out with me?"

"Uh, I've enjoyed my time with you so far and last I heard... single moms still need to eat," I offer, hoping she'll see she's making it a bigger deal than it is. It's dinner—not a wedding proposal or anything.

Sure, I don't know a lot about kids but why would being a mom make her less interesting to me? If anything, I'm more intrigued. How has she managed to go to school, work, and raise a kid? I've always known Vanessa's different. I've felt something for her since the day we met. I'd be a fool to walk away just because she comes with a package deal.

Cocking her head to the side, her eyes roam my face as if she's trying to find what I'm holding out on her. Instantly, I'm reminded of trying to slip something past my mom in high school. Yeah... Vanessa's most definitely a mom, and that thought alone brings a smile to my face. She's freaking adorable.

"What's so funny?" she asks speculatively.

Shaking my head, I school my features then admit, "You."

Well, this appears to shock her as her mouth drops wide, and her hand comes to her chest as, "Me?" escapes.

"For the record, I asked you out because I'm interested in getting to know *you* better. I like that you're witty, kind, and make me smile. But let's be real, Vanessa. This is only our first date. I understand you have a kid and need to take her into consideration, but don't you think you ought to give us a shot before you're marrying us off in your head or completely shutting us down? But going on a date would help clue me in if you're still interested... that is."

Rolling her eyes, I'm rewarded with the most beautiful grin. "I'm being ridiculous... I see that."

"Not ridiculous," I instantly correct her. "You have every right to be nervous, but please know I'm interested in you—not just the side of you that *you think* I want to know. Being a mom is a part of you and has made you who you've become today. So far, I happen to like that part... but after going out with me, for all I know, you could think I'm an ass and drop me to the curb. So, don't stress out too much. I can still find a way to annoy the crap out of you and all this worry will be for nothing. All I'm asking is that you at least give me a shot before you shoot me down."

Vanessa full-on belly laughs at my unusual antics.

Mission accomplished—I've eased the tension.

Holding out the flowers I've been carrying like a fool, I offer, "These are for you—whether or not you choose to come with me tonight. I didn't know your favorite but if I make the grade and earn a second date—maybe you'll consider telling me."

With that, Vanessa visibly relaxes and opens the door further. "Come on in. Let me put these in water, and I'll grab my purse."

Following her inside, my eyes are immediately drawn to a framed photo on the wall in the foyer. Vanessa and a girl that could pass as her mini-me smile brightly as they build sandcastles at the beach. Happiness radiates from both of them, and I feel it flow through me. When Vanessa stops to see why I'm not following her, I offer, "I'll just wait here, unless you'll be awhile."

"I'll just be a minute," she says as she turns and walks through the open living room into what must be a kitchen on the other side.

I'm drawn to more pictures as I wait. There's one of Vanessa and a man who looks too similar not to be her brother.

His hair is darker, but they share the same features. There are a few pictures of Vanessa and her daughter as well scattered in the collage frames further in the living room.

Before I can inspect their similarities any further, my thoughts are interrupted with, "I'm ready," from Vanessa.

"You just have one final thing to decide before we leave." My tone comes across more serious than I intend, stopping her in her tracks.

"What's that?" she asks hesitantly.

"You haven't told me what you like to eat. I have a few options in mind, but I'd like your input, if that's all right with you?" I offer, stepping toward her as I reach for her hand to give it a squeeze. A live wire shoots through me the moment we touch, which I quickly force myself to ignore it.

A wide grin splits Vanessa's playful face in two. "I think I can handle that. But fair warning... I've been a ball of nerves all day wondering how you'd react to the news of Julia—and now I'm starving."

Chuckling, I pull her toward the door. "I think we'll manage."

9

DAMIEN

WE END up at a Korean restaurant on the other side of town. Neither of us have tried it, but according to Mal, the place is to die for. We both order bulgogi, a beef dish that has my mouth watering when it arrives. When I finally take a bite, my taste buds explode with so many flavors at once. Soy sauce, sesame oils, brown sugar, Asian pear, and a mixture of spices practically make me moan in pleasure. I'll definitely be returning.

Vanessa and I have kept up a casual conversation since we've arrived. I'm quickly learning I enjoy seeing the side of Vanessa when she's no longer in work mode. She's much more talkative and animated.

I love that she talks with her hands when she gets excited. For instance, when she tells me about an absurd customer I missed this morning, I almost die. "So... this woman comes in just after you leave. She's probably in her mid-seventies, barely five feet tall, and that's being generous. She comes up to barely here..." she says, pointing to the part of her arm just below her

shoulder. "She and Jack start up a conversation, and she's inde-
cisive about her order. Jack being Jack suggests she just get it
all... and it was all I could do not to let my jaw drop when she
does. She orders the biggest stack of pancakes, bacon, and a
cinnamon roll from the menu. She also ordered orange juice
and coffee. Mind you—she barely weighs a hundred pounds if
she's soaking wet."

"What's so interesting about that?" I ask, wondering what's
the big deal. There has to be more to this story.

"Jack bet her the cost of her meal... that if her eyes weren't
bigger than her stomach and she finishes the entire thing, he'd
have to take her to dinner."

"Jack asked her out?" Damn. The man still has game.

Vanessa nods enthusiastically. "Yep, Martha gobbled the
whole thing down like a frat boy after a binger. I couldn't
keep my eyes off Jack when he realized she was winning their
bet."

"No kidding? I can only imagine what was going through
that head of his."

"I know, right?" Vanessa shrugs as if that should explain
everything. "It was cute as can be when she took the last bite of
cinnamon roll. Jack's eyes practically bulged out of their sock-
ets, and he swallowed so hard I could hear it. Then in typical
Jack fashion, he flippantly states, '*Well, I guess that's that.
Would next Sunday afternoon work for you? I can pick you up
at six.*'"

"I wanna be Jack when I'm older," I admit with a chuckle.
"Though I do hope I'm not single at that age... Hell... I'd settle
for being more like him now," I admit when I recall how I'd

almost botched my date with Vanessa. "Did you hear the way he was harassing me earlier?"

Rolling her beautiful hazel eyes, she swats a hand in the air between us. "Oh, please. He was just trying to get the show on the road."

Two can play at this game. "So, that's how it is?"

"Well, according to him, it was." She shrugs. "He wished me luck tonight before he left but if you want to know the truth, I think he's rooting for you, too."

My shoulders raise on their own when I admit, "I guess I'll take all the luck I can get. Though I have to admit the old man is right to some degree. I've been interested in you for a while now." I'd rather Vanessa know my intent than to ever wonder.

Genuine shock fills her features. "Did ya now?"

"Yes, ma'am," I tease, but honesty rings through my words. "Why else do you think I always ask random questions to keep you around each morning?"

She stares at me blankly.

Damn. She is cute—and apparently clueless.

I can see her wheels spinning out of control.

"Wait... you're serious?"

I simply nod. What else can I say?

Blinking her confusion away, she quietly asks, "But why?"

"We've been over this," I remind her as the waitress interrupts, asking if we need anything else. When both Vanessa and I shake our heads, I change the subject to something that will hopefully make her less uncomfortable. "Tell me about Julia. How old was she in that picture of the two of you at the beach?"

"Oh, that was taken when we went to Long Beach last summer. She just turned five last week and was the reason I was busy."

"She's adorable. She looks so much like you. I take it the guy in the picture is your brother, right? There's definitely a family resemblance."

Nodding, she agrees, "Yeah. That's my baby brother—and yes, those seven minutes count." She smirks adorably, then continues, "He's been amazingly supportive of me since having Jules. He wasn't supposed to attend CRU, but at the last minute, he changed his mind because he wanted to guarantee I wouldn't be just another teenage statistic."

"That's a commitment. Just from what you've told me though, I'm not surprised. You seem close."

"Yeah, we've lived in the same house since the womb, is our running joke." She grins. "But I'm not complaining. Not many people would want to spend their college years living in family housing and helping me care for a toddler."

The way she says it, I get the feeling Julia's dad isn't in the picture. I wonder where her parents are.

"I'm sure you're right. But under your circumstances, I'm not surprised. I'd do the same if it were my sister and we went to school. Family is everything, and you gotta stick together."

"You have no idea how true those words are." She sighs almost to herself. Then she straightens her spine and lifts her chin as if she's forcing herself to change gears with her thoughts. "But you asked about Julia... I'll warn you... I'm pretty fond of her, and you may get sick of hearing about her if I start..."

Damn. This girl. She sure knows how to make me smile. "Sounds like the words of a proud mom. You have every right to talk about her... she's a part of you, and I'd love to hear anything you're willing to share."

Sitting up, her hands fly in front of her face as she adoringly talks about Julia. "Well, she's a spitfire—so be warned. She's cute as a button one minute, but don't let that fool you." Vanessa shakes a finger in warning. "She's filled with spunk and will always keep you on your toes. She's smart as a whip—and I'm not just bragging. She just turned five, and she already can read a lot of basic books. She loves numbers and will question everything about how the world works. She's strong-willed and won't give up once she sets her mind to something. For instance, she insisted she learn to ride a big girl bike a month or so ago and wouldn't stop until she was flying solo down the sidewalk."

If I had to guess, I'd bet the apple doesn't fall far from the tree. From the tone in her voice, I'm fairly certain she could be listing traits of her own. "She sounds incredible."

"I have no idea where she gets her daredevil ways because now she wants to learn how to long board. She saw a kid from her class do it at the park the other day, and now she's begging for a board of her own." Vanessa's hands cover her face as she shakes her head. "I swear she'll make me turn gray in no time at the rate she's going."

Laughing at a memory, I admit, "My mom said the same of me and my brothers. I was the one who rode skateboards. My brother Derek rode when we were kids, and I had to be just like him."

"I can only imagine." Vanessa's light laugh makes me join her.

"Do you or Vince know how to ride?" I ask.

"Uh... that would be a Big. Fat. No."

"Long boards are easier to ride, so it's probably best if she starts on one of those should the time come. There's guaranteed to be road rash at some point—even the best crash eventually does. But if she's wearing a helmet and pads, the risk isn't any greater than riding a bike."

"If you say so." Vanessa's tone tells me she's not quite buying what I have to sell, but she's not dismissing it either.

"I'd never lie about safety. Trust me. Sure, I've been known to take risks in my youth, but I'd never willingly put anyone in jeopardy. I also used to snowboard when I got the chance, and in my day, I may have been a punk, but I've been told I've grown out of it," I tease.

"You're such an old crony now, Damien. I'm surprised you don't need a walker."

"Okay, brat. I get your point. All I'm saying is I wouldn't be going off jumps anytime soon, but long boarding isn't that dangerous. If you need some pointers, I'm sure I can help."

Did I just volunteer to teach her daughter?

"We'll cross that bridge when we get there," she says. "She also wants a kitten. We'll see which of the two wins out."

"Oh, you're in for it," I say, remembering how relentless Dani could be when she wanted something.

"One thing's guaranteed. Life is never dull with Jules."

"I can only imagine."

The waitress comes with our check, but I'm nowhere

ready for our evening to end. Glancing at my watch, I realize the night is still young and suggest, "It's a beautiful evening. Wanna walk along the riverfront?"

Vanessa's face lights up as she nods in agreement. "Sounds amazing. I haven't been down there in forever."

It doesn't take long for us to find a place to park along the Columbia River and walk along the paved pathway. Mt. Hood and all its beauty is a prominent feature as a backdrop for our walk. There are a few others enjoying the evening along the boardwalk, but for the most part, I'm oblivious to anyone but Vanessa.

"This is so different from seeing Mt. Rainier in Seattle from the campus of U-Dub," I admit as I stare at the beauty of the Columbia River Gorge. "In the U-District, sure you have the water from Lake Washington, but it's surrounded by the bustling of the city. Here just feels more peaceful."

"I'll never tire of this view," Vanessa sighs as she stares at the mountain before us. "Did you grow up near Seattle?"

I shake my head. "No. I grew up near Leavenworth. My parents own and run a store outside Cashmere. Well, Dad runs the store, and Mom does the books. I moved to the city for school."

"I grew up just south of Seattle, but I'm familiar with the U-District. I can see the pull, but I wanted a school with a traditional college feel, not as urbanized. So, I chose CRU. I liked their nursing program, so that helps, too." Vanessa's adorable the way she shrugs her last comment. Though I'm quickly finding there's not much I don't like about her.

"After coming to work at CRU, I'll admit, I totally see the

draw." I watch a large bird in the distance dip down and pick up something out of the water. "You don't see things like that every day."

"No kidding. That was freaking incredible."

We stop for a moment and lean against the rail to watch the bird swoop down again. This time he glides along the water and pulls out a larger fish.

"Look at those talons," Vanessa says in awe, and all I can do is shake my head in agreement.

When the bird disappears into the trees in front of us, I return my attention to Vanessa. I'm surprised to find her staring at me with a look of wonder in her dancing hazel eyes.

"What?" I ask, suddenly feeling as if I have something on my face to make her stare at me that way.

Shaking her head, she mutters, "It's nothing."

Nope. Not buying it. Her expression is quite serious. So, I push a little, "I highly doubt that. Something's on your mind. Just spit it out. Please know you can say anything, and there will be no judgement."

Rolling her eyes to the sky, she shakes her head.

After a long pause, she looks me in the eye. "You're right," she admits. "I was thinking of something."

"Okay..." I prompt, hoping she'll continue. I don't want to push her, but my curiosity gets the better of me. I can't read her face entirely, but I suddenly feel as if I need to know what's behind it, as if it will unlock a door to knowing more about her.

"Well, if you must know..." Her voice fills with a playful

tone, then she sighs heavily before continuing. "I want you to know I'm having a wonderful time tonight."

"Okay..." That doesn't match her expression, but I'll take it.

Vanessa's soft hand reaches up to push my hair from my face. I know I need a haircut, but damn, if it keeps her touching me, I might have to reconsider. She has my full attention. When her fingers trace my jawline and cup my chin, I freeze.

I have no idea what's holding me in place in this moment. As her emerald eyes stare into mine, it takes everything in my power not to close the distance between us and kiss the hell out of her.

"So total truth..." she whispers, and it's the sexiest thing I've ever heard.

Instinctively, my body draws closer to hers as we get lost in each other's eyes. But I keep from closing the gap completely because I need to keep my focus on her eyes, so I won't miss anything. Somehow, I manage to ask, "Truth?"

A mischievous grin distracts me, and I barely notice her raise on her toes and get closer. "I was wondering what it would be like to do this..."

I feel a light tug on my chin a split second before her hand rests on my shoulder for balance, and she presses her lips to mine. They're soft, yet strong, and know what they want. There's the perfect amount of pucker and suction, making me want more.

My lips smile against her lips as I pull her body flush to mine. "You mean this..." I say as I glide my free hand along her shoulder to the base of her neck where I guide her head ever so softly, so my lips can align perfectly with hers to continue what she's started.

Nodding, she moans, "Yes," into my mouth, and I'm done for.

I run my tongue along the seam of her lips, and they part for me. She tastes of the mint Chapstick I saw her apply along the ride and something entirely her.

I. Can't. Get. Enough.

Her hands cup my face as she shows me exactly how she likes to be kissed. When she captures my lower lip in hers and pulls ever so slightly, I almost forget this is our first date, and we're in public.

Almost.

As much as I'd love to get carried away, I manage to keep my wits about me. When we eventually break away, both breathless and panting for air, I can't help the triumphant grin that forms. "Is that what you were expecting?"

Damn, if the cutest blush doesn't fill her features. Though all thoughts of her being shy fly out the window when she says, "I'm not sure. I may have to try that again."

What. A. Vixen.

Grinning, I close the distance between us and kiss her for all I'm worth. If she has any hesitation by the time I'm through with her, then I haven't kissed the fuck out her properly, and I don't deserve her.

Who gives a damn if we're in public or only on our first date? If this woman wants me to kiss her, I'll happily oblige. Though with lips like these, it's hardly out of obligation. The more I nip, suck, and taste, the more I want. It's like her lips are the gateway drug I was warned about as a teen. Once you start, you won't want to stop.

But eventually, we must.

Because well... we're in public.

And I may have my mind on a mission, I haven't forgotten my reasons for slowing things down in the first place.

This time, when we pull apart, Vanessa's beautiful eyes are wide as she catches her breath and blinks a few times. Then she nods slowly. "So much better than my expectations," she says in a tone I'm not sure if she's talking to me or herself.

Leaning in to kiss her once more chastely, I reach for her hand and give it a squeeze before I playfully reply, "Sweetheart, you have no idea. What do you say we continue our walk while I still can?"

10

VANESSA

BY THE TIME Damien walks me to my door, I swear I've been living in an alternate reality. Things like this don't happen to me. I don't make the first move, and I certainly don't have a guy's full attention for an entire evening. Don't get me wrong, I know I'm worthy... I'm just not used to being the focus of their attention. From the day I found out I was pregnant with Julia, I've known that I was no longer the center of my world.

"Can I see you again?"

I'm barely able to nod in agreement before his lips slant over mine, and I'm lost in the moment.

The way his tongue dances with mine sends sparks of electricity zipping through me. My stomach flitters as if a swarm of butterflies are dying to escape as my pulse skyrockets. He manages to control the kiss so that I'm on the brink of being completely satisfied, yet when he pulls away, I'm left wanting more.

Before I can say anything, he says, "Goodnight, Vanessa. I'll see you in the morning."

With that, he turns and walks away.

I guess the girls were right. Dating *is* just like riding a bike. I may be out of practice, but I certainly remember how. Though let's be honest, I've never kissed a man like Damien. Holy shit, he can kiss.

I swear I could feel the heat from my toes to the tips of my hair as the energy that flowed between us caught fire. I've never been so consumed by a kiss that I forgot my name when I came up for air. Maybe it's because he's older and knows what the hell he's doing, but I've never experienced this kind of whole-body kiss. What's weird is things never moved beyond the basics. It was only a few kisses. Nothing more. Yet I feel as if I've had an out-of-body experience. I can't even find words to describe it.

Damien drops me off a little before ten. Thank goodness, Julia's sound asleep, and Vince and Sydney are busy watching a movie when I come in, so I can excuse myself to my room without any fuss. The knowing look on Sydney's face tells me she's dying to know what happened, but she'll wait to ask when Vince isn't around.

My mind is a muddled mess as I replay the events of this evening on a loop. Knowing I have an early morning, I hop into my jammies, getting ready for bed on auto pilot. I brush my hair and teeth and check on Julia one last time before I make the final descent onto my mattress.

Peeking through the door, I see she's conked out and won't be any the wiser of my presence. Her hair's strewn about her pillow, and her arm rests above her face as if it's blocking the light. One leg is kicked out, and her blankets are already a rumpled mess. She's freaking adorable when she's in dreamland. I can't help but close the distance between us to give her the goodnight kiss I missed this evening.

God, I hate being away from her, but I'll admit I totally enjoyed my time with Damien tonight. After tucking her in, I can't help but stop and stare. She's the best thing that's ever happened to me. Sure, she wasn't expected, but I've come to learn that the best things in life never are.

Rubbing a finger over my swollen lips, thoughts of Damien drift through my mind.

Knowing I can't stay up much longer, I force myself to end my fantasizing and return to my bedroom. Four forty-five will be here whether I want it to or not. Even though I'm eager to see Damien again, I'm not one who functions well on zero sleep.

Drifting off to sleep, I'm reminded of the soft musk of his cologne, the way he held my hand, or guided me as we walked with his hand at the small of my back. I was so in tune with him, it was crazy. I swear, before he touched me in any way, it was as if my body sensed it as a premonition. Like a slight tingle would prick at the base of my spine and tingle through my limbs. Then when he made contact, I would be grounded and calm in that same instant.

Maybe I'm just overthinking this and being ridiculous, but I'm dying to know if this is just a one-off or will it be like this every time I'm with him. I do know one thing for certain. I can't wait to see him again.

ODDLY ENOUGH, when my alarm goes off, I don't even feel the need to hit snooze. I practically bounce out of bed, rushing though my morning routine. Somehow, I manage to make it out the door earlier than usual for my shift. I know I'll likely crash early this evening, but I'm eager to see if what happened between Damien and I is real—or just a figment of my vivid dreams in the night.

Knowing Damien usually doesn't show for a while, I busy myself by cleaning unnecessarily between customers and restocking what I can from the already full shelves to prepare for a rush.

"What's got you actin' like a long-tail cat in a room full of rockers, Vanessa?" Jack asks as he sips his cup of coffee. "You look at that door one more time, you're gonna wear the paint off it."

"What?" I scoff, realizing he's caught me redhanded, indeed looking at the door again. "I'm just waiting on the daily rush," I attempt to pass off.

But he's not buying it. "Uh, huh..." he slowly draws out as a grumble. "You keep tellin' yourself that."

Not knowing what to say, I just stop my bustling and stare at him.

"I'm thinkin' it might have somethin' to do with that young fella who finally got the nerve to ask you out." He sucks in a deep, exaggerated breath as he glances at his watch. "If I'm not mistaken, he's due any moment..." Then he looks to me. "I take it you had a good time, or you'd be avoiding the front counter.

Am I right?"

Not that I want to divulge my personal life to the patrons in the diner, but this is Jack, and he's the only one at the counter at the moment. So I allow my excitement to show. "Yes. We had a great time—thank you very much," I tack on at the end, sounding sarcastic, so he won't read too much into it.

Jack's light-blue eyes dance with delight, and his genuine happiness can be felt from where I stand. "Good for you, honey. You deserve every ounce of happiness offered to you. Damien seems like a good-enough fella, but if you find out otherwise—or if he ever hurts you—I know a guy who will take care of him, and we'll never see the likes of him again. You just say the word—ya hear me?"

Oh. This man.

My heart pangs when I realize just how much he cares. Sure, he teases like crazy, but over the years, he's become the long-lost grandparent I never had. He's so easy to talk to, and he's gotten me to open up in ways I never imagined I would with a stranger. I love that he cares enough to threaten bodily harm—though I doubt it will be necessary.

"Oh, Jack." My voice fills with emotion. "Thank you."

He cocks a thick brow in my direction, and his once-teasing features turn serious. "He already do somethin'?"

Swatting that thought away, I quickly assure him, "No... No... Damien's been nothing but a gentleman, but it just feels so nice to have someone looking out for me. That's all."

"Honey, you know I do." He nods in reassurance, but then his tone turns mischievous once more. "But I'm serious—

I know a guy. I grew up in the South and know which bushes to bury someone under—and you'll never hear from them again."

As I fight to hold my laughter in, I assure him again, "I don't think that will be necessary. Besides, we don't have any plants like that around here, so I think Damien's safe."

"Damien's safe from what?" I hear from the sexiest voice imaginable.

Oh. My. God.

How did I not see him come in?

Crap, what did he hear?

Jack laughs aloud as he motions for Damien to take a seat beside him. "Have a seat, son."

As Damien sits, Jack pats him on the shoulder. "Vanessa and I were just talking about the fact that if anyone ever hurts her, I know a guy who can make things happen."

"If anyone hurts her, they'll have to stand in line," Damien says.

"That include you?" The words fly out of my mouth before I can stop myself.

"Most certainly." Damien nods without hesitation.

Jack slaps Damien on the back as he grins wide. "Well... now that that's settled... When will the two of you be going out again?"

"Jack," I gasp and admonish simultaneously. What the hell is he doing? Our first date was just last night, and he's already pushing for another?

"As soon as she's able," Damien says, and my focus stays on him.

Staring in disbelief that he'd be so bold, I'm at a loss for what to say.

I know he wants to go out again, but I didn't think he'd make that proclamation to Jack—after only one date. Maybe I'm not the only one feeling our connection.

But what is it with Jack and his sudden need to play matchmaker? What if Damien hadn't wanted to go out again? That would've made things awkward.

Damien's soft tone somehow grounds me and keeps my emotions at bay when he looks me in the eye and adds, "I know Vanessa's busy and has other obligations. But anytime she's willing to make time for me, I'm happy to go along for the ride."

"Be careful what you wish for," I tease. "My life is a circus sometimes. You may live to regret that."

Damien's deep smile makes my stomach flip and my heart melt. "I think I'm willing to take that risk." His tone is just as playful, but the meaning packs a punch. I feel his words in my bones, and I'm not sure what to make of it.

Needing to keep things casual, I ask, "Want your usual before you're off to conquer the world?"

"That and some coffee would be great," he says as he clasps his hands and leans on the counter in front of him. The sleeves of his dark-blue button up are rolled to just below his elbows and when his hands clasp, I find myself staring at his corded forearms.

When I realize I'm staring, I quickly turn and grab the carafe, fill a mug, and place it in front of him.

I don't get the chance to say anything because a group of

ten college students come in and sit in my section, causing us all to watch their silly antics.

"I'll get this order in and be back when I can."

"Take your time. I know you're busy." I hear as I bustle off to take care of the start of the morning rush.

Though I'm aware of nearly his every move, I hardly get to talk much with Damien. I'm not sure what's in the water, but everyone is out and about, and the rush never lets up until I'm nearly off shift. Damien manages to say goodbye and mentions texting me later, but I'm too busy to do more than deliver his food and take care of his check.

By the time I'm off shift, I'm exhausted. But knowing I have a full day of classes and Julia tonight, I push through—what choice do I have? Just as I get to campus, my phone buzzes with an incoming text, so I pull if from my jeans pocket and read as I walk to class.

Damien: Hope the rest of your day goes well.

Knowing that he's thinking of me brings a smile to my face.

Me: Thanks. You, too. Sorry we couldn't talk much today.

Damien: Maybe we can talk tonight?

My thoughts instantly go to last night, and I want much more than talking. When I nearly bump into the person who has stopped to pick up something they dropped, I force myself to pay better attention to my surroundings.

Me: Julia's usually asleep by 8. Can I text you after she goes down?

Damien: You can text me anytime. I gotta run to my next meeting, but I'll get any messages you send when I'm free. Have fun in class.

Before I can respond, another text comes through

Damien: I didn't get the chance to tell you—you looked beautiful today.

Aww... he thinks I'm beautiful.

Yeah, there goes my concentration. I manage to make it to class on auto pilot. Thank goodness, I have time to spare; my mind is lost on him until my professor starts class, and I'm forced to pay attention.

11

DAMIEN

KNOWING Vanessa isn't available until this evening, I bust through my list of chores when I get home so I can talk when the time comes. She is never far from my thoughts today, but as I start installing the cabinets in my kitchen, I'm forced to concentrate on them rather than her. There's no way I'm redoing any of these. Not only are they a bitch to install on my own, they're too expensive to replace.

I stop earlier than normal to take a shower before Vanessa calls. I want to give her my undivided attention. When I have a half-finished project, I've been known to keep working while talking on the phone, just to get it done.

With my kitchen out of commission, I'd ordered a pizza earlier, and I'm finally able to sit and eat my meal. Settling into the couch to watch some TV, I grab a slice from the box using the paper plate they provided and wait.

When the phone rings, my heart races like it did in high school with my first crush. But I'm quickly disappointed when

I see it's my sister Dani. Swiping to accept the call, I greet her with, "Hey."

"Hey to you, too, Dame. Everything okay?"

"Yeah," I sigh heavily. "I'm just watching TV."

"Are we still on for this weekend?" Dani asks.

"Yeah, I wouldn't miss it. Do you want to stay here? I have an extra room set up. Though at the moment, the kitchen's out of commission."

"Thanks for the offer, but Luke and I need to get back. I'm on a deadline, and Luke's leaving to see his parents for a few days on Sunday."

"Why aren't you going?" Those two are usually connected at the hip, and I'm surprised she'd pass up the chance to travel with him.

"I have a book signing next weekend, and I'm traveling to Chicago. I can't afford to travel so much if I have any hopes of meeting my deadline. Besides, Luke and his dad are going fishing, and I'd just be in the way."

"Makes sense. What time do you think you'll be free Saturday?"

"I'm meeting with Sam at ten, and we should be free after noon. She usually doesn't work on the weekends, but she's making the exception for me; it was the only time we could meet in person and catch up this month."

"You do know there's this thing called video conferencing, right?" I tease.

I can hear her eye roll when she sighs. "Yeah, but we've learned that when we're both in the same room, we're far more effective. Besides, this is also an excuse to visit my brothers. I'm dying to see this new place you've got."

As I look around my home, I see all the work I've done—and all the work left to do. "It's coming together, but it's still a work in progress," I admit.

"It'll be great. Look, Luke just got home, and I gotta run. I'll see you Saturday. Love you, Dame."

"Love you, too, Dan." I laugh as I hear the click of the line. That girl is always on the run. I'm glad Luke makes her so happy though. He's definitely one of the few who gets my sister and her quirks.

Hell, I'll never forget the day I met Luke. I'd been visiting my sister at my grandparents' cabin on Anderson Island. I'd been watching something on TV when there was a knock on the door. I had no idea who was at the door, but obviously Dani knew. She launched herself into the stranger's arms and kissed the hell out of him. It got to the point where it was uncomfortable to watch, so of course, I cleared my throat to remind her I was in fact in the room when they came up for air. I was about to leave them alone when I recognized the stranger. Who wouldn't know the Rainier Renegades newest head coach? Given the fact that at the time, he was the youngest in the league, I think I said something along the lines of "*Holy shit... Luke Leighton is kissing... you? When did you crawl out from the rock you live under and meet a guy like him?*"

I swear, as long as I live, I'm not gonna let Dani live that one down. Of course, they've had their moments where their fame has gotten in the way but overall, they're perfect for one another. And let's face it... as long as she's happy, I'll be happy for her.

My phone buzzes with an incoming text, and I'm instantly pulled from my memory.

Vanessa: Are you busy?

For her—never.

Me: Nope.

Instead of replying, the phone rings, and I'm blessed with Vanessa's sultry voice. "Hey, you." Her voice is deeper than in person, but it could be that she's tired from an extremely long day.

"Hope you don't mind. I'd much rather talk than text," she admits.

"I'd rather talk in person—but I'll settle for the phone," rolls off my tongue. So much for playing it smooth. But really? Why wouldn't I tell her? After last night, I'll always choose the option where I get to kiss her at the end of the night.

"Sorry. Julia's in bed by eight usually—and although I can talk on the phone, I don't get much of a social life."

Shit. I never meant for her to feel guilty. Quickly, I backpedal to explain, "You have nothing to be sorry for. You're a mom, and Julia will always come first. That was just my pathetic way of telling you I enjoy being with you in person."

"Oh." She's quiet for a moment, and fear sets in that I'm blowing it.

"Oh, what?" I clarify.

Please let me be wrong.

"I... uh... just wasn't expecting that."

"Expecting..." I draw out because this is *not* the time to make assumptions. I've likely already made an ass out of myself, and I don't the need to dig the hole further.

"Expecting you to say you want to spend time with me?" she questions.

Holy shit. She couldn't be more wrong.

"For the record—and so we're clear. I like being around you. I'm kind of a selfish bastard and will take you any way I can get you. If it's just time at the diner in the mornings, in person, or on the phone. I just want the chance to know you better. If you don't want me around, you'd better tell me. After last night, I hope we see a lot more of each other."

"Okay... wow," she whispers on the other end.

Fuck, what does that mean?

Thankfully, I'm quickly put out of my misery when the most beautiful laugh fills my ears. "Okay... I guess I can live with that. Thank you for your honesty. I guess I'm so out of practice, I was trying to give you an out."

"Vanessa," I say firmer than I expect, "if I don't want to be around you—you'll know; life's too short, and I'm too damn old to play games."

"On that we can agree." She's quiet for a moment but then changes the subject unexpectedly. "So how was the rest of your day? I didn't get the chance to text because my classes were back to back, and Jules wanted to go to the park to ride her bike until nearly dinner. Then of course, it was bath and story time before bed. I still have a paper I need to work on due later this week."

Holy shit. She ran circles around me today. Is this what her life is like every day? "Well, my day was nothing compared to yours, Wonder Woman. I just had a few meetings, came home, and installed a few cabinets in my kitchen."

"You mentioned you were flipping your house. What all have you done?" she asks with interest.

I fill her in on my progress. She asks questions, and I explain the state of the house I bought it in. She surprises me by saying, "Wow, I'd love to see that someday."

"I'd be happy to show you anytime you'd like. Speaking of seeing you, do you have any time free soon?"

Vanessa sighs heavily. "Uh... I probably won't have time until the weekend. I have an exam and a paper due on Friday. But you're busy with your sister then, right?"

"Are you free Sunday?" I ask, filling with hope. Maybe we can make something work. I meant what I said about being okay only seeing her at the diner, but she typically doesn't work much in the later part of the week.

"Can I check with Vince and get back to you?" Regret fills her voice, and that line of thought needs to stop.

"Of course. I should be home most of the day, so just let me know when you'll be free. I'd love to show you my place. I'd offer to cook, but my kitchen isn't an option."

"I'm sure we can figure something out," she says on a yawn.

"What time do you have to be up tomorrow?"

"My alarm goes off at four forty-five." Her voice is gruff

and filling with sleep.

Glancing at my clock, my eyes nearly bug out. "Uh... I'd better let you go. You have a long day tomorrow, and it's nearly eleven."

"Is it really?" she asks in awe. "I could've sworn it was earlier than that."

"Get some sleep, Wonder Woman. I'll see you at the diner in the morning."

"Okay," she says on another yawn. "I'd better go before I fall asleep on you."

She's freaking adorable.

"Night, sleepyhead."

"I'm not that tired," she protests, but her voice is far more gravelly than usual. She's exhausted, and I've just kept her up late. I'll have to remember that in the future. But I swear we said hello—and the next thing I know, it was hours later.

"Sure you're not," I tease. "Well, I'd better get *my* beauty sleep if I don't want to look like a zombie in the morning."

This earns me a beautiful laugh. "Night, Damien. See you in the morning."

"Looking forward to it." I chuckle in response.

When I hear the line click off, I end the call from my end.

Smiling, I stand and gather my trash from dinner, then get ready for bed.

As I crawl between my cool sheets, my mind drifts to Vanessa.

One thing is certain, the clock flies when I'm with Vanessa, but the minutes drag when I'm waiting to see her again. I never thought I'd be dying for my alarm to come the next morning.

12

DAMIEN

SEEING Vanessa each morning never gets old. I pop into the diner a little earlier than normal each morning she's worked this week to spend as much time with her as I can. Even though she's busy with school and Julia, we manage to talk each evening as well. It's been hard as hell not to kiss the ever-loving shit out of her the moment she's in my sight, but we've managed to keep things fairly casual while she's at work. I don't think anyone she works with would notice her subtle wink, or the way her hand lingers long enough for me to brush mine with hers for the briefest of seconds.

It's hard being on my best behavior and not flirt or talk in depth like we do on the phone each evening, but we manage. The more I get to know Vanessa, the more I'm intrigued by her. I can't wait to spend more time with her.

Of course, our flirting doesn't go unnoticed by Jack's eagle eyes. When Vanessa drops off my coffee this morning, my hand brushes hers as she hands me the mug. When our eyes lock, we stare wordlessly until we're brought out of our revelry by Jack's grumbles.

"I don't reckon I could get that kinda reaction from her when she *finally* gets around to serving me a cup. Lord knows, it'll be cold by the time she gets to me, if the two of you keep making googly eyes at each other."

Vanessa drops her hand like I'm a hot potato and stares at Jack as my eyes whip to his.

Shaking his head, he grumbles at me, "Oh, don't get your boxers in a bunch. I'd just like to get my coffee while it's hot. The way you two were starin' at one another, the world could disappear, and you'd be none the wiser. Don't get me wrong. I remember those days. I was just the same way when I met my Mary. She was somethin' of a looker, and God only knows how she ended up with her sights on me. But when your lingering looks come between a man and his daily dose of caffeine... a man's gotta do... what a man's gotta do."

"Well, we certainly wouldn't want the beast you become without coffee to appear. I heard that's a sight no one wants to live through. Let's get your daily fix to you right away," Vanessa says without missing a beat. "I'd hate to ruin this perfect perception I have of you, Jack."

"Oh, honey." Jack chuckles. "I'm far from perfect. I'm just givin' the two of you a hard time. Someone's gotta do it, and it may as well be me. It's not my fault you're easy targets. But you give an old man like me hope. So keep flirting the way you are... and remember—if anything happens—invite me to the weddin'."

Seriously? Did he just say wedding?

Vanessa's not fazed by it at all, in fact, she pushes back at him, giving as good as she gets. "Okay, Jack. But if you hit it off with Martha and wedding bells start ringing, I'd better be invited. I was here when you met, so I call dibs."

She didn't just say that.

But when I look to Jack, his mouth opens and closes like a fish, and it's all I can do not to laugh. Holy shit. She's rendered him speechless and me as well. I've wondered if he ever went out on a date with Martha but haven't had the nerve to ask—knowing it's none of my business. Leave it to Vanessa to lay it on the table.

Vanessa fills his cup and smirks. "That's what I thought." Then she reminds him, "You'd better not back out on Martha. That poor woman went to great lengths to get your attention. You at least owe her dinner out of it."

Jack sighs exasperatedly, "I'll have you know... we're goin' out tomorrow evening, Miss Know-it-all. But that's all the details you're gonna get from this old man—ya got it? I don't kiss and tell."

Holy shit. I want to be him when I grow up.

Vanessa's beautiful laughter fills the room. "You can keep whatever you want to yourself, Jack. Just promise you'll give her a fair shake."

"Same with you, Missy." Jack laughs as he nods in my direction. "Same to you."

The rest of my time with Vanessa goes quickly and while she waits on other customers, Jack and I make small talk as I finish my breakfast. After I pay my bill, I chat with Jack some more. When I'm forced to leave for work, I notice Vanessa's still busy with other customers, so I text her instead of saying goodbye.

Me: Talk tonight. BTW—You look beautiful today.

Knowing she won't be able to reply for a few hours, I make my way with a full belly and a smile on my face. I can't wait until we can see one another again. As I walk away, once again, I wish I hadn't made plans with my family tomorrow. I have no idea how I'll make it until Sunday before I see her again.

THE NEXT AFTERNOON, just as I pull into my brother's apartment complex, I receive another text from Vanessa. Sure, we talked into the late hours of the night and a few times this morning, but my heart still races as a smile forms when the notification goes off.

Vanessa: Have fun with your family. I'm off to the park with Jules.

Me: Thanks. I just got here. Picking up Davis so we can meet Dani in a few.

Vanessa: I won't keep you. Jules wants to ride bikes, so I'd better go.

I haven't ridden a bike in years. Maybe I should get one so I can join them sometime. I almost text as much, but then think better of it.

What the hell, Dame? You just met this girl.

Slow your roll and see what happens next. You know what happens when you're not on the same page.

A knock on my window startles me.

As my heart races out of my chest, I see my brother's dopey grin waiting outside the passenger door. "Dude... you gonna let me in?" he says, muffled by the closed door.

Christ. Where's my head?

Chuckling, I roll my eyes at his pathetically begging face.

Some things never change. "Geez,, Davis... have some patience," I mumble as I click the locks. "I would've come to the door."

"I know... but I heard your truck pull in and waited forever for you to turn it off. What the hell were you doing in here?"

"Just returning a text," I admit. But then I don't miss the chance to razz my little brother. "You know... that thing people do... in some circles, which is considered socially acceptable or expected?"

"Geez... you're starting this shit already?"

"If the shoe fits..." I playfully tease as I pull out of the parking spot to head to the restaurant we're meeting Dani and Luke at. They'll all come to my place to check out my progress later, but Dani insisted we eat first.

When Davis remains quiet, I ask, "How's school?"

He releases a heavy sigh. "Good, I guess. I'm in labs for

hours on end, and I'm starting my clinical experience next month, which will make me have even less of a life. When I can finally practice... it will be worth it."

"What you're doing is amazing, Davey." The use of his childhood name has him rolling his eyes. But I continue with the truth. "We're all proud of you."

"Speaking of social life—wanna go out tonight? I need to let off some steam and thought I might crash at your place if we get too wild."

Thinking about my date with Vanessa tomorrow, I shrug. "You're more than welcome to stay, but you'll need to drive your car. I'm busy tomorrow and won't have time to bring you back."

Nodding, Davis agrees, "Sounds good. God... I need a night out. I haven't had one in I don't know how long..." he trails off as if he's trying to remember.

Knowing Davis, it's been awhile. He rarely lets loose and relaxes these days, so I offer, "I'll even be your wingman tonight."

"Why won't you be scouting for your own possibilities?" he asks with interest.

Instantly, Vanessa's beautiful face fills my mind, and I smile. Her expressive hazel eyes, pink full lips, and a smile that melts me from the inside out. But it's too soon to say anything, so I stick with vague details. "I... um... just started something new... and until I know what's going on there, I'm keeping my focus on her."

"Sounds serious..." Davis picks up on my mood. "Does she happen to be part of your plans tomorrow?"

Yeah. Davis knows me better than anyone, so there's no use in hiding anything. I find myself nodding as I quickly reply, "Yep."

"I see..." Davis draws out.

Pulling into the parking lot of the restaurant, I ask something only a brother can. "Can we keep this between us? I'll fill you in on the details later but for now, I'd rather not mention it to Dani. You know how she gets when she thinks one of us might be serious with a girl... I'd rather just enjoy our time with her and Luke and keep my personal life out of it."

"Hmmm..." Davis puts a finger to his lip as he looks out the window. "If I didn't know you better, I'd almost think you *were* getting serious with a girl... but we both know you don't do serious relationships—after Amber." He opens the door and hops out before I can respond.

Fuck. The last thing I want to think about is Amber. But this thing with Vanessa is nothing like that. Could it be? No... it's nothing like that. In the short time we've known each other, I'm certain of that. Vanessa is nothing like Amber.

Hopping out of my truck, I spot Dani and Luke getting out of his SUV. Heading in that direction, I holler a greeting to get their attention, "Look what the cat drug in..."

Dani rushes to me and launches herself into my arms for a hug. "Dame. God, it's been too long." Being a good six inches taller, I lift her like I always do when we hug. From the moment I've been able, this is our thing. Her curly hair springs to life and assaults my face unintentionally. When I set her down, Luke's there to shake my hand.

"Good to see you, Luke," I offer as I pull him in for a bro hug.

"Damien," Luke offers as I release him.

"What about me?" Davis asks as he approaches.

"Oh, Davey, we won't forget you," Dani says as she hugs him just as fiercely. "God, I've missed you, too. We have to get together more often."

"Can't breathe," Davis exaggerates, and she finally lets him go. He's just as big as I am, so we all laugh at his response, since Dani's a dwarf in comparison. But we all know she's a hugger. She always has been.

When she releases Davis, she announces, "I don't know about you, but I need to eat. Let's go. Luke made reservations."

The restaurant isn't that fancy, but I'm not surprised he's gone to the effort. We've learned it's easier to let him do his thing and get a more secluded place in the restaurant. Most don't recognize him—but now that Dani and Luke are pretty famous in their own worlds, it's best not to risk it.

When we get inside, we're immediately escorted to a back room where our table is ready and waiting for us. After looking briefly at the menu, we give the waitress our orders.

Davis asks Dani about her meeting today, and we spend the entire time waiting for our food listening to how her book might have a movie option—which is huge news. Since this is the first she's been able to tell anyone, she's more excited than usual about the possibilities. She gushes over the potential actors who would play the part, and I'll admit, I'm impressed with the A-List names that roll off her tongue.

"I mean... can you imagine... with names like these, my books will become household names."

"Uh, Dan," Davis interrupts. "You kinda already are... not to burst your bubble. The last girl I dated was more into you than me, I think... once she found out who my sister was."

Dani bats the air in dismissal. "Oh, I doubt that..."

Davis looks to me and shrugs. Obviously, he isn't joking but won't argue with Dani. She'll never believe him anyway. She's like the only one on the planet that hasn't realized now that she's with Luke—they've pretty much become a social icon.

"So, Damien," Luke draws out in his barely there accent from Tennessee—clearly changing the subject. "Dani says you're almost done with your kitchen. If you need any help, I can give you a hand before we take off this evening."

"I'd appreciate that, Luke. The top cupboards will go in much easier with a second set of hands. It honestly won't take more than an hour or so if you're serious. I was gonna ask a guy from my crew if he'd be able to help me, but I'd much rather get them done sooner."

"You know all you had to do was ask," Davis reminds me.

"I know. I know." I put a hand up to stop his train of thought. "I was gonna ask you either way to give me a hand with the top cabinets tonight—whether or not Luke volunteered. But if the three of us work on it, we can knock them out in no time."

"I can't wait to see what you've done to the place. Dani showed me your before shots on the ferry ride this morning."

"I've done quite a bit since I last sent pics, trust me. You can see for yourself, so I won't bore you with the details. Tell me—have the two of you been staying out of trouble now that you're in the off season? I know Dani's working on her next book—as usual. But what have you been up to?"

Luke draws a hand down his face and sighs heavily. "I swear, I'm just as busy in the off season—doing things people don't usually talk about. We've been spending more time at the Island, so Dani has less distractions, but sometimes it's unavoidable, and we have to stay in town. Do either of you have plans the week of July fourth?" He looks to Davis and me, and Dani's excitement gets the best of her.

When each of us shrugs, she practically jumps out of her seat. "Good! See what you can do to take the entire week off— we're giving you plenty of notice. We'll have a reunion at the end of the week, and we can celebrate the Fourth together as a family. The 'Rents are on board, Grandma and Pops are coming into town, and Derek is free, too."

"I... uh... don't know if I'll be able to take the whole week off," I say hesitantly. I'm not sure how my bosses will feel with me taking time off around an already short week. But with just one glance at the pleading look in Dani's eyes—I know without a doubt I'll be asking for it off. This is important to her for some reason, and I won't be the one to disappoint her.

"Will there be enough room? Or should I look into getting an Airbnb for us?" I offer, knowing I'm too damn old to be camping out, and my grandparents' cabin is only a three-bedroom place with a pull-out couch as well. Technically, we can all sleep there, but I'd rather have some space.

Luke's the one to offer. "Why don't you give Derek and

your parents the rooms at your grandparents' cabin, and the two of you can stay in each of my guest rooms? If we need more space, I'll see what I can do about accommodations."

We don't have much family besides what's been mentioned. Who else would we need accommodations for? Maybe Luke's family will join us? When Davis and I just stare at them, waiting for further explanation, we get nothing. Whatever they're planning, I won't push. Knowing my sister, sometimes it's best not to ask.

By the time we finish our meal and make it to my place near the CRU campus, it's only mid-afternoon. Knowing Dani and Luke have to still travel back to Anderson Island, I offer we forget about hanging the cabinets, but Luke is insistent.

True to my word, by the time the hour is up, we're hanging the last of them. Everything is in place, and all that's left to do is put my new appliances in when they arrive and have the countertops installed. Since I'm going with a marble slab, I'm leaving that to the professionals.

By the time Dani and Luke take off, Davis is ready to grab some dinner and head out to the bar to unwind for the evening. Being new to town, I'm not sure where to go, but then I remember the bar Vanessa told me about—the one her brother's girlfriend works at. Apparently, there's a live band most weekends, and a great crowd gathers. If Davis is in the mood to hook up with a girl, it'll likely be the place for it to happen.

Just as we're finishing dinner, a text comes through from Vanessa.

Vanessa: Hey, how was your day? Are you still with your family?

Me: Davis and I just grabbed a bite to eat. Later, we'll grab drinks. I know you're busy, but I won't lie... Wish you could join us.

Vanessa takes a few minutes to respond. At first, I'm afraid I've upset her.

When her text finally comes through, I'm relieved.

Vanessa: Sorry. Jules woke up. I had to get her back to sleep. Are you having fun?

Smiling that she'd care enough to ask, I quickly tap out a reply.

Me: Yes. Finished installing my cabinets this afternoon, and we're just hanging out now.

Vanessa: Well, don't let me keep you.

As much as I love my brother, I'd rather talk to Vanessa on the phone than hang out in a bar.

Me: Davis just walked back into the room. I'll check in with you in a bit.

Davis looks to me questioningly. "Everything okay?"

Stowing my phone in my pocket, I reply as casual as I can manage, "Yeah. Just texting a friend."

"Is this that same *friend* you happen to have plans with tomorrow?"

"Yes," I admit. I don't have anything to hide. Maybe it's because everything's so new. But I think I'd rather see how things pan out than hang my hopes on something that might not be what I think it has the possibility of becoming.

"Just checkin'... Your goofy grin tells me she makes you happy, and if you're happy, I'm happy. Are you ready to get out of here and be my wingman?"

Soon, we arrive at the bar where the band's just started. We're a little early, but if Davis and I want to grab a beer and just hang for a bit, this is the time to do it. The dance floor fills as the bass beats through the room.

When Davis spots a few women dancing together with just one guy, he nods in my direction to see if I'm interested.

"Naw... you go ahead. I just started my beer, and I'd rather drink it while it's cold," I offer. Besides. if he's on the dance floor, I won't catch a bunch of shit about checking in on Vanessa.

"It's your loss, Dame." He shrugs as he makes his way to the dance floor.

Pulling out my phone, I quickly tap out a text.

Me: How is your night going? Did Julia get back to sleep okay?

Vanessa: Yeah. I'm working on a paper, so I can go to the game with you.

Damn. Does this woman ever take a break? Hands down, she accomplishes so much more than me, and I typically put in at least ten-hour days before starting on any projects at home.

Me: What's the topic?

Vanessa: Ethics and patient rights.

Yeah. I have no input to give there. But I'm still interested in what she has to say.

Me: How close are you to finishing?

Vanessa: I'm on page four of seven but should finish soon. Research is done, just getting the words on the page.

I certainly don't miss those days. I can write a great paper, but it doesn't mean I enjoy it. I'd much rather put my plan into action than write about it.

Me: Better you than me. I'll be around if you need a break.

Vanessa: Aren't you out with your brother?

Me: He's on the dance floor. I'm enjoying my beer and chatting with you.

Her reply is instant.

Vanessa: You're supposed to be having fun with your brother—not texting me.

I can't help but laugh as I tap out my reply.

Me: There's only one woman I want to dance with at the moment, and she's writing a paper. I can watch from afar and hang with him when he returns. Besides, knowing Davis, it's only a matter of time before I'm ditched for a better offer.

As I reread what I've written, panic hits.

God, I hope she doesn't think the two of us came out to hook up. Davis rarely does this, and I'm well past finding a one-night stand. Been there, done that. Over it.

Vanessa: Don't let me stop you from having fun tonight.

Shit. Please don't think I have any interest in anyone here tonight.

Me: It's not my scene tonight. I'd much rather be home talking with a beautiful girl about her paper than be sitting in this bar. But Davis doesn't let his hair down often. If he's out looking for a good time, I won't stop him. Med school takes its toll on him, and I can't begrudge him a night of fun.

Vanessa's reply is faster than I could've imagined.

Vanessa: I didn't mean anything by it. Time with family is precious. Just enjoy it while you can. You said he could end up anywhere in the world if he does the Doctors Without Borders program. Relax, Damien. I just want you to have fun and not feel the need to text me all night.

Me: I happen to like texting you.

Vanessa: Hahaha! You know what I mean. Don't be the creeper that hangs out in a public place on his phone all night. It's rude. Enjoy your night with your brother. I'll be up until I finish this freaking paper that never seems to end.

Realizing she has a point, I look over to Davis, who seems to have hit it off with a particular brunette from the group of women dancing. They're dancing to the slow song that just started. As the words from the song drift in my direction, I tap out one last reply to Vanessa.

Me: For the record, I like talking with you.

Vanessa: Noted. Now go have fun. Even if I'm sleeping—will you text me to let me know you've made it home? If you need a ride, I can come and get you. Please—Just don't drink and drive.

My chest tightens at the fact she cares.

Me: We'll Uber. But I'll let you know when we get there. I can't wait to go to the game with you tomorrow.

To my surprise, I'm blessed with my first picture of Vanessa in the form of a selfie. She's wearing a pair of dark-rimmed glasses that gives off the sexiest librarian vibe imaginable, and I'm hard in an instant.

Me: Keep sending pics like that, and I may be tempted to crash your study session. Damn, you're gorgeous. Do you wear glasses for reading?

I wait a few seconds before I see the dots of her reply.

Vanessa: No—they're for blue light reduction.

They help my eyes not hurt when I'm forced with screen time. Now stop talking to me and go spend time with your brother. I'll see you tomorrow.

So that she won't worry, I offer.

Me: Hope you get to bed soon. I'll text you when I get home.

But in reality, I'm just counting down the minutes until I see her again.

13

VANESSA

GOD, it's been one hell of a week. I manage to finish my paper, study for my exam, and most importantly, talk to Damien every night before bed. Thank God, I'm good at completing class work during the day, while Jules is in class, or there's no way I'd be able to talk with Damien as much as I have. Who needs sleep, right?

Vince has no idea I'm going out on a date with Damien again, but neither he nor Sydney said anything when I asked if they could watch Jules this afternoon. Damien's invited me to watch the opening game for Portland's baseball team. I'll admit, I'm not a huge fan of this team, but time with Damien is worth the sacrifice.

I've learned many things about Damien over this past week. Not only does he make me laugh, he's also an amazing listener. He's not bothered when I talk about Jules and her incessant need to get a cat, or how she managed to track paint all over my house when she tried making a footprint for me with fingerpaints. Thank God, I got the paint off my kitchen floor and she sat still long enough so I could clean her up.

As I pull up to his home, I'm far more eager than I'd ever admit. I haven't been able to kiss him since our last date. But every freaking morning when I've seen him at the diner or talked with him on the phone late into the evening, I've wanted to do nothing but. What is it about this man who keeps me wanting more? I swear, it's like I'm never satisfied with my limited time with him.

Of course, it'd be much easier if he met Jules. We could have dinner together or go to the park after he got off work or something, but I'm not sure I'm ready to take things to that level. It'd also be easier if Vince knew because I hate keeping things from my twin.

There's no reason to hide Damien. But meeting someone's family is big under normal circumstances. But Vince and Jules would take things to a whole new level for him. My track record hasn't been the greatest when it comes to men, so I'm sure Vince will grill him—like Dad would've.

My heart pangs at just the thought.

I know without a doubt, Dad would've liked Damien. Yeah, he may have thought he was a bit old for me, but I know Mom would have made him see just how happy I am. Maybe it's because we're forced to get to know one another by talking late into the night after Julia's gone to bed. But I'm quickly learning, the more I get to know Damien, the more I like him. He's smart, funny, and extremely considerate. He wants my success just as much as I do. He was thrilled to hear I should've aced my test today and even offered to help me study—though I didn't take him up on it.

When I walk up to the porch, his front door swings open, and I'm greeted by the beautiful man himself. "Hey, Vanessa," he practically growls as he closes the distance between us. His hand reaches for my hip as the other cups my face as he pulls me close and devours me. When his tongue slides along the seam of my lips, mine part. I'm sure we're putting on quite the show for his neighbors, but who the heck cares. I've waited way too long for this.

"So good," he moans between fevered kisses.

Running my hand through his hair, I pull at his neck, keeping him close. His arm around my back lifts me with ease to make up for our height difference. I have no idea how long I'm suspended in the air, but after all too short of time, I feel my feet touch the ground again, and Damien breaks our kiss.

"I've been dying to do that all week," he growls after putting me back on the ground.

Grinning, I nod in agreement. "That was well worth the wait," I admit.

He runs a thumb over my bottom lip as he grins. "I... uh... could get quite used to that. Please don't get me wrong, I'm not complaining..." He shakes his head as if he's reliving the memory as I am in this moment. "But if we're gonna make it to the game on time, I'd better give you a quick tour so we can leave."

I'm not sure what look I have on my face when suddenly Damien says, "You're so freaking adorable," as he kisses me chastely once more. "Come on... I'm beginning to think you might be a bad influence on me..." With that, he grabs my hand and pulls me inside the door.

I'm the bad influence?

"What does that mean?" I say through a laugh.

Shaking his head, he rolls his eyes and sighs. "It's nothing. I'm just highly distractible around you, that's all. I'm used to being able to keep my wits about me... but when you look at me like that..." He points to my face. "I just want to kiss the living hell out of you."

"Well, there are worse things..." I tease as I point my finger to my chin and pretend to look to the sky as if I'm contemplating something serious.

"What am I gonna do with you?" He chuckles. "Come on," he says as he squeezes my hand. "Let me give you the tour."

"Well, what are you waiting for?" I tease as I eagerly look around.

Man, this place is amazing.

It's obvious he's done some major renovations. The dark wood throughout looks perfect with the cabinetry he's installed in the kitchen, even if it's missing countertops. I can't believe he's done this all himself. From the hall, he shows me a makeshift office and his guest bedroom. He's put crown molding and painted accent walls in each room to give each its own unique feature.

When I see the window seat he's installed in the guest room, I gush, "Oh, I've always wanted one of those. If I ever get the chance, I'm putting one of those in my bedroom. I love reading and would love to just curl up with a book."

"My sister was a huge influence in me using this space this way. She's always had her nose in a book."

"She sounds like my kind of people," I admit.

"Oh, I'm sure the two of you would get along." He nods in agreement, then shrugs. "Though I'll admit, I also put that there for some built-in storage. This house doesn't have a ton of it, and I know that's a hot commodity when looking for a new home."

"True," I say as he leads me to another door.

"This is the master bedroom. You have to see the tile work I completed in the bathroom. I've never done it before, but I'll admit I think it turned out pretty kickass if I do say so myself."

I've been impressed with the entire house so far, but his master bedroom is by far my favorite room. Not only does it smell incredible—just like him, but there's a huge king-size bed as well as enough room for a sitting area if you wanted furniture in your bedroom. I can easily picture my favorite over-sized chair in the corner and a love seat along the wall, to become a special place for someone to just relax.

When we walk into the bathroom, my mouth drops.

There's an over-sized walk-in shower to one side and an enormous sunk-in tub I could practically swim in, lining the other wall. Between the two is an entry to a walk-in closet I will kill for. He's got custom built-in shelves on one side with a few shelves occupied, as well as clothes hanging on the other side. But it's nowhere near capacity.

"You okay?" he asks when I still haven't said anything.

"Oh... don't mind me. Just wishing I could have a bathroom like this. Vince took the master bedroom, so I share my bathroom with Julia since our rooms are next to one another. Someday, when I get a place of my own, I'll have to hire you to custom build it."

"Oh, I don't build, but I can remodel," he teases. "Some things are worth hiring out for."

"You've done an amazing job. Why are you working on apartments when you could be doing this?" I ask in wonder.

"Well, for starters, this is just a hobby. I like the challenges of orchestrating big projects and watching them come to completion. Let's be real... the other one has great benefits that include a 401K. Maybe someday, after I've flipped a few homes, I can do this full time but in the meantime, I'm happy being the lead engineer on the biggest project of my career. But enough about me... we've got a baseball game to get to."

The way he says it, I can tell he means it with all his heart. Could Damien be cuter? His humility is just another characteristic I'm beginning to like about him. "That's impressive—on its own," I say, not letting him dismiss his accomplishments.

"What can I say?" He shrugs again. "I moved to a new town and didn't know anyone, so I picked up a project to occupy my time."

"Do you miss your family?" I ask as we reach his living room. I'd be lost without Vince. Maybe it's a twin thing—or the fact it's just the two of us now. But Damien comes from a bigger family.

"Yeah," he sighs. "We get together as often as we can. But even though we're miles apart, we're only ever a phone call away."

"I can't imagine having so many siblings. Are you closer to some of them more than others?"

This earns a laugh. "Oh... we all have our moments. Growing up, I was naturally closer to Davis as he was my younger brother. Dani and Derek paired off because they were older, but honestly, I'm close with all of them. It was a built-in friends thing with three siblings. We either loved each other—or loved to hate each other and would gang up accordingly—at least that's how Mom described it to anyone who asked."

"That's Vince and me. We'd be the best of friends and the worst of enemies when we were little. But in recent years, I can't even remember the last time we had a disagreement. I guess it was something we outgrew." I shrug.

"That is one benefit of growing up. Petty things don't become disastrous. Now that we all live on our own, we're just grateful to be around each other. Though we haven't forgotten how to bicker if we're pitching each other shit about something. There's just some things you can't let your siblings get away with."

"Oh, we can still bicker, too." I giggle. "Especially when it comes to deflating egos."

"Right?" He conspiratorially nudges me with his elbow.

"I've already put a blanket in the truck in case it gets cooler this afternoon. Do you need anything before we leave? I have an extra jacket if you need one." He looks me over from head to toe, and I feel every inch of his gaze, which emboldens me to make my next move.

"I just need one thing," I say, taking a step toward him.

Reaching to the side of his face, I brush my hand along his

jaw as I apply pressure to the base of his neck to encourage him to bend in my direction.

Damien's eyes darken when he realizes what I need, and a smile spreads across his face, as our lips align.

Pressing my lips to his, I feel his smile widen as he mutters the words, "I could get used to this."

I may have started this, but Damien soon takes control. His tongue deliciously swipes across my lips, and they eagerly part, so I can taste him more. Damn. This man tastes amazing. There's a hint of mint from his toothpaste, but something entirely him all the same. I never want this kiss to end.

"Mmmmm..." I moan as he pulls away. "I'm not done yet," I admit.

I feel his chuckle before I hear it. "Van... I could do this all day... trust me... but we've got a game to be at."

"There you go... being all adulty," I tease.

His beautiful brown eyes roll, as a smirk forms. "There you go with the old-man jokes... I see how it is."

Reaching up to peck him once more, I pat him on the cheek. "Well, if the shoe fits," I tease, then turn and walk out the door to his driveway.

14

DAMIEN

OH, this woman.

She may be the death of me—but what a way to go.

Discreetly, I adjust the effects of our kiss and follow her out the door. Her dark jeans fit her like a glove, and her red hoodie comes just to the top of them, leaving me a spectacular view of her ass. I lengthen my strides so I can reach for the door before she can. "Here. Let me help you," I offer.

I drive a full-size F350 with a crew cab. Thankfully, it came with running boards, or most would have difficulty getting in. Back in high school, I drove a jacked-up truck that most had to crawl into, especially shorter women—don't think I didn't use that to my advantage. But I quickly learned running boards were a necessity when I constantly had to help Mom or Dani get into the cab—hence the reason for these when I finally upgraded.

As soon as she's settled into the truck, I close the door and move to the driver's side, excited to spend more time with her.

I could give two fucks what we do for the day as long as I'm with her.

When we arrive at the ball field, the place is packed. Thank goodness, I'm a pro at parking this beast of a truck, so I back into a spot with ease. We make our way through the gates, and I'm thrilled to find our seats six rows up from first base.

"Wow, your boss has great season tickets," Vanessa says as she takes off her hoodie and reveals a fitted black tee underneath. It's a beautiful spring day in Portland. The clouds are high, and the sun shines through. Taking Vanessa's lead, I pull off my black hoodie and take the seat beside her.

"Yeah. I had no idea what to expect," I admit. "Do you watch much baseball?"

Vanessa's face turns a light shade of pink as her nose wrinkles in the cutest of ways. "Uh... not really."

"Then why did you come?" comes out on a laugh I can't hold in.

"You asked?" She shrugs as both a question and an explanation.

I just stare dumbfounded. *Why subject yourself to something you don't like?*

"For the record, I happen to like baseball. I watched it a lot with my dad. But you asked if I watch it much. Since senior year in high school, the answer would be no."

There's so much to tackle in that one sentence alone. I'm not even sure where to begin. So of course, I just stare, hoping she'll explain. Of course, I'm not that lucky. She turns her attention to the field for a few moments and watches the first baseman pick up an in-fielder as practice.

With her eyes on the field, she says, "I played fast pitch growing up. That is, until I got pregnant with Jules. It was something my dad and I did. Vince didn't play. He was the kid out there picking flowers in the outfield. No, he was more musical, and I was the athletic one. I was also daddy's little girl. We did everything together." The way her voice changes at the end has me on edge. Did something happen? Was he not supportive of her pregnancy?

Her eyes blink rapidly, as if she's fighting back tears.

Shit. What am I supposed to do?

Needing to do something, I place a hand on her thigh and squeeze, letting her know I'm here for her. When she doesn't respond, I ask, "You okay?" for assurance.

With a voice barely above a whisper, she nods. "Yeah, I'll be fine. Just give me a sec."

"Take all the time you need," I offer. When I pull my hand away, she reaches out to keep it in place. So, I do the only thing I can. I hold her hand and hope she'll let me in on what's bothering her when she's ready.

True to her word, a few minutes later, she looks to me with a smile. "Sorry about that. I don't mean to be a Debbie Downer. It came out of nowhere... just as it usually does." Sucking in a deep breath, she squeezes my hand. "I'm okay. Honest."

Curiosity gets the better of me, so I ask, "Does this have something to do with Julia?"

Instantly, she shakes her head. "No. He loved Jules. From the moment he found out about her..." She lets out a low laugh. "Well... maybe not his initial reaction. No, that was at best—an over-protective father freak-out... But he was quick to come around. No... there was... an accident... and..." she trails off.

My heart sinks, and my stomach plummets.

Holy shit. He died.

Squeezing her hand, I stop her from saying the words. "It's okay. You don't have to say anything."

Vanessa's eyes whip to mine, and the unexpected fierceness catches me off guard. "Please understand grief is hard and hits me at the most inopportune times. But I *am* getting through this. I have to. Curling up in a ball and giving up has never been an option. I was thinking happy thoughts when it hit just now... honest. I'd been thinking about the first time he took me to the field. I was barely big enough to hold a bat, and he'd taken me to the game in Seattle. It was the first time I'd ever realized baseball was a sport. My dad was so eager to show Vinny and me all about it."

"I can imagine." My dad had been the same way when he took our family to the football stadium.

Before I can say anything, she continues, "There's not a day that goes by that I don't miss 'em. My dad would be so proud of what I've become. Do I wish he were here to see this? Of course, but he isn't."

"If it's difficult for you to be here, we can leave," I offer, trying to give her a way out.

"Absolutely not," she says in a tone that distinctly reminds me of my mother. "I'm not a basket case. I'm just reminded of 'em at the most random of times. Dad would be pissed if I stopped doing what I love just because I feel sad and miss him." She shakes her head, and her eyes soften as if she's trying to comfort me. "Someday, I'll tell you the full story—I'd rather not get into the whole thing now in such a public place."

"Only when you're ready," I suggest. As much as I'd like to know the details so I can support her in any way that I can, I know she has to tell me on her time, and not a minute sooner.

When the players are announced, I'm caught off guard. Vanessa suddenly stands and whistles louder than anyone I've ever heard, by sticking two fingers between her teeth as she cheers on the home team.

Holy shit. I'm glad she's closer to home plate than me!

As the anthem is sung, I watch from the corner of my eye as Vanessa sings along under her breath. Then she cheers with the crowd as the game begins, eager for things to get underway.

I swear, if I hadn't seen her reaction to the field just a few moments ago, I wouldn't have ever known what she's been through. I stare at her in awe.

Not only was she a teen mom, but to lose a parent at such a young age? If it had been me, I would've probably gone off the deep end and have been derailed from my plans of becoming an engineer. But no—here she is working almost full time, taking a full load of classes, and being the best mom possible to Julia. One thing is certain. Vanessa's one hell of a woman. The more I learn, the more intriguing she is.

By the time we're in the fourth inning, Vanessa and I have finished the hot dogs and beer I ordered. We've kept a playful banter with the fans around us, but most importantly, Vanessa is at ease with the stadium again. She cackles at the ump for bad plays and whistles when our team does something well. If it were socially acceptable, I'd spend the game watching her—and I'd be thoroughly entertained.

At the bottom of the sixth inning, right as our team takes the lead, Vanessa gets a call. Knowing it's her brother, she accepts it as she presses one finger to her ear to hear him.

Instantly, her playful expression turns serious.

"What? Give me a sec. I need to get to where I can hear you better." I hear over the crowd. She starts for the stairs and when I start to follow, she shakes her head and points a finger at me to wait here.

Once she's assured I'm staying put, she pivots and ascends the stairs two at a time. I watch her disappear, but there's no way in hell I feel comfortable with this. It takes everything I have to follow her wishes. I have no idea what she's told her brother about today, but since Julia's with him, I hope nothing's wrong.

After giving Vanessa almost five minutes of privacy, my nerves can't take it anymore. I gather our hoodies and climb the stairs to find her. Maybe she just had to go to the bathroom while she's out there—and I'm overreacting. Or maybe my gut is right. Either way, if we need to leave, we'll be closer to the exit when I find out.

When I get to the concourse, Vanessa's leaning her shoulder to the wall. One hand covers one ear as she talks into the phone. Even from behind, I can tell she's disagreeing with whatever is being said because her head shakes often.

Finally, I hear part of her conversation. "Are you sure?" she asks hesitantly. Then sighs heavily. "But...."

"Will you let me know the second you find out?" she pleads.

"I know... I know. I *am* enjoying the game, Vin, but I can meet you if you need me."

To keep from startling her, I walk in front of her and wait for her to fill me in on what's going on. When her eyes meet mine, regret fills her features, and I know in that instant, I'll do whatever it takes to fix things.

She squeezes her eyes shut as she shakes her head. "I know... I know. I understand. Promise you'll call the minute you know anything."

Fuck. What the hell is going on?

When there's a moment of silence, I mouth the words, "You okay?"

She shrugs as if she's not sure herself. After a few more moments, she pleads again, "Just keep me informed."

When she hangs up, her expression remains unsettled, which in turn rubs off on me. She just stares in my direction but doesn't see me. It's as if she's weighing a heavy decision, and I'm not even here.

When I can no longer hold in my concern, I ask, "What's going on?"

Closing her eyes for a moment, she takes a long breath as she shifts her head from side to side. "Vince says she's fine..." she trails off.

"But..." I nudge, hoping she'll continue her thought.

At first, I'm certain she'll keep her worries to herself, but then words she'd been holding in release as if the flood gates have been opened. "I guess he asked her to re-shut her door...

because his hands were filled with groceries. When she went to slam Sydney's car door shut, her fingers were caught in the crack. Apparently... she was using one hand to steady herself against the car, and her fingers got in the way when it closed."

Taking a moment to process what she just rambled, I ask, "She... as in Sydney?"

Vanessa looks to her toes as she shakes her head and whispers, "Jules."

Damn. I was afraid of that.

"Is she okay?"

Vanessa pulls her lower lip in. "I think so..." comes out on a wince. "But she may have broken her finger."

"Do you wanna go?" I ask, pointing in the direction of my truck.

Surprisingly, Vanessa says, "No."

She's quiet for a moment, then pulls in a deep breath and releases her explanation. "Vince says I *should* stay here and keep watching the game. He says she's not crying, and there's nothing we can do but wait to see what the x-rays say. He's heading to urgent care now."

"You sure? I'm totally okay with leaving."

At first, she hesitates, and I swear she'll change her mind, but then her shoulders square as her chin lifts, and the confident woman I'm beginning to fall for makes her presence. Then she reaches for my hand and says, "No. Vince is right. He's got things handled, and there's nothing I can do. Besides, there's only a couple of innings left, and we'll be on our way soon enough. Let's go see how this game ends."

Reluctantly, I follow her back to our seat, not sure we're doing the right thing.

From the corner of my eye, I watch as she settles into her chair and props her elbows on her knees. Clearly, she's going through the motions and attempting to get back into the game, but every so often, she pulls on that bottom lip of hers, which I'm quickly learning is her tell, and I'd bet my last paycheck it's killing her to sit here.

I don't have kids—but I'm not buying her *let's pretend to relax* expression. Clearly, she's upset about her daughter, and she should be there with her. God, I hope she's not staying for my account. I could give two fucks about this game if something's bothering her.

When her leg starts bobbing up and down, and she wraps her arms around her waist, I can't take it anymore. "Vanessa?"

Of course, something happens out on the field at the exact moment I try to call her name, and the crowd screams in adoration, so she doesn't hear me. Reaching out, I tap her on the leg to get her attention. When her hazel eyes reach mine, they're filled with confusion. "What?"

"Are you sure you want to keep watching this game? You didn't even cheer when they just made a major play."

"I... uh..." She stops and pulls on her lower lip.

That's it. We're outta here.

Standing, I reach for her hand. "Come on. Let's go."

Relief washes over her as she nods. "Thanks."

With the crowd inside the stadium, it's effortless to reach the freeway. Vanessa hasn't said much, but I can tell she's glad we're closing the gap between her daughter and us. Thankfully, traffic is light, and I'm able to make good time.

Eventually, I break the silence in the cab. "Hey, Vanessa?"

From the corner of my eye, I see her look at me as she says, "Yeah?"

"If you wanted to be with Julia, why did we stay?" It's been puzzling me since we returned to our seats.

"Well... I was having a great time... and I like you. I haven't dated since finding out I was pregnant with Julia, but..." she trails off.

When the silence lasts longer than my curiosity can handle, I prompt, "But..."

"But... I didn't want you to think..."

Ah, shit. This *does* have something to do with me.

Not acceptable.

"You can just stop that thought right there," I interrupt. "Let's be clear about something. I know I don't have kids, and I'd never proclaim to be an expert... Hell, I've hardly been around kids... but I want you to clearly know where I stand..." I draw in a deep breath so I can choose the words she needs to hear. "I will *never* judge you for putting Julia first. From what I know of you, you're an amazing person and an incredible mom. I've seen what you've done to keep her a priority. Please don't ever think that I'll be offended if we cut our time short so you can be with her. I've got plenty of ego to go around, and I guarantee it won't be bruised if I'm not first."

"Okay," she says quietly as she looks down at her hands. "Good to know."

"I'm serious, Vanessa. Please don't ever feel like you can't say what you want or need. I'm a big boy and can handle whatever you throw at me. Will I miss you if we can't hang out—sure. But I promise I won't be butt hurt or make you feel as if I should take priority. That's not fair to any of us. Maybe someday I'll be included in your plans with Jules, so you don't have to choose. But until that day comes, I just want you to know I appreciate the time we do get together."

When Vanessa remains quiet for an unusual amount of time, I risk glancing in her direction.

To my surprise, her jaw hangs slack, and her eyes are wide.

"What?" I ask, replaying my words in my head.

Did I say something wrong?

No, I don't think so.

I meant every word.

But why hasn't she said anything?

"Vanessa?" I ask hesitantly.

"Wow..." she says with both wonder and accusation. "Just wow."

Shit. Maybe I did say something wrong. "Wow what?" I prompt.

She remains silent.

For the love of God, just put me out of my misery already.

As casual as I can manage, I prompt her again to continue as I return my focus to the road. "Vanessa?"

From the corner of my eye, I see her head shake.

"Wow... as in I didn't think my mom would be right..."

"About..." Damn. This girl needs to learn to finish her thoughts. She's killing me.

"Mom said... someday I'd meet a guy who'd understand my

need to put Julia first and wouldn't be selfish when it came to spending time with him."

"Your mom sounds like a smart lady." Who wouldn't recognize the situation of Vanessa being a single mom and where her priorities should be?

"She was... especially in this case. I remember finding out about Julia and thinking my life as I knew it was over. But Mom, being the amazing mother she was, just said. *No honey. Just your turn at being the center of your world is over. This is only the beginning of an amazing adventure. Trust me. One day, you'll find someone who recognizes your need to put this little one above both of your needs and love them for who they are to you.*"

I mull over her words and realize just how true they should be.

But then it hits me. *Was Julia's dad ever in the picture?* I mean—she's never mentioned him. But if things ended poorly, why would she?

I don't get the chance to voice my thoughts because Vanessa continues, "I'm not saying that we're at that stage, but I'd been so certain that nobody would ever look twice at a single, teen mom." She sucks in a deep breath, then continues, "But then again, my priorities were focused entirely on Julia, so I never even imagined the possibility could be a reality."

"For the record, I'm glad you think better of that now. I most certainly think you're worthy of looking at a lot more than twice. Why else do you think I visit the diner so frequently? I mean—don't get me wrong. The food's great... but something else holds my attention more than the cuisine."

"Seriously?" she asks in wonder.

Does she not know the effect she has on me? Clearly, I've done a shit job of showing her. "As a heart attack."

"Okay, then." I'm unsure if she meant it for me or herself.

With her arm leaning against the console, I reach out and take her hand in mine to give it a squeeze of reassurance. "Vanessa, why wouldn't I be interested? Not only are you sexy as fuck, but you're an amazing woman. I've enjoyed my time with you, and I know without a doubt, having Julia in your life has shaped you into the person you are today. Anyone who thinks otherwise, frankly, is an idiot. My mom didn't raise an idiot. So please trust that I'm telling the truth."

"Okay," she says on the most beautiful laugh, and I feel the tension release from her hand. "I believe you. I may question your sanity from time to time. But I do believe you."

As I find a place to park at urgent care, I squeeze her hand once more. "Now that that's settled, are you ready to go see for yourself if Julia's okay?"

15

VANESSA

I'M STILL REELING over Damien's words as I exit his truck. He takes my hand in his, and I'm so much calmer than I would've been without him in this moment. I have no idea how he has this effect on me in such a short amount of time, but since I'm not being a nervous nelly and completely freaking out, I'll take what I can get.

As we walk through the sliding doors to urgent care, I'm startled when I hear, "Momma, you're here."

The next thing I know, Julia launches herself at me.

Instinctually, I drop Damien's hand and catch her with ease as I bring her to my full height to hug the crap out of her. Obviously, things aren't too serious if she's able to fly into my arms—so maybe I've overreacted.

Trying to play off my concern, I tease, "What's this I hear about a door?"

Julia winces as she brings a bandaged hand up to show me. "I hurt it pretty bad. It bled, and Unks thinks it might be broken. He made me wrap it in this white stuff and taped my two fingers together. He says I have ta see a doctor." Then in a suddenly nervous voice, she asks, "Am I gonna be okay, Momma?"

God, her uncertainty breaks my heart. Not wanting to lie until I know for certain what's the matter, I will the words to be true. "I'm sure you will be... eventually."

When I look up, Vince and Sydney have joined us.

Vince's expression clearly shows both annoyance and relief. "I thought I told you to stay and watch the game. I had this handled," he reminds me the way only my brother can. I know without a doubt he won't begrudge me for being here, but he also loves me enough to worry enough for the both of us. He also knows I am finally doing something for myself, so he won't begrudge me for being away.

"I know..." I shrug. What else can I say?

"I'm glad you're here, Momma," Julia says as she squeezes me in a vise grip once more.

"There's no place I'd rather be," I whisper in her ear as I set her back to the floor. Then I turn to Vince, who's looking with interest at Damien behind me. He then raises his eyebrows in question at me.

Shit. This isn't exactly how I'd planned on Damien meeting my family.

Before I say anything, Damien steps to Vince, reaching out his hand. "Hi. I'm Damien. You must be Vince."

On instinct, Vince returns the handshake. "I take it you're the *friend* who scored tickets to the Portland game?"

That little shit. Why couldn't he leave that part to

himself? Of course, I'd said I was at the game with a friend. I just didn't specify because I'd been keeping my dating Damien to myself.

Damien handles Vince like a pro. "Yep. I'd be the one. It's nice to meet you." Then he turns to Julia, who's standing beside me and bends to her level. "You..." he points at her hand, "you must be Julia. I heard you had a run-in with a door. I'm sorry to hear you were hurt."

"Dameinum?" Julia completely butchers his name. "Are you a friend of Momma's?" She looks from him to me, but back to him.

Of course, Damien also handles her with ease. "Yes, I am. But you can call me Dame. That's what my friends and family call me."

"Momma was with you at the baseball game?" she asks, and my nerves frazzle because I'm not sure where she's going with this. But her inquisitive brows furrow, and God only knows what she'll say next.

Attempting to influence the conversation, I say, "Yes, he was, sweetie." Damien nods in agreement.

"Good. Momma loves baseball. Did you know she used to play when she was a kid like me? She says next year, I get to start playing once I'm in school."

This kid. Could she be any cuter?

"She mentioned something about that," Damien says as he returns to his full height. "I'm sure she'll teach you when you're ready."

Her eyes whip to mine. "Do you think you can teach me next time we go to the park?"

"Uh... we need to see what the doctor says about your finger first," I remind her.

Clearly, she may be injured, but she isn't devastated by any means.

"I wanna play, too, squirt," Sydney pipes in as she reaches for Vince's hand. "I loved playing as a kid."

Remembering my manners, I introduce Sydney to Damien. Then Vince suggests we take a seat while we wait to be seen. Julia climbs in my lap, and Damien takes the seat beside me as I ask, "Do you know how much longer the wait is?"

"We should be called back any minute. They've already triaged us, but they said the wait was another forty minutes or so when we arrived," Vince offers.

Looking to Damien, I offer him an out. "I'd totally understand if you don't want to stay for this. It could be awhile before we're done."

"I'm good for now," Damien says as he relaxes back into his chair and crosses his leg over his knee. "I can head out once you go back to see the doctor—or I can wait here to find out the verdict. I'll leave it up to you, Vanessa."

Surely, he has better things to do. But could this guy be any sweeter? I've completely derailed our plans for the day, and he's choosing to sit in a waiting room for God knows how long, just to hang out with us?

Jules buries her head in the crook of my neck, and I feel her body relax. Her hurt hand rests on my opposite shoulder. As I feel her breaths slowly even out, I listen to Vince and Sydney make small talk with Damien. Sydney, being the master of manipulation, uses her skills as a bartender to get Damien to tell her why he's here at CRU. When Damien asks about what they're going to school for, Vince and Syd explain their degrees in business. I don't even bother to be a part of the conversations as I'm too focused on Julia being in my arms, safe and secure.

Eventually, a nurse comes into the room asking, "Julia?"

Instinctually our entire group stands, and her eyes widen. Though she quickly regains her composure as she calmly asks, "For now, let's just go with immediate family."

"I'll be right here, sweet girl, when you get out," Sydney says as she ruffles Julia's hair.

When I look to Vince, he's torn. I can tell he wants to come with us yet wonders if he should stay with Sydney in the waiting room. Not knowing the extent of her injury, I'd feel better if he were there to listen carefully—should things go awry. I remember all too well what it was like being alone at the hospital last time. Reaching for his hand, I whisper, "Come on, Vinnie. Jules may need you."

Turning to Damien, I say, "Thanks for an amazing day. Sorry it had to end under these circumstances. I'll let you know when I know what's going on."

"Please do." He nods.

I don't have time to say more because we're whisked out of the waiting room. God knows there's no place I'd rather be than here with Julia in this moment but am I selfish that a small part of me wonders what it would've been like to have the opportunity to finish our amazing date and kiss him goodnight?

16

DAMIEN

AS I WATCH VANESSA LEAVE, I see her face flicker with regret for having to end our date like this. Or maybe it's just me projecting my feelings into the situation. The moment I see Julia fly into Vanessa's arms, I know without a doubt, we'd made the right decision to be here. A girl needs her mom, and I'll never stand in the way of that.

As I turn around, I contemplate whether I should retake my seat or just leave.

Sydney makes my decision for me when she offers, "If you're not busy, I'd love the company while we wait. I'm a nervous wreck, and I'll be bouncing off the walls while I wait—if I'm left to my own devices."

"Well, that wouldn't be good for anyone," I say to put her at ease. Though let's be real, I'd take just about any excuse to stay. Knowing Julia's injuries aren't vital. I saw the way Vanessa zoned out once she got her baby girl in her arms. I'd much rather see for myself that she's holding out okay, than wait around for a text that may take hours to come.

As I return to my seat, Sydney looks at me closer, making me on the verge of being self-conscious. Then she shakes her head, and I'm forced to ask, "What?" to satisfy my curiosity.

"It's nothing. I'm usually good with faces, and I swear I've seen you before—but for the life of me, I can't place where."

She stands out enough that I doubt I'd forget meeting her. I just shrug in response. "Sorry?"

"Wait... were you out with a guy that looks like you but has shorter hair last night?"

"Uh, I was with my brother Davis last night."

Sydney smacks her leg. "I knew it," she rushes out. "He ordered a few drinks and danced once with my roommate Chloe and her friends. Though I think he ended up spending more time with one of her friends. You were glued to your phone at the booth, right?"

Damn. This girl is observant. To clear any misconceptions she may have, I admit, "I was texting Vanessa most of the evening."

"I knew I liked you. I saw your brother bring a few girls back to your table at one point, and you showed zero interest— and they were coming on hard."

Shrugging, I admit, "I... uh... am only interested in one person."

"That Vanessa's a lucky girl." She smiles. Then her expression turns serious. "I know it's new with the two of you, so I won't say much, but I need to mention one thing. She and her brother have practically become family to me. If you fuck up—

you won't just have to deal with Vince. He'll be the least of your worries."

Holy shit, her conviction is fierce.

If she lives up to the stereotype of redheads, I seriously doubt this is an idle threat.

"That won't be a problem," I assure her.

"No—you don't get it. Those two have been through *so* much, especially Vanessa. Hell... she's one of the strongest women I know, but if you're just looking for a quick fling, move along sooner than later for her sake. She rarely lets anyone in— and the fact that you're even sitting here—means you're lucky enough to make the cut."

That's saying something.

Though I already know this about Vanessa for the most part—based on our evening talks. I'll gladly hang on every word Sydney shares if it means learning more about Vanessa.

Sydney shakes her head as if to clear her thoughts as she takes in a long and steady breath. "I'm probably making a horrible first impression. I'm usually not the type who gets into others' business. But there's *nothing* I won't do for that family. So, if I come across as a complete bitch, I'll gladly be that person, especially if it saves any of them a chance at heartache. The amount of shit they've experienced brings out the mama bear side of me. I won't even say I'm sorry... because let's face it, I doubt either of us will ever meet three people who've been through more at such a young age."

Remembering Vanessa's father and her teen pregnancy with Julia, I nod in agreement. "I have no intentions of hurting her," I say with conviction.

Then I realize another truth.

"Of course—I'm a guy who happens to be human—so I'm bound to mess up at some point. But I'll never hurt her on purpose."

She shrugs. "I guess that can be expected. But since we're on the same page now... how was Portland playing today? I haven't heard the highlights yet."

I chuckle at how quickly she switches topics. With the relaxed expression on her face in this moment, you'd never know she'd just threatened to end me mere seconds ago. I appreciate her boldness though. From the sounds of it, Vanessa needs someone in her corner, and I'm glad Sydney can be that person.

If Vanessa lets me, I'd like to be in her corner, too. Knowing everything is still new between us, I'm not sure where this will lead, but I can't imagine wanting to end things anytime soon. Sure, I may have been gun-shy about relationships since Amber. But Vanessa is different. I can't quite describe it, but I'm old enough to know when to listen to my gut instincts all the same.

Needing to distract myself from all that is Vanessa, I tell Sydney about the triple in the third inning as well as a few amazing infield plays. We chat about baseball, then the conversation easily flows into basketball and football. Sydney's knowledge of sports is impressive.

When we get on the topic of favorite football teams, I quickly learn she loves the Rainier Renegades. She's jealous when I reveal I've had season tickets the last few seasons. Sydney can quote stats about some of my favorite players, like very few people I know. I don't bother telling her how I get my season tickets because I don't like explaining my sister's business. Eventually, it'll come up. But there's no need go there today.

When Vanessa, Julia, and Vince return to the waiting room, I'm surprised time has flown by. Originally, I hadn't planned on staying.

Vanessa's beautiful smile stops me mid-conversation with Sydney.

"I thought you were leaving?" she asks in wonder.

"He kept me from wearing a hole in the tile floors," Sydney offers. Then she turns her attention to Julia. "Hey, squirt. What's the verdict? You gonna live?"

"Oh, Sydney... you're silly." Julia laughs then scrunches up her face like she's eaten a sour apple as she says, "They poked a hole in my nail, and I got two stitches. They're making me wear this, too." Julia holds up her finger that's now in a metal brace and bandaged.

"I'm glad you're okay though," I offer Julia.

"There's also a hairline fracture on her finger. Thankfully, it didn't have to be reset and should heal quickly," Vanessa offers, and I wince. Holy shit, that must've hurt. She's a freaking trooper for being so calm when we got here.

"They also said she needs to keep her hand elevated to keep the swelling down," Vince reminds Julia, who nods her understanding reluctantly.

"Do you think cinnamon rolls will make you feel better, Jules?" Sydney asks.

Julia's hazel eyes, the same shade as her mother's, widen to saucers. "Uh-huh." Julia leans in to hug her.

"Okay, let's get out of here," Vince announces as we exit the waiting room.

As Vince, Sydney, and Julia walk out ahead of us, I quietly ask Vanessa, "Do you wanna ride with them? I can make arrangements to drop your car off."

Vanessa shakes her head. "That's not necessary. Vince already suggested I ride with you to pick up my car." She worries her hands together as she asks, "You don't mind... do you?"

"Not at all." Time with her is always a blessing.

I watch as Vanessa gets Julia settled into Vince's Jeep. Then we wave as they pull out of the lot. The moment they're out of sight, Vanessa turns to me. "Thank you."

"For?" I haven't done anything. Why is she thanking me?

She places her palm on my chest. "For staying. For helping me keep my cool. And most importantly—for just being you."

She reaches up on her tiptoes as she places her palm on my cheek to pull me closer to her. The scent of her perfume is a mixture of calm and excitement for me. This woman can turn me on from zero to sixty in a nanosecond. She's like a siren, and I'm drawn to her in ways I could never imagine.

When our lips meet, I feel her body melt into mine. The tension she's been holding evaporates, and I loop an arm around her waist to not only bring her closer but to give support if necessary. I can't imagine what it would be like to go through the events of the last few hours and not be exhausted.

When her tongue sweeps along the seam of my lips, they

part, and I'm lost in all that is Vanessa. I run my fingers up her spine to the base of her neck and bury them into her soft hair.

Her soft moan makes me growl in appreciation.

When a car door shuts nearby, I'm reminded that we aren't alone. I slow the pace of our kiss and end it much sooner than I want. Pulling apart, I'm breathless as I suggest, "Should we get to my place so you can get home to Julia?"

She's absolutely adorable as she sighs heavily and mutters, "I suppose."

Vanessa's unusually quiet on the ride to my place. When I pull into the driveway, I can't stand it any longer. "Vanessa, is everything okay?"

"What?" she asks with a shocked expression as she focuses her attention on me. "Sorry. Just lost in thought."

I can't help the smile in my response. "I figured as much. Wanna tell me what's got your mind spinning? When we talk on the phone, you never hold back—so why stop now?"

"Now that you've met my family... would it be weird if I asked you over to dinner tomorrow night?"

For her or me?

"Why would it be weird?" I finally ask when I can't be certain.

Vanessa takes in a long breath, squares her shoulders, and finally looks me in the eye. "Okay... so I'm totally being selfish. But now that Julia and Vince both know we're dating, I'd like to spend more time with you." She shrugs at the end as if it's the worst thing imaginable.

Could she be any cuter?

"Uh... I don't think it's selfish at all. I'd love to get to know your family more."

She pulls on her lower lip with her teeth. "You sure?"

"No... I just totally lied to you." I roll my eyes at her audacity. Why the hell wouldn't I want to spend time with her? I barely get to see her as it is.

"I'll cook dinner," she offers. "That way you can have a home-cooked meal and not have to eat out again."

"I can pick up dinner, too," I offer, knowing her busy schedule each day.

"How about this—I'll cook. You bring dessert. Jules and I will love anything that involves chocolate!"

She leans in and presses her lips to mine once more. There is zero innocence in the way she lights me from the inside out. Just as things are getting good, she pulls back and smiles like the Cheshire cat.

"I'll see you tomorrow then... Dame."

The vixen that she is hops out of my truck and has a lot more swing in her step as she walks to her SUV.

Damn. Now I want a hell of a lot more than chocolate.

17

DAMIEN

EAGER TO SEE VANESSA, I do everything in my power to leave work at a decent time. I'm not sure what to expect tonight, but if it means being with Vanessa, I'm game for anything. The only wild card for me—is Julia.

I'll admit I know next to nothing about young kids—except for when I was one. I may have done some sleuthing during my lunch break today to look up some of the cartoons and games Vanessa's mentioned while on the phone these past few weeks. At least I won't be completely in the dark if she talks about those things.

I know with my years of being a camp counselor through high school at the Lake Wenatchee YMCA camp, the best thing I can do is relax and be myself. I worked with pre-teen boys on the verge of puberty rearing its ugly head, not five-year-old little girls who are young, innocent, and so impressionable. What worked on the boys most likely won't work with Julia.

As I pull up to the curb in front of Vanessa's home, I throw my truck into park. I quickly grab the chocolate-covered strawberries that were calling my name at the bakery and the chocolate chip cookies that looked just at tempting. I'm guilty of having a terrible sweet tooth. Besides—strawberries count as fruit, right?

I stopped myself from buying flowers since I thought it'd be awkward showing up with flowers for Vanessa, Julia, and Sydney—so no one was left out. Three bouquets made it weird. Besides. I'd rather keep official dates with Vanessa special.

When I ring the bell, I hear the sound of feet running, and a "Look to see who it is first," coming from somewhere inside.

A small head pops into the window beside the door, then I hear the rattle of the locks. "It's Dame... Momma, can I let him in?" I hear the little voice say.

I have no idea if she gets an answer because the next thing I know, the door's flung open, and an eager Julia bounces with excitement. "Did you bring that for me?"

"Well... I brought it for all of us to share if that's okay with you?"

"Of course I'll share," she says dramatically. "That's waaayyy too much for just me. I'll get a tummy ache if I eat it all."

"Well... we wouldn't want that," I tease in return. "Tell me. Do you like cookies or chocolate-covered strawberries better?"

Julia's adorable as she puts a finger to her chin and contemplates this decision as if her life depends on it. "I think... cookies. I've only had chocolate strawberries once at a birthday party, and I can't remember what they taste like. But I do like strawberries. They're yummy."

"What are yummy?" Vanessa asks as she towels off her hands from behind Julia.

"Dame brought cookies and chocolate strawberries. Can we eat them now?"

"You know the drill, missy." Vanessa bops her daughter on the nose. "Dinner before dessert."

"Okay," Jules whines sadly, and it takes all that I can to keep a straight face.

"Go tell Vince and Sydney dinner's ready. They're in the garage putting Syd's things in the attic."

"Okay, Momma!" Julia hollers as she sprints past Vanessa, heading toward the living room.

Once she's out of sight, Vanessa turns and steps to me with a beautiful grin filling her features as she greets me, "Hey."

Stepping closer, I reply with, "Hey, yourself," bending to greet her with a kiss. I keep it short and to the point, letting her know I've missed her.

When I pull back, she brushes a thumb over my lips. "Lipstick," she says as explanation.

"Thanks. I'm sure it looks better on you," I tease.

"Oh, I could get used to seeing my lipstick on you. But don't get your hopes up. I don't wear it often."

"It wouldn't matter either way," I admit. "I'll still think you're gorgeous." Not being able to help myself, I slant my lips over hers and chastely kiss her again.

"You're silly," she says on a light laugh as we end our kiss. "Let's get inside before they send out the calvary."

As soon as I enter the house, my senses are on overload. Instantly, I'm reminded of Sunday dinners with my family growing up. It smells like a roast has been in a crockpot all day slow cooking. Or at least that's how my mom always did it. My mouth waters as I anticipate its savory taste. God, it's been forever since I had a home-cooked meal like this.

"Hope you don't mind. I threw in a roast to cook with all the fixings before heading off to class, so it'd be ready when you arrived. It's one of Julia's favorites. Though there will be a side of broccoli—because that wouldn't taste as good if it had cooked all day. I like broccoli, but having it mushy? No thanks."

"Need help with anything?" I ask, setting dessert on the counter out of the way.

"Nope. Julia helped set the table. All we need to do is sit down to eat."

Julia's feet tap out a rhythm as she reenters the house from the garage. "They're almost done and will be right here."

"Okay. Go wash up. The sooner you eat, the faster you'll get dessert."

There must be two modes to Julia, speedy and practically asleep. I have yet to see anything else in my short time with her. She makes me smile as I watch her zoom out of the kitchen.

"Kids..." Vanessa sighs exasperatedly. "If I've told her to walk once, I've told her at least a million times. I need to get that girl into track or on a soccer field. Softball might be too slow of a sport for her. If you'll put this on the table, I'll join you in a second," she says as she hands me a large bowl of broccoli.

There's laughter from the hall off the kitchen that interrupts my mission. When Sydney and Vince round the corner, she swats at him. "You did not just say that."

"If the shoe fits, Syd. You have so many cookbooks, you'll never use them all."

Pointing a finger at him, she waves it. "See if I bake for you again..."

"Hey. You know my favorite recipes by heart. I'm sure you'll manage with a few books in storage for a while. Besides... if you ever need them, you know where to find them."

When they spot me staring, Vince explains, "Sydney's moving in, and she has no less than forty cookbooks. I've never seen that many. It's a good thing we have storage in the attic, or we'd have to add onto the kitchen to put them in a cupboard."

"I don't need them out for the next year or so. But I *am* keeping them, Vincent Daniel Larson. Some were Gram's and others I've picked up along the way."

Vince's smile disappears. "We can pick up a shelf if you want them inside. You know I'm just giving you a hard time, Syd. I didn't realize where they came from."

"I'm good with the attic for now. But if I change my mind, I'll let you know."

Julia runs into the room. "All washed up, Momma."

In a matter of minutes, all of us sit at the round table. Vince and Sydney on one side pair off, and Julia plops beside them. "Dame. You can sit by me. Remember—You'll get in trouble—you have ta take a no thankyou bite... even if you don't like it. Or Momma gets mad."

"That's a good rule to live by. But rumor has it we're having roast. I happen to love it." I grin at her cuteness.

"Don't worry, the broccoli will be good. If you don't like it though..." she trails off as her eyes linger on the bowl in front of her. Then she whispers, though I'm sure the room can hear, "You can just pass it to me, and I'll eat it before anyone knows, 'mkay?"

God, this girl is adorable!

But being the adult I'm supposed to be, I keep a straight face as I whisper back, "Thanks for the offer, I'll keep that in mind."

As I look up, I don't miss Vanessa rolling her eyes and shaking her head. She doesn't get the chance to say anything because Vince clears his throat and says, "So, Damien, you work on campus?"

"Yeah, I just started a few months ago."

"Does that mean you'll be leaving soon... I mean, when your project's over?" Vince clarifies. His face doesn't show any malice, just curiosity. Though I'm sure it has something to do with being a protective brother—That's what I would do with Dani, so I can't blame him.

"I suppose I will, in about a year from now."

"Where will you go then?" Julia asks.

"I guess I'll go wherever my company takes me. I was working in Tacoma before moving here."

"Why did you move here?" Julia asks with a prong filled with broccoli and a facial expression I've seen mirrored on her mother when she's being inquisitive.

"I moved here to help build apartments that families like you could live in, on campus."

"Really?" Julia asks.

"Yeah," Vanessa answers for me. "Students like Unks and I have kids, and they all need places to live. We're lucky we live in a house with a yard you can play in. Some families live in apartments and like to be with other families, instead of with other students."

"So you mean places like my friend Kate lives?"

"Yeah, squirt. Exactly like that," Vince answers.

We spend the next few minutes discussing the student housing project. Vince impresses me with his ability to see the need for family housing on campus. But then again, he and Vanessa have a unique situation. I doubt many students live with a toddler as freshmen. I sure wouldn't have thought much about family housing at their age. Hell, the only reason I've thought about it at all is because it's a part of my job.

"Hey, Van, I have something I'd like to run past you," Sydney says as she wipes her mouth with her napkin. "I want to give Abby and Drew a going away party before school gets out in a few weeks. With our place turning into a storage unit for boxes, would you mind if we host it here?" Before Vanessa can answer, Sydney rushes out, "It will only be us and Drew's roommates most likely. Maybe a few players from the team and a friend or two from Abby."

"If you're living here, this is your place, too." Vanessa shrugs. "I don't see a problem with it. Do Jules and I need to make other plans for the day?"

Sydney's head shakes profusely. "No. Not at all. What do you think of having a barbeque and just hang out in the back-yard if the weather holds? Abby wouldn't want you to miss her going away party."

Then Sydney turns to me. "You're welcome, too, Damien. If you're not busy. I still need to run the date by Abby and Drew. They're leaving in a little over three weeks to check out apartments in Baltimore, so it might happen next weekend or the one after."

"I... uh..." I don't even know where to begin. Does Vanessa even want me here? Under the table, I feel her hand squeeze my leg and from the corner of my eye, I see her nod in a silent invitation. "Okay. That sounds good. Just let me know when."

As soon as everyone finishes their meal, Vince says, "Hey, squirt, help Syd and I with the dishes. Let's let your mom and Damien go relax for a bit."

"Do I have to?" Julia pleads the way any kid with better plans would.

Sydney bops her on the nose as she walks past her. "You do if you want dessert."

"Okay. But I wanted to show Dame how fast I can ride my bike."

To buffer the situation, I assure her, "I'd love to watch you ride when you're ready."

Vanessa motions with her head that we should leave, so I take her cue.

As soon as we're out of the kitchen and away from prying ears, she says, "I hope my crazy isn't too much for you?"

Puzzled, I ask, "Uh, what was crazy about it?"

"Well, Vince giving you the Spanish Inquisition and just a typical evening with Julia."

Reaching for her hand, I give it a squeeze. "I hate to break it to you, but there wasn't any crazy about tonight."

Rolling her eyes, she shakes her head. "Okay... if you say so."

Tipping her chin to meet my eyes, there's a sense of unease I've never seen before. So, I assure her, "I'm having a great time."

Leaning in, I slant my lips over hers and kiss her until she grasps one simple concept. I enjoy her company—simple as that.

I pull apart when a dish clatters to the floor in the other room.

Without missing a beat, Vanessa calls out, "Everything okay?"

"Sorry, Momma, it slipped. But it didn't break," Jules calls from the kitchen.

A devilish grin forms on Vanessa's lips as she whispers, "Hey, I'm not done with you yet."

Damn. I love her feistiness. "Well," I say on a low chuckle. "We can't have that now, can we?"

But before my lips can reach hers again, Julia bursts into

the living room. "Momma, we're done with the dishes. Can I show Dame how fast I can ride? Can I?"

"Go grab your helmet and bike. We'll meet you out front." Then she turns and whispers to me once we're alone again, "Rain check?"

Like I'd ever turn down a kiss from the beautiful woman before me.

18

VANESSA

THREE DAYS LATER, I can't stop thinking about my brazenness with Damien. Every chance I get, I am like a teenager with her first crush. I steal kiss after kiss, and Damien doesn't seem to mind. I swear that man is like catnip or something. All he has to do is breathe in my direction, and I'll gladly come running.

But reality strikes—especially when Julia hits her witching hour. Yeah, she's been much worse, but when she starts getting hyper, I know my time with Damien has to end, so I can get her settled at a decent time for bed.

I've never been more thankful for my regular customers at the diner than I am this morning. I doubt I'd get many new orders right with the state of mind I'm currently living in. When Jeff hollers, "Order's up," I don't even notice it's mine until Tara nudges me.

"Uh, earth to Van. Come in, Van?" she says as she waves a

hand in front of my face. When my eyes meet hers, she laughs. "Where the heck were you?"

"Right here." I attempt to pull off but fail.

"Naw... she's here in body, but her spirit is elsewhere," Jack guffaws. "If I was a bettin' man, I'd guess I know exactly where her mind is."

Ignoring him, I pick up my order and deliver it to the couple it belongs to. Damien has an early meeting and won't be stopping in today, but I can't help but wish he'd walk through the doors. My shift drags on, and I can't wait for it to end.

When I finally make my rounds to refill coffee, I end with Jack, knowing he'll likely talk my ear off. "Anything else I can get for ya, Jack?" I ask, topping off his mug.

"I'm good, sweetheart. Where's that fella of yours? I haven't seen him around today."

Sighing, I release a heavy breath. "Oh, he had an early meeting this morning. I'm sure he'll be in tomorrow."

"That makes sense," Jack says on a sigh. "I remember the days before my wife and I were married. I'd hardly go a day without wanting to see her. Ah... to be young and in love again..."

Love. Did he say love?

"Aww, honey, shut that mouth of yours before you catch something in it. I'm not so much of an old fart that I can't see what's going on. But as you're clearly not ready to hear any of that, I'll just keep my opinions to myself for the time being."

"Ha—that'll be the day," I chortle. That man will never

keep his opinion to himself. And frankly, I wouldn't have it any other way.

"I'm just glad to see you smilin'," he says as he sips on his coffee.

Just then, Sydney's roommate Abby and her fiancé Drew enter the diner and draw my attention with "Morning, Van," as she settles into a booth she and Drew typically sit at.

"Mornin'. Can I get you two some coffee?"

"Yes. Please." Abby eagerly nods. "Finals are kicking my ass, and they don't start until next week."

"You'll do great, Abs. We're ready," Drew assures her by reaching across the table to squeeze her hand. "We're studying and doing all we can. Besides, we're already accepted at John's Hopkins—so the pressure's off."

"True. But you know I won't settle for anything less than an A."

"Trust me, I know," Drew sighs.

"You want your usual?" I ask as I point at the menus still sitting in their slot near the wall.

Abby nods as Drew says, "Sure. Thanks again for hosting next weekend. Abby and I are looking forward to seeing our friends one last time before we take off."

"Anytime. It should be fun. Though Syd's in full planning mode, so I'm just along for the ride." When another customer comes through the door, I offer, "Let me get your order in, and I'll stop by when I can."

"Thanks, Van," Abby offers as I rush to the kitchen.

By the time my shift is over, I'm tired and ready for classes to be over. Tomorrow's class is cancelled—my professor is out of town for a conference this weekend in Chicago. Lucky me, I practically have a three-day weekend. Since I traded my coworker a shift earlier this week, I don't have to work at the diner until Monday.

Just as I get to class, my phone buzzes with a text.

Hoping it's Damien, I eagerly retrieve it from my pocket. To my surprise, it's from Jana, a mom to one of Julia's friends.

Jana: Would Julia be up for a sleepover this weekend? We're going to the beach Saturday and would love to have her join us. We should be home by bedtime. If you're up for it, she can stay with us again, or we can drop her off when we get back to town.

Wow, a kid-free day.

Knowing Jana is one of the few people I've learned to trust Jules with, I quickly tap out a reply.

Me: That sounds good. Let's see how she feels about Saturday night before deciding.

Jana: Sounds good. I'll text you tomorrow night.

Me: Gotta run to class. Talk soon.

Just as I sit down in my seat, the text I'd been expecting comes through, and my smile widens even further.

Damien: Thinking of you. Hope you got to class okay.

Is it possible to physically swoon from just a simple text?
I swear my insides feel gooey, and I can't erase the perma-grin on my face if I try. Knowing my time is limited before my professor starts class, I quickly tap out a response.

Me: Just sat down with a few minutes to spare. Busy conquering the world?

Damien: Today could've been better if I'd seen you this morning. But overall the meeting was productive, so it's good.

Me: What if I told you I have a kid-free night tomorrow evening? Know anyone who wants to hangout?

Damien: I think I might.

He might? What does that mean?
Before I can respond, another notification comes through.

Damien: How does pizza and a movie at my place sound? I'd offer to cook—but no functional kitchen. If you'd rather go out, we can do that, too.

The thought of being alone with Damien sounds quite promising. We've talked for hours on the phone, but I'd much rather be with him in person. Besides, then I can get more of those lips on me that I can't stop thinking about.

My professor stands to teach, and I know I need to cut this short.

Me: Your place is great. Class is starting. Talk later.

Class flies by and instead of picking up Jules early, I settle into my usual studying room at the library. With the semester coming to an end, I have a paper and a few exams to study for. If I use my time well, I could have an entirely free weekend—which would be rare.

One thing Jules has taught me is the necessity for time management. I've learned to utilize every free moment to make my time work for me. That means I stay ahead of my studies and be disciplined enough to stay on campus to finish what I can. Once I get home, all my perfectly laid-out plans can fly out the window—so I've gotta *make hay while the sun shines—as* Daddy used to say.

He'd be so proud of me and what I've become.

In less than one year, I'll have my nursing degree, and the fear of being another teenage statistic will be abolished. I'm determined to be among the two percent who graduate from college before the age of thirty. Sure, I wouldn't be where I am without Vinnie by my side, but I'll be dammed if I'm giving up.

Within two hours, I've finished my paper and feel

prepared for my exams. Knowing I've got thirty minutes to spare before picking up Jules, I swing through the on-campus coffee shop to pick up a treat for my accomplishments.

Sipping on my caramel macchiato, I walk across campus to my car. I'm not sure what it is about this sweet concoction, but when I treat myself to one—the day always goes better. My mood is light knowing I only have one class keeping me from my weekend. Sure, I'll use the time to finish studying, but I feel ready. I can't wait for this semester to end.

My load will be much lighter once summer break is here. Not only will the college students go away, and the town has way less people living in it, but I'm only taking one class this summer. Sure, I usually pick up a few more hours at the diner, but most of my days will be spent with Julia, and times like that are priceless.

"Momma," Julia gushes as she rushes into my arms for a hug when I pick her up from daycare. "Guess what?"

"What?" I ask, amused by her eagerness.

"Cora says her momma might call and ask me to sleep over."

Putting her down on the ground, I bop her on the nose. "She did. She even asked if you could go to the beach with them on Saturday. Are you sure you can handle that?"

As the beach is one of our favorite places, her eyes pop wide as saucers. "Really? What'd ya say?"

"I said I'll talk it over with you. Do you promise to listen and be on your best behavior?"

Nodding excessively, she assures me with a "Yep."

"What about going near the waves?" I ask, wondering if she'll remember our rules.

"Not without an adult. And I have to be close enough to hold their hand... So.... Can I go?"

Nodding, I make her day. "Yeah. You can go."

"This is the best day ever!" she squeals as she hugs me fiercely around my waist. "But do you know what would make it even better?"

The scheming gleam in her eye tells me she's up to something.

"What's that?"

"Maybe we could make cookies and take some to Dame? We ate all of his, and he can't make them himself. You said his kitchen is broken."

"Hmmm..." The thought of seeing him sooner than tomorrow is promising. "Why do you think he needs cookies?"

"Unks loves it when Syd bakes for him. I'm sure Dame needs treats, too. The store-bought ones were okay, but we could make 'em better."

Not knowing what his plans are for the evening, I offer, "We can whip up a batch of no-bake cookies and drop them by his place if you're interested. But if he's busy, we'll just leave them on his porch—you okay with that?"

Jules simply nods and grabs my hand to pull me toward the car.

Yeah, I'm thinking I'm not the only one eager to see Damien.

19

DAMIEN

JUST AS I pull into my driveway, my phone vibrates with an incoming text message. A second later, it goes off again. Once I've put my truck in park, I pull my phone from my pocket and smile at the image on my screen.

Vanessa and Julia's smiles are almost identical and extremely infectious. They're taking a selfie holding up a plate of cookies.

When I read her next text, I burst out with laughter.

Vanessa: Know anyone who might want these? We're hopping in the car now but wanted to give you some warning. If you're busy, we'll leave them on the porch.

Me: Can I take the two of you to dinner first? I know your rules about treats.

She doesn't respond and with the possibility of her driving, I don't want to bother her. Besides, she'll be here soon enough. I occupy my time by getting the mail and hauling up the garbage can from the street. When I see her SUV pull onto my street, I walk out to meet them.

As soon as she parks, Julia's door bursts open. "Dame! You're home. Momma said we were just going to drop these off." She shoves a container of cookies in my direction.

"Have you had dinner yet?" I ask Julia, but it's meant for the two of them.

"Not yet," Vanessa offers. "We made these first and wanted to deliver them before you got off, but obviously you beat us here."

"Were you just going to do a dump and run?" I tease. "I guess I can go to dinner by myself, but I'd much rather have two beautiful women join me."

I'm rewarded with two of the most beautiful smiles in the world. "I think that can be arranged." Vanessa nods, then asks, "Do you mind if I drive so I don't have to change over her car seat?"

Shit. I haven't even thought about that.

"Of course. Can I take a moment to change out of my work clothes? Julia, if it's okay with your mom, you can watch a show while you wait," I say as I open the front door to my house.

Julia nods as Vanessa says, "That's fine. Just take your time. We didn't mean to crash your evening." She smiles apologetically.

"You're not crashing anything," I assure her as I get Julia

settled in the living room with the remote. Just as I'm about to leave the room, I step close enough to Vanessa so only she can hear. "My plans included talking to a beautiful woman on the phone and ordering takeout. I'd much rather it be in person." Leaning in, I peck her quickly on the cheek, so Julia won't notice.

Pulling back, I brush a strand of hair from her face. "Is it weird that I missed you this morning?"

Shaking her head, she agrees, "No, I felt the same way. That's part of the reason I agreed to Jules wanting to bring you cookies."

"I'll never turn down the chance to see you but know... I don't need any bribery. I'll gladly spend any chance I can with you."

Vanessa's smile turns mischievous. "Well, in that case..." She reaches for the cookies still in my hand. "I guess I can take these back."

"Not so fast..." I tease. "I thought we were sharing these *after* dinner. I'm a lonely bachelor with no kitchen... You wouldn't deprive me of a home-cooked treat, would you?"

Sighing heavily, she exaggerates, "I suppose I won't." Then she points in the direction of my room. "Go get changed. We'll be here when you return."

The vixen she is glances to her daughter who's completely engrossed in a show on television and sank deep into the couch facing away from us. Then she lifts to the tips of her feet and kisses me chastely on the mouth. As she pulls away, I swear I hear her mumble. "God, I've wanted to do that all week."

Then she swats at my arm. "Go. Or you'll get to meet a hangry Julia and trust me—no one wants to see that."

Within fifteen minutes, we're loaded into Vanessa's SUV. Julia's picked a Thai restaurant I have yet to try. Vanessa's bopping along to the low music that plays on the radio. Apparently, she and her daughter listen to music regularly because they can sing every word the artist sings.

When "Lose Yourself" by Eminem comes on, I'll admit I give in and sing along with him. Yes, I was in elementary school when it came out, but I remember my brother Derek playing it all the time growing up. As we each give it our all, I can't help but internally laugh. Never in a million years did I expect to be rapping with a child in the back seat, going on a kid-friendly date. But with Vanessa, I'd do it a million times over. I may not have known her long, but something about being with her just feels right and being with Julia... well, that's just an added bonus.

By the time we get our meal, I've quickly learned Julia has the ability to talk the ears off a grasshopper, as my grandpa would say when one of us jabbered. I've learned that she can't wait to start school in the fall, she loves playing with Barbies, riding her bike, and *really* wants a cat of her own. Of course, Vanessa expertly evades that topic by bringing up the topic of summer break and asks which beach she wants to travel to celebrate.

When I tell them how I used to spend my summers with my grandparents on Anderson Island, I get peppered with questions I wasn't prepared for.

Julia's eyes are wide with disbelief when she asks, "You have grandparents?"

"Yeah. They live near Olympia now. But we still have a family home on the island," I offer.

"No... I mean, yours are still alive?"

"Jules," Vanessa says in warning.

"It's okay," I assure them both. "I don't mind talking about them."

"Sorry, Dame." Julia looks to her plate. "I don't remember mine. They died right after I was born. But I know my momma misses them. I do, too."

Them? Does she mean both of Vanessa's parents died right after high school? Fuck, I had no idea. No wonder she doesn't talk about them. My mind reels for what to say. I can't imagine losing one of my parents, let alone both—and at such a young age.

When I look to Vanessa, I don't find sadness on her face. Just an understanding smile toward her daughter. "You're right. There isn't a day that goes by that I don't miss them. But fortunately, most people aren't like us, Jules. They have living family members well into their eighties and nineties. Grams and Pops were taken from us way too soon in that car accident."

Julia nods slowly in understanding. "I know. But Damien still has his grandparents... and he's old—like you... how does he still have grandparents?"

Too shocked by the old comment, I can't help but laugh. "Uh... for your information, I'm only twenty-six. My parents are in their mid-fifties, and my grandparents aren't even eighty yet. I'm not a dinosaur..."

Vanessa covers her face with her hand, and I'm not sure if it's to hide her embarrassment—which she has nothing to be embarrassed about—or to hide her shock about the old comment.

"Momma, you're twenty-one, right?" Julia asks.

When Vanessa uncovers her face, I'm relieved to find it was laughter she was hiding from. "Yeah, squirt. I am."

Julia shrugs as she looks to me. "I guess you're not *that old*."

Holy shit. What do I say to that?

Rolling her beautiful hazel eyes, Vanessa sighs heavily. "Well, that's good to know. Why don't you finish your meal before Damien thinks better of it and takes us home for being so rude?"

"I'm not offended, but I'm glad to see both of you think I'm an *old man*," I say when Vanessa finally makes eye contact, reminding her of our earlier conversations. Thankfully, she smiles at the memory. "I'm sure I'm old—compared to someone her age. I used to think my teacher who was thirty was practically a senior citizen. God, I'm glad I know better—now."

Vanessa lets out a beautiful laugh. "No kidding. Still, Jules, you'd better eat up. It's almost your bedtime. If you want some of those cookies for dessert, we'd better hurry up."

By the time we get back to my house, it's after seven. I could hear Julia's yawns from the front seat on the way home, but the girl insists she isn't tired. Since I promised I'd share my cookies when we get back to my house, Julia's doing all she can not to fall asleep. She insisted that her mom blast the music and sang at the top of her lungs to Lady Gaga, Adele, and Maroon 5. Even tired, the girl behind me is adorable.

When we make it inside, you'd never know she was sleepy mere moments ago. Vanessa insists she sit at the coffee table to keep the crumbs over the table and not on my floor. I could care less. That's what brooms are for, but I won't interfere with Vanessa's parenting.

Eventually, Vanessa excuses herself to use the restroom, and I'm left on my own with Julia. The minute we're alone, Julia turns to me with a serious expression. "You like my momma, don't you?" It's not a question but an accusation.

Honesty is always best, so I nod as I say, "Yeah. You okay with that?"

Fuck. The approval of a five-year-old has never mattered more than in this moment. What if she says no? I'd never come between Vanessa and her daughter.

After what feels like forever, she slowly nods. "Yeah. It's okay. But do you like her—as in you want to be her boyfriend? Like Unks and Sydney?" Her expression is a younger version of her mom's when she's dead serious.

Knowing I'll never lie about my feelings about Vanessa, especially to Julia, I admit, "Yeah. You okay with that?"

"Can I meet your grandparents someday?"

Well, that's out of left field. "Sure. Maybe someday you'll get to meet my parents *and* grandparents," I offer. Then I hope like hell I didn't just lie to her. I have no idea what Vanessa feels, but for the first time in forever, I'm eager for my family to meet the women I've never been happier to have in my life.

"Okay. Can I have another cookie?" she asks as if we didn't just have the most serious conversation in the world.

"Uh... one more. Then you'll have to wait for your mom, 'mkay?"

By the time Vanessa returns, you'd never know her daughter just gave me the what for mere moments ago.

"Okay, squirt. We need to get you home. We both have to be up early. Let's say goodbye to Damien and get on the road."

As soon as I stand to walk them out, Julia surprises me by bolting in my direction and launching herself at me. Her arms fly around me like a spider monkey, and she nearly squeezes the breath out of me. "Night, Dame."

"Night, Jules," I whisper when my breath returns as she releases me. Then I turn to Vanessa who looks mystified, yet I can't entirely read her expression as she blinks at us a few times before shaking her head. "Can I walk you out?" I offer so she can get Julia home to bed.

Julia grabs my hand and says, "Yes." Then she pulls me toward the door.

"Okay, then." I chuckle, following after her.

After helping Julia in the car, I walk around the car to help Vanessa with her door. Wishing I could kiss her goodbye, it takes everything in me to keep things at a G-rated level. "Night, Van," I whisper. "I had a great time. I'll see you tomorrow night."

"Can't wait," Vanessa mouths in return as I shut the door, and she rolls down her window.

Then loud enough for both to hear, I duck into her SUV and say, "Thanks again for the cookies. See you later, Jules."

As I watch them drive off, an indescribable feeling spreads throughout my chest. There's a tightness I've never felt before. One thing I do know, I can't wait to see what tomorrow night brings.

THE NEXT NIGHT, I'm folding laundry when there's a knock on my door, I practically run to get it from my bedroom.

"Coming!" I holler, racing to the door.

Breathless, I swing the door open and what little breath I had left in me vanishes as my jaw drops to the floor. Vanessa's there gorgeous as ever. She's done something to her hair, so it flows in waves past her shoulders. She's wearing a fitted black top and a pair of skinny jeans that do nothing but make me notice her sexy figure. When my perusal returns to her face, I notice she's wearing makeup. Her eyes are lined perfectly to accent the depth of the color of hazel in her irises. Her lips are painted a beautiful shade of pink, slightly darker than her natural color, and the way she grins makes me want to kiss it right off her.

"Hey?" comes out as a question, and I want to smack myself for staring.

Blinking, I force myself to use words. "Damn, Van. You look amazing. Are you sure you just want to hang out here looking that good? Don't get me wrong, I'm happy to keep you to myself, but you look like you're ready for a night on the town, not hangin' with my sorry ass."

"Crap. I knew I put too much effort into this," she mumbles to herself as she looks to her feet.

"Stop," comes out more forceful than I intend, and her eyes dart to mine. "You're one of the most beautiful people I know. This outfit... well, it makes you basically drool worthy. Trust me. That was just my dumb-ass way of asking if you'd like to actually go out for dinner rather than order in."

"I... uh..." she stammers.

Needing to stop her self-doubt, I step closer and pull her to me, slanting my lips over hers. "I'm more than happy staying in. The choice is yours, Van. I just need to know if I should go change or not."

Without giving her the opportunity to answer, my lips are on hers. Goddamn. I've missed this woman. I know we saw each other yesterday, but my lips haven't touched hers since Monday.

Vanessa's hands reach up to cup my face and pull me closer, and I happily oblige as I deepen our kiss. When her tongue tangles with mine, she tastes of mint and something entirely her. When I hear the sexiest sound imaginable come out of her, I'm hard as granite instantly. It's a cross between a moan and a sigh as she presses her body closer to mine. I need more. When a car alarm blasts through the air, we jump apart in a panic. Spinning to see where it's coming from, Vanessa shouts, "Oh shit! Where are my keys?"

She frantically pats down her pants until she practically rips them out of her pocket. If she weren't so worried, I'd almost laugh. Pressing the button over and over, it finally disengages about the fourth try.

Her cheeks are flaming red as she turns to face me. "Ohmigod! Let's go inside. I can't even..." She points to her car and then the neighborhood.

Wanting to put her at ease, I quickly pull her through the door and slam it shut in my haste.

With wide eyes, she looks from me to the keys in her hand. "I blame you... this is all your fault..."

"Me... what did I do? You're the one looking hot as sin, setting off alarms and all."

Her mouth opens wide, then shuts immediately. Then she sets her keys on the table by the door. "You think I'm hot as sin, do you? Well, I'll show you just how hot I can be." Wrapping her arms around my neck, she pushes her body against mine and kisses the fuck out of me.

Holy Fucking Hell. This woman is perfect for me.

When she uses her teeth against my lower lip, I'm fucking done for.

My mouth fuses to hers, and I use my hands to lift her ass, so that she's closer to my height. As if we've been practicing this for years, her legs wrap around my torso without breaking our kiss. With her holding most of her weight by hanging on to me, I slide one hand up her back to the base of her neck to control the kiss further.

Suddenly, the fucking doorbell rings, and we pull apart, startled once again.

Fuck. I'd forgotten about the pizza I'd ordered.

Setting her on her feet, I look down at the effect she has on me. I'm not even sure I can walk the five steps to the door in this state. Seeing my hesitation, she asks, "Want me to get that?" as she points at the door.

When the offending bell rings again, I slowly nod and pull out my wallet. Handing her more than enough cash to pay for the pizza, I say. "Yes, please."

Taking a moment to straighten her hair and glance in the mirror hanging by the door, she shakes her head and smiles. "At least I'm not as obvious as to what we've been up to."

Her swollen lips and tousled hair make her look as if she's been thoroughly fucked, but she doesn't have a raging hard-on that's practically bulging out of her pants. So, yeah... she's the less obvious between the two of us.

Opening the door, she greets the delivery person as if she hadn't just climbed me like a tree and kissed the ever-loving fuck out of me. She hands the money over and pulls the large box through the door before shutting it.

With wide eyes, she looks at the extra-large box and bag of breadsticks and says, "Uh, is this just for us?"

Shrugging, I nod. "I can always put it in the fridge for leftovers."

Giggling, she walks past me to the living room and sets it on the coffee table. Then she turns and walks back to me. Using her thumb, she runs it along my lips. "Lipstick," she says as explanation. "I'm pretty sure all that I had on is now trans-ferred to you."

"If that's the sacrifice I have to make to be kissed like that, I don't even care if it's not my shade."

"Very funny. Are you ready to eat..." she trails off, and her innocent expression transforms to mischievous. "Or... if you have something better in mind, I'm game for that, too."

"Van," comes out as both a plea and a warning, "I'm trying to do the right thing here." From our conversations on the phone, I've gathered that she hasn't dated much since Julia was born. But this bolder side of her isn't only a major fucking turn-on but completely uncharted territory for her. I don't want to rush things if she isn't ready to take things beyond the level we're at now.

"I know you are, Dame—and I appreciate that. But I'm not done with you yet." When she reaches out her hand and those confident hazel eyes meet mine, I know in this instant, I'll do anything to make her happy.

Pushing the coffee table out of the way, I sit on the couch and wait for her to join me.

When she hesitates, it's clear her confidence and bravado may have some cracks. This just won't do. "Come here, Van. There's no pressure. It's just me. We can sit, eat pizza, and watch a movie, or we can keep making out like before. I never mean to make you uncomfortable, 'mkay?"

"Oh, I'm uncomfortable all right," she says teasingly as she plops down beside me.

"Uncomfortable how?" I ask for clarification.

"Well," she huffs out. "If you must know, I haven't been able to stop thinking about your magnificent lips all week. We've hardly had any time alone since you came over for dinner, so yeah... I've been all out of sorts. I haven't felt this way... ever... so I entirely blame..." She points at my chest. "You."

Fuck, she's adorable.

Laughing, I pull her onto my lap, so that she's facing me. "Well, we can't have that now. If you've been thinking about kissing me *all week, then* I can definitely help you in that department right this very second."

The moment my lips meet hers, we're right back to where we started before the pizza arrived. Her hands run through my hair and along my neck, making my senses become overloaded. She may kill me with how much I want her, but at least I'll die a happy man.

When her hand slips under my t-shirt, as her fingers trace along the planes of my abs and up my chest, I break the kiss to give her more of what she wants. Ripping my shirt over my head with one hand, I'm pleased when her eyes widen, and she whispers, "Oh, I could get used to this."

Chuckling, I suggest, "All you had to do was ask."

"Good to know." She rolls her eyes. "Now get over here, so I can admire you." Her flirty confidence makes me like her more than I thought possible. When her lips meet mine, the inferno picks up where we left off. My hand slides down her back, and I run my fingers along her exposed skin at the top of her jeans.

When she breaks our kiss to look me in the eye, heat radiates from them. "Damien," comes out slow and seductive. "I want nothing more than to take my shirt off and feel your skin against mine—but with your lack of curtains, I think we might need to move this to another room."

Fuck me. Why did I take them down last week in the first

place? Oh, right. I'm replacing the windows next week and wanted to be ready for the installers.

Why the fuck am I thinking about that now though?

"There is privacy in my bedroom," I admit. God, the thought of having her sprawled out across my bed and taking my time to get to know her better sounds like the best idea —ever.

Without saying a word, Vanessa stands and reaches for my hand. "Then let's go."

The moment we walk through my bedroom door, I shut it for an added layer of protection from my neighbors, then step toward her predatorily. "Is this private enough?"

20

VANESSA

"YES," I whisper, tilting my face to meet his. With one hand, Damien grips the base of my neck as my other snakes around my waist, pulling me closer. "Mmmmm," I moan as my fingers sprawl across the light dusting of hair on his chest. Damien feels incredible.

When his hand slips under my shirt, and his fingers run along my spine, I'm reminded of why we came in his room. Reluctantly breaking our kiss, I hastily pull my shirt over my head, tossing it to the floor.

Damien's dark eyes widen in appreciation, and I feel even bolder than before. I'm entirely in uncharted territory, but I've read a lot of romance. For some reason, this man makes me feel confident in ways I've never imagined.

Sure, I've had sex before—hello, I'm a teenage mom. But I'm extremely limited in my experience.

Damien doesn't even have to touch me for my breast to feel heavier and my bra tighter. Gazing at me with such adoration has my clit thumping and heart racing. I might not have had an orgasm without it being a solo mission, but I do know what it feels like to anticipate one.

Glancing at the bed, I'm reminded of just how long it's been since I've had sex. Exactly nine months before Julia was born. I'd lost my virginity and gained a daughter all in one night. I don't regret it for anything. But Damien should know, so if things progress that far, he can be prepared.

What if he doesn't want to be with me once he finds out?

Damien senses my hesitation and completely misreads it.

"If you'd rather go back to the living room, I'm fine with that, too," he offers.

Knowing the truth is the quickest way to put my fears at ease, I straighten my shoulders and begin, "No. I want to be here. But before things go any further, I think there's something you need to know."

The look of uncertainty that flashes across his beautiful features has me quickly spouting my truth to put his unease at rest. "I..." Where the fuck do I begin?

Just start with the beginning.

"I... need you to know something." I look to the floor, hoping to find the answer for how to rip off the proverbial bandage and get this over with quickly.

With a finger, Damien lifts my chin to meet his eyes. "You can tell me anything, Vanessa. Please know that."

"I'm sure you've been with lots of girls..." I start but stop as soon as I realize I don't want to go down that slippery slope. I'd rather not think about him with other women right now.

"Okay..." he draws out, but neither confirms nor denies my

accusation. When I remain quiet for longer than necessary, he attempts to prompt me with, "But...."

"But I haven't..." Jesus Christ, just spit it out, Van. "I mean... I don't have a lot of experience."

A sexy, yet reassuring smile spreads across his lips. "This isn't a competition, Van, and I'd rather not keep score."

"Obviously, I'm not a virgin—with Julia and all—but the night I got pregnant was the one and only time I've had sex."

There. I've said it.

Damien's jaw drops right along with my stomach.

Crap. Maybe I shouldn't have said anything.

Then he quickly recovers as his eyes fill with sincerity. "Thank you. That is something I'd much rather know... but please don't feel pressured to do anything."

"I don't," I spit out faster than I intend. "What I mean is... I want to be here with you. I just don't want to do something... or not do something that you would or wouldn't expect." Fuck. "That made no sense."

Damien steps closer, places a hand at the base of my neck, and guides my eyes to meet his while cupping my cheek. "Okay... let's get one thing straight. Communication is everything. I need to know what you're thinking and feeling, so I can be what you need, too. I have zero expectations for us in terms of how far we go—or don't go. I'm man enough to know that I want you to be a thousand percent ready for when we take that next step together and if you're not ready or feeling it, I'm perfectly okay with that, too."

This man. He's so sweet. But if honesty is what he's asking for, honesty is what he'll get—even if I have to swallow my pride in doing so. "I guess... I'm... just afraid that you won't want me... you know... because I'm not very experienced. You've got plenty of other women who'd happily be with you... and..."

Damien furiously shakes his head. "Stop. Just stop. No more self-doubt. Let's get one thing straight. I will *always* want you. You're smart. You're sexy. You're fucking unbelievably driven. You're one of the best moms I know, and most importantly, you make me feel things about myself I've never felt before. You make me want to be a better man. You make me want to take a chance on being in a relationship, and most important... you're making me fall for you."

He takes in a slow and steady breath but never loses eye contact.

"I could give two fucks about whether or not you've screwed one man or a million. No—I take that back. I'd go insanely jealous with the thought of a million guys knowing what an incredible woman you are... so let's just stick with keeping things between you and me. When you're ready to take things to that next level—we will. Until you are—we wait."

Holy shit. Did he just say that?

"I didn't want things to end," I admit. "I just wanted to let you know, so you didn't think I was hiding things from you. I rather liked how things were progressing. I honestly won't know until we get there... if I'm ready for sex. But I know for the first time in over five years, I'd like to consider it a possibility."

Dipping his head so we're eye to eye, he says, "You take the lead, Van. I enjoy being with you, but I'll never make you feel pressured to do *anything*, 'mkay?"

"Got it. Now can we go back to making out?" I suggest. Coyly, I smile in his direction as I push him toward the bed. "I rather liked that—and I definitely want to spend time with my tongue on your abs."

Shaking his head, he chuckles as he backs toward the bed. "You're quite the vixen, Van."

When his legs bump against the foot of the bed, I playfully push on his chest. "Glad you think so. Now get on that bed, so I can go on a treasure hunt."

"Holy fuck..." he mumbles through a shocked grin.

When he falls back, he brings me with him. The moment we land, he tickles my waist, and I burst into fits of laughter. "Two can play that game. Be careful what you wish for," I warn as we roll around the bed, filling the room with laughter.

It doesn't take long before my lips find his, and I kiss him for all I'm worth. This man understands me in a way no other has. It's like he was given a key to a locked chamber, and I'm coming alive in his presence.

His fingers trail over my rib cage and along my back. When I reach back to release the clasp of my bra, he beats me to it. The moment my breasts fall free, he takes one into his hands and guides my nipple to his mouth to nip and suck in such a way that all I can do is throw my head back and enjoy the sensation. Holy... Ohmigod, what is he doing to me? "More.... Please..." I pant.

Shifting our bodies so that I'm lying on the bed, Damien covers me with his body as he trails hot kisses from breast to breast, along my collarbone and down my stomach. In this moment, everything I've always been self-conscious of disappears. I no longer care that I carry extra weight around my middle, that I have stretch marks, or that I haven't been with a man in years. All that matters in this moment is him and how he makes me feel.

I squirm like hell under him, trying to find a way to release the pressure building inside me. My ears thunder with my heartbeat, and my clit strums at an even faster beat. God... I need... more...

"Tell me what you want," he says between kisses along my ribs.

Had I said that aloud?

Pressing my pelvis into his thigh, I practically beg, "I'm so close..."

I feel a deep chuckle rumble from his chest at the words, "Can I help you with that?"

"Heck yeah! You're the one that got me this needy..." I practically whine.

"For the record, my pants are staying on tonight... but would you be opposed to yours being removed... ya know... so I can be of assistance?" His tone is teasing, but his face is watching my every move.

Nodding so hard I think my head may separate from my neck, I reach for the button of my jeans.

"Let me, Van," he says as he brushes my hands aside and returns to kissing my belly. Holy hell. When did that become an erogenous zone?

Damien's in no rush, and he takes his sweet time making

sure my senses are on overload as he slowly removes my jeans. He skips over the places my underwear covers, instead trailing kisses down each leg and back. When he stops at my inner thigh, I can't take it anymore.

"Dame... You're killing me." Reaching for his head, I fist my fingers through his soft hair. I've never realized the importance of longer hair on top than I do in this moment.

Damien stops to make eye contact with me, and I nearly die. "You sure?"

"If you don't, I'll be liable for taking matters into my own hands."

"Someday, Van." He smiles deviously. "I'd like to watch— but today isn't that day."

Slowly, he lowers the last barrier between us, kissing those same trails he made with my jeans. Shivers sprawl throughout my body in anticipation. I've never been so exposed to anyone except my gynecologist, but in this moment—I've never felt more comfortable with another human on the planet. Damien makes me feel so alive as I relish in the sensations he creates. And the heat coming from his eyes as he takes all of me could make me burst into flames on its own.

As he crawls back up my body, he settles naturally between my legs, stopping in just the perfect place. "God-damn, you're beautiful," is one of the last coherent things I hear. When his lips and tongue finally make contact with my most sensitive places, I'm taken out of this world. Damien's ability to nip, suck, lick, and pull has me quickly barreling toward ecstasy. I just can't get enough.

As my outer extremities tingle, and a ripple runs up my spine, I have the biggest release I've ever experienced. My trusty vibrator has nothing on Damien. Wave after wave of pleasure rolls through me, and I chase each sensation to the very end.

When I'm nothing but a puddle of goo, Damien kisses his way back up my body to lie beside me. His fingers roam across my body, elongating the sensations he's created that continue to flow.

I can't even form coherent words when he asks, "You okay?"

A euphoric smile and a nod are all I manage.

"God, you're gorgeous blissed out like this," Damien says on a laugh. "I might have to do this to you more often."

"Yes, please," I whisper, and that sets him into a full belly laugh.

His amusement is infectious.

I want to explore his sexy body, but I can't even lift my head at the moment.

He must have the ability to read my mind because he bends closer to me and brushes his lips against mine. His lips taste of me combined with him, and I'm not sure what to make of it. The fact that it doesn't seem to bother him eases my fears.

When he breaks our kiss, he whispers, "Damn, you taste amazing. When you've recovered, I'm totally doing *that* again."

"Wha..." I start, but he kisses me into silence.

After things get heated again, my stomach rumbles, causing us to burst into laughter.

Damien pulls back, waggling his brows. "How about we go eat our real food, then come back here and I'll get my dessert?"

Swatting at him, I pretend my shock. "You did *not* just say that."

"Oh, trust me, Van. I'll make it worth it for both of us. I'm nowhere done with you yet."

21

VANESSA

I WOULDN'T SAY I get much sleep with Damien. After eating pizza in only my underwear and a t-shirt he lets me borrow, it doesn't take long until he's ready to devour me again. I have no freaking clue what he does to me, but he is like a drug I can't get high enough on.

I must have dozed off again because when I wake up, I find the sun is up and the bed empty. In Damien's place, I find a note on the pillow.

Morning Beautiful,
Went to grab breakfast. Hopefully, I'll be back
before you wake. If not, make yourself at home.
Rumor has it I have a tub you claimed you wanted
to get lost in.

That's exactly where Damien finds me when he returns. After washing my hair, I get lost in his ginormous tub. It's so big I can float and not touch the sides. I've never been in so much space. I have music playing on my phone, so I don't hear him when he enters the bathroom.

"Well... that's certainly something I don't come home to every day." His words bring me out of my hypnotic state.

"Ahhhh!" I scream as I bolt to an upright position. Water splashes everywhere, but thankfully, it stays in the tub. "You scared me."

"Uh, you left the door open... and I did knock." Damien somehow manages to look me directly in the eye.

Pulling my knees to my chest, I sigh. "This tub is amazing. I can't remember the last time I soaked without interruption. Or have ever been in anything so big."

"Doesn't this count as an interruption?" He points between the two of us as he cocks a brow in my direction.

"Uh... it's your house," I offer in explanation.

"I'll make you a deal. I'll wait for you in the living room. Take your time. Then if you'd like, we can go do something."

"I'm fine with staying here," I offer. "I don't need to be entertained."

"I know that, Van. But if we stay here, I'm gonna want to join you. Then if I join you, I'm gonna have to taste you. If I taste you, I know we're never gonna leave." By the end, his smile is crooked and downright sinful.

"Then you'd better scat, and I'll finish up in here. I don't want to make this any harder on you than necessary. Do you mind if I borrow another one of your shirts to wear until we can stop by my place to change my clothes?"

"You can borrow anything you'd like," he offers. "I'll be in the living room. I've got some coffee and some pastries from the local bakery down the street. I figured you'd rather not eat at my usual place, as it's your day off."

"You figure right. Are you gonna make me let this water get cold? Or are you gonna go wait in the living room?" I tease.

"It's not like I haven't seen it all before, Van. If I recall, you quite liked it when I tasted every square inch of you."

If that's how he wants to play, two can play this game.

A surge of boldness rushes through me as I lift my chin along with my entire body from the water as I stare directly into Damien's wide eyes. His jaw drops as I reach for my towel and step from the tub. Bending at the waist, I start at my toes and dry myself off like I would without anyone watching. I rise slowly, toweling off along the way. Wanting to put on more of a show for the stunned man before me, I quickly wipe off my chest and arms, then flip the towel to my backside to dry off my back. Then to prove a point, I flip my hair over my head and wrap my head, then stand to my full height.

"As Jack would say, you're gonna catch some flies if you don't close that mouth of yours," I tease.

I have no idea where this brazen woman inside me came from, but the look of appreciation I see on his face has my inner critic cheering myself on. Confidently, I walk to him and ask, "See something ya like?"

Damien's tone is clipped as he says, "Vanessa, you're gonna be the death of me. I'm trying so fucking hard to do the right thing here. But you're making it... really difficult."

"It's your own fault, mister. You're the one standing there enjoying the show, when you could be eating pastries and drinking coffee. We both know how much you need to consume to make it through the day."

"I enjoy the view no matter the location—though this takes the cake if I'm being honest. There's no way I'm walking away when the sexiest woman I've ever seen is flaunting all her goods. I may not be the smartest man in the world, but I'm not dumb enough to ignore this either. For the record, this might be my favorite memory in this house." Damien smirks, then adds, "By the way, did you ever think I might drink that much coffee each day to keep talking to you?"

How the hell is he keeping casual conversation like this? I'm standing here as naked as the day I was born... and he's talking about coffee?

As my need for him grows, I'm forced to make a decision.

Feeling bold and empowered by the confidence Damien gives me, I rip the towel from my hair and let it drop to the floor between us. I take the necessary step toward him to close the distance as I reach for the fly of his jeans and pull him close.

Damien's eyes darken as the air crackles between us.

"I think it's my turn to have dessert first."

I have his fly undone and am sliding his pants and boxers over his perfectly sculpted hips before he can find the words to respond.

When I drop to my knees, his denial sounds weak. "You... don't have to..." But it's too late. The moment my hand cups his cock and slides down to the base, he lets out a guttural, "FUUUUUCCCKKKK," and I'm certain I've never felt more powerful than in this moment.

Taking my free hand, I push his pants to the floor, and he quickly steps out of them and kicks them to the side.

When I focus my attention on his raging hard-on, I swear it bobs in greeting.

His thick cock is smooth and corded with veins as I guide him to my mouth. With the tip of my tongue, I trace around his head, and I'm rewarded with another sexy moan. "God, Van. That feels incredible. But we could spend the day out of the bedroom..."

With a mouthful of him, I manage to mutter, "Later. I'm busy."

Flattening my tongue, I run it along the underside of his length, and I swear he gets even harder. So, of course, I double down on my efforts, bringing my hand into the mix to complement my movements. I easily slide up and down his shaft, finding a rhythm that drives him wild.

I may not have done this in years, but I certainly remember enough of the basics to practically bring him to his knees. Sure, this would be easier on the bed, but he was so patient, kind, and perfect last night, I want to show him how he makes me feel. Besides, there's something sexy as hell about catching him off guard and bringing him the most amount of pleasure possible. I came more times than I could count last night—and he never asked for anything in return, other than to do it again.

"Oh, God. Vanessa." His moan sounds sexy as hell repeated on a loop.

When I'm reminded of a technique I've only read about in one of my romance novels, I give it a try. Taking my free hand,

I cup and massage his balls. Then I apply pressure to the spot just behind them, and I'm rewarded with, "Van... I'm close."

Sucking harder, I apply more pressure. "Shit. Van. I'm close. You may wanna stop."

To which, I shake my head no as I continue my efforts. He pushes on my shoulders to let me know he's serious, as I take him in deep and suck hard as my tongue rotates around his shaft. "Fuck... Van... Can't stop it... Pull off, so I don't come in your mouth."

No way in hell am I missing this experience.

Taking as much of him in as I can, I suck even harder, and he erupts. Pulse after pulse, I continue the rhythm I've set, as Damien lets out a string of curses telling me how amazing his orgasm feels.

When I'm certain there's not another twitch left in him, I pull off with a pop, and he mules. "Fuck... Your mouth should come with a warning label, woman."

As his eyes roll to the back of his head, I ask. "That's a good thing, right?"

Grinning, Damien's eyes dart to mine. "A very fuckin' good thing," he assures me.

"Good." I stand, bringing the towel before me to my mouth and wiping off my lips. "Let's go eat some *real food* and get started with our day."

Leaning up on my toes, I kiss him chastely before asking, "Which shirt can I wear? We both know neither of us will get any real food if I stay naked."

"If you insist," he sighs. "Though I'll always vote for naked breakfast when it comes to you, if given the choice."

"Why must I be the adult, Dame? Shouldn't you be the responsible one?"

Turning, I walk to his closet, and he swats me playfully on the ass. "Oh, I'll show you adulting, my little temptress. You just wait and see how I rock your world next time."

"Promises. Promises," I tease. Leaving him half naked, I turn and pick out the first t-shirt I can get my hands on and pull it over my head.

When I turn, he's slipping on his jeans. "If this is a typical morning with you, I can't wait to see your adventurous side."

You and me both, Damien. You and me both, I giddily think to myself. He may have just opened Pandora's box with all my pent-up sexual tension over the years. I just hope I live up to the brazen woman he's turned me into today.

22

DAMIEN

TO BOTH OUR SURPRISE, Vanessa and I are rewarded with an extra night together when Julia is invited to spend a second night with her friend Cora. Waking up with Vanessa in my arms is something I can get used to. I've loved every moment I have spent with her this weekend, too.

Though I'll admit we spend most of Saturday at my place, after getting the call from Cora's mom, we venture out to get her a change of clothes and grab some dinner. Afterward, we walk along the river and end the night actually watching the movie I'd originally invited her over for.

Early Sunday morning, the sun has barely made its presence, but enough light shines through my curtains to make out the beautiful woman beside me. My over-sized tee she asked to wear to bed is pooled around her waist, and her blue cotton panties are sexy as hell. My fingers itch to trace circles along her spine but knowing she rarely gets to sleep in, I keep my interaction to eyes only.

The more I get to know the amazing woman beside me, the more I'm in awe of her. Thoughts to the conversation at dinner with Julia come to mind. I can't even imagine what it would've been like to be a teen parent. Then to lose her parents? Fuck. I'd be rolled up in a ball, rocking in the corner—not conquering the world one day at a time.

Leaning back against my pillow, I stare at the ceiling, recalling Julia's comments about their accident. As much as I want to know more, I haven't allowed myself to ask Vanessa about the details. We've been having such a great time. Why would I dampen her mood? Clearly, it still upsets her—as evidenced at the baseball game.

Resilience is just another attribute I'm learning to love about Vanessa. Hell, my life has been like Pollyanna, compared to the tragedies she's endured. Punch after punch, Vanessa just gets back up and swings back at the world that's tried to knock her down.

Yes, she has Vince's help but from what I can tell, the two of them are essentially on their own. My siblings are basically adults, with the exception of Davis in med school. But we have amazing extended family we can count on, too, to get us through whatever life throws at us. Who does Vanessa, Jules, and Vince have besides each other?

When Vanessa rolls over and flings her leg across my torso, I know in this instant—if she'll let me, I'd like to be someone she can count on, too. I've never been one for commitment—my family can attest to that. But with Vanessa... the thought of not going all in physically makes me ill.

I'm drawn to her in a way that's more than just attraction.

Ever since Amber, I've been scared as hell of letting someone close to me. Not only did she give me a royal mind fuck, but she made me realize I was better on my own. Thank fuck, I finally saw the signs and ran—not walked in the other direction from her.

But Vanessa's different.

Vanessa's kind and loving and won't think twice about putting others' needs first. Hell, she does it each and every day. Not only is she an amazing mom, but she's a supportive sister and will make a fantastic nurse someday. I just know it.

"What are you thinking about over there so seriously?" comes out on a long, adorable yawn. "It's waaayyy too early for contemplating world domination, Dame. What's going on?"

The hand that had been resting on my chest comes up to cup my cheek. Her thumb naturally brushes along my scruffiness and it feels amazing.

"Honestly, just how amazing you are."

"Oh, geez. You haven't. You're not allowed to be so sexy *and sweet* in the morning. That's just not fair to all of mankind."

Now who's being cheesy?

"I'm not being sweet. Just telling the truth," I admit. "I guess I was wondering how you do it all? Raising Julia. Going to school. Sure... you have Vince, but you're essentially on your own. I'm in awe—that's all. Can't I admire you?"

"You're ridiculous," she guffaws. "I'm more of a hot mess than a hot catch, Dame. Trust me. Half the time, I'm just fakin' it 'til I make it. If I believe it enough, it has to come true, right?"

If only she could see herself through my eyes.

"Have you been up long?" she asks, changing the topic.

"A while." I shrug.

"Ohmigod. Are you—like—naturally an early riser? I'd never willingly know there are two five o'clocks in a day if I didn't pull the early shift at the diner so I can spend my evenings with Jules."

"I'm afraid it's out of habit. Once I started working full time, I've never been able to sleep in—no matter what time I go to bed."

"That's just.... Wrong." She shakes her head. "Though Julia is the alarm I never have to set, so I don't sleep in much these days either, I guess. But it's not natural. Just a necessity."

"Speaking of Jules..." I trail off, wondering if this is the wrong time to ask about her parents. "At dinner the other night, she said something."

"Oh, God. What did she say?" she asks as if she's trying to recall our conversations. "It wasn't bad, was it?" She cringes at the end.

"No. Not really. It's just..." I start but quickly clarify, "I'm curious about something.... But... I'm fine waiting until you're ready, too."

Vanessa's face fills with alarm, so I sputter out the rest of my thought so that she doesn't have to worry about something Julia may have done.

"It's just... Julia mentioned there being an accident..." I trail off, then quickly add, "We certainly don't have to talk about anything. But I wanted to make sure I heard her right."

Nodding slowly in understanding, she says, "Yeah. I lost both my parents when Julia was two months old. She's never known them, but we've let them live on through our memories."

Holy shit. She had a newborn and lost her parents within months of each other?

Fuck. I shouldn't have brought this up. Why couldn't I have been patient and waited for her to share when she was ready?

"I'm sorry," I say as I reach for her hand. "I don't mean to upset you."

"I'm not upset. I knew this conversation would come up eventually after dinner that night. I'm surprised you haven't asked sooner, honestly."

"I didn't want to upset you," I admit. "I also don't want to pry. I'm okay with waiting until you're comfortable talking about it with me, too."

"I've come a long way since the accident. Time and therapy have helped, as well. For the longest time, I blamed myself. But now, I've come to realize it was just a horrific accident, and there's nothing I could've done to prevent it."

Why would she think her parents' accident was her fault?

"What do you mean?" I ask for clarification. Now isn't the time to assume anything. My mind races to all sorts of conclusions, but none of them seem viable.

"At one time, I thought it was my fault they were involved in the accident in the first place. The night of graduation, my parents stayed home with Julia so I could celebrate at our senior party. They'd made special arrangements for me to drive home before midnight, and then they left to take the two to six a.m. shift as chaperones.

"I made it home safely and was sound asleep with Jules when it happened. I was none the wiser." She shakes her head as the memories assault her, making my chest ache.

"If this is too hard, please don't feel like you have to tell me," I reassure her.

"It's easier if you know," she quietly whispers.

Vanessa inhales deeply, then releases it slowly as if she's fortifying herself for what's to come. My chest tightens and even though I know what's coming, I mentally brace myself so I can force myself to keep my reactions to a minimum.

"Thankfully, I wasn't alone. Vince got home before my parents... but at the time, we didn't think anything of it. Maybe they'd stopped somewhere or something. We were both playing with Jules in the front yard when the officers arrived."

Slowly, she exhales, and my heart breaks as I watch her trace the patterns on my sheets absentmindedly. God, what this woman has gone through in such a short period of time.

I'm surprised when a small smile forms as she says, "Jules was adorable that day. She'd actually slept in, and we'd been having a relaxing morning. I took her outside so we could soak up the sun for a few minutes before I put her down for her early morning nap. Little did I know that'd be my last memory of life as I knew it..."

Her smile fades as she shakes her head, as if to rid herself of a painful thought. Fuck, I wish I could erase that pain for her, more than anything. Not being able to help myself, I pull her close to comfort her. Though she snuggles closer, her eyes are fixed on her hand still tracing patterns on my sheets.

Her voice is low and almost mechanical as she reveals

more. "When the officers pulled into the driveway, all it took was one look at the grave expressions on their faces, and my stomach filled with lead. I pulled Jules closer to me, trying to find comfort in her as I watched them approach. My blood turned to ice as I tried to imagine why they were visiting. Vince must've sensed it, too, because to this day, I distinctly remember his arms coming around the two of us as an added layer of protection. We knew something was wrong. But never in a million years did we expect the news we received."

"I can't imagine," slips from my lips without my permission.

"I went numb the moment they got us inside and explained what had happened. They calmly went through the facts as they explained how my parents had been run off the road. Apparently, it was a hit-and-run, and the driver was caught a few miles down the road when he wrecked his car once again.

"Ironically, he'd up-ended our entire world, yet he was so freaking drunk, he didn't have a scratch on him. At the trial, he claimed he had no recollection of the events of the day. He even tried to get off, using his disease of alcoholism as an excuse. I do feel sorry for him because he obviously had a problem. But that doesn't excuse his choices. He chose to drink. He chose to drive. It took me a long time to realize it was a horrible accident, and I had nothing to do with it, but his choices that day had monumental consequences, which impacted us all."

"What happened to him?" I ask, in fear of making this harder on her than it should.

"He's still in jail because there were witnesses. Apparently, this wasn't his first hit-and-run. Though it was his only accident involving a homicide." She takes in a deep breath, and her voice is watery when she continues, "I honestly believe he didn't remember what had happened. But it doesn't change the fact that it did, ya know?"

Holy shit. If I categorized Vanessa as being only one of the strongest people I've ever known before, she definitely holds the title now. I can't imagine what she and Vince went through. The thought of losing one of my family members would bring me to my knees, but to lose both parents at once...

Awe and wonderment also flood my thoughts about this strong, independent woman before me. She not only picked herself up by her bootstraps, but she did it with a kid in tow. Not only is Julia thriving, but she and Vince are, too.

Half the people I know, myself included, would have given up, but no—not Vanessa. I admire her strength and determination.

"I'm so sorry," I say, giving her a much-needed hug. However, I'm not sure if it's more for her or myself. I'm wrecked just hearing her story. I can't even begin to imagine what it was like to live through it.

Instead of acknowledging my compliment, Vanessa continues with the rest of her story. "The coroner who'd performed the autopsy said they died on impact. Like that's supposed to bring you comfort."

"I'm sure it doesn't. But at least you know they didn't suffer," I offer.

"Yeah, but it doesn't mean I don't miss them every day. Some days are harder than others, but my parents wouldn't want us to give up on our dreams. In fact, that was one of the reasons Vince transferred to CRU to be with me."

"That's admirable," I admit. I've heard this part before but knowing more about her parents puts things into an entirely new perspective. I can't imagine the hardship and sacrifice their family has gone through.

Shaking her head, she admits, "I have no idea where I'd be without Vinnie. Yeah, we've been together since the womb, but he didn't have to make the sacrifices he has. I'm so happy he's finally putting himself first and allowing himself to get close to Sydney. Can you believe he almost broke up with her because he thought Julia and I needed his undivided attention?"

"Are you serious?" I know they're close, but he and Sydney seem perfect for one another. There's no reason he couldn't date and still be there for his family.

Shaking her head, she smiles. "Yeah. When I found out his plans, I nearly kicked his stupid ass myself. Why the hell would he need to put his life on hold for Jules and me? He's sacrificed so much for us, but enough was enough. His reasons for pulling away from Sydney were ridiculous. I mean... my brother is one of the smartest people I know, but he was being stupidly ridiculous. Thankfully, he pulled his head out of his butt and made things right with Sydney before I had to intervene."

There's no way I'm asking what he did, not with her being so worked up about it.

"Sounds like things have worked out—with her moving in and all."

Sighing heavily, she says, "Yeah. I love her. She's the sister

I've never had. But most importantly, she gets Vince and brings out the best in him."

"You all have been through so much. I'm glad he's found someone who's made him happy."

"Speaking of happy..." Vanessa's voice turns playful. Then she suddenly scoots to her knees to face me.

"Yessss," I draw out and play along with her sudden change in mood.

"If I recall, you made me quite happy last night, too."

"Is that right?" I draw out, enjoying this playful side of her.

"But do you know what would make me even happier?"

Whatever it is—it's hers.

But I can't give in that easily. "Nope. No clue," I tease.

"I say we soak in that ginormous tub of yours, grab some breakfast, then head to my place so we can be there when Julia's dropped off in a few hours. I'm not ready for my time with you to end."

That I didn't expect. But as I have nothing planned except spending time with her today, I'm totally on board. "I think I can manage that," I say with a slow grin.

You know that saying about good intentions?

I'd like to say I'm the perfect gentleman who stayed entirely on his side of the tub. But the moment her perfect breasts floated above the bubbles and her eyes darkened with heat, I was in for.

Vanessa is sexy as fuck when she drifts to her knees and crawls toward me. "I... uh... think I have something else I'd like to do before I have to adult again."

Oh, she's fucking adulting right now.

She's sexy as sin and knows exactly what she wants.

Keeping my fists clenched underwater, I fight like hell not to reach out and devour her. "Really?" Comes out hoarse, so I clear my throat and ask, "What's that?"

For a split second, she hesitates but it's gone just as fast. "I'm pretty sure I'd rather stay here and feast on you."

She totally stole my line and my breath.

What did I ever do to deserve her?

Straddling my lap, she hesitates again when my dick bobs, making his presence known. Yeah, he's just as eager as I am to be with her, but I won't let him do the talking for me.

"What do you say we get out and dry off? I'd much rather take my time with you on the bed. We've still got a few hours, right?"

A sultry smile splits her face. "I think that's the best suggestion you've had all day. I sure hope you have plenty of condoms."

Not being able to control my need for her any longer, I crash my lips onto hers. Her hands dig into my hair and her body presses against mine. She feels fucking amazing. When my cock presses against her heat, I know I need to slow things down or I'll be inside her without protection.

"Hold on to me," I growl as I hoist the two of us out of the water.

Her laughter fills the room. "I could've walked."

"But then your sweet naked body wouldn't be clinging to mine and where's the fun in that?"

The next thing I know, she bites down on my shoulder and sucks.

Not only does she shock the hell out of me, but my dick could now pound nails thanks to her. "Hey now."

"Hey now, yourself. Put me down, you big ox. Let me dry off, then you can have your way with me."

I do as she requests, but still feel the need to mutter, "Promises, promises," as I hand her one of the towels I grabbed along the way.

Slowly the temptress she is draws a towel up each leg. When she's dried to her satisfaction, she almost wraps the towel around her body, but hesitates. "I guess there's no use in covering up when all I want is this."

I can't even take a breath before she closes the distance between us and my towel is long forgotten.

"I... uh, may be out of practice, but I have to admit. I love the things you do to me, Damien." With that, she reaches up and kisses me.

Words no longer need to be spoken, as our bodies speak for themselves. Her tongue dances with mine as her breasts press into my chest. This woman makes me feel things that have been dormant for years. I may only have a few hours, but one thing is certain. I'm nowhere close for my time with Vanessa to end.

23

VANESSA

AFTER SPENDING the weekend with Damien, it's been hard as hell snapping back to reality. With finals next week, I've stretched myself thin between studying, picking up a few shifts to cover for my coworkers, and staying up way later than I should, talking with Damien.

Late-night video chats have nothing on the real thing. But with Julia being in bed early, I don't have any other option. Damien's come over a few times but when Julia's witching hour approaches, he usually leaves, so I can get her to bed without distractions.

He's learning firsthand just how temperamental five year olds can be. One minute, she's sweet as can be, then the next, she may as well grow horns for as ornery as she becomes. I swear one minute, she worships the ground he walks on; the next, she's crabby and demanding—especially when she's exhausted in the evenings.

I almost died the other night when I walked Damien to his

car to say goodbye. Of course, it was so I could kiss him one last time—without an audience. But Julia didn't know that. Nope. My stinker of a child just opened the door and shouted for the entire neighborhood to hear, "Go home, Dame! We don't want ya! Momma needs to come inside, and you need to leave!"

Thankfully, Vince intervened and stopped her from shouting more, but I could barely look at Damien to see his response. When I tried to apologize to him—he wouldn't hear anything of it. He simply said, "Stop. She's tired, and you have no control over what she says and thinks."

"But..." I start, but he placed a finger over my lips. "But nothing. Give me a kiss goodnight, and I'll be on my way."

He then proceeded to kiss the argument right out of me.

Why he keeps coming around is beyond me—especially when she's being a giant turd. I'm surprised the crazy man just smiles and rolls with it.

I'm thankful for the weekend because I get to spend more time with Damien as well as my friends. I'm just getting off the morning shift, and everyone will be here this afternoon for Abby and Drew's farewell party. Even on his day off, Damien pops into the diner for breakfast. His counters should be installed this morning, so I wonder if he'll eat more at home in the mornings.

Pulling into the garage, I can smell the delicious aroma of baked goods coming from the kitchen. Sydney worked last night, but she must've gotten up early to be ready for the party this evening.

"Hey, Van." Sydney smiles as she pulls a pan of cookies out of the oven when I enter the kitchen. "How was work?"

"It was good. Where's Vince and Jules?" I ask, looking around when I realize the house is way too quiet.

"Oh, they're at the store picking up propane for the grill. We thought there'd be enough, but you know your brother... He likes to be prepared. Besides, it's not like we won't use it this summer."

Vince has already mowed the yard a few days ago. He's also pulled out the extra lawn chairs we store in the attic for the winter.

"You okay?" Sydney asks, pulling me out of my head.

"Yeah..." I say on a sigh. "Just thinking about Mom and Dad—and how Mom insisted on getting the patio furniture. I'm happy Vince and I get to entertain like she would've wanted with it. How many people do you think will show this afternoon?"

"I honestly don't know. I know Chloe, Abby, Drew, and his roommates DeShawn and Grey for sure. Abby mentioned her friend from class might show as well as a few of Drew's other teammates who want to wish him well. He's promised they won't let things get out of hand. He mainly just wants to chill and visit with those he won't see for a while—now that they're moving across the country. God, I'm gonna miss Abby." Sydney ends with a sigh.

"I know. But it's not like you won't ever see her again. Thank God, we live in the age of video chatting and cheap flights."

"Speaking of cheap flights, did your brother mention we found an amazing deal for a quick getaway this summer?"

This is new. I had no idea they'd planned to travel anywhere.

"Yeah. I was stressed the other night while studying for finals. The next thing I knew, I was looking at trips to New York City. I've never done anything like it in my life. But since I've saved up for first, last, and deposit on a new apartment, I've got a little extra I can afford for a mental health getaway."

Realizing I haven't vacationed since the summer before Julia was born, I easily agree. "Yeah? Tell me about it."

"Well, when I found a killer deal on flights to New York, I jokingly made the mistake of telling Vince about it."

Knowing my brother... I cringe. "What did he do?"

"That silly man grabbed his wallet and purchased the damn tickets on sight."

"Seriously?"

"Yeah. I nearly shit my pants. Here I was looking at a fantasy vacation and now in a matter of weeks, we're going on vacation."

"Wow." I know he's been wanting to take her someplace special to get away from it all. But New York City? That's a big getaway.

"You're telling me. I've insisted on paying for our accommodations, since he bought the tickets. But knowing Vince, he'll fight me every step of the way."

I love that she won't let my brother pay for things. I'm not sure what he's told her, but Vince can afford this trip if he wants to—without any hardship. Each of us work for spending money and to cover the cost of insurance, but if we chose not to, we could afford to not work as well—with our monthly allotment from our parents' inheritance and settlement from the accident. Once we turn twenty-five, we'll also have access to the trust funds my parents created for us as well.

Instead of revealing this, I simply laugh. "You know Vince. He's just as stubborn as you when it comes to getting his way. I'd love to be a fly on the wall when that conversation goes down."

"He's already insisting I live here dirt cheap. Only having to pay for cable and part of the utilities is one hell of a bargain," Sydney says, shaking her head. "And that's after I threatened to get a place of my own if I didn't at least pay for something."

Ohmigod. I love Sydney. But she's as stubborn as they come and lives up to the feisty redheaded stereotype. "I get where you're coming from, Syd. I do. But we're not paying for it either. This house is paid for, and all we have to do is pay taxes and utilities. We have enough set aside to pay for itself until we're out of college. Those are the only bills we have."

Sighing heavily, Syd concedes, "I know. I just wasn't looking for a handout. That's all."

God, I love her even more for that. "We both know that. But let's call a spade a spade. You and Vince practically spend every night together. It's ridiculous for you to get your own place and throw away that money each month. Besides, now you can use that money for tuition and not have to worry about getting a second job or going into debt."

"God, I hate it when you and your brother make logical sense." Her tone is teasing when she adds, "It's just not fair."

"What's not fair?" Vince says as he enters the kitchen from the living room.

"Oh you know... you and your sister... when you point out logical things about why I should be grateful for letting you help me." Sydney pretends to pout, causing my brother's grin to widen.

"Syd told you about the trip to New York, I take it?" Then he turns to me. "I've been meaning to tell you, Van. We're going over the Fourth of July weekend. I hope that's okay with you?"

"Uh... why do you need my permission? Last I checked, you're both of legal age and can make your own decisions."

"Will you be okay with Jules on your own?" Vince asks, his face filled with concern.

"I can't imagine why we wouldn't." He should know better by now.

"What about when you work the early shift at the diner?" Sydney asks.

"Worst case scenario, I take the week off," I admit. I hardly ever ask for time off. I'm sure my boss will be okay with it if I give him enough notice. The thought of truly taking a vacation from work and school sounds promising. This may be the excuse I need to get away from it all for a few days.

"I'm sure Chloe would help if you're in a bind. She's sticking around this summer, and you know Jules adores her," Sydney offers.

"I've got time," I assure them both, then I look around the room, realizing it's much too quiet. "Uh... speaking of Jules, where is she?"

"She's playing in her room." Vince points in the direction of our living room. "She said something about setting up her doll house in case anyone wants to play with her this afternoon. What time is Damien coming?"

"His counters are being installed this morning, so he'll be over later. Why?"

"No reason." Vince shrugs. "I figured with it being Saturday, he'd be over when you got off shift."

"Uh, he does have better things to do than hang out with all of us," I remind him.

Vince steps up to Syd and kisses her on the cheek. "Need help with anything?"

"No... I've got it. Did you hear anything from Ryan?"

"Yeah," Vince says, taking a cookie that's cooling on the counter. "He'll be here in a little bit. He says he needs a study break day because finals are kicking his ass."

"I can totally relate," I admit. I'm ready for my exams, but I'll be so freaking happy when next week is over.

I'VE JUST PULLED my shirt over my head when I hear a knock at my bedroom door. "Van, you in here?" comes from the sexiest voice I know.

"It's open," I call, and my pulse races. Sure, we've seen each other this morning, but that doesn't mean I'm not eager to see him again

When the door opens, I'm greeted by the gorgeous man himself. His dark hair is tousled perfectly, and a devious grin forms as his long legs eat up the distance between us. "Hey, you," comes out on a growl as he leans in to kiss me.

In that moment, I'm overwhelmed by my overload of senses. Traces of his masculine cologne send shivers down my spine as I instantly recall our last night together. His lips taste even better than his cologne. When his tongue sweeps across my lips, I part them, letting mine tangle with his.

Knowing there's a house full of people due any moment, it takes everything in my power to keep from getting carried away. Who the hell knows where Jules is—but in this moment, she's the least of my worries. All I want is this man.

When I fist his hair, intensifying our kiss, a light chuckle pulls from his chest as he lets me have my way for a few minutes. Then, he pulls back, panting. "Okay, then..." he muses. "Guess you're happy to see me."

"Yeah." I feign innocence—as if he didn't just rock my world with a single kiss. "I'd say you're right."

Quickly kissing me once again, he pulls back and playfully says, "Wouldn't have it any other way, Van. But unless you want me to lock us in here all night, I suggest we get out to the crowd forming in your backyard. Or I won't be held liable for my actions."

"Promises, promises." I pretend to pout, but he has a point. I could get carried away if we were left to our own devices for an evening. Why did I have to agree to host this party again?

"Did you finish the counters?" I ask, wiping lipstick off his perfectly formed lips.

"Yeah. I'm pretty happy with them." He nods, wiping his palm down his face, getting the remains of my lipstick.

The sound of Julia running in our direction has Damien stepping back from me.

"Momma?" Julia calls from the hall.

"In here, Jules. What's up?"

Even though she's breathless, her eagerness is infectious. "Dame, you're here. You wanna play cornhole with me? I was gonna ask Momma, but I can play with her any ole' time." She looks to me and shrugs apologetically.

Yeah. I've clearly been replaced with him as her shiny new toy.

Damien looks to me, looking for approval, and I nod an assurance.

Of course, my eagle-eyed girl sees this and squeals with joy, then grabs his hand. "Great. Let's go. I need to beat Unks. He's silly and thinks he's the king of cornhole."

"Well, we'll have to see about that," Damien encourages her competitiveness.

By the time we enter the backyard, I see Drew and Abby have arrived as well as Chloe, Ryan, and Drew's roommates. I quickly make introductions and visit while Jules whisks Damien to the back of the yard where the game is ready to play. Vince and Ryan have a game started, and they each shake Damien's hand in greeting.

"Where can I put this?" Grey, Drew's roommate asks, holding two bags of ice.

Pointing to the cooler by our back door, I say, "Over there."

"I've brought a fruit tray, too," he adds. "God knows, no one wants me to cook anything."

Drew chuckles. "Hey... everyone needs ice. But God help you when I leave."

Grey straightens after putting the ice in the chest, then

brings an offended hand over his heart. "Hey, I find ways to fend for myself... but I will admit I'm gonna miss the hell out of your cooking."

"I know you will, brother," Drew says as he pats Grey on the back. "Maybe someone will take pity on you and start a feed Grey fund. Instead of donating food to you, they will take the food you buy and give you a home-cooked meal once in a while."

My jaw drops. Is he that bad of a cook that he won't even try for himself?

"Drew," I start to admonish, but Grey cuts me off.

"No... he's not lying." Then he rolls his eyes dismissively. "You burn one pot of boiling water, and you never hear the end of it with this crew." He points between Drew and DeShawn.

"Seriously?" How the hell can you burn water?

"The place smelled for weeks. The Teflon pan was toast," DeShawn joins in. "Though let's be real. No one cooks like our man Drew. He may be our lead scorer on our team and gonna make a fine doctor, but he's missing his calling. This man should be a chef."

"Ah, I'm sure the two of you will survive... somehow." Drew's expression turns wistful, making us all burst into laughter.

"At least Syd's offered to bake once in a while. I'll just have to take some of this stash home with me, so I can stay out of the cafeteria for the next week."

DeShawn chimes in, smacking him on the back. "Don't look at me. You know I can cook—but I'm not cooking for your sorry ass every night. Take some lessons, man. It's not that hard."

Grey pretends to pout, as if the situation's hopeless.

Of course, I take pity on him, too. "Good grief, Grey. That's pathetic. You're welcome to come to dinner, too. Granted—you'll have to spend time with a five-year-old who will fight you tooth and nail for the broccoli, but we can't have you starving to death now that Drew's leaving."

Grey's eyes light up, and DeShawn warns. "Oh, be careful, Vanessa. You've just offered to feed the stray that will never leave."

"I do clean," Grey offers hopefully. "I even do dishes and scrub toilets."

Holy shit. This guy is hilarious. "You run a hard bargain," I tease. "Here... hand me your phone. I'll give you my number. When you're craving a home-cooked meal, just text me, and we'll work something out. But you get what you pay for, and you can't complain about the company. Jules will chat your ear off." Then I look to DeShawn. "You're welcome to come, too. I know you all are friends with Syd. No reason now that she's moved that you can't stop by as well."

All three guys look as if I've just offered to sacrifice a puppy.

Shit. Am I being too hospitable?

Growing up, our house was always the go-to spot for hang-outs. Sure, my mom may be gone, but there's no reason I can't carry on the tradition. Something about these guys makes me put the offer out there. Besides, Grey's pretty bad off if he can't even boil water.

When none of them say anything, I quickly backpedal. "It's just dinner. If you're not interested, I'm not pushing it on you."

"No," Grey quickly interjects. "I'll be there. I'm just shocked that you'd offer."

Okay, then... I read that wrong.

Straightening my spine, I hold my chin up high. "Well, I just did."

"Just did what?" Vince asks with Damien and Jules right behind him.

"I invited poor Grey and DeShawn to dinner. Did you know Grey's not even allowed to boil water at his house? As in —he'll burn it if he does?"

"Hey, now... it was one time," Grey interjects.

But I ignore him. "Vin, growin' up, our place was the spot everyone came, especially to eat. There's no reason we can't do that again." Pointing at our house, I continue, "This place is plenty big enough. If Grey wants to learn to cook—we should take pity on him and help him out."

Burying his face in his hand, Grey says, "Oh, God. What have I gotten myself into?"

Vince just smiles. "Uh... she just went mama bear on you, dude. She means well... promise."

Grey uncovers his face and looks to me. "I swear, I'm not a charity case. I buy food and clean. The cooking doesn't always turn out so great, and it's become the butt of most of our jokes."

DeShawn pipes in, "He does make a mean sandwich."

Bless Jules' heart when she adds to the conversation, "My

momma and Unks cook the best, Grey. You can take cooking lessons with me. We can learn together."

Can my daughter have a bigger heart?

Instead of brushing her off, Grey bends his knees to get to her level and handles her like a pro. "I'll tell you what. If you're willing to give lessons, I'll be there."

"First, you gotta play cornhole with me," Jules says as if she's a professional con artist.

"You drive a hard bargain, missy. But I think I can manage," Grey says as they walk away.

When I turn to Damien, he remains silent, and his expression is unreadable.

24

DAMIEN

WATCHING Vanessa put these two D-1 athletes who tower over her in their place is something else. The fact her heart is so big, and she won't let the poor guy go without a decent meal, just makes me fall for her even more.

Then Jules offering to help—damn, her heart is just as big as her mother's. The more I get to know each of them, the more I can't imagine my life without them. Vince and Vanessa don't have much family but each other, but they've definitely made up with that by their group of friends.

Sure, when I first got here, I'd felt old as hell with the people around me. I mean—I have a good five years on them, and I'm in an entirely different stage in my life, but then I got to know them. None of the people here today are your typical college student just looking for a good time or a way to unwind before finals next week. Yes—that's what they're essentially doing, but they each seem to have a strong head on their shoulders and are more mature than I expected.

I'll admit I hung with a different crowd in college, and I acted much younger and carefree. I didn't spend much time with the athletes, but in my short time here, I see they like to have fun—but there's a lot more to them than being able to handle a ball.

HOURS LATER, Vanessa's putting Julia down, and Ryan, Vince, Syd, and I are cleaning up from the party. Ryan and I move the lawn furniture to the garage, while Syd and Vince finish the dishes in the kitchen. Ryan seems like an easy-going guy, until he corners me in the garage.

"So... what's the deal with you and Vanessa?"

Okay. That's unexpected.

"Well, not that it's any of your business, but we're seeing each other." I take this moment to stand to my full height to look him in the eye. Sure, Ryan towers over most everyone, but I've got about forty pounds of muscle on him, and I'm not intimidated by him in the slightest.

"I've come to love Vince like a brother—which in turn makes Vanessa like family."

But the look in his eye tells me he doesn't think of her as a sister. No, if I had to guess—he very much likes Vanessa. So, I do what any man in my situation would do—I poke the bear he's becoming further. "And your point is?"

"Vince and Vanessa have been through so much shit. Vanessa, in particular. She needs a man in her life that will put her first above all else and not just be poking around for a good time. She deserves better than that."

"Yes, she does," I agree. But I drive my point home. "And for the record, I do put her first—not that it's any of your business. But I know neither of them have many people in their corner. The fact that you feel the need to play the role of protective brother means that you care about them, too. So, I respect that. But if you think for one minute I'm taking advantage of her—that's where you're wrong. Vanessa and Jules are a package deal, and I'm not dumb enough to walk away from them anytime soon."

Ryan's face morphs from stern to friendly in an instant. "Good. I thought Vince had been too easy on you, but you're the right person for her, dude. We good?" He reaches out for a fist bump.

I'd rather punch him in the face for pulling this shit with me, but the fact Vanessa has a friend who'd care tells me just what type of person she is. She's a true friend. Loving and most of all—Loyal.

Returning his fist bump, I say, "Yeah, man, we're good. Let's get these chairs put away, so we can get back inside. Rumor has it Sydney's dishing up her famous cinnamon rolls."

By the time we return inside, everyone who's left is gathered in the living room. Vanessa pulls me to her over-sized chair, and I sit. She starts to sit on the arm of the chair, but not wanting to make her uncomfortable, I pull her onto my lap instead.

Sydney, Vince, and Ryan take the couch, and Sydney asks the room, "So, are you all ready for finals?"

Ryan groans, but Vince and Vanessa shrug as if they'd practiced their response to be in unison. It must be a twin thing. Sydney notices and laughs as she points in their directions. "God, you are so much in tune with each other."

Ryan practically whines. "I've been studying for weeks. I just want next week to freakin' be over."

"You and me both," Vanessa agrees, and Vince nods.

"Hey, Vin? I know we're leaving for New York in July. But what would you say to a weekend getaway once finals are over? Traditionally, Chloe, Abby, and I take a girls' weekend after finals each year, but that isn't in the cards. Abby's going to Baltimore that weekend, and Chloe bailed. I need to get away. I can go alone—but would you want to join me?"

Rolling his eyes, Vince laughs. "Gee... a weekend alone with you... It'll be such a sacrifice... but one I'm willing to make."

Sydney claps with excitement. "Great. I can't wait. I've already made reservations. I'd much rather have you with me than go alone."

"You're lucky you get to get away," Ryan sighs. "I start my internship on Monday, so I'm spending the weekend traveling to Boston to get settled."

"You're gonna have the best time," Vince encourages.

We spend the rest of the evening chatting and keeping up casual conversation. Eventually, Ryan leaves, and Vince and Sydney decide they're ready for bed. Knowing I've been watching Vanessa stifle yawns for the past hour, I stand to make my exit, too. If things were different, I'd love to take her home with me. But that wouldn't be fair to Jules—especially not given her warning about a sudden change in her schedule.

When she walks me to the door, I thank her for an amazing evening and let my kiss show my feelings for her. God, why does it hurt to walk away? She has responsibilities, and it would be weird for Julia if I were here in the morning—so that isn't an option either.

As I walk to my car, I can honestly say I wish things were different.

25

VANESSA

FINALS WEEK officially kicks my ass. Between working a few extra shifts at the diner, studying, and actually taking my exams, I have barely seen Damien. To make matters worse, Julia must sense my stress because she's been a pill for the last three days. She's not typically this whiny—like ever. But something has crawled up her butt and festers more each day. I'm seriously at my wits end by the time Friday evening comes.

Of course, I don't get any relief because Vince and Sydney left after their last final for a weekend away. When Damien calls to check in for the day, I find myself unloading on him way more than I should.

"Hey, you," he says when I answer his call.

"Hey, Dame," I sigh heavily, trying with all my might to get my emotions in check.

"What's wrong?" His voice fills with concern.

"What isn't wrong..." I spit rhetorically.

"Was your final that bad?" he asks.

"No. Finals went fine—thank God. But all evening, Jules has been hell on wheels. It's like everything I do is a constant battle. The more I try to discipline her, the more she's pushing back. I swear... it's like she's been inhabited by aliens or something, and I'm left wondering where the heck my sweet girl went."

"What can I do to help?" the man sweetly offers.

Knowing there's nothing he can do but hug me, I sigh. "There's nothing you can do." She'll go to bed in a few hours hopefully, and we can reset her mood in the morning. Though she's been a piece of work all afternoon, it may carry over to tomorrow. But, God—let's hope not.

Just then, I hear Julia call, "Momma," in a panic as she runs down the hall.

When I hear the sound of retching from the bathroom, I quickly mutter, "She's puking. I need to call you back."

Hanging up the phone, I rush to my poor daughter as I mutter, "This explains everything."

God, why didn't I think she was getting sick? Hell, I thought this was just a horrible phase for the last two days. But no, I should've known better. She only gets this way when she's about to get the stomach flu.

Rubbing her back, I offer words of encouragement. "I'm right here, Jules. I'm right here."

"Momma," her struggling voice calls out. "I don't feel so well."

"Oh, sweetheart," I say, rubbing her back and trying to comfort her. "I know."

When her head slumps to the toilet, I know I need to assist

her further. "Do you think you're done?" I ask, hoping she's put out of her misery soon.

"I think I'm done..." She takes some tissue and wipes her mouth. "But my tummy hurts."

Grabbing a towel, I lay it on the floor to make her more comfortable. "I'm gonna run to the kitchen to grab a bowl. Stay right here, and I'll be back as soon as I can."

On my way back to the bathroom, I grab a few extra beach towels. If I don't want to wash sheets all night, I need all the reinforcements I can get to help her.

Stopping by her room, I add the layers of towels to her bed, making sure I drape them over the side and along the floor, so I can put the bowl on the floor near her. When I hear her moan, I rush to the bathroom to be with her.

My poor baby.

My heart aches seeing her in pain. There's nothing worse than knowing something is wrong, yet knowing there's not much I can do but let it run its course.

When I enter the bathroom, her hair's in complete disarray, and I realize I didn't get it out of the way earlier.

Fuck. Now she needs a shower.

Gone is the strong, proud, boisterous kid that I'm usually blessed with. In her place is a tiny, weak girl needing her momma. "I'm here, baby. Let's get these clothes off you and get you in the tub. I'll make it quick."

Within a few minutes, I have her showered, dressed in jammies, and her hair pulled out of her face. She's usually so independent, it's hard seeing her so reliant on me. Don't get me wrong, I would be here no matter what, but having a sick child definitely makes you appreciate when they are well.

By the time we get her into bed, she's spent. Her head hits the pillow, and she's out before I can even pull her blankets around her. Instead of using her thick comforter though, I lay that aside and pull over a fleece blanket instead.

Leaving her door open, I return to the bathroom to clean up and disinfect. Knowing I may need more towels, I take any dirty ones we have and shove them in the wash. Checking on her one more time, I see she's still sound asleep.

When my phone rings, I'm relieved to see it's Damien.

The moment the phone connects, I hear his worried voice. "Everything okay?"

Sighing, I plop onto the couch. "It will be. Jules likely has the flu. I've got her cleaned up and in bed, so we just have to wait it out and let it run its course."

"Anything I can do?"

"No. Not really. I've just gotta be here to wait it out with her."

"Do you have saltine crackers and bottled 7-Up? That was my mom's go-to when one of us got sick as a kid."

"Ugg... no, I don't," I admit. "None of us have been sick in ages."

"Tell you what. I'll run by the store and pick up a few things for you. Anything in particular that would be a treat for you?"

Oh my heart... "That is so sweet of you. But you don't have to."

"Vanessa," comes out stern with little room for argument. "I'm doing it."

"Okay. Crackers and soda would be amazing."

"What about you, Van? If I'm left to my own devices, you'll end up with half the store," he says in warning.

The thought alone makes me laugh and is just what I need in this moment.

"All right... all right. No buying half the store. Maybe pick me up a caramel macchiato on the way along. I know it's late, but I need to stay up for a while to make sure she's okay."

"Got it. I'm hopping in my truck now. If you need anything else—text me."

"I doubt I will. But thanks for offering."

"I'm serious, Van. You need anything... you let me know."

I settle into the couch. "I will, Dame. Thanks."

It isn't long before Damien knocks quietly on my door. At first, I'm afraid to let him in, but when he reminds me that he's likely already been exposed, I agree.

Taking a sip of coffee, I settle into Damien's side on the couch. "Ahhh... thank you. This is amazing."

"I just wish I could do more," Damien says as he squeezes me in a side hug. "Do you think she'll sleep through the night?"

"It would be amazing if she did, but I highly doubt it."

"I know you're exhausted, but now that finals are over, maybe you can get some rest."

"Yeah. I'm only taking one class this summer and will be done by the end of June. Things should be a lot lighter."

"One class in less than six weeks? That oughta be intense."

"It will be. But by doing this, I can start my clinicals next year and graduate in four years. Vince and I have been working our asses off to meet this goal. It's so close, I can taste it."

"I seriously don't know how you do it. How will you do clinicals with Julia? She starts school next fall, right?"

"Yeah." How is my baby old enough to be in kindergarten? "Some days, it feels like just yesterday she was born; then others, it feels like forever. Funny how time does that. Isn't it?"

"I have something I'd like to throw out there, but I don't need an answer right now—there's no pressure. Promise."

What the hell is he talking about? I pull away so I can sit up and look him in the eye.

"Relax, Van. It's not that big of a deal. But I know Vince and Sydney are taking a trip over the Fourth of July, and I'm already off that week for a family thing. What would you say to coming with me? We could head out to Anderson Island for a few days, then maybe up to Seattle to get away."

Uh... of all the things he could possibly say, I wasn't expecting this.

The thought of getting away sounds amazing. Especially if I get to do it with Damien. God, it would be amazing to get away. I did already put in for the time off. So maybe it could work out.

"I..." I start then remember all the reasons I can't. Well, one... "But Julia..." I start, but he cuts me off.

"Uh, you and Julia are a package deal. Of course she's invited. I'm only asking now because I need to let my family know about lodging. I'd honestly blow off my family—but for some reason, Dani is insistent on everyone being on the island that week. You don't know Dani—but this family reunion is a big deal for her, and I can't let her down."

"Are you sure you want Jules and me tagging along? You should be spending time with your family."

Damien levels me with a hard stare in an instant. "Uh... I want to spend time with you and get to know Jules better. What better way than a mini vacation? We can go kayaking; she'll experience a ferry ride, and we'll have some fun in downtown Seattle."

Millions of thoughts hit me at once, and I'm unsure of where to begin. I'm not even sure how I feel about taking Jules away with him for a week. So, I stick with the logistics.

"Isn't Anderson Island small? Do they even have hotels there?"

"Most likely, I'll just rent a cabin on the island for a few days, so we'll each have our own room."

"Where would you stay if we don't go?" I hedge, knowing he wouldn't spend the money on just himself.

"Um, I'll likely stay at my grandparents' cabin, or at Dani and Luke's place. If It's just me, all I need is a bed to sleep in, and I'm good."

"That doesn't make sense," I argue.

"Look. You don't have to give me an answer right now, but I'd like to spend the week with you... and Jules," he tacks on at the end. "If you don't come with me, I'll likely just go for a day or two, then come back home. There's no reason to stay an entire week away, when I know the entire time I'll be wishing I were here."

I open my mouth to say something, but he cuts me off.

"This is my choice. I love my family, but I only need to see them for a few days to catch up with them. I'd much rather spend my one and only vacation this year with you."

"Well..." I huff. "When you put it that way... there's no pressure at all." I smirk at the end, knowing I've made my point.

Damien groans, and I can't help but laugh. "That's not what I'm saying... Like I said, nothing has to be decided tonight. I'm just throwing it out there, so you *could* plan on going if you want. Not to put pressure. Not to force you into a decision, and certainly not to make this weird for you. I like spending time with you—period. No hidden agenda."

"Okay, okay. I'll think about it," I promise. Though let's be honest, I doubt I'll think of anything but until I make this decision.

"Good." Damien smirks, and I want to kiss that smug expression right off his face.

Just as I lean in, I hear muffled cries from Julia's bedroom.

"Momma?"

"Coming, baby girl. I'll be right there," I say as I pop off the couch.

Looking to Damien, I whisper, "I'm not sure how long I'll be."

He smiles in understanding. "Go. I'll be right here. If it gets late, I'll just lock the door before I leave."

Leaning in, I give him a quick kiss, though it's nothing like what I'd planned earlier. "In case I forget to tell you, thank you for everything."

When I get to Julia's room, her face is covered in a sheen of sweat, and she's curled into a ball with the blankets kicked off. "What's wrong, love bug?" I say as I rush to her side.

"I need to go potty," she whines, and it's obvious she doesn't have the strength to move.

Lifting her with ease, I carry her into the bathroom. Her clothes are soaked and sticking to her skin. She looks so miserable, and I feel utterly useless.

"Wanna take another bath?" I offer when she finishes.

Shaking her head, Julia moans, "No... too tired."

Once back in her room, I strip her down to her undies and use a wet cloth from the bathroom to wipe her face and neck down. "That feels good, Momma, thanks," she moans.

"I just want you to feel better. Want a sip of soda?" I offer, reaching for the 7-Up Damien brought for her.

Shaking her head, she whispers, "Yes." She takes a small sip, then slinks back onto her pillow. "Just wanna sleep... hold my hand?" she whispers as she places her hand in mine as she drifts back off to sleep.

After a few minutes, I try extricating my hand from hers, but she stirs and holds on tighter. "Don't go, Momma."

Well. Shit. Now what am I gonna do?

Walking around to the other side of her bed, I crawl in beside her and reach for her hand again.

Eventually, Damien's large figure fills the frame. "Can I help you with anything?"

Looking to Julia's hand in mine, I whisper, "She won't let go. You can head on home, and I'll call you in the morning."

His expression is torn as he looks from me to her. "Can I get you anything before I go?"

Since I just drank coffee, I'm nowhere near ready for bed. "Would you mind grabbing my Kindle from my nightstand? I'll just stay in here and read for a bit if you don't mind."

"Not at all. I'll be right back."

I expect him to just hand it off and run out of the room, with all the germs floating around. But that fool of a man walks it over and kisses me goodnight. I'm sure he'll think better of it if he comes down with the flu.

"Night, Van. I've brought your phone from the living room, too. Don't hesitate to call. I'm only a phone call away."

"We'll be fine," I assure him.

He kisses me one last time, then lets himself out of the house.

LITTLE DID I know mere hours later, *we'll be fine* would be my famous last words.

Never has the cool tile and porcelain throne felt so good against my cheek.

Death warmed over feels a thousand times better than I do in this moment.

Fine?

I'm not sure I'll ever be fine again.

26

DAMIEN

I TRIED TEXTING Vanessa when I woke up a few hours ago. But no such luck. I knew it was early, but surely the two of them are up by now. When I text again with no answer, I resort to calling.

"Helllllloooo?" croaks out like a tortured cat.

Holy shit. Is this Vanessa?

"You okay?" Maybe she's been sleeping.

She's silent for a moment, then groans, "Can't get off the bathroom floor. Puke is everywhere. We don't have any sheets left in the house that are clean. Julia's finally asleep on the couch, and I'm feeling better with this cool tile on my face. But other than that, I'm peachy."

Gathering my keys and wallet, I rush to the door. "I'm coming over..."

"No..." the stubborn woman protests... "You'll get sick. You don't need my crazy life. Stay away while you can..."

"I'm coming over," I insist.

"Why? Why would you come over? My life is nothing but a fucking mess. Trust me... there's nothing pretty to see here. I'm disgusting, and you'd be better off staying far... far away." She pants at the end, then gasps. "I gotta go. I'm gonna get sick."

Fuck. I locked the door when I left. How am I gonna get in?

Thank God, I have Vince's number, and he's on the East Coast, so I won't be waking him when I call.

He answers on the third ring. "Damien?"

"Hey, man," I say in greeting but don't have time for chitchat. "Van and Jules have the flu. I'm fairly certain they'll be fine, but I want to go check on them. Is there a way to get into your house without a key? Vanessa says she's camping out in the bathroom at the moment," I try to explain, so I don't sound like a creeper.

"Wow... Okay... Um... go through the garage." He rattles off the code, and I commit it to memory.

I end the call promising to keep him updated.

I'm sure I've just thrown a wrench in his day, but he thanked me for it all the same.

There's nothing he can do—and besides, I'm here.

I text Van to let her know I'm here, but I don't wait for an answer.

The house is quiet, and Jules is where Van said she'd be as I walk by the couch.

When I get to the bathroom, I announce my arrival. "Hey, Van? You in there?"

"Go away," she moans. "You don't need to see this."

As if.

"I'm here. Let me help you," I say, pushing the door open. She can push me away later—for now, I'm helping her in any way I can.

I find her on the floor curled around the toilet. There's a floormat under her head as a pillow, and she looks absolutely miserable sprawled across the floor. Her hair is piled on top of her head, most likely to keep the puke away, and she isn't even able to lift her head to scold me properly.

"Do you think you're done getting sick?"

"No idea..." she moans softly. "Just when I think I'm done, I rush back in here. Just easier to stay..."

"I'll be right back," I assure her as I search the house to see what state it's in. Seeing a clean bowl beside Julia on the couch and her covered with beach towels, I head to her room to survey the damage. Yep. Vanessa was right. Her sheets are soiled on the floor. I head to Vanessa's room, and I find the bed in the same condition. Poor girl doesn't even have the strength to get them into the wash.

Grabbing a large pot from the kitchen, I walk back to Vanessa.

"What about Vince's room? Think you'd be okay if I put you in there?"

"It's... too far... don't wanna walk."

In a split-second decision, I bend down and haul Vanessa into my arms. Of course, the stubborn woman chooses now to protest again. But I just ignore her. His bed is made and at this point—I could give two shits what state his room is in. Pulling back the covers, I gently deposit Vanessa onto the bed and assure her I'll be right back with a bowl. I'm grateful to see there's a bathroom off his bedroom, so she won't have to travel across the house in this state.

Thankfully, Vanessa crashes the minute her head hits the comforts of his pillow because I'm not arguing with her over this. There's no way I'm letting her curl up around a toilet when I can help her to bed.

Once I get her settled, I quickly check on Jules again. She's out like a light as well. I change over the towels in the wash to the dryer then stain treat each set of sheets to wash. After that, I scour her bathroom and fold towels from the dryer when they finish, so I can switch over the sheets. Seeing that Julia's blankets need washing as well, I throw those in next. Hopefully, by the time either of them wakes up, I can have their house back in order.

Just as I've finished folding the last towel, Julia stirs on the couch. When she sees me, I'm blessed with an adorable grin. "Dame? Why are you here?"

"It seems both you and your momma need my help. Is that okay with you?"

Julia nods slowly. "Did Momma get sick, too?"

"Yeah. How are you feelin'?" I ask, wondering if she needs anything.

"My tummy feels like I may be hungry," she says, rubbing it softly.

"Want to start with some crackers and soda? If you can keep a little of those down, I'll get you something else."

She nods, and I hurry to the kitchen to retrieve them.

By the time I return, Jules looks a lot better. She's sitting upright, and her grogginess from sleep has disappeared. Handing her the bottle of 7-UP, I warn, "Now don't drink this too fast. Just a couple of sips for now."

As she warily looks at the food in front of her, I send a silent message to the universe hoping she's over the worst of her illness.

After a few sips, she hands it back to me with a quiet, "Thanks. Can we watch a show?"

"What do you have in mind?" I ask, sitting in the over-sized chair beside her.

She gives me a look that would have been accompanied with *Duh,* in my days and says, "*Descendants*... of course. Hand me the remote, and I'll start it."

As soon as she has it in her hands, she uses the voice demand to cue it up. I'm impressed by her ability to navigate as well as she does. Before I know it, the opening lines are starting. Needing to make sure she's comfortable, I ask, "Can I get you anything?"

Sheepishly, she looks in my direction and pauses before quietly asking, "Will you snuggle with me? Momma or Unks always rub my back to make me feel better when I'm sick."

Okay... I can do this. "I'm all yours," I offer as I stand to sit on the couch beside her. She lifts her pillow and points for me to sit on one side, so I take her lead. As soon as I sit down, she plops a pillow in my lap.

She's a lot like her momma in that she knows what she wants, I suppose. As she adjusts her blanket, I can't help but notice she's wearing an over-sized tee that must be Vince's. As soon as she adjusts the blankets around her legs, she turns on her side to watch the movie. Just when I think she's settled, she turns her head to look at me. "Dame?"

"Yeah?" I ask, wondering what's wrong now.

"You gonna rub my back? Momma does it in small circles."

Shit. I'd forgot about that.

Quickly, I do as she asks, and her body relaxes immediately.

Not having watched a Disney movie since I was a kid, I absentmindedly rub circles along her spine as I immerse myself in the movie. The songs are catchy, and the plot keeps my attention as I do what I can to be here for Jules.

When she falls asleep, I don't even think about moving because there's no way I'll risk waking her up. She needs her rest after the night she's had. When the movie ends, I quickly click on the sequel. Who knew I'd want to find out what happens next to the kids of main characters from my youth. Kicking my feet onto the coffee table in front of me, I relax further into the couch.

The next thing I know, I feel someone touching my face.

Startled, my eyes pop open, and I'm blessed with a much better form of Vanessa staring back at me. Her hair is fresh from the shower, and she's changed into a pair of leggings and t-shirt.

"Hey, you." I smile in greeting.

"Hey, yourself," she whispers back. "I see Jules woke up and subjected you to her shows."

Shrugging, I focus my attention to her. "How are ya feelin'?"

"When I saw the two of you sleeping, I snuck into the

shower. I couldn't stand the smell of myself, ya know? By the way—you didn't have to do laundry. I would've gotten to it."

"I wasn't gonna just let it sit there when I can help, Van. Besides, it's not a big deal. The sheets should be ready to make your beds, but I didn't wash your comforter yet. Obviously, Jules wanted to be snuggled, and I wasn't about to say no to her."

Vanessa lets out a huge huff of air as she shakes her head. "Why you willingly subject yourself to this crazy is beyond me...."

She doesn't get it, does she?

"If I can't handle your crazy, I don't deserve your calm," I admit.

This stops her in her tracks. "I mean..."

How can I put it so she'll understand?

She stares expectantly into my eyes, and I'm lost for a moment in her beauty.

Clearing my throat to refocus my attention, I do my best to explain what she means to me. "What I'm saying is that if I can't handle you and all that comes with your life, I don't deserve you when you're alone with me either. Jules is an amazing girl and frankly, you're a package deal. Life is messy, I get it. But nothing I've seen from either you or Jules—puke included, makes me want to run away."

"But you have so many better things you could be doing..." she protests.

"Uh... last I checked, the only person I'm in love with is you... and you come with an incredible sidekick... so why would anything else matter?"

Vanessa's hand flies to her mouth as she asks, "What did you just say?"

Slowly, it dawns on me what I've just revealed. Making sure I make my point clear, "Why would anything else matter when I'm in love with you and your adorable sidekick?"

"You love me... too?" Julia's voice groggily asks, waking from her nap as she stretches in my lap.

Looking her straight in her eyes, I touch her nose as I repeat my words. "Yes. I love you, too, Jules. That okay?"

Within an instant, she pulls herself to a sitting position. "Good. Because I love you, too, Dame." Then she throws her arms around me in an unexpected hug.

All I can do is hug her back and look at the beautiful yet shocked expression on her mother's face.

As I look into her eyes, I mouth the words, "I love you, Vanessa."

Vanessa's eyes well up with unshed tears.

Is she crying?

Fuck.

Before I can say anything, Jules releases me from her hug, rushes to her mom, and throws her arms around her waist. "Are you feeling better, Momma?"

Blinking heavily, Vanessa continues staring at me. "Yeah, sweet girl. I'm feeling better. Careful though, I'm still a little weak."

"Oops, sorry," Julia says as she pulls away.

Hopping up from the couch, I offer, "I have Gatorade if you think you can handle it. It might help to get some electrolytes into your system."

"That sounds good," Vanessa admits as she sits in her favorite over-sized chair.

When I return from the kitchen, I offer Vanessa a Gatorade and place containers of Jell-O and two spoons on the coffee table. "If you're up for it, here's some Jell-O for you, too."

Before either can say another word, I excuse myself to use the restroom. While I'm down the hallway, I take the sheets to Julia's room and quickly make her bed. Just as I'm pulling Vanessa's sheets from the dryer, I find her leaning against the laundry room door. "You don't need to do all this."

"I don't *need* to do any of it," I admit. "But that doesn't mean I don't want to help you. Just how many hours of last night were you hanging on the bathroom floor, while I was sound asleep in my cozy bed?"

Wincing, she actually admits, "I got sick around three this morning."

Holy shit! She spent five hours on the floor? Laundry is the least I can do to lighten her load.

"Why didn't you call me?" I stand, closing the distance between us and cross my arms over my chest.

"You were sleeping..." she says to her hands. "Jules woke up—got sick in my room, and it all snowballed. I went to clean our bedding, and the nausea hit me like a ton of bricks. One minute, I was okay, and the next, I was very much not okay, ya know."

"Still... Why didn't you call? You shouldn't have to handle all this alone."

For the first time since I arrived, she meets my eyes. "I

meant it when I didn't think you deserved to be subjected to my crazy life."

I stare at her for a moment to let what I'm about to say sink in. "And I meant it when I said, if I can't handle your crazy, then I don't deserve you in the calm," I remind her. "I've fallen for you hook, line, and sinker, Vanessa. If I love you, I have to love all of you—not just the pretty parts."

Electricity crackles between us as she stares into my eyes, then her nose crinkles adorably. "Well... I certainly wasn't very pretty when you found me praying to the porcelain gods."

"*You* were still gorgeous—no matter what. But I'll admit, I hated how sick you were."

"Oh, Damien," she says through rolled eyes. "What am I gonna do with you?"

"Just be you—and I'll be more than happy."

I won't settle on this one—she needs to get it through her thick, stubborn skull, I'm not going anywhere.

Vanessa looks down the hall, then back to me with a torn expression. "I'm terrified of getting you sick... but I did just brush my teeth..."

God, I love this woman.

Chuckling, I brush the loose strands from her face. "I think it's safe to say that I've already been exposed. And kissing you —well, that's a risk I'm willing to take."

"Well, what are you waiting for?"

Slanting my lips over hers, Vanessa tastes strongly of mint. When her tongue tangles with mine, I want more. I need more. Electricity sizzles through my spine and crackles through the air.

Unfortunately, Julia chooses this time to come looking for us. "Momma... Dame? Where are you?"

Breaking the kiss, I run my thumb across Vanessa's swollen lips. "We're in the laundry room!" I holler as if Vanessa didn't just rock my world with a single kiss.

When Vanessa's eyes meet mine, they twinkle with mischief as she bops me on the nose playfully. "That right there... is only one of the reasons I love you, too."

Stunned, I just stare.

Did she just say that?

Vanessa shrugs her explanation. "You understand she comes first and have no problems with it." Then she chuckles. "That and the fact you're sexy as hell and give the most magnificent O's, pale in comparison."

Holy shit... when she swings, she knows how to knock it out of the park.

I'm fucking stunned, and all I can do is pick my jaw off the floor to greet Jules in time when she says, "Wanna watch another movie?"

"Sure thing, Love Bug. Let's finish making Momma's bed, then we can spend the evening binging on your favorite shows," Vanessa suggests.

"Dame, do you wanna pick the movie?"

Though I'm flattered she's let me choose, this is completely out of my wheelhouse. I only know the classics I grew up on—and I'm sure she has something better in mind. "You can choose, squirt. My favorites growing up were *Aladdin* and *Flubber*. Do you even know what those are?"

"Uh... what's *Flubber*?"

"I haven't seen *Aladdin* in forever," Vanessa jumps in. "Let's get my bed made so we can watch that."

When Julia returns to the living room, Vanessa turns to me.

"Rain check on that nearly orgasmic bliss?"

Like I didn't need an excuse to love her more. God, she sure knows how to keep me on my toes.

Leaning in, I kiss her once more. "Just wait until we're alone—I'll show you orgasmic."

Thank fuck, she's feeling better.

27

VANESSA

THE NEXT FEW weeks fly by. Between cramming an entire semester's worth of work into five weeks, work, and balancing my time with Jules and Damien, I'm running myself ragged. Plopping into my favorite chair, all I want to do is curl up with a great book for the day and relax.

That's exactly what I plan to do with an unexpected Friday off.

Before knowing my class had been cancelled, Syd and Vince invite Jules to go up to Mt. Hood for the day. Apparently, they're driving through the Columbia Gorge first, so Syd can pick up some fresh berries to make pies and cobbler.

I could've gone with them but seeing how tired I am, Vince insisted I enjoy a kid-free day. Hell, he even encouraged me to make plans with Damien tonight and told me he'd see me in the morning. I could've kissed him for being so thoughtful. And I'm not missing this opportunity. Damien doesn't get off until six and at the rate I'm going, I see a long nap in my future.

But first, I'm diving into my long-lost book by Charlotte Ann. It's been ages since I've been able to binge read. It doesn't take long before I'm completely immersed in the story. I feel each and every emotion along with the character. Gah, Charlotte Ann always does this to me. I can't believe what her characters have to endure to find their happily ever after. My heart breaks into shards before she puts me back together again—I'm sure. It's what she's known to do. Tears stream down my face as I frantically race through the pages.

When there's a knock on the door, I groan in frustration, quickly rushing to the door so I can get rid of my unexpected visitor. It's only three o'clock, and I'm clearly not expecting anyone.

Grabbing a tissue on the way, I brush away the tears, so I don't look like a complete wreck. Swinging open the door to greet what I'm sure is a solicitor—who can't read the sign, I'm shocked to see Damien's beautiful brown eyes mirroring my expression.

"What's wrong, Van?" comes out before I can even say hello.

Rolling my eyes, I bat at the air. "Oh, don't mind me. Just got lost in a book."

Apprehension is clear when he asks, "Seriously? You'd tell me if something was wrong, right?"

Widening the door, I pivot to return to my chair.

"Of course I'd tell you. Brody—the character in my book just had to make the ultimate sacrifice so Lanie could follow her dream. I'm not even close to halfway through the book. But they have to end up together—they have to."

Shaking his head, he sits on the couch beside me. "You have no idea how much you sound like my sister right now."

"I think I'll like your sister," I admit.

"Speaking of my sister, I just got a text—a text no less—saying that I need to bring a suit for family photos—something to do with my parents' anniversary. She couldn't be bothered to call, so she group-texted all of my brothers. We all have suits, so it won't be a problem—but why would we want family photos in clothes we only wear to weddings and funerals?"

"I think that's sweet," I gush, quickly forgetting my book—now that I'm picturing him in a suit.

"If you say so," he states, though he clearly doesn't agree.

"I wish I had more family photos," I remind him. "Don't take this opportunity for granted."

Sighing, he agrees, "You're right. I'm sorry. I shouldn't ruin my sister's fun. But If I'm dressing up—so are you."

"Whoa... why would I need to dress up for *your* family photos?"

"If we're getting dressed up—I'll at least take you and Jules someplace special, so we have a place to go. Might as well kill two birds with one stone."

"Wow—way to make a girl feel special," I tease.

"If you want to dress up for every meal, I will. I'm not opposed to it. I think I'm just pissy because Dani pulled rank as older sister and is bossing us around."

As if I speak fluent sarcasm, "I'm sure that must be very

annoying," rolls off my lips. "I'm sure you and Vince can take notes and compare how awful older sisters can be."

"That's not what I meant, Van—and you know it."

"Well, I for one can't wait to see what you look like in a suit. I'm sure you'll be sexy as hell. Wait... Didn't you say your brothers look like you?" I pretend to fan myself. "I'm not sure I could handle three hot Fallon men, dressed in suits."

"There's only one Fallon man you need to worry about," he says with a growl as he darts in my direction.

"Really? Who's that? I've always had a thing for older guys. Maybe Derek will catch my fancy."

Damien's jaw drops, and my teasing is so worth it. "Did you just say, 'Catch my fancy? What are you, ninety?"

Bursting out with laughter, I counter with, "Well... I am into older men."

"Men... as in a harem?"

Tapping my chin, I look to the sky. "That does sound promising..."

"Oh, really." He leans in so we're nose to nose.

"No—not at all. But I love that it bothers you because I love teasing you... For the record... I only want one man." I point into his chest. "And he's about to have his way with me... if I'm not mistaken."

"Oh, he'll have his way with you," he promises. Then he crashes his lips to mine and reminds me over and over why he's the right man for me.

"Bedroom," I whisper, knowing I want to explore more of him, and this chair doesn't lend itself to making it easy.

The next thing I know, Damien stands and hoists me over

his shoulder to carry me in a fireman's hold, making me giggle as I smack him on his ass. "I could've walked, you Neanderthal," I say through bursts of laughter.

"This is faster," he practically growls as my hallway zips past me at an inverted angle.

True. With our time being limited, we've had to get creative over the last few weeks. But one thing is certain, each and every time we're together—I want him more.

The next thing I know, my body is flying and lands on my soft bed. The sudden movement gives me the same thrill of being on a rollercoaster. I scooch up the bed as he purposely stalks toward me.

Shivers tingle up my spine as I take him in.

His eyes fill with need as they roam over my body. I've never felt more beautiful than in this moment with the way he wants to devour me. Not wanting to draw things out, I reach to the hem of my shirt and rip it off.

"Ahh..." he moans. "Two can play that game."

Slowly, he unbuttons his shirt, then drops it next to him.

Oh. My. Hell. This man is sexy as sin. My mouth dries, and I have to remind myself to breathe as I watch his every move. To keep him going, I squirm out of my leggings—though I'm sure it's not nearly as sexy as watching him undo his fly and drop his pants to the floor with a thud, due to whatever was in his pockets.

"I'm likin' this show," I murmur. "Keep going..."

"I thought we were playing a silent game of Simon Says... I'm only mimicking you," he says as he straightens and waits for my next move, locking his eyes with mine.

Hmmm...

Reaching behind my back, I unclasp my bra and fling it to the floor. Then I get up on my knees to face him as I slide my panties over my hips. Not knowing how I can get these things off gracefully, I laugh at myself as I realize I have to somewhat stand to get these suckers off.

Smooth, Van... real smooth.

But the moment Damien slides his thumbs into the waistband of his black boxer briefs all laughter vanishes. When his thick cock springs free, my stomach flips in anticipation. As he reaches down to grab a condom from his wallet, my core clenches. I don't think I've ever needed him more than now.

Throwing the condoms on my bed, he says, "For the record, I had planned to take you out to dinner."

"Later," I whisper as I reach out to pull his face closer. When his lips meet mine, I'm blessed with the glorious taste that is all Damien. I nip, suck, and let my inner goddess flow. Being with him gives me a sense of power I've never experienced. Sure, he likes to give as good as he gets, but in these moments when I'm in control, he savors it as much as I do. As if he was built just for me, my body comes alive, and my inner vixen roars in anticipation.

Reaching between us, I cup his balls, rolling them in my hand just the way I've quickly learned he likes. With my other hand, I stroke the length of his cock and elicit the sexiest moan imaginable. He fists my hair and intensifies our kiss in the sexiest of ways.

My nipples rub against his chest as my hands work my magic along his length, knowing I won't get to do this much longer because he'll want to slow things down, claiming he wants to make it good for me, too. Not that I'll ever complain, but sometimes I love being in control of things. I mean... what girl doesn't?

When I break our kiss to trail hot kisses down his collarbone and onto his chest, a guttural moan escapes from deep from within. The kind of moan that if I had panties on, they'd melt on the spot. The sound only spurs me on further.

Just as I'm about to go for gold, I murmur, "Lie down." I change positions with him and once he's on his back, I slowly crawl up his body to continue feathering kisses where I left off. My lips trace along his jawline, down his neck, and across his well-defined muscles forming his abs. His heavy breaths let me know I'm on the right track. Keeping enough space between us so I can grip his cock and slide my hand from the root to the tip over and over again, I slowly kiss my way down his body.

Grabbing for the condom beside us, he shoves it at me. "Need you... Van," comes out in a guttural cry. "We can go as slow as you'd like—next time. But for the love of God, get that sexy ass of yours on me—now! Ride me like there's no tomorrow."

It's not what I had in mind, but it will certainly do. I love being on top with him.

Ripping the condom open, I have it on him in no time. Knowing I'm practically dripping with need, I do exactly what he asks. The moment I bottom out on him, he lets out another sexy moan. "God, Van, you feel incredible."

He's not the one being filled in the most glorious way from the inside out. We quickly find a rhythm that has my body tingling in no time. I feel every nerve ending come alive and sizzle as my orgasm builds. I swear it's like he's cracked a secret code that only he's been able to find.

The moment he takes one of my breasts into his mouth and creates this perfect rhythm between sucking and pulling, my need for him grows. It's as if his mouth is live wired to every nerve in my body, and he sets me on fire. Before I know it, I'm teetering on the edge of ecstasy. Wave after wave of sensation tingles from my lower spine through the roots of my hair and to the tips of my toes, and I let out a scream I can no longer contain when he pushes me past the point of no return with the squeeze of my other nipple.

I make every effort I can to ride this orgasmic high until I feel him stiffen and curse as he finds his release. Feeling his pulses sets off another wave inside me. Christ, what this man does to me.

I am ruined.

Each and every time I am with this man, it gets better.

Breathless, I collapse onto him. My entire body is a gooey mush, and I'm sure I couldn't stand if I tried. Hell, I can't even lift my head to look at this glorious man. No—instead, I just rest my head on his chest and listen to his heart race as he pulses inside me.

While both of our heart rates return to normal, Damien traces his fingers along my spine. I don't want to move a muscle as I'm afraid of popping this blissful bubble I'm in. Eventually, all good things must end, and he excuses himself to get rid of the condom.

When he returns, he slips back into bed beside me and asks, "So, when will Jules be back?"

"Late this evening, I think. Vince and Sydney had an entire day planned." Then I laugh at the memory of Sydney's parting words.

Damien quirks a brow in wonder. "Mind fillin' me in?"

Gah. Syd and her craziness. "Oh, I'm just remembering how Syd left this morning. The second Jules and Vince were out of earshot, she turned, and I quote, *'Girl, you'd better get it on with that sexy man of yours. We've got Jules covered until tomorrow, so we'd better not see you curled up with a book when we get home. Go get yourself some Bow-Chicka-Wow-Wow! You deserve a night off.'*—All I could do was stare because who the hell talks like that?"

I feel Damien's laugh before I hear it. "Apparently, Sydney does," he says in a shrug. "But I'm more than happy to volunteer anytime you're up for some Bow-Chicka-Wow-Wow time."

"Ohmigod, you did not say that—I swear, if you call it that again, I'm never having sex with you again," I threaten, but there's no way I'll ever follow through. After what we've just experienced... hell no. I'll take all the Bow-Chicka-Wow-Wow time he wants—but he doesn't need to know that.

"I won't—but you gotta admit, that's funny as fuck..."

No longer able to keep my composure, I crack. "Yeah." I nod through laughter in agreement.

28

DAMIEN

WATCHING her effortlessly juggle her schedule never ceases to amaze me, but we steal as much time together as possible. We always make it a priority to put Jules first. Sure, I may stay later than her bedtime on weeknights, and we've found creative ways to be together, but I always go home to my own bed. Besides, Vanessa works early and is off before most college students even think about getting out of bed in the morning, so it just makes sense.

The thought of going away with her and Jules is equally thrilling and terrifying. Hands down, there are no two other people I'd rather spend my vacation with, but the fact that I'm bringing them to meet my family could prove interesting to say the least. God help my brothers if they turn into jackasses and make Van or Jules uncomfortable.

Until I know for certain the girls will join me, I don't bother to tell anyone. Why get anyone's hopes up—especially my own? It isn't until Mom asks if I am staying with them, I admit to renting a place of my own for the long weekend. Of course, Mom being Mom knows something is up. First, I've never bothered to get a place because it's usually just me and though I'd prefer a bed, I can sleep just about anywhere. Second, I hesitate a second too long before any explanation.

Yep, her super-sleuthing skills are put to task, so of course, she expertly asks, "Will your brothers be staying with you?"

To which I all too quickly reply, "Uh... That would be a hard no. Vanessa's agreed to come with me, and I'm not subjecting her to those fools for our entire stay. Nope. No, thank you."

"The fact that you're bringing her at all says a lot, Dame."

Sighing, I know I may as well tell her the story. "I think you're gonna like her, Mom..." And before I know it, I tell Mom everything. From the first moment I saw her in the diner, up to finding out she has a daughter, and the basics of these past few months. She's my mom, so I leave a lot of the personal details out—but she gets the gist of things.

I love my mom more than anything when her only question is, "Tell me more about Julia."

"Mom, she's quick as a whip and always calls me on my shit—whether she knows it or not. She's so much like Vanessa in that she's smart, independent, and beautiful from the inside out. The two of them have been through a lot in a short time, but you'd never know it for as well adjusted as they are."

"What do you mean?"

"It's a long story, but Vanessa and her twin brother Vince lost both their parents right after Julia was born. Ever since, it's basically been the three of them against the world."

"Wow, that's something." I can tell she wants to ask more but somehow refrains.

"Mom, I know this is all still new—so I don't want to say too much to everyone, but she's special—and so is her daughter. You'll see."

"Dame. I have no doubt if you're bringing them around our crazy crew. I'll do what I can about your brothers—hopefully, they've gained some maturity with age... but this is still the first woman you've brought around... since... well...." She pauses for a moment and immediately, I know where her mind's gone.

Quickly, I spit out, "She's nothing like Amber, Mom. Vanessa's everything Amber wasn't and then some. Vanessa may be a few years younger than me, but she's got a strong head on her shoulders and knows what she wants out of life—and the truth is—she'd do it fine with or without me."

"Okay... Okay... calm down." She laughs into the phone. "I only want to see you happy, Dame. If you're happy, I'm happy for you. Now I've gotta go see what trouble your dad is getting into. You tell both Vanessa and Julia I'm looking forward to meeting them."

After Mom and I get off the phone, I can't help but smile. She's still an expert at pulling any secret—big or small—out of me effortlessly. It's not like I have anything to hide, but Mom has a way of knowing all the same.

Pulling into Vanessa's driveway, my eagerness to see her outweighs my nerves. I barely get the truck in park when the front door flies open, and Jules sprints out to the porch.

Hopping out of the truck, Jules rushes toward me and

flings herself in my direction for a welcome hug. This is the first time she's been this ecstatic to see me, but I'll take it. She has that effect on me, too. Bending to welcome her, I hoist her to my height. "Hey, Jules, you ready for a road trip?"

Nodding fervently. "Yep! Momma packed me a swimsuit and says we're going on a ferry?" This comes out as a question but before I can answer, she asks, "Did you grow up on an island? I get to meet your mom and grandma, right?"

Shaking my head, I do my best to answer her rapid-fire questions.

"Yes, we're going on a short ferry ride and no, I grew up outside of Leavenworth. My grandparents lived on the island, so I visited them every summer and on holidays."

"What's it like?"

Needing clarification, I ask, "What's what like?"

"Having a big family. You have two brothers... and a sister... I've always wanted a big brother, but Momma says it doesn't work that way."

"No, I'm afraid it doesn't work that way. More than likely, you could get a little brother, so I hate to break it to you—you'll always be the oldest."

Though I suppose if Vanessa were to meet someone with older children, it could happen.

Fuck.

I tap that thought down as soon as it surfaces.

I'm not thinking about her being with anyone else but me.

"Dame.... Dame..." Julia waves a hand in front of my face. "Did you hear me?"

Busted.

"Uh... sorry. Can you repeat that?"

Exasperated, she repeats, "I said..." she draws out the way her mom does when Jules hasn't been paying attention. "Do we get to ride in your truck?"

Setting her down to the ground, I say, "That's the plan. Should we go see if your momma needs help, so we can hit the road?"

As if we've done it a million times, Jules clasps my hand in hers and leads me to her mom. In this moment, I'm certain Vanessa's not the only one I'm falling for.

WHEN WE ARRIVE at the ferry terminal, I'm relieved to see we'll make it on the next boat, without having to wait. Julia's been a trooper for our car ride, but I'm not sure I even want to wait an hour or more for our turn on the ferry. Julia's chatter is infectious as she gives us a play-by-play of what's happening with the ferry. When we actually drive onto our spot, her mood shifts to disappointment, since we're stuck behind a utility van and can't see much of anything from the cab of my truck.

It's a beautiful summer day on Puget Sound. Big puffy clouds are high in the sky, and the sun reflects on the rippled waves in the water. Knowing it's a short ride, as soon as it's safe, I ask the girls, "Wanna go up on the deck so you can get a better look?"

In no time at all, we're on top of the deck and have prime real estate against the rail at the front of the ship. Our unobstructed view of the sound as we cross to Anderson Island makes me miss this place even more. As a kid, I loved hanging out here on the deck, with the wind on my face as I scoured the water for any sea life.

"Dame!" Jules gasps, getting my attention. "Did you see that?"

She points in the direction of two sea otters playing along the side of the ferry and squeals. "Can you believe it? They're adorable."

Vanessa pulls out her phone and records them for a few minutes, then turns to the two of us. "Say cheese." Leaning into Jules, we both grin wide as she takes our picture.

"Your turn." I grin as I snap a few shots of the two most beautiful people in my world. Their matching hazel eyes twinkle in delight, as their long hair flows around them with the wind. Before we return out attention to the otters, I suggest, "Let's do a selfie."

While the girls watch the otters, I find myself watching them. They're so happy and free in this moment, all I can do is smile and enjoy the magnificent view. It's hard to believe these two have become an intricate part of my life in such a short time.

Hell, mere months ago, I barely looked at any girl twice. I'd been so focused on work and was convinced I didn't have time for more than that. Fuck, let's face it. I haven't done more than hook up with a woman in a few years—and frankly, I was happy about it.

God, I had no fucking clue what happiness was.

This. This right here—watching this beautiful woman and

her daughter laugh so carefree, is exactly what I'd been missing in life. Ever since Amber, I've sworn off getting seriously involved with anyone. Maybe I had it all wrong.

Or maybe I was meant to wait for these two.

As much as I don't want to admit it, the fact I'm bringing someone home to meet my family is significant. Mom knew and of course, I dismissed it. I know I can handle any shit my brothers sling at me—but if they even think about giving Van a hard time—they won't know what hit them.

Sure, they'd just be protecting me, but Vanessa's nothing like Amber, and I need to make that point clear. I wonder if Mom's said anything—or if she wants to let me tell them. I'm sure Dad knows. Those two never keep secrets.

Snapping a few more photos to capture this moment, I'm startled when there's an announcement to return to our vehicles as we'll be docking soon. Knowing our vacation rental is just a few houses up from my grandparents', I make my way off the boat to our final destination with ease. Once we've unpacked and get things settled, I suggest we visit my family.

Julia's adorable as she insists on holding both our hands on the walk along the rural road to the cabin. Anderson Island hasn't developed enough for sidewalks, and it's a straight shot to my grandparents' house. I tell her how I used to play in the woods on the vacant lot as we pass, as well as where I like to kayak. She peppers me with questions the entire way.

I swear Mom still has a homing beacon on me because we don't even step foot on the front porch, and the door bursts open. "Damien! I'm so glad you made it."

Mom may be barely five-foot-four on a good day, but man,

she's a fierce hugger. I don't even get the chance to let go of Jules' hand, and the breath is squeezed out of me. Squeezing her back with my free arm, she finally releases me and steps back.

"Well... who do we have here?" She looks to Vanessa and Jules who each smile in greeting.

"Mom. This is Vanessa and Julia." Then I turn to the girls and shrug. "This is my mom Daisy."

Vanessa doesn't miss a beat as she reaches out a hand to greet my mom. But Mom just shakes her head. "That just won't do." Then she steps toward Vanessa and wraps her arms around her to welcome her properly. Thankfully, Vanessa seems at ease and simply returns the hug—as if they've been doing it all along.

When they're finished, Mom pulls back and squats to Julia's level. "I've heard so many things about you, Julia. I couldn't wait to meet the girl that's got Dame wrapped around her little finger. I'll have to share some secrets to help you keep him that way," Mom says with a wink to me.

"Great... you're already ganging up on me." I pretend to pout. But that's all it takes to put Jules at ease.

She drops my hand like a hot potato and steps in to give Mom one of her famous squeezes. Those two are a match for sure. They both can squeeze the life out of you and not know any better of it.

I glance over them to Vanessa to see if she's okay, and she just shrugs it off with a smile. Reaching for her hand, I squeeze it, letting her know I'm here for her if she needs me. I know she was nervous to meet my mom, but hopefully, any doubts she had will soon disappear.

When Mom stands up, she's business as usual. "You two are the last to arrive—except for your sister. She had some business to attend to off island, so she and Luke will join us tomorrow."

Before I can ask about Dani, Dad greets us, "Hey, Dame. Who do you have here?"

I go through the necessary introductions. When Julia hears his name is Trent, she turns and asks me quizzically, "I thought all the names started with a D."

"Well, I'm his dad, does that count?" Dad teases.

Jules just shrugs. "Dad does start with D."

"What starts with D?" Derek calls out from inside the house.

Mom quickly invites us to come inside so the girls can meet everyone.

Obviously, Mom hasn't spilled the beans about my company because my brothers' shocked expressions are downright comical when they've realized I've brought the girls with me. Derek's eyes nearly bug out, and Davis's jaw drops to the floor, but both of them quickly school their features when Mom side-eyes them as she makes introductions. Thankfully, Jules and Vanessa are none the wiser, but each of my brothers have that look on their face that tells me we'll be discussing this later. Clearly, they want to know what's going on.

"Well, now that you've met everyone," Mom turns to Julia. "I know you've had a long drive. Dinner won't be ready for a few hours. But are you hungry? I have some chocolate chip cookies with your name on them, if it's all right with your mom."

Julia's eyes dart to Vanessa eagerly, who only smiles and nods.

"Does that mean we can finally eat some, too?" Davis hedges.

"Yes, I suppose you can." Mom pretends to be disgruntled, then turns to Vanessa. "I had to turn them off until our company *at least* had a chance to be offered some." Then she turns to Jules. "We'd better hurry if you want to get more than a few."

Laughing, we follow Mom into the kitchen, where we find my grandma at the counter, peeling potatoes. "Hey, Grandma. Where's Pops?"

"You have a Pops, too?" Julia asks innocently.

"Yeah. That's what we call my grandpa," I explain.

Then she looks to the man in question and says, "Hi. I'm Julia. I had a Pops, but he's in heaven. But it's nice to meet another one, though."

Vanessa's face reddens in an instant. "Jules."

Totally unaware she's just told the entire room of Vanessa's parents' death, she asks, "What?"

Before anyone can say anything, Pops says the sweetest thing he could as he bends to her level. "You know what, Julia? I think I like you. I've always got room for more people to call me Pops. Especially from beautiful girls like yourself. Would that be okay with you?"

Julia nods emphatically.

Grandma leans over in their direction and tells Julia, "Just so you know, he rarely answers to anything else. So, if I were you, that's the *only* thing I'd be calling him."

"Hey... hey... hey.... This young lady can call me anything... but late for dinner..." Pops teases, making us all laugh at his silliness. Pops hasn't changed a thing in all the years I've known him.

Julia's wide eyes dart around the room, then return to my grandma.

Grandma, being the expert at putting everyone at ease, leans in and grins. "You're welcome to call me Grandma if you'd like. I've long lost my given name with this crowd. Besides, who wants to be called Beatrice? Grandma is *so* much better, don't you think?"

Jules looks hesitantly to Vanessa who just nods in agreement.

"Okay," Jules agrees. Then she turns to my mom. "Did you say there were cookies?"

"You'll fit right in here." Davis laughs as he reaches over the counter to snag one from the platter set out.

"No kidding," Derek agrees.

I completely agree. Having Jules and Van here with me is as easy as breathing. I have no idea what I'd been worried about.

29

VANESSA

OKAY, I'll admit I'd been nervous when we first arrived, but Damien's family quickly puts both me and more importantly, Jules, at ease. I nearly die when she tells everyone my dad's in heaven, but at the same time, I'm glad she feels comfortable enough to share.

I haven't met anyone's family since high school. I don't realize how nervous I am until we arrive. Knowing how important Damien's family is to him puts more pressure on me than I anticipated. My stomach is tied in knots, and my hands are sweating. Thank goodness, I bring comedic relief in a pint-size package, right?

From the moment his mom squeezes me in her arms, the worries I'd fret over disperse. By the time everyone's enjoying fresh-baked chocolate chip cookies, I hardly remember why I'd been nervous in the first place. As I listen to the conversations around the room and see the way they do their best to put Julia and myself at ease, I feel a sense of belonging I haven't had unless I'm with my family.

Eventually, the men in the house disperse to hang out on the back deck. Julia eagerly goes with them when Damien offers to play frisbee with her. Seeing his mom and grandma preparing dinner, I do what I do best—offer help.

"Oh, honey," his sweet grandma guffaws. "You're only a guest for the first time in this house. You're welcome to stay, but you can just sit and visit with us. The next time you come— you're on your own and are expected to help. Do we have a deal?"

Ohmigod. I love her.

"I think I can handle that, Ms. Beatrice. But know I've got two working hands if you need them."

"I meant what I said, Vanessa," Beatrice warns. "You may as well call me Grandma, too." Her warm smile melts my heart. "Everyone else does."

"I think I'd like that." Then I admit, "My grandparents passed when Vince and I were little, so we hardly knew them."

"I'll never try to take the place of your kinfolk, but if our Damien's bringing you around, you're more than welcome to join my fold. He's special, that one—and if he likes you, I'm fairly certain we all will. That girl of yours is just precious."

"Damien mentioned you attend the university he's working at, what are you studying?" his mom asks after putting an enormous casserole into the oven.

"I'm in nursing school at the moment. I'll graduate next year."

"Where will you go from there?" Beatrice asks.

Shrugging, I admit, "Wherever a job takes me. Though I can't imagine living far from my brother Vince."

"I'm glad you're close to your brother. Family is everything." Beatrice nods as she finishes peeling one last potato.

"Maybe it's because we're twins, but we've always had a special connection."

"Damien mentioned he attends CRU as well?" Daisy prompts as a question.

"I don't know what I would've done without him." I nod. "After graduation, our parents died in a car accident. He and Julia are the only reasons I survived it. He was supposed to go to an Ivy League school back East but changed his mind and transferred to CRU with me, so I'd finish school in four years."

"I'm sorry for your loss, but that's commendable," Beatrice sighs, and Daisy nods in agreement.

Gah. My emotions get the best of me as a lump forms in my throat from trying to hold back tears. I don't mean to dump everything on them, but I'd rather get the elephant out of the room—with Jules putting it out there so matter-of-fact.

"Thank you," I manage. Then I swallow back the rest of my bubbling emotions. "It certainly hasn't been easy. But like I said, with the help of Jules and my brother, we're doing more than just surviving now."

"I can certainly see why our Damien is so smitten with you," Beatrice says.

Smitten? Wow... I guess... but how would she know that?

Daisy must read the confusion on my face. "Of course he's smitten with you, sweetheart. The fact that you're here in the first place is enough proof for us."

Before I can say anything, his grandmother interjects, "That poor boy hasn't brought a girl round in ages. We know you're special to him. Please don't fret over anything. If he's happy, we're happy for him."

Wow. Okay. I guess there's just one more elephant to get out of the room. "And you don't care I come with a five-year-old?"

"Should we?" Daisy smirks as if she knows the answer. "Last I checked, single moms are a package deal."

"Besides," Beatrice interrupts. "I'm getting old, and none of these grandchildren of mine are bringing me great-grandbabies anytime soon. She's just one more person I get to love. One thing I've learned in my old age, darlin'—there's always room to love more—your ticker is the one organ that expands without you even being aware."

Holy crap. I think I love this woman already. Raw emotions return in an instant as I blink back unshed tears that rapidly form.

How can they make me feel so welcome in such a short amount of time?

Of course, this is how Damien finds me.

"You okay, Van?" he asks, rushing to me. Once he's by my side to put himself between me and his family, he looks to his mom and grandma as if he's deciphering who he needs to protect me from first.

Gah. His adoration is the final act that breaks the dam. Tears flow freely as I explain, "I'm fine, Dame. Really. Your grandma just said something very touching, and I got emotional."

Suspiciously, he looks between his mom and grandma with a raised brow.

Beatrice stops his brooding in an instant. "Boy, don't look at us like that. You know better, and you shouldn't worry. We like Vanessa, and we're just havin' a moment here—before you so rudely interrupted. You get off your high horse and let us finish."

Damien ignores the matriarchs in the room as he focuses on me. "You're okay?"

Nodding quickly, I blurt out, "Yes. Grandma's right. We're just having a moment. You can just go away and stop worrying." I smile at his overprotectiveness, and an unshed tear breaks free and rolls down my face.

Gah, what is it with this family? They're making me so emotional. Quickly, I brush it away and attempt to deflect, "Is Julia being good with your dad and brothers?"

"Don't worry about her," Daisy assures me. "Davis is a med student, and this isn't Trent's first rodeo. If he survived Dani, I'm sure he'll be fine."

"Speaking of Dani," Damien changes the subject. "She's the one who planned this little reunion. Why in the world is she in Tacoma?"

I swear, I see something flit across Daisy's features, but it's gone so quickly, I could've imagined it. "She'll be here tomorrow. She's left strict instructions to be ready by noon for the photographer. We're meeting over at Luke's to do our family photoshoot on his beach."

"I still don't see what the fuss is with suits," Damien grumbles.

Beatrice chimes in, "Hey, mister-too-big-for-my-britches, I for one can't wait to see us all in our Sunday best. I'm not gonna be around forever, ya know. So pipe down and let me enjoy this."

"Geez, Grandma. No need to lay it on so thick. Dani's just extremely vague and has been ghosting me when I text her these past few days."

"You know Dani. She's probably working hard. You know how stuck in her head she gets," Daisy explains.

"That's an understatement," Damien grumbles as he shakes his head. "I'd better grab the drinks and get back out there."

Seeing his hands are full, I offer, "Here, let me help you."

Before leaving, I turn to Beatrice and place a hand on her shoulder. "Thank you. I appreciate what you said earlier."

"It's not a problem. Now go enjoy that sweet girl of yours. We'll be out in a bit to join you."

I'm surprised to find a large deck with an enormous yard beyond it. Julia's playing on a rope swing that looks like it's seen better days. But the rope looks sturdy enough for what she's doing, so I let that worry go.

Sipping on my bottled water, I take in Damien and his brothers as I listen to their steady conversation. It's evident they're related. Each is well over six-feet tall. They all have the same shade of brown hair, but each is styled uniquely to himself. Their family traits also include broad shoulders and square chins. Damien's hair is tight on the sides, but a bit longer on the top. Davis looks the most like Damien, but he's skinnier, and his hair is cropped short. Derek, on the other hand, has longer hair and is bulkier than the rest, but the similarities remain. With all these handsome men in the family, I wonder what their sister looks like.

It's interesting to see their family dynamics. It's been Vince and me for so long, I find it entertaining to see how the nuances of a large family play out. There's laughter, ribbing, and jokes to go around but under it all, I can tell they care for one another. Their antics may be loud and boisterous, but as time goes on, they subtly check in on one another and have meaningful conversations among themselves.

"How's the house coming along, Dame?" Trent asks with interest.

Damien fills him in on the remodel. His brothers interject here and there to ask questions, and since I already know most of this, I focus my attention on Jules. I can see her smile from here as she swings back and forth. She's thoroughly entertained, and I can feel her joy from here.

Damien must notice because he whispers, "Don't worry, I tried that thing out myself. If it can hold me, I'm sure she's safe."

That would've been a sight to see. Yet, my chest tightens over his simple gesture all the same.

"Oh, I wasn't worried," I admit.

"That thing was around when we were kids. We were placing bets on which one of us would break it—but no such luck," Derek admits.

"It may have been my suggestion," Trent interjects. "Though I had nothing to do with the bets these fools placed. I didn't want that sweet little girl getting hurt. Though I'm sure she got quite a laugh watching these idiots do their best to break it. I think it's safe to say that rope isn't going anywhere anytime soon."

"Speaking of going places..." Derek pipes in. "How long is your job at CRU?"

"It's scheduled to last a year, so I'll be done next spring."

"Then where are you heading off to? Is that project in New York still the next viable option?"

My heart sinks to my stomach at the thought of him leaving—period. But New York? Why hasn't he told me anything about this?

I feel Damien's eyes on me as I focus intently on the suddenly fascinating water bottle in my hands. I can't look up if I tried, in fear of showing the thousands of thoughts racing through my mind.

Damien reaches for my leg and squeezes it once as if he can read my mind.

"I... uh... am not sure where my next job will be. A lot can happen in a year. But I'm not so sure about the East Coast."

"True... a lot of things can change in that time," Trent agrees. "What about you, Derek? What's going on with you?"

"Things are good, Dad. I'm enjoying the firm I work with for now, but if a few of my side projects become bigger than they are, I am considering making it my full-time gig. The great thing is I work remote and can travel either way, so I can't complain."

Damien turns to me and explains, "He's a graphic designer and works for an advertising agency."

I nod and continue listening to them check in with one

another. Davis tells us about a few interesting cases he's been working on during his recent clinical rotation. Then Trent talks about the family business he and Daisy run outside of Cashmere.

When Derek asks, "What's gonna happen when you and Mom decide to retire? Do you think you'll sell the place?" Trent raises a brow at his eldest son.

"Well... none of you want to run it, and I don't see any of you poppin' out kids anytime soon, to leave it to as their inheritance. I guess your mom and I'll have to cross that bridge when we get there. For now, she enjoys running the books, and I'm not anywhere close to retiring."

"We've got good people helping us run it now," Daisy chimes in as she sits down in a chair beside her husband. "Did your father tell you we're taking an actual vacation this fall?"

"Nope." Trent smiles. "I was waiting for you to tell them."

"Well..." she gasps excitedly. "I've finally convinced your workaholic dad to take me to Australia for three whole weeks in September. I've always wanted to go and once school starts, the store slows down a bit. Besides, it's our thirtieth anniversary, and it's about time we went on that honeymoon we never seemed to get around to."

"Wow... you sure you can survive not working every day?" Davis teases his dad.

"I might find I like the travel bug and will have to do it more often." Trent shrugs.

"I've always wanted to go to Australia," I admit. "That and New Zealand. I'm sure you'll have a wonderful time."

Julia rushes up to the porch with a panicked expression. "Momma... I gotta go..."

Crap. I know that look. Before I can do anything, Damien stands and promptly says, "Come on, squirt. I'll show you the way."

Could this man be any sweeter?

As I watch them leave, Beatrice, who's taken a seat beside me, whispers, "You're not the only one that boy's smitten with."

30

DAMIEN

JUST AS WE FINISH DINNER, my sister sends a group family text.

Dani: Don't make plans for after the photoshoot tomorrow. Luke and I have made reservations for us all in Tacoma. We have you dressed up—now you'll have a place to go. (Smiley face emoji)

"What is she up to?" Derek asks the table.

Mom's smile is huge. "Oh, Derek. We know *you* hate surprises. But let Dani have her fun. Besides, she's right. If we're getting all dressed up, we may as well go somewhere special, too."

Dad's in agreement with Mom on this one—which is interesting. "Let's just go along for the ride. Who knows? It may be fun."

"Does this mean we get to go on the ferry again?" Jules asks the room.

"Honey, anything off this island does," Pops chimes in.

Davis's response has us all bursting out with laughter.

Davis: We'll go—but we won't make any promises beyond showing up.

Of course, Derek can't keep out of it.

Derek: Just because you're the only girl doesn't make you the Queen Bee. When will you stop bossing us around?

Dani's reply is instant, and I'm thankful Jules can't see it.

Dani: NEVER!!! Pull that stick out of your ASS, big brother, and loosen up. I promise it'll be fun, and I'll bet you $100 you won't even hate me for it later.

Out of nowhere, Grandma chimes in, and I nearly fall out of my seat with laughter as she shakes a fist at Derek.

GMA: Don't you worry, Dani. I've got this handled. I'll drag that stick in the mud kicking and screaming if I have to. ALL these boys will be at the photoshoot with bells on by noon. Or they'll

answer to me. That includes Damien's sweet Vanessa and her baby girl Julia. You're gonna love them. Whether they stick around these fools after this week, that's their choice.

Dani's reply is instant.

Dani: Wait!?!? Damien's sweet Vanessa? What am I missing?

Me: If you'd been here today, you would've met both Vanessa and her daughter. You snooze, you lose, sis. That's what you get for ghosting me all week...

Mom: You'll love them both. You just get what you need to get done. We will ALL be at Luke's place by noon. Dressed and ready for family photos.

Dani: Luke's family's flying in tonight for the long weekend. It should be a blast. Gotta run. See ya tomorrow.

"What is Dani scheming now?" Davis asks the room. "You gotta admit. This is weird—even for her."

Dad takes a drink of his beer, and Mom just shrugs. "No idea. But this seems important to her. Just go along for the ride, and I'm sure you'll have fun."

"Yeah," Davis snorts. "Famous last words—Just go along for the ride—right before you end up in the ER or something."

"You worry too much, Davy," Grandma chides. "Stop acting like you're ninety with one foot in the grave. Hell, I don't even act like that, and I'm a lot closer to it than you are."

"Okay... Okay..." Davis grumbles.

When I look to Vanessa, she's got her mouth covered with a napkin, but I'd bet my last dollar she's doing all she can to hold in laughter. Julia, on the other hand, just giggles right along with Pops. This shit is funny even if she isn't fully aware of the string of texts.

I'm not sure what I expected it to be like but having Jules and Vanessa here with me is as natural as my heart beating. My family has welcomed them with open arms, and I couldn't be more grateful.

Before we leave to get Jules settled at a decent bedtime, Mom pulls out some of my favorite books from childhood for Julia. Mom or Grandma must've found them in some closet because I thought those treasures were long lost over the years. I haven't seen them in ages.

Tonight is the first time my dad's even mentioned wanting grandkids. Maybe Jules has sparked something, or maybe it's the fact we're all getting closer to thirty, but I can see where he's coming from. Now that I've met Vanessa and opened myself to the possibility of more—kids of my own don't seem like such a far stretch.

When Derek had brought up the possibility of moving, my gut physically ached at the thought of leaving Vanessa and

Jules. Sure, New York has been my next logical step, but I'm not even sure I want that as a possibility for my future.

THE NEXT MORNING, Jules, Vanessa, and I enjoy a lazy morning together. With Jules being an early riser, I'd packed a few things for her to munch on until it's a decent hour for breakfast with my family. We even go for a walk down to the beach near my grandparents' house to kill some time, before getting ready for family photos.

Vanessa spends time doing Julia's hair and helps her get into a dress, while I slip into the master bathroom to take a quick shower and put on my suit. I volunteer to hang with Jules while Vanessa finishes getting ready.

We're deep into coloring a page from one of her books when Julia asks, "How big is your family, Dame?"

"You've met almost everyone but my sister and her fiancé Luke."

She stops coloring and looks quizzically at me as she asks, "What's a fiancé?"

Shit. What do I say to a five-year-old?

"Well... Luke has asked Dani to marry him. I guess a fiancé is someone you plan to marry?"

"Do you have a fiancé?" she asks, her brows drawn as she scrutinizes my face like no five-year-old should manage.

"Uh... no. I don't have a fiancée." When Julia's shoulders sag and her lips form a frown, I quickly ask, "What's wrong?"

Suddenly, she seems unsure. What the hell is wrong?

"Well... you said a fiancé is someone you want to marry." She bites her lip, then looks to her coloring page as she whispers, "So... you don't wanna... marry Momma?"

Shit. How did she jump to that conclusion?

It's not that I don't want to marry Vanessa.

Hell, I can't imagine being with anyone else. And the thought of making her and Jules a part of my family has certainly crossed my mind—but she's not my fiancée.

Because you haven't asked, dumb ass.

Jules is asking if I want to marry her mom—isn't she?

Fuck... why can't kids come with a training manual?

"Dame?" Julia asks when I remain silent for too long.

Think, Fallon. Think.

"Jules..." I start but hesitate when I'm at a loss for words. "A fiancé means that you've asked someone to marry you—and they have said yes. It has nothing to do with want. It just means the decision has been made."

Julia's face is like a pinball of emotions. First, she frowns, then smiles, then it morphs into the most calculated expression I've ever seen. "So... you're saying you don't have a fiancé because you haven't asked. Does that mean you might... someday?"

This kid.

God help the man who sets his sights on her someday. She'll most definitely keep him on his toes.

The minute the thought hits me, another thought flashes just as fast.

I'd like to be there to see it happen.

I can picture the entire thing. Her in a white dress, me

walking her down the aisle. Her mother and I sitting beside each other as we watch her marry her future husband.

Where the hell did that come from?

Evading the question to a point, I suggest, "I'll tell you what. When I decide I'm ready for a fiancée—you'll be the first to know. Would you be okay with that?"

Nodding fast, Julia gushes, "Yes. If Momma becomes your fiancée, does that mean you'd become my daddy?"

Daddy... I hadn't thought of myself as that. But I'd gladly fill the role if she'd let me.

Looking into her hopeful eyes, my chest tightens harder.

"If she and I were to get married, I suppose I could be—if you wanted me to."

"I've never had a daddy. Only an Unks. But I'm sure we'd figure it out if we work together. That's what Momma always says."

I know I've fallen for Vanessa, but until this instant, I didn't realize I've fallen just as hard for Jules, too. I will make this happen for us.

Trying to act calmer than I am, I take a steadying breath. "I'll tell you what. Let's keep this between us. When the time is right, we'll surprise your momma together, 'mkay? Can you be patient?"

She looks at me as if I've lost my mind. "Dame, I'm five. There's no reason to rush things. We've got our whole lives to be together."

She sounds just like Vanessa when she tells Jules to not wish her life away and just focus on what you can enjoy today. How can a five-year-old school me so easily?

"Okay," Vanessa sighs, entering the room. "I'm ready."

One glance in her direction, and my mouth dries. She's wearing the most gorgeous shade of green dress that makes her eyes pop. It wraps around her body like it was made just for her alone. The V in the neckline doesn't reveal anything but accentuates Vanessa's natural beauty.

Slowly, she draws out, "Do... I...." She swallows nervously. "Do I look okay?"

Fuck. Unstick your tongue from the roof of your mouth and compliment her, you idiot.

Shaking my head to regain focus, I stammer, "You... Look..." Words, you fool. "Amazing. No..." Shaking my head. "That's not right, you look breathtaking."

Julia pipes in, "You look pretty, Momma."

Blushing, Vanessa looks to her sandal-covered feet and murmurs, "Thanks."

This just won't do. Stepping closer, I cup her chin to look at me. "Vanessa, you're gorgeous, mouthwatering, and even though we're getting photos to remember this occasion, in this moment, you'll forever be etched in my memory."

Leaning in, I kiss her chastely, keeping in mind my audience, yet at the same time, unable to stop myself.

Not only is it the day I've told her daughter I'd be her daddy, but it's also the day I realize I need a plan to make my fantasy from earlier become a reality.

31

DAMIEN

WHEN WE ARRIVE at Luke's, Dani's nowhere to be found. According to Luke, she'll be ready shortly. After introducing Vanessa and Julia to Luke's family, the photographers they've hired gather us to get started without Dani.

Maybe it's the unexpected amount of people here, but from the moment we've arrived, Vanessa's been unusually quiet. Of course, I don't get much time to worry about it because I'm quickly pulled into a photo with all of my brothers and Luke.

I'll admit, we're gonna love these photos as the sun pops in and out of the high clouds. With the view of the sound and Mt. Rainier in the background, the backdrop is phenomenal. To my surprise, Dani and Luke have gone all out, with three photographers as well as a videographer. Maybe they're doing some PR for Dani's books or the team with Luke, and they've forgotten to mention it. Dani said she wanted to do a photoshoot for our parents' anniversary, but this is overkill—even for her.

Not wanting to miss this opportunity, between one of the shots of us guys and Luke with his family, I ask one of the photographers if they'd mind taking a few shots of Vanessa and Jules together as well as the three of us. She happily obliges and pulls us aside to get the job done.

At first, Vanessa's apprehensive, but the minute Jules joins us in the photos, she finally relaxes into my arms and enjoys herself. When the photographer asks to photograph Jules alone, I lean into Vanessa's ear and ask, "Are you okay?"

"I'm fine. Why wouldn't I be?" But it's a little too rehearsed, so I'm not buying it.

"You'd tell me if something was wrong, right?"

"There's nothing wrong. Relax," she commands. "It's nothing."

I may not have been in many relationships, but *it's nothing* clearly means there *is* something. But given the fact we're in a large crowd, I grant her wish and drop it... for now.

When she reaches up on her toes to kiss me, my worries are soon forgotten.

Apparently, the photographer focuses her attention on us because she asks, "Can you do that again? I'd like to capture that on camera."

I don't need an excuse to kiss Vanessa again, so of course, I oblige.

When we break apart, I notice a few more people have joined us. I'm not sure why Stacey Gardner, Dani's personal assistant, is here but obviously, she's helped orchestrate this.

Seeing Mike Townsend, the owner of the Rainier Renegades, Tony Marcelli, the team's general manager, and a few coaches like Brandon Michaels and Sean Peters all arrive as if on cue with a handful of players, I realize this elaborate ordeal must have something to do with the team. I thought this was a family photoshoot.

What the hell is going on?

Davis must be wondering the same thing as he hollers, "Where's Dani?" across the beach to Luke. "She's made all the pomp and circumstance, but she has yet to show her face."

Stacey answers quickly, "She'll be right here. Luke, can I talk to you for a minute?"

After a few minutes, one of the photographers shouts, "Can I have everyone's attention?"

Turning to see what the fuss is about, my jaw drops in complete shock.

Holy shit. Is this happening?

There's my sister in a long white dress, billowing in the light breeze.

Her hair's done professionally in one of those up-dos, and she's wearing a tiara with a veil hanging from somewhere in the back. She looks absolutely stunning.

Gasps can be heard all around.

"Holy shit, they're getting married," Davis mutters.

"If it looks like a duck and quacks like a duck," Derek says under his breath.

But what gets me is the elated expression on Dani's face. I've never seen her happier than in this moment. I'd never dream of taking it away from her.

"Surprise!" she shouts, then quickly adds, "With our crazy schedules, we didn't want to make a big deal of things. Soooo..." she exaggerates, "We're having a small private wedding here, then a reception tonight at the Glass Museum in Tacoma."

Looking to my parents and grandparents, there's not an ounce of shock on their faces. Clearly, they're *all* in on this. But I don't begrudge them.

This obviously is important to Dani, and I'll never complain about her happiness.

"We've got less than an hour to get the rest of these photos taken," Stacey announces. "Then a few more guests will arrive, and we'll get this party started."

I barely have time to check in with Vanessa and Jules as I'm ushered from photo to photo, with the soon-to-be bride and groom. When I finally get my chance to have a solo picture with my sister, I lean in and hug her fiercely, though I'm careful not to wreck her dress.

"Congratulations, Dan. I'm happy for you."

"I'm so glad you could be here with us," she says as she squeezes me in return.

"You know, all you had to do was ask, and we would've been here anyway."

Dani's eyes dance as she grins from ear to ear. "Where would the fun be in that? Besides, we didn't know if we could pull it off, until everyone agreed to come."

We pose for a few photos, then she gushes, "I can't wait to meet Vanessa and her adorable daughter Julia."

"If you'd been at the house last night, you would've," I counter.

Dani sighs dramatically. "I know. But you know me and secrets. This was so hard to keep under wraps."

"Okay..." I drag out, hoping she'll explain.

"Every time we've set a date to get married, something came up. The minute we had all of our family committed to be here, we decided to kill two birds with one stone."

"Great analogy for a wedding. I thought you were the romance writer. Nothing sounds more romantic than killing more than one bird by stoning it to death," I deadpan.

Rolling her eyes, she smirks. "You know what I mean. Today will be so crazy... so promise me, you'll have to bring the girls back up for a football game once the season starts, and I can get to know them better then."

"I'm sure I'll be bringing her around plenty—if all this," I point around the crowd, "doesn't scare her away."

Looking to Vanessa and Jules who currently are occupying their time away from the crowd by skipping rocks into the sound, Dani says, "They're adorable."

"They're special to me... that's for sure."

"Look at the camera," the photographer calls out as she clicks away, taking multiple photos as my sister and I smile.

Once we're done, Dani moves on to take photos individually with the rest of my brothers.

It's then I notice Dani and Luke have hired a crew to set up chairs for guests as well as brought some food for us to munch on while we wait. Right before more people arrive,

Dani disappears so she can make her official appearance as the bride.

Walking to the shore to check on Vanessa and Jules, I can't help but wish this day happens for us, sooner than later. I know she's in school and has dreams she needs to accomplish on her own, but it doesn't mean I don't want to start my forever with her as soon as possible.

Hell, I'm not even sure when I went from being a perpetual bachelor to wanting a life like this with her, but hearing their laughter echo off the water is exactly the reason why. Somehow these two have burrowed their way into my once-stony heart, and I'm sure I never want to let them go.

Walking up behind Vanessa, I slip my arms around her waist and pull her close. Whispering so only she can hear, I let her know just what she means to me. "God, I love you, Van. I'm so glad you're here with me."

Leaning into my chest, she laughs lightly. "Okayyyy... what's gotten into you?"

"Can't I just tell you what you mean to me?"

Turning to face me, she asks, "Did you have any clue this was happening today?"

"You know exactly what I knew. This is a total surprise."

"Uh... is there a reason you never bothered mentioning your sister is like... The Charlotte Ann who happens to be marrying Luke freakin' Leighton, in just a matter of minutes?"

Shit. Now she thinks I've hidden something from her.

Shrugging, I explain, "To me, they're just Dani and Luke?" But it comes out as a question. "She's my bratty older sister who I love more than anything, but honestly... I never think of her as Charlotte. Sorry. I just can't. I'm happy she's a successful author, but she told us long ago it'd be awkward if we read her books, so I buy each and every one—to support her of course, but I never read a page."

"Well, I do." She gapes. "You know that book I was crying about when you showed up at the door?" I point in the direction of his sister. "It was hers. Heck, I'm even a member of her fan group online. Do I say something... or just ignore it and pretend like she's *only* your sister?"

Before I can say anything, she interrupts, "Wait... it's totally weird for you that I'm completely fangirling and freaking out, isn't it? I'll stop." She's fucking adorable when she sucks in a deep breath and visually goes through the motions of calming herself down.

"I take it her books are good?" I tease, trying to get her to laugh, but all I get in response is wide eyes and a slack jaw.

"Are you kidding me right now?" she whisper-yells at me. "She's freakin' incredible. I've literally read every book she's written. That's why I'm a bit weirded out right now. I've never been around anyone famous, and your sister is Charlotte Freaking Ann." Then she takes a deep breath. "Okay. I'm done freaking out. This is her wedding, and I won't ruin it for her. She deserves this—especially with all the craziness in their lives."

"You do realize Luke is likely way more famous than her—globally, right?"

Okay, captain obvious.

"Sure, he's famous—but if I'm being honest, I'm a bigger fan girl of your sister. Luke's just the hot football coach—who happens to be dating my favorite author. No offense to Luke, but once you realize they're real people, in real relationships—with other women you respect—you can admit they're still attractive, but for me at least—the fandom just isn't the same as before when they're just basically anonymous eye candy."

Her logic kinda makes sense—but it's very convoluted.

"So, I have nothing to be jealous of then?"

"Gah... of course you'd make this about you. Yeah, Luke's handsome—but if I'm being honest—you're my type, not him." Then she wrinkles her nose. "He's pretty old for me—no offense."

"I'll have to tell him you said that," I tease. Though seriously, it would be hysterical to see his reaction.

"If you do, I will never speak to you again. Gah. I need to shut up now."

Pulling her close, "It's okay, Van. I get it. People can be attractive—but it doesn't mean you'll act upon it. Over the years, I've had my own celebrity crushes."

"Stop. I don't want to hear about any. I'd rather stay in ignorant bliss. Trust me, jealousy doesn't look good on me and I'd truly rather not know."

"I love *you*, Van. For the record—NO ONE holds a candle to you. Famous—or not—You're all I'll ever need."

"I love you, too, Dame," she whispers as she hugs me tight.

Jules rushes up. "You never said we'd get to see a real princess, Dame."

"Princess?" I ask, looking around.

Pointing to Dani, she whisper-shouts like her mom. "She's right there. It's like a fairy tale." Even though Dani's in the house and away from the crowd, she's not doing a great job of keeping hidden. It might be her wedding day, but I'm sure she'd never pass up the opportunity to meet my girls.

Reaching for her hand, I grab Vanessa's with the other. "Let's go meet the princess, then."

I swear I hear Vanessa groan, "Ohmigod."

"But I'll warn you, Dani's not really a princess—even though she may act like one today. She's just my sister, so don't be disappointed."

Walking across the back deck, Mom opens the door. "Mind if we meet the bride?" I ask, eying each girl holding my hands.

"Not at all!" Dani shouts from behind her. "Get in here, so I can meet 'em."

Vanessa's hand squeezes mine tighter as we approach. I return it to let her know everything will be fine. "Jules, this is my sister Dani. She's the *princess* you're dying to meet. But trust me—she may be wearing a tiara, but she's very much like you and me."

"Aww, you're so sweet to think I'm a princess. Is it Jules?"

"Julia. But you can call me Jules. All my friends do. I think princesses should, too. Besides, you're Dame's sister, and that makes us friends, doesn't it?" She adorably looks to me for assurance, and I nod in approval.

"Well, you can call me Dani—It's short for Danika," my sister says as she bends to look Jules in the eye. "You'd better consider me a friend. Damien's my baby brother and if you're a friend of his—you're stuck with me, too."

"See? Told you nothing special about her," I tease.

"Damien," Vanessa chides as she tugs on my hand. Like that would stop me from harassing my sister.

"Dan—I'd like you to meet my girlfriend Vanessa. Fair warning—she's read all of your books, and I completely didn't think to mention your alter ego. So, your rule of family not reading your books won't stick with her, got it? And for the record—I had no idea she read your books when we started dating—so I can't be found at fault either."

Laughing, Dani stands to pull Vanessa in a hug. "It's so nice to meet you. And don't worry, I'm not that scary. I just didn't need my brothers or Dad reading my smecksy scenes, if ya know what I mean?"

Laughing, Vanessa agrees, "I can see that. It's nice to meet you."

"Nice to meet you, too." Then my sister cocks her head from the side and looks between Julia and Vanessa. "Wait... you're Vanessa Larson, right? I thought I recognized you from your profile pic. It's of Julia and you, right?"

"Ohmigoodness," Vanessa rushes out. Then her jaw drops. "You recognize... me?"

"Well, you've been in my fan group for years. Of course I do. We'll have to catch up sometime." Then she shrugs. "Probably won't happen at the wedding, but next time. Promise you'll come up for a game with Dame. We can make a girls' weekend out of it," she says, including Jules, and my heart soars. I could kiss my sister for her kindness toward Vanessa. "Besides, who else will fill you in on all the dirty details of all that is Damien?" She smirks in my direction, and my adoration for her is lost.

"It's time. All the guests are here." Stacey pops her head in the sliding glass door.

"That's our cue," Vanessa says as she ushers Julia toward the door. "By the way, you look breathtaking. Congratulations, Dani. I'm so happy for you and Luke."

An emotional "Thank you" is uttered as we walk out the door.

To my surprise, more guests have arrived. There are a few couples seated on both sides of the aisle. From the looks of it, they must be Renegade players—based on their size alone. The others must be close friends of Luke and Dani. I recognize some faces but don't quite remember their names.

Taking a seat alongside my brothers, Vanessa, Jules, and I sit behind my parents. "I can't see," Julia whispers to her mom, and I motion for her to come sit on my lap since I'm taller.

Luke, his dad, and Sean Peters, the team's get-back coach stand at the front of the gathering. With their backs to the water, they wait for the ceremony to begin. The view of Mt. Rainier and Puget Sound as a backdrop, they couldn't have picked a more beautiful place for their wedding.

With Vanessa's hand in mine and Julia on my lap, there's no place I'd rather be, so I'm glad I didn't make that bet with her last night. As I look to Derek, he's clearly enjoying himself as well—so it looks like he's out some cash when all is said and done.

When the music indicates the ceremony's beginning, I hoist Jules right along with me so she can see as I stand to greet my beautiful sister. Stacey walks down the aisle separated by chairs, and Dani waits eagerly at the edge of the deck.

Dani's stunning. Sunlight glistens off the intricate beads on her dress and sends a glow around her. Dad stands beside her and whispers something to make her smile even wider, and I can feel her excitement from here.

Glancing to Luke, his expression is priceless. A combination of love, adoration, and excitement all in one. His father pats him on the back and he exhales slowly as he waits impatiently for Dani to meet him.

Once the music stops, Sean speaks to the crowd. "I've been told there once was a time when Dani was jealous of my relationship with Coach. But rest assured, I only got handsy as part of my job."

The crowd hoots in laughter as Dani's eyes dart to Luke. "Ohmigod, you did not tell him that."

Luke simply shrugs. He is so guilty.

Sean clears his throat to continue. "Now, I'm here to guide both Dani and Luke in matrimony, with you as our honored guests. Thank you for joining us. You may be seated."

As Sean recites an opening prayer then performs the ceremony, I never let go of Vanessa. Maybe it's my conversation with Jules earlier, but I know I want to propose sooner than later. As I watch my sister and Luke, I process what needs to be done to make this happen.

When Sean states, "It's my understanding that you wrote your own vows. With her being the romance writer, I wish you the best of luck, Luke. Just remember marriage isn't a competition."

"Yeah, right," can be heard from across the aisle, and the crowd erupts again.

Dani clears her throat and begins, "I'll keep this short and simple. Luke, the moment I crashed into your life, I did more than fall for you. You became a part of me, and I can't imagine my life without you. You push me to be better, you're understanding when I get lost in my head, and you support me with each and every endeavor I can think of. You're more than just my ride or die. You're my best friend in the entire world. You're my heart, my soul, and a part of my every breath. I know I'm capable of walking in this world without you—but I choose to be with you because you've made me see that life is better when you can share your ups and downs with someone. You've made the world more colorful, and I can't wait to start this magnificent adventure with you."

Sean looks to the groom. "Luke?"

"I'm not a professional wordsmith... so bear with me."

The crowd chuckles as Dani shakes her head.

"When I came home that week for a much-needed break, I got a lot more than I bargained for. Little did I know this fiery, fierce female who flew over her handlebars would quickly become the center of my world. Who knew something as suave as fixing a bike tire would lead to this, right?"

Luke has to wait for the crowd to settle before continuing.

I can feel the love Luke has for my sister when he pins her with his eyes. "Danika Marie Fallon, it certainly has been a wild ride so far. To the world, I'm Luke Leighton. But for the first time in forever—in your eyes, I was just Luke. You saw the real me and loved me anyway. You put up with my hectic schedule. You understand that I'm far from perfect but at the end of the day—you're my true partner in life. I can't wait to grow old with you, travel the world with you—even if it means attending your book signings, and I can't wait to start forever with you. I love you so much. Thank you for saying yes to this amazing adventure."

The rest of the ceremony goes by in a blur. The next thing I know, Sean announces that Luke can kiss his bride.

After some jeers from the crowd, like "Get a room," Luke and Dani break their kiss with wide, unapologetic smiles. Love looks amazing on them.

Instead of walking down the aisle, Luke stops to address the crowd. "As many of you know, we've chartered a boat and arranged cars—well, my amazing assistant Harlow planned everything—let's give credit where it's due." Everyone laughs, and Luke waits to continue, "Cars are at your disposal for the rest of the evening. Please join us for our reception at the Tacoma Glass Museum—where we'll dance to my wife's favorite music." He turns to Dani. "Wife. I love the sound of that."

"Luke." She points to the crowd, and we laugh at the fact he's forgotten about us.

"We'll dance, eat, and party the night away. Thanks for being here on such short notice. It means the world to Dani and me to have you here to celebrate with us."

The crowd erupts in cheers, and Dani and Luke proceed down the aisle.

The reception is everything you'd expect and then some. Except, instead of dancing with old aunts and uncles, we're rubbing elbows with the majority of his team as they're close friends.

Jules is excited to dance with some newfound friends as she quickly finds a few guests her age to dance once the music starts. Vanessa and I join her, and we dance the night away.

I offer to take Jules home early, but Vanessa just shrugs. "She'll make it for one night staying up late. Besides—how often does your sister get married? Just be warned, she'll still wake at the crack of dawn and will likely be crabby."

Knowing what we're in for, I follow Vanessa's lead. Besides, the reception ends at ten, so I'll take my chances with Jules. Holding Vanessa close in my arms, I whisper, "I think I can handle that. By the way, have I told you I love you?"

32

VANESSA

THANKFULLY, we've planned a lazy day on the island before traveling to Seattle. Julia actually sleeps until after ten. Damien was the sweetest as he carried her from the limo all the way to his truck at the marina. Jules didn't even move as he buckled her into her car seat or transferred her from his truck to her bed. I'm sure a bomb could've detonated, and she would've been none the wiser, in her exhausted state.

Today, we're exploring downtown Seattle. Damien insists on making it fun for Jules. We'll walk along the pier, check out the aquarium, hit Pike Place Market, and explore the City Center. We have two entire days, so we're not in a rush and can let things flow with our schedule.

As we drive past the Rainier Renegade Stadium in Tacoma, it's hard to believe only days ago, we hung out with the team as if it were any given Saturday, and I wasn't at my favorite author's wedding. I still feel the need to pinch myself when I take stock of the events of this week. Sure, I may have freaked out, but once I started to see her through Damien's eyes, I managed to rein in my inner fan girl. I still can't believe she recognized me among her thousands of fans. It was an honor, to say the least. Don't even get me started on the fact she wants to hang with me—and we'll attend a Rainier Renegades game.

Jules has no idea she just spent an entire evening among famous athletes and a few of their families. They were warm and welcoming. It was amazing how at ease they made us feel.

We let Jules wake up on her own this morning before saying goodbye to Damien's family. They are the sweetest when they insist we return soon. They also promise to see Damien's new place soon and can't wait to see us girls again, either.

I absolutely love how accepting they are of Jules and me. His brothers are a riot. They made me laugh non-stop. Knowing Davis lives in Portland, before we left, I invited him to visit when he has a chance. Damien was on board with it and insists if they go out, I join in the fun. We'll see how that goes.

From the moment we arrived, his mom and grandma treated me as if I were one of their own. Even though we just left this morning, and it feels weird to admit, I miss them already. I hadn't realized how much those day-to-day conversations with my mom meant to me. You know the ones you take for granted because you can just pop into their room and hang out with them for a bit. Daisy and Beatrice made me feel as if Mom was watching over me this week as well.

"Everything okay over there?" Damien asks, squeezing my

hand as we walk along the crowded boardwalk. We're almost to the aquarium, and Damien has Jules hoisted on his shoulders so she can see above the people passing by. I'm sure some of it has to do with the fact she's eager to see everything, we keep having to practically run to keep up with her, but she hasn't complained once since she climbed aboard.

"Yeah. Being with your family's amazing—but it also made me miss mine." I shrug, then quickly add, "It's not a bad thing. I just miss girl time with my mom. Being with your mom and grandma reminds of happy times." When he doesn't look convinced, I quickly add, "Don't worry, I'm just reminiscing."

"My family adores both you and Jules. For the record, I'm sure they'll be down to visit sooner than later, for your sake more than mine."

I stop in my tracks and turn to him. "What do you mean?" That makes no sense.

Shrugging, he sighs. "It's nothing. Just a hunch. That and the fact my dad actually said he'd better get down our way to watch Jules ride her bike and learn to skateboard. Apparently, she's invited them to check out her new tricks."

"But your parents live like six hours away..." I say in disbelief.

"I'm sure that won't stop 'em. They've driven further for less important things for us as kids. She's made quite an impression."

I'd say. Jules, Trent, and Daisy danced song after song at the reception together, much like I can picture my parents doing if they'd been here. She has everyone wrapped around her finger. I just hope they realize she's not always smiles and sunshine. Sometimes she's a torrential terror, too. Thankfully, those moments are few and far between, because when her head starts to spin, no one's having a good day.

As we walk past a shop, Jules shouts as she points, "Look," at a giant unicorn that's likely bigger than her standing on its own in the window.

"Whoa, that's the biggest one I've ever seen!" Damien exclaims. "I don't even think that would fit in my truck."

"You're silly, Dame. You have a *truck*. Isn't that what the back is for?"

"I meant the cab. That would be precious cargo—it would need to ride up front, wouldn't it?" he hedges.

Before either of them gets any crazy ideas, I quickly interject, "There's no way we're packing anything like that around when we've got an aquarium to explore."

Damien shrugs in disappointment. "She's right, squirt. I'm already carrying you—and I'll want my hands free for the hands-on exhibits. Last time I was here, I pet the coolest sea anemone and octopus."

"Really?" Jules gasps in excitement. "Momma said we might see a giant dogfish that's a shark and looks nothing like a dog. Do you think we'll see that, too?"

"We won't know until we get there," I remind her.

"Well, what are we waiting for? Can't your long legs move faster?" Julia encourages.

"Hold your horses, sassy pants," I admonish. "We've got all day."

Thankfully, the aquarium is only a few blocks away, and it's our first stop for the day.

Having purchased our tickets online, we skip the line for admission. Julia's excitement to explore the hands-on exhibits is almost comical as she hop-skips to each station. Oh,

to be young and full of energy.

Damien grabs my hand as we trail behind her and whispers in my ear, "Don't ya wish we could see the world through her eyes? So much excitement and wonder. I was just like her at that age."

"True," I admit. "Though, there's no way I would've willingly touched an octopus at that age. Something about their tentacles creeped me out."

"I can see that." Then he admits, "I was shy at first but couldn't let Dani outdo me. Then once I did, I got over it, ya know?"

"Oh, I totally get sibling rivalry. Trust me."

Damien leans in and kisses me quickly. "Damn, you're adorable, Van."

His lips on mine make me momentarily lose my train of thought.

Then he whispers, "I absolutely love that look on your face, too," he whispers then pulls me in the direction of Jules.

Shaking my head at his absurdity, I get about two steps, and my stomach plummets. I swear my heart rate slows, and I feel each pulse flow through my ears.

God, I must be seeing things.

Of course, Damien notices and quickly asks, "What's wrong, Van?"

As if my tongue is glued to the roof of my mouth, I can't find the words.

This can't be happening... I must be seeing things.

Damien's face fills with concern. "Van, you're pale. Talk to me."

"I... uh..." I start, but my eyes dart to Julia instead. There she is completely unaware and carefree. "I swear I just saw Julia's biological father," I whisper so Jules doesn't hear.

Damien's eyes dart around, but Zach is nowhere to be found. Besides, the room is full of men, how would he know who to look for?

"He just disappeared," I whisper. "But I swear it was him."

"Are you okay? He won't hurt you or anything, will he?"

"Zach?" I shake my head. "No, he won't hurt me. But I haven't seen him since the day I told him I was pregnant. It's just... weird," I trail off when I can't find the words to describe my emotions aloud.

"Dame, do you see this?" Jules gushes over a tidepool.

"I'll be right there, Jules," Dame assures her but before he moves a step in her direction, he turns to me. "What do you want me to do?"

Hell, I don't even know what to do. Should I talk to Zach, or just ignore it? It might not have even been him, and I could be making a mountain out of a mole hill.

"Let's just enjoy the afternoon with Jules," I offer, trying not to let my nerves get the better of me. Even if it was Zach, what difference does it make? "I'm not even sure it was him."

"Van," Damien warns. "I'll follow your lead, but please don't pretend for my sake. Clearly, seeing him has upset you."

"I know," I agree. "But I don't want this to impact Jules. I... I just haven't thought about him in so long... and I didn't expect to see him after all these years. Honestly, it might not have been him, so I'd rather not talk about it right now if that's okay with you."

Damien pins me in place as he contemplates his next move. I see questions in his eyes, but his lips remain pursed. Slowly, he takes a deep breath and sighs. "Okay. But this conversation isn't over."

I nod in understanding as I turn my attention on Jules. "What did you find, squirt?"

She gushes about a sea creature. I may be here in person, but my mind feels a million miles away. What on earth would Zach be doing here? He hated this town and once he left, he swore he wouldn't come back.

If it is him, what will I tell Jules? She's never asked about her father, so I haven't bothered to explain. Have I been a shitty parent in doing so?

No. Zach terminated his rights before he even laid eyes on her. I haven't done anything wrong. We were young and nowhere near in love. Hell, we broke up before I even found out I'd missed my first period.

When Damien squeezes my hand, I'm brought to the present. "Van, you sure you're okay?"

Okay? I have no freaking clue how I feel. But when I look to Jules, I nod and attempt to smile, but Damien knows me well enough to see right through me.

Spotting a restroom ahead, I say, "I'm just going to pop in here for a minute. Do you mind keeping an eye on Jules? It's not that big of a place that I won't be able to find you if you move on from this area, too."

Torn, Damien looks from Jules to me. Clearly sensing I need a moment, he sighs as he pulls me in for a hug and kisses the top of my head. "Sure. Take all the time you need." He's quiet for a moment as he looks over my head. I shouldn't be surprised when he says, "Hey, there's a café over there with caramel macchiatos. Why don't you get yourself one of those and relax a bit? Don't worry about Jules. We'll just keep exploring." But I am. I may be out of sorts, but when he squeezes me once more, I relax into him.

Of course, Jules takes this exact moment to grab our attention, "Hey, Dame, check this out!"

Chuckling, Damien shakes his head as he releases me. "Duty calls. I've got this. Go," he points to the café, "and relax."

Walking into the women's room, I'm relieved to find myself more or less alone. There's just one person at the sink when I step into a stall. After doing my business, I find myself at the counter, staring at myself in the mirror as I wash my hands.

As I catch my own reflection I lock eyes on myself and mentally ask, *What the hell is wrong with you? Why the hell are you freaking out? You've done nothing wrong. Fuck, you don't even know if it was Zach out there.*

Clearly, I have issues I still need to deal with. I thought I was past all this. Why am I being this way? This isn't me.

I finish washing my hands and reach for the paper towel under the mirror. Knowing I have to let this go, I give myself one last message before leaving.

You're not that same young and naïve girl anymore. You've

got your shit figured out and despite everything, you've raised one hell of a girl out there. You've got this. No matter what life throws at you—you will get through it. For her sake and yours.

With that, I dry my hands and promptly leave.

With a newfound confidence, I fling open the door and make my way to the café, where I place my order and wait for it. The moment I hear the barista call my name, I step up to the counter to grab my drink, only to turn around and bump into someone.

"Umph." Thank God, I manage to keep my caramel concoction safe.

"I'm so sorry, Vanessa," a familiar voice says. "I thought it was you, and I was going to say something. But you turned around unexpectedly before I could say anything."

"Zach." My voice clearly shows my shock though I'm not sure why. I was certain it had been him.

His dark-brown eyes are wary, and his lips purse. I know this look. It's the look he has when his confidence is gone, and he's unsure of himself. After a few moments of awkward silence, his eyes dart to a nearby table, and he tilts his head in that direction. "I... uh..." He looks to me then the table once more. "I... uh, know I have no right to ask you, but can we sit for a few minutes?"

Zach's well over six feet and from the looks of it, he's even better physically fit than I remember, but his cocky swagger I remember from high school is nowhere to be found. He's never been a shy person, so this must be difficult for him.

Somehow, I manage to remain calm and much more

collected than I feel. My mind swirls with questions, but it's best to just let him get what he has to say out there.

"Sure," I agree, knowing I'd rather confront whatever he has to say head on.

I'm no longer the young, gullible girl he knew in school. I've always known at some point we'd need to have this conversation; I just didn't expect it to be today.

"Thank you," comes out rough and whispered.

With much more confidence than I feel, I slip into the seat at the high-top table beside me, and he takes the chair across from me. Looking him over, there's something different about him that I can't quite pinpoint.

"How have you been?" he asks with genuine concern.

There's no malice in his voice like the last time we spoke. But I can't help but wonder, "Why do you care?" I shock myself by saying it aloud, which causes him to smirk as he nods.

"Okay. I deserve that."

We're both silent for a few moments as he looks to the sky then back at me. When our eyes meet, his narrow. He inhales deeply, and a hand runs down his face as he releases it. He starts to say something but stops.

It takes everything in me not to pepper him with questions, but somehow I manage to stick with my original one.

"Seriously..." I start, needing to know why he approached me. This awkward silence is killing me. "Why do you care?" This time, of course, all snarkiness has disappeared because there's something about the way he's looking at me that makes me feel as if this isn't the time to be petty.

"Look," he sighs and looks to the table for a moment. "I know I have no right to ask. But I genuinely am curious how you are. I know I pulled a total dick move back then, but I'm not that same person anymore."

"Trust me. None of us are," I agree.

"No. You don't get it. I couldn't tell you everything."

"Couldn't or didn't want to?" I hedge. Everyone has a choice, and he clearly made his.

His head hangs in shame, but his eyes find mine. "Couldn't."

"You made your choice a long time ago, and I have written proof of it," I remind him sternly. Nothing he says or does is going to change the choice he made.

His eyes widen in shock, and he quickly shakes his head. "No. You've got it all wrong. I'm not here to make things more difficult for you. I honestly want to just know how you're doing and clear the air, so to speak. I certainly don't expect or deserve anything from you..." he trails off then shrugs. "Including this conversation."

All I can do is nod in agreement because everything he's said is true.

But pulling a dick move on him won't make things better either.

Summoning all my inner strength, I pull in a long breath, then take a sip of my drink.

"To answer your question, I'm doing much better now." My manners get the best of me, and I tack on, "How are you?"

He ignores the question and presses on. "I heard about

your parents. I'm sorry for your loss. Your dad was a great man. I owe him everything."

What? Why would he owe my dad anything?

"I don't understand?" I admit, trying to connect the dots.

"You see, I'd been in a group home when we met," he starts as he plays with the bottled water in his hand. "I guess at the time, I didn't tell you because I'd been too proud to admit I'd come from nothing. I was put in the system when I was six and bounced around from home to home, until I ended up being too old. I knew I would age out before anyone adopted me."

Holy shit. How did I not know this?

"I was young and stupid, Vanessa. But that's no excuse."

"What does any of this have to do with my dad?" I interrupt because I don't want to hear why he broke up with me after we'd finally had sex. We'd dated for almost six months, but the moment we had sex, he broke it off.

Zach lets out a low, humorous laugh. "You see, your dad knew I was turning eighteen in a matter of weeks when we were last together. I'd done something stupid..." he trails off as his focus returns to his water bottle.

"You mean besides getting me pregnant?"

"For the record, I broke up with you before we even knew. Your dad found out I'd been involved in a heist that would land me in jail, if I didn't take his deal."

Did Dad force him to break up with me? Yeah, Dad was a lawyer, who worked in the DA's office. But he wouldn't stand in the way of justice to protect me. What am I missing? "Explain," I demand.

"You see, I was innocent, but I was still guilty by association. My buddies at the time, you remember Jared and Paul? Well, they broke into someone's house and stole enough that it was considered a felony."

Knowing there's more to his story, I probe, "What did you have to do with it?"

Grimacing, he rolls his eyes. "I was stupid enough to store some of their shit in my backpack. When the arrest went down, I went down with them. But your dad saved me."

"First, he told me I had to break up with you, and he'd represent me. He didn't want his daughter dating anyone who was stupid enough to get himself into this situation. I cared about you enough to agree with him." He hangs his head for a moment, then returns his sad gaze to me. "But when he learned about my past, he took pity on me and worked his magic. I gave the prosecutors all the information they needed, in exchange for the charges being dropped."

"How did I not know any of this?" I ask in disbelief.

"Part of my deal was to use what tools I had to get out of the system. I'd already been accepted to the Navy Academy. By some miracle, my ACT scores and the help of Mr. Barnes, our school counselor, I'd procured letters from Senator Beck and a few local law enforcement officers before any of this went down. Your dad told me it was in all of our best interest to let him take care of things and get me out of town. My so-called friends were pretty pissed that I'd rolled on them, and it wasn't safe for me to stick around at the time."

"Why are you back now then?" I ask as I process this information dump he just gave me. I'm not sure which weighs more on my heart, the fact that Dad went behind my back to get rid of Zach, or that Zach thought he was in danger.

"I'm home on leave visiting my biological sister. We were separated as kids, but now that we're older, we're in touch with one another. She was only a year older than me but couldn't care for herself, let alone me back then."

Looking around, I ask, "Are you safe now?" needing to know if my association with him in this moment might bring trouble to my door.

"Yeah," and I instantly relax. "Those guys only did a few months and were released. Paul didn't learn his lesson and is back in with a ten-year sentence. Jared, on the other hand, cleaned up his act and found a way to contact me through our guidance counselor at the high school. Well, we've always stayed in contact. He's the reason your dad helped me, too... Anyway, Jared reached out, and we've made amends. He never blamed me for taking the deal. He was one of the few who knew my real situation and knew I didn't need anything else holding me back."

"So... I was holding you back?" I'm not sure why after all he's told me, that this is the most shocking.

"No!" he says adamantly. "I promised your dad I wouldn't drag you down with me. The night... we ... uh... well, that was my idiotic way of saying goodbye to you. You meant a lot to me. I'm so sorry for what I've put you through."

"What? Say goodbye and leave me with a baby?" I practically squeal.

"No. Fuck. We found out you were pregnant right as the trial was starting. Your dad didn't want any of my shame touching you or the baby. Not knowing what I know now, I agreed. I was just a good-for-nothing kid who grew up in the system. I wanted more for my child's life than to have a chump like me as their father. I thought they deserved better, and your dad agreed. It was a part of the reason I went to Running Start our senior year at the local community college, so we wouldn't see one another, if I could help it."

Wow. Just wow.

"I'm so sorry I wasn't there for you when they died. I'd shipped off a week earlier to boot camp and didn't hear about it until almost two years later when I'd finally come back on leave. By then, you'd moved, and I didn't want to bring drama into your life. You'd already been through so much. You certainly didn't need my sorry ass coming around. Besides, I'd signed away my rights, and I didn't want to cause you any problems. I made a promise to your dad, and I intended to keep my word to him after all he did for me."

I have no freaking words. This is unreal. Someone must be pulling one hell of a prank on me. In a matter of minutes, he's unraveled my entire perception of what went down between us—and my dad played a part in it. How did I not know? When I signed the papers to have sole custody of my unborn child, I thought it was because he'd just completely abandoned us. I knew he wanted to join the Navy, but when he disappeared, I never knew what happened to him.

Well, I never wanted to see him again either. So, there's that, too.

Out of the corner of my eye, I spot Damien with Julia. The moment our eyes meet, he gives me a silent nod and steers Julia in the opposite direction of Zach and me. God, that man is a saint. I have no idea if Julia should meet Zach. This would upend her world. I'm not sure either of us are ready for that.

Watching my gaze, Zach quietly asks, "Is that her?"

"Yes," I whisper, not knowing what else to say.

"Her name is Julia, right?" He surprises me once again by knowing her name.

He quickly adds, "Your dad sent me a picture the day she was born, but I was only told her first name."

Holy shit. "Was Dad ever going to tell me?"

"Van?" he whispers, drawing my attention. "I'm so sorry. I think he would've once he knew I'd made good on my promise and straightened my act. You have to understand, I was trying to do what I thought was best for you. We were so young, and all the shit I was in would've brought you down right along with me."

Millions of questions rush to my lips, but I stick with the most important. "What do you want from me now?"

"Nothing. I can't ask anything of you. I lost that chance years ago. But I wouldn't be opposed to being friends—well, at least not enemies. I'm sure you hate me for all that I've done—and I deserve that. I get it."

"I never hated you," I admit. "I knew we were young and as much as I liked you—we weren't in love. I just didn't expect you to disappear the way you did. But thank you for shedding some light on that. Julia's the best thing that's ever happened to me. Without her and my brother Vince, I would've never survived my parents' death. I've never regretted getting pregnant with her, because from the moment I came to grips with my pregnancy, I loved her."

Zach says nothing but nods in understanding.

"It hasn't been easy, but I have zero regrets. Does that make sense?"

His voice is filled with emotion as he whispers, "Yeah. I think I understand. But what... what does she know about me?"

Guilt flashes through me as I see the deepest regret in his eyes.

"Uh, I honestly don't know. She's never brought it up, and neither have I," I admit.

"Do you think...?" he starts, then stops, and stares at a hole in the table as he chooses his next words carefully. Once he's formulated his thoughts, he looks to me with unshed tears. "Look. I don't want to cause any trouble for you or more importantly, her. But do you think..." he trails off as he swallows hard. "Do you think I could meet her?"

I seriously have no idea what to say, as I swallow down the swarm of emotions engulfing me in this moment.

"It's completely up to you, and I have no right to even ask. I understand that more than you know. I'm not looking to upend her life or change anything. You can even introduce me as a friend from high school. She never has to know if that's how you want it. I totally respect that, too. It's just... it's hard to be this close to her and not at least say hello."

"I... uh..." God, what do I do? Can I just go over there and introduce the two of them, as if he's my long-lost friend? Should I tell her who he is? Someday, she'll want to know.

"Look, I'm not trying to create chaos in her life. If you want to tell her who I am *someday*, I'll respect that. I will. And if you never want to say anything, I'll live with that, too. If you need me to walk away and not look back, I'll accept your choice. I'm not trying to pressure you in any way. Please know that."

The sincerity in his eyes lets me know he's telling the truth.

"I know," I mutter, taking a long pull of my drink through my straw to buy me more time.

Looking to heaven, I ask the universe, *what should I do?*

And the universe answers as Julia hollers, "Mommy, look. Look What Dame got me!"

33

DAMIEN

THIRTY MINUTES EARLIER...

"VAN, YOU SURE YOU'RE OKAY?"

Blinking as if she's just been brought back to reality, Van glances at the restroom doors nearby. "I'm just going to pop in here for a minute. Do you mind keeping an eye on Jules? It's not that big of a place. I'm sure I can find you if you move on from this area."

I want to be there for her, but I can tell she needs a moment to herself, too. Sighing, I pull her to me and hug her, and I kiss the top of her head. God, I love this woman. I'd do anything to take this torment away from her. Who knows if she's seen her ex, but either way, she needs a break from Jules to reset herself.

"Sure. Take all the time you need." Holding her longer than necessary, I spot something that just might bring her out of this funk she's in—and give her a way to relax. "Hey, there's a café over there with caramel macchiatos. Why don't you get yourself one of those and relax a bit? Don't worry about Jules.

We'll just keep exploring." I know I've said the right thing when she relaxes into me.

In all too short of time, Jules exclaims, "Hey, Dame, check this out!"

Chuckling, I shake my head and release Vanessa. "Duty calls. I've got this. Go." I point to the café. "Relax."

My feet feel as if they're filled with cement as I walk away from Vanessa. But knowing Jules needs my attention, I make the most of it. Being with her is effortless, and my worries melt away momentarily as I get lost in her world.

To give Vanessa a chance to relax, I encourage Julia to explore a new part of the museum. We're in luck when we round the corner and find they're starting a live octopi presentation. We're lucky to grab a front row bench. Jules can barely contain her excitement as she eagerly looks at the different tanks in front of her.

As soon as Chris, our official guide to the world under the sea, introduces himself, he starts by asking the crowd questions. Jules participates eagerly by sitting on the edge of her seat and raising her hand, in hopes of getting called on. We quickly learn everything from the fact there are over three hundred different octopi species, to what they eat, and even that they can live up to five thousand feet under the ocean.

Jules practically jumps out of her skin when he asks her, "How many brains does an octopus have?"

Eagerly, she guesses, "Three?"

Her eyes nearly bug out when he simply shakes his head. "Nope. Besides the central brain, each tentacle has its own mini brain. So, that's a total of nine."

Jules' jaw drops as she mutters, "Holy cow."

Chris just nods and continues his presentation.

She's so freaking adorable. She's like a sponge absorbing the wealth of information Chris shares. Every once in a while, she turns to me and whispers, "Can you believe that?" as she repeats her newfound knowledge.

My heart melts when she grabs my hand from my lap and locks her fingers in mine. I'm not sure how this one little gesture can have such an impact, but it does. She's wormed her way so deep into my heart, there's nothing I wouldn't do for her—or her mom for that matter.

When the presentation ends, Julia looks around quizzically as she finally remembers her mom is missing. "Where's Momma?"

"She stopped off to get some coffee. She'll catch up to us in a bit."

Julia smiles innocently. "Momma *loves* coffee. 'Specially when it's quiet. Does your momma like her alone time with coffee, too?"

Chuckling, I admit, "She did when I was your age, that's for sure." God knows how Mom handled four of us under foot all the time.

Knowing Van hasn't sought us out, I try to buy her more time. "What do you say we check out more things and let your momma have her quiet time?"

It's been over twenty minutes, and even though I'm enjoying my time with Jules, my mind isn't far from Vanessa. The longer she waits, the more I worry something might be bothering her more than she let on.

When we get in view of the café, my chest tightens when I see her sitting at one of the high-top tables, across from a guy her age. Clearly, she's not comfortable by the way her frame remains rigid as they speak. Her expression reads more of shock than anger, upon further inspection.

As if she can sense I'm looking at her, she glances up to me with an unsure expression. I'm dying to know if she's okay, but I don't want to drop a bomb on Julia either.

Shit, if I wait too long, Julia will notice her mom, too. Fuck, should I take Julia over to meet him, or give them their space?

Is this Julia's biological father? He doesn't look much like her—but then again, she's all Vanessa.

Does he want to be a part of her life after all these years? I have no fucking idea why he's even been away. Since Julia's never met him, I'm guessing there has to be a good reason. I just wish I knew what it was.

Glancing over, I see Vanessa's expression relax. She nods once at me, assuring she's okay—for now.

In a split-second decision, I offer to Jules, "Wanna check out the gift shop?"

Oblivious to my sudden panic, Julia's eyes widen, and her face splits in two with one of the largest grins. "Where is it?"

Since it's in the opposite direction from her mom, I steer her in there and occupy her time for as long as possible, walking around the shop to ensure she sees everything before we purchase the one item I promised her.

I'm not sure how convincing I am when my mind's stuck on the café outside, but Julia's so eager to find her one prize for the day, she hardly pays me any attention. Eventually, she's made her decision. After listening to the octopi presentation, she wants a small stuffed gray octopus to remember the occasion.

As we walk out of the gift shop, my eyes immediately find Vanessa. She's still in deep conversation. Shit. Where else can I focus Julia's attention?

Unfortunately, I can't give Vanessa any more time because Julia spots her and gushes, "Mommy, look. Look what Dame got me!"

Vanessa's smile doesn't quite meet her eyes as she pretends to eagerly ask, "What's that, love bug?"

Julia rushes into her mom's awaiting arms, holding up my most recent purchase.

When Vanessa's eyes meet mine, I shrug and mouth, "Sorry. I tried."

Vanessa nods in understanding as she refocuses her attention on the plush octopus in Julia's hands.

The man at the table makes a movement which catches all our attention. Then he shifts awkwardly as if he wasn't quite ready for us to notice him.

His eyes never leave Julia as Vanessa clears her throat. She suddenly looks unsure of herself as she starts, "Um... Jules? This is... um... a friend of mine from high school. His name is Zach." Then she turns to Zach who's doing all he can to keep his face free from emotion.

Unknowingly, Julia turns to greet her biological father in the way she would any friend of hers. "Hi! Did you know an octopus has nine brains? Can you believe each tentacle has a mini brain in it? Isn't that crazy?" Then Julia turns to me,

"Dame just took me to see this man who told us all about it. You missed out on so much fun, Momma."

"I'm sure I did," Vanessa agrees.

Zach's stoic expression cracks as well as his voice, as he says his daughter's name. "Julia... it's so nice to finally meet you. Your mom's been telling me a lot about you."

Julia scrutinizes Zach the way she would anyone new in her life, then smiles. "You have a lot of tattoos. What does that one say?" she asks innocently, and my heart drops through my stomach.

"April twenty-third," Zach admits quietly.

Julia's eyes widen as she asks, "Really?"

Zach's eyes blink rapidly as he nods once, but his lips press in a straight line, as if he's holding back from saying more.

Julia misses this as she rushes out, "That's my birthday."

"It's a special day for me, too," Zach admits quietly as he keeps his eyes trained on her.

I have zero doubt this is a coincidence.

When I look to Vanessa, her eyes are wide, and the pit in my stomach churns as a sense of déjà vu hits me. Ohmigod, it feels like Amber all over again. He may have been absent for the last few years, but he hasn't forgotten Julia—or Vanessa for that matter—with a tattoo like that. Clearly, they still mean something to him.

Julia smiles innocently. "That's cool. Momma says I can only have the fake kind of tattoos. But yours are real, right?"

This earns a genuine laugh and a smile that looks just like Julia's. "These are real, all right. Most of them have to do with something from the Navy, but a few are personal, too."

True to form, Jules begins to pepper Zach with questions. "What's the Navy?"

"It's a branch of the military. You know—the men and women who protect our country?" Vanessa intervenes.

"I start kindergarten next year. Did you know Momma then?"

Chuckling, Zach's posture relaxes. "No... I didn't meet your mom until high school. But just lookin' at you, I'm sure you're gonna grow up just like her."

Julia rolls her eyes. "Unks says I'm her mini-me."

"How is Vince?" Zach asks Vanessa.

"He's good. He attends Columbia River University with me and is vacationing this week in New York City," Vanessa answers.

Zach nods and quietly asks, "Are you still pursuing nursing?"

Apparently, he wasn't just a one-night stand. He genuinely cared about her at some point.

Vanessa nods. "I'll graduate next year."

"That's great." Zach nods. "You always knew what you wanted and never let anything get in your way."

For some reason, Vanessa finds this funny. "Nope. My family wouldn't let me, even if I tried."

"Yeah. I never thought they would," Zach agrees then turns his attention to me.

Vanessa quickly blurts out, "Geez, where are my manners?" With an apologetic smile, she says, "Zach, this is Damien."

Zach stands to shake my hand. "Nice to meet you, Damien."

The verdict's still out whether this is a good thing, so I just nod an acknowledgement.

"Momma, can I get something to eat? I'm hungry."

Vanessa looks at the long line at the counter and back to Julia and then to Zach with an expression that makes me wonder if they still have unfinished business. Instead of letting things get awkward, I offer, "Come on, Squirt; let's get you something to eat."

When relief washes over Vanessa's face, I know I've done the right thing. Julia hops to my side in an instant and reaches for my hand. "Thanks, Dame."

Looking to the table, I ask, "Anyone need anything else while I'm at it?"

Vanessa quickly says, "No, thanks. I'm good," as Zach shakes his head. His eyes keenly lock onto his daughter as she leans into me and wraps her other arm around mine. His lips flatten into a straight line, and his eyes become guarded.

Yeah, man, I'm a lucky bastard. I know without a doubt how amazing this girl beside me is. Whatever his excuse, he's missed out, and no amount of time or effort will change the fact he'll never get those days back.

Hell, I have no idea if he regrets not being in her life, or if he's just a sorry good-for-nothing, deadbeat dad. I probably shouldn't judge his situation until I hear more from Vanessa. But as Jules clings to me, I can't help but wonder his story.

As soon as Jules tugs me in the direction of the line, I look to Vanessa to ensure she's okay with being left alone again.

With a quick nod from her, I focus my attention to Jules. "Okay, Jules. What looks good?"

As we wait in line, Jules rambles over her decision of what to get, while I pretend not to focus my attention on the conversation at the table nearby. I'm far enough away that I can't make out their actual words over the noise around us, but I'm certain Vanessa's at least open to talking with Zach.

Once Julia and I get to the counter, she orders a chicken sandwich and an apple juice. Surprisingly, instead of running back to her mom, like she'd normally, she stays by my side. Grabbing my hand, she leans into me again as we wait.

By the time we return to the table, Zach looks to his watch then stands reluctantly. "Look, I've got a ferry to catch if I want to see my buddy in Bremerton. You've got my number. I'd love to stay and chat, but he's expecting me."

"I understand," Vanessa says. "I'll call you when we're back home." Then she stands and quickly hugs him. "I'm glad we ran into each other. I'll be in touch."

Zach turns to Julia and stares for a wordless moment. Then he swallows and finds his words. "It was nice meeting you, Julia. I hope you enjoy the rest of your time in Seattle."

"Dame is taking us to the Space Needle tomorrow!" she exclaims.

Looking between the three of us, Zach smiles and nods. "The view from the top is spectacular. I'm sure you'll have a great time."

An alarm buzzes from his phone. Apologetically, he looks between Vanessa and Julia. "I gotta run, but I'll be in touch."

Those simple words have my heart clenching and my mind

racing as déjà vu hits me like a ton of bricks. Those final days with Amber flash before me. At one time, I thought I was in love with her, but my feelings don't even hold a candle to the way I feel about these girls in front of me. There's so much more at stake, and I'm not sure I can handle the repercussions if this ends the same way.

When Vanessa nods, he doesn't say another word but pivots in a well-practiced move from being in the Navy and walks away. I'm surprised he doesn't look back as he retreats. He's either got his heart on lockdown, or he doesn't care. Either way, I find myself watching him exit the building because now more than ever, I'm afraid of what I'll find when I finally make eye contact with Vanessa.

34

DAMIEN

VANESSA and I go through the motions of sightseeing with Julia for the rest of the day. For the most part, we do our best to ignore the giant elephant in the room and just focus on the here and now. Hopefully, Julia is none the wiser to each of us being distant throughout the day. Obviously, we can't discuss anything in front of her, and the tension between us thickens as time wears on.

I manage to make it through the day by repeating the mantra, *this is not the same. Vanessa's not Amber.* However, no matter how I spin this in my mind, it's exactly the same—and my gut twists even further.

By the time we get back to the hotel later that evening, I offer to go out and get some snacks, while Jules takes a bath and gets ready for bed. We have promised she could watch a movie at the hotel and as the smart five-year old she is, she has claimed we can't watch a movie without snacks. So here I am, driving to the nearest grocery store.

When my phone rings, I accept it without looking at the caller ID because I'm sure it's likely Vanessa thinking of something she's forgotten.

"Hey, what did we forget to put on the list? I'm pulling into the store now," I say on a laugh.

"Well, dear..." my brother Derek chortles. "A million bucks and a nice juicy steak sounds amazing."

"Wouldn't we all like that," I snort.

"I was gonna ask if this is a bad time, but I'm sure you've learned to multi-task and can talk and shop at the same time."

"Yeah, I've picked up some skills... adulting and all." I pretend to grumble, but he knows better.

"Hey, man, I've got something I wanna run by you," he says, all joking aside.

Putting my truck in park, I stay in the vehicle so I can give him my full attention. "Okay. What's up?"

"I've got a major gig lined up that's gonna be all I need to venture on my own. Like I think I'm gonna put in my two-week notice and head to Denver so I can work closely with this client."

"Whoa, this is huge," I agree.

"I'm not stupid, am I? I mean, I've got over a year's worth of salary stalked away because I've been trying to venture out on my own and needed the start-up capital. But with this opportunity, I'd be a fool to stay with my current company. I still need to work out things like health care and depending on how long I stay down there, I might put my things in storage and rent out my home, but those are minor details. I can always fly home later to take care of it—if it turns into a long-term thing. For now, I've just gotta be there for the next few months or so as they get their branding in order company wide."

"Uh, what exactly do you need from me? It seems like you've already got it worked out."

"Yeah, I guess I do," he agrees quietly then adds, "There—I hit send. I've officially put in my notice."

"Well, that was quick. What the hell did you even call me for?"

"To make sure I wasn't losing my mind—to be my voice of reason."

"Dude, you already work remote—and from what you told us this weekend, you've had this plan in place for some time. I'm sure you're gonna kill it on your own."

"Yeah, you're right. It's just a huge risk to walk away from the benefits of this job. I have a feeling they'll want me to stay on as a consultant to finish some major projects they had planned for the next year, but if not, I've got plenty of other clients to keep me busy."

It takes a hell of a lot of guts to bet it all on yourself, but if anyone can do it, I'm sure it'll be Derek. "I'm proud of you, man. I am."

"How's your trip to Seattle? Is Jules enjoying the sights?"

"Yeah," I sigh as the events from today replay in my mind. "We went to the aquarium today and walked around Pike Place Market."

"What's going on, Dame? You don't sound like the man who was on top of the world—just yesterday."

I chuckle with no humor at his description. "I guess I was, wasn't I..."

How do I explain so he'll understand?

Concern echoes through the phone as he prompts, "Dame, what's going on?"

"Vanessa ran into Julia's biological father at the aquarium."

"No shit," Derek says in disbelief. "I got the impression he hasn't been in the picture. Was I wrong?"

My chest feels heavy as I admit, "No, D. This is the first time she's seen him since before Julia was born. She went to get a latte and relax after thinking she saw him—and when I returned with Jules from exploring a bit, I found them sitting at a table, talking."

"Okay..." he draws out, hoping I'll explain more.

I'm silent for a moment as I come to grips and release my biggest fears from the day. "Fuck. I feel like this is Amber all over again."

"It's not the same, Dame. It's not the same, trust me." Derek's voice is stern.

"How can it not be?" I ask, then proceed to tell him the unfortunate events of this morning. When I get to the part about Zach giving Vanessa his number and her saying she'll reach out, I ask, "What do I do, Derek?"

"I may not be the smartest man when it comes to a track record with women, but have you considered talking to her?"

"I haven't been able to with Jules around. So, I have to wait until we're alone or back at home," I sigh heavily.

"For what it's worth, I don't think this is the same as Amber—at all."

"You know..." I draw out, wondering where to start with the similarities. "I was thinking about proposing to Amber right before we ran into Xavier—her ex. Then they started talking again and within a month or so, she'd moved on and was living with him."

"Shit. I knew something happened, but I can see why you're freaking out now. Why didn't you share those details at the time, bro?"

Ignoring his question, I focus on Vanessa. "The thing is, D, I'd do anything for those girls. I love Julia as much, if not more than I love her mom. They're a package deal. But is it a dick move to not encourage her to be with the father of her child?"

"Do you know why they aren't together?" Derek asks quietly.

"That's the thing. I got the impression they broke things off even before she found out she was pregnant. I'm not sure he's ever been in the picture."

"Only you and Vanessa will be able to talk this out and get to the bottom of things. But if she loves you the way I think she does, I'm not sure any of this worrying will be worth it."

"Fuck, man, I even talked with Jules about possibly marrying her mom this weekend. Did I just give her the biggest mind fuck of all if her mom decides she wants to give Zach a chance?"

"Run that by me again?" Derek demands.

"Jules asked if I had a fiancée, and I told her no. She got upset."

"What did you do then?" His voice fills with concern.

"She asked what it meant to be a fiancée, and I told her it's what you call the person you intend to marry. And she didn't understand you weren't someone's fiancée until they agreed." Then the part about being her dad rips through my mind. "Fuck, man, she completely melted me when she told me she has an Unks but never has had a dad and asked me to be that person for her."

"Holy shit, what did you say?"

My emotions get the best of me, and my voice cracks when I admit, "I fuckin' promised her she'd be the first to know when it happens."

"The only thing you can do, Dame, is talk with Vanessa. Find out what's going on in her head and tell her how you feel. This isn't the time to pussy foot around though. You have to lay it all out on the table, so she knows her options. This also means you're gonna have to suck it up and have the patience of Job, if she needs some time."

Heavily, I sigh. "I know. But it won't be easy."

In my mind, this is the only option, but my heart has zero fucks for being patient. Hell, I'd ask her to marry me tomorrow if I knew it wouldn't freak her out. This trip has proved nothing but the fact I love her deeper than I've ever known. That goes for Julia, too.

"Brother, nothing worth having ever is. If everyone took the easy route, we'd all have Stepford wives. Boring and the same. I've seen the way that woman looks at you, as well as her daughter. They love you, too. I'm positive."

My darkest fear comes to light. "But with Zach back in her life, she may not have room for me."

"Grandma always says the heart is the only organ that has infinite room for growth," Derek reminds me.

Leave it to my fucking brother to pull out the big guns.

"Are you still sittin' in your truck?" Derek asks when I don't reply.

"Yeah."

"Get your ass in that store so you can get back to your girls."

God, the way he says 'my girls' makes me want to stake my claim and leave nothing unsaid to Vanessa. She needs to know where I stand and then if I have to, I'll give her all the time in the world.

Derek continues, "When Jules goes to bed, talk to Vanessa. I'm sure things will work out."

"Thanks, man," I say as I turn off the engine and climb out of my truck.

Unexpectedly, he chuckles.

"What?" I ask, curiosity getting the best of me.

"Looks like we're both at a crossroads, and major change is happening. With Dani getting married, maybe we all are— Davis doesn't count since he's not out of college yet. Though, his life is constantly changing."

"I guess you're right," I solemnly admit.

I just hope the path Vanessa chooses, leads to me.

35

VANESSA

MY MIND'S been spinning all day. Thankfully, Damien's given me space, and I've been able to process. I never in a million years expected Zach to reenter my life, especially with the way he abruptly left. But apparently, Dad had a big hand in it all. I wonder if Dad had been alive, would he have told me the full story someday.

I guess I'll never know.

Seeing that tattoo of Julia's birthday hit me harder than I expected. Hell, his entire backstory did. How could I date someone for so long and *not* know they lived in a group home? Either I was completely naïve, or he was good at hiding it. But that's not the point, is it? I'm sure he had his reasons for not disclosing things. No wonder we spent so much time at my place.

I liked him, but I'd never say I was in love with him. When he left me right after we had sex for the first time, that stung and left deep scars. Now that I know the circumstances, those wounds I thought I'd dealt with will finally heal.

Damien's been here all day, yet distant the same. At first, I was so lost in my head, I didn't even notice. But as I sit beside him on the couch, I notice he's not reaching for my hand or snuggling me like we usually would.

Sure, Jules is sprawled out on his other side, lying across his lap for a pillow. When she reaches for his hand and takes it, my chest tightens at his thoughtfulness. He loves Julia as much as he loves me, and I can't imagine my world without him.

She doesn't even make it thirty minutes into the movie she had chosen, but Damien and I have continued to sit here and watch the rest of it in silence, all the same. I'm not sure where his head is. Hell, I'm barely sure where mine's been. But one thing is certain, before we sleep tonight, there are many things he needs to hear.

As the ending credits roll, Damien yawns. "I'm gonna put her in her room. Be right back."

Damien had been sweet enough to rent a two-bedroom suite, so we'd have our space, and Jules would have hers. Thankfully, the living space is between each room, so we can have this much-needed talk—without interruptions.

"I'm gonna clean up our snacks, then we can head to bed," I offer quietly.

Within a few minutes, we're both in the bathroom brushing our teeth and getting ready for bed. I've been in my jammies since he returned from the store with more snacks than we'll ever eat on this trip. While he changes into his sleep pants, I make use of the privacy in the bathroom.

When I enter our bedroom, I notice he's shirtless and leaning against the headboard to the king-size bed. That act alone is sexy as sin, but when I look into his eyes, instead of need and sexual desire, I find them guarded and filled with worry. If it were any other night, I'd be climbing right onto that bed and having my way with him, but there's an elephant in the room that needs to be addressed before either of us will relax.

"Hey," I whisper as I make my way to my side of the bed.

"How are you holding up? You've had quite a day." Of course, he worries about me and puts my needs first.

"I'm doing okay," I admit. "It's been a lot to think about, that's for sure."

"I can imagine." Damien's voice is laced with concern, and I'm sure a million questions are on his mind, yet he won't voice them aloud if I'm not ready to talk just yet.

"I've learned some things that spun a different light on what I thought my reality was today. It's truly been a lot to process, to say the least."

Damien's brows knit together, and his worry line forms above his nose. "What do you mean?"

Knowing I need to start at the beginning, I sigh. "Apparently, Zach got into some trouble while we were dating, and my dad helped him. I was none the wiser. I also had no idea he'd been in a group home and had been in the foster care system growing up. He was too proud to share that part of his life with me."

"How did your dad help?"

"Well, I guess Zach was charged with a felony for possessions of stolen goods. He was able to work a plea deal, to roll on his friends, as well as who they worked for, and Dad helped him get off."

Shit, I need to explain more.

"This all happened before we even conceived Jules. Dad made Zach promise to walk away from me if he helped. Once we found out I was pregnant, Dad and Zach thought it best if he stayed away in case any of the gang members wanted to retaliate. That's why Zach signed over his rights as a parent. When Dad told me not to put his name on the birth certificate, I agreed because I was so pissed at the time. I wanted nothing to do with him."

"Wow. That must've been hard to hear."

"Not as hard as you'd think," I admit. "I knew I liked Zach —the way anyone would with a high school crush, but when he slept with me, then essentially disappeared, I became jaded. At the time, I was more infatuated with him—than ever being in love with him, ya know. It was exciting to do things with your first real boyfriend and easy to let lines cross."

"I can only imagine," Damien says as he shakes his head. "I wasn't in love with my first either, so I get what you're saying."

"I guess Dad sent him a pic on the day Julia was born— hence the tattoo. He never intended to be a deadbeat dad, but since our lives were at risk, he thought it best to keep his distance. Dad convinced him the only way he would get out of the system and break the cycle of poverty was to continue with his path to Annapolis—once he was declared innocent and the charges were dropped, of course. Apparently, when we started dating, Dad also helped secure his acceptance.

"Zach thought Dad was just keeping his distance when he no longer sent photos of Julia. He had no idea about the accident until years later—and by then, I'd moved, and he didn't want to interrupt my life."

Damien's voice is laced with concern when he asks, "How does that make you feel?"

"Honestly, I have no idea how I would've felt. I was working so hard to just get through the day and be the best mom I could be to Jules, I'm not sure I would've accepted his story back then."

"True. You've gone through so much," he says, reaching for my hand to place in his lap.

"For complete transparency, he'd like to at least stay updated in Julia's life. Neither of us are sure to what capacity he'd be. He's leaving the decision up to me. He's aware she knows nothing about him, and he'll accept even being a family friend, if that's what I want. But since he has such little family, I guess we'll have to cross that bridge when we get there. I need to do right by her and lying to her doesn't sit well with me."

Damien squeezes my hand and sighs. "She'll hate you for it if she finds out later."

"That's my gut feeling, too. I'll tell her the truth, but I think I'd like to talk it over with Zach some more, so we can figure out another time for them to meet. No one's ever prepared to drop a bomb on their child like this—trust me."

No kidding. But she never expected this to be the case.

"I have a feeling she'll handle this better than you'd imagine. She's so resilient and if you're honest with her, she can't fault you for it later. You didn't even know where he was until today—so eventually, she'll understand."

"True," I sigh, leaning into his chest. When he pulls me close, the tension I've been holding onto all day eases.

When he leans in and kisses the top of my head, for the first time all day, I feel like it's all gonna be okay—eventually.

"The thing is—I get what it's like to have limited or no family. It's been just Vince, Jules, and me against the world for so long. I can't fault Zach for wanting to be a part of his daughter's life."

"Do you think he'll be around often?"

"He's still at the Naval Academy in Annapolis, Maryland. Then if I got it right, he'll be a commissioned officer for at least five years after he graduates, so I'm sure what time he gets will be limited."

With that, Damien relaxes further, though I'm not sure why, so I ask, "What's going on?"

I feel the heavy sigh before I hear it, and Damien stays quiet for an unusual amount of time. When I can't take it anymore, I probe, "Talk to me, Dame. What's going on?"

"You've had plenty to deal with today. You don't need my insecurities added to the list."

What the hell is he talking about? He's one of the strongest people I know. Turning my entire body to face him so I can read his face better, I ask, "What insecurities?"

Looking to the ceiling, he bites his lower lip. "Do you remember when I said I hadn't dated anyone serious in a long time? Well..." he sighs. "There's a reason for it. You see, when I was in college, I got pretty serious with this girl Amber. We made plans, and I was about to propose to her. Like I seriously thought she was the one."

"Okay..." I draw out, wondering when the other shoe will drop; stories like this always do.

"Well, one day... we were walking through the U-District, and we ran into her ex-boyfriend. He'd graduated a few years before us, and he'd gone back home to Michigan. I thought things were fine until she dropped a bomb about two months later."

Oh, shit. She didn't.

But clearly, by the look on Damien's face, she did.

"Apparently, she'd been in contact with him since the day they reunited, and he wanted her back—she just didn't know how to tell me."

"I'm so sorry, Damien." There's no excuse for cheating. If you want to be with someone else—just end things.

"It was the end of the term, so over spring break, she packed her shit and moved to Michigan. Last I heard, she's married with a couple of kids."

Oh, this poor man. What he must've been going through today with Zach returning out of the blue. My chest squeezes when I realize he's probably waiting for me to do the same.

Trying to lighten the suddenly dark mood, I tease, "Well, I've got news for you, Damien...."

His dark brow arches skeptically. "Really? What's that?"

I wait until I have his full attention. "I'm not going anywhere."

A smile plays at his lips, and his eyes crinkle. "And why's that?"

"Well, I happen to be in love with *you*. I'd bet my last check Jules feels the same."

Reaching out, he cups my face. "Well, that's good because I love you both just as much."

Reaching for my hip, he guides me to straddle his lap. "If you keep looking at me like that, I might just have to show you how much I love you right now."

This sexy man. I swear all he has to do is smile as he runs his hands along my spine, and my panties melt off. When he pulls me in for a searing kiss, all my worries disappear. I love this man more than I could ever imagine.

Once he's kissed me senseless, I pull back and smile. "I guess life is like that old Garth Brooks' song. Thank God for unanswered prayers."

"I'm sorry you were hurt, don't get me wrong," I quickly spit out. "But maybe we were both meant to go through everything because it wasn't our time yet. We needed to meet now. When we were ready."

Damien doesn't have to say anything; his expression says it all. This man loves me so much. Leaning in, I kiss him once more.

When our kiss breaks all too soon, his brows pull together. "Wait... you're a country fan?"

What. The. Hell.

"After all I said, *that* is what you took from it?" I push against his chest to pull away, but he won't have it.

"Just where do you think you're going?"

"To sleep because I *obviously* was mistaken—you're *not* the one for me."

Pulling me in for a bear hug, he laughs. "Uh, country fan born and raised—I'm just shocked you are, too. That's all."

"My mom loved Garth. I swear I could sing every album by the time I was three. He and George Strait were her favorites. Why else do you think I call Jules Love Bug?"

Damien's deep laugh is felt before the sound erupts from his chest. "Vanessa—make me a deal. Let's never stop learning about each other."

"I think I can live with that." I grin then add cheekily, "Her favorite movie was *Top Gun*. *Take me to bed or lose me forever*." I mimic.

Damien doesn't miss a beat. "Show me the way home," as his lips land on mine.

36

DAMIEN

THE REST of the week with Jules and Vanessa flies by. We watch fireworks from the Seattle Center. We make it to the Space Needle, and we even manage to tour the Museum of Pop Culture. Julia loves the music exhibits and being able to play all the different instruments. Personally, I enjoy Paul Allen's sci-fi collection, too. By the time we get home, we aren't quite ready for our adventures to end, so we make a trip into Portland before picking Vince and Sydney up from the airport.

When I pull up to the curb at the airport, Vanessa doesn't wait for me to come to a complete stop before she's hopping out to hug her brother and Sydney.

When she pulls back from Sydney, she screams. "Ohmigod!" then she turns to her brother and squeezes the living hell out of him. He may be nearly a foot taller, but in this moment, I doubt he can breathe.

"What, Momma?" Jules hollers when she can't take not knowing anymore.

Sydney beats Vanessa when she shouts loud enough for the entire airport to hear, "Vince proposed!"

"Really, Unks?" Julia beams.

"I sure did, Squirt. Sydney and I are getting married!"

Immediately, Julia's eyes go to me, and her mouth snaps shut, sending me a clear message to get the ball rolling already.

"Congratulations!" I holler through the open door, and Julia repeats the sentiment adorably.

Vanessa offers Vince the front seat of my truck while she and Sydney hop in the crew cab, next to Julia. Vince quickly drops their luggage into the bed of the truck before joining us in the cab.

"We need to celebrate, and I need details," Vanessa gushes.

I only catch half of what they say, as I focus my attention on the heavy airport traffic. I'm sure Van will fill me in later. Turning to Vince, I offer, "Wanna grab a drink later this week to celebrate?"

He's quiet for a moment, likely listening to the girls in the back before he answers, "Yeah. Sure. Sounds good. I'm free tomorrow if you're interested."

"Tomorrow is good." I pretend to nod casually. Now, if only I can wait that long.

"Let's stop at that Thai restaurant, Vin. You know... the one we went to on our first date?"

"Sounds good to me," Vanessa quickly adds.

"Show me the way." I laugh. "Thai it is."

VINCE and I are heading out for drinks after dinner, and I have to say, I love this family. Hell, I want to make them mine, but they take *forever* to finish a meal. Especially when they have no clue I have important things to do tonight.

By the time Vince and I make it to the bar, I'm strung so tight, I need the beer to help me relax. We took an Uber since Syd's working, and Vanessa works in the morning. I do, too, but not nearly as early as her.

I would've preferred somewhere out of the way, but when Vince suggested the place where Syd works, I couldn't tell him no without raising some red flags at the dinner table.

When we get to the bar, I suggest sitting at a booth. I'm a nervous ball of energy, though I'm doing everything in my power not to let it show. I have no idea what he'll say, but knowing how important he is to Vanessa, his opinion certainly matters.

When I stare at my bottle of beer instead of taking a long pull, he asks, "Hey, man, is something going on?"

Shit. It's time to speak now or forever hold my peace.

Squaring my shoulders, I meet his gaze and nod. "Yeah."

This gets his full attention. Setting down his beer, he asks, "What is it?"

Swallowing one more time, I say, "I love your sister and Jules."

Chuckling, he says, "Well, thanks, captain obvious. I wouldn't know by the way you're over for dinner almost every night these days, or the fact the three of you went away for the week."

Just like his sister, he knows how to put me at ease, so I

laugh right along with him. "I know, right? Anyway..." I draw out. "I can't imagine my life without either of them in it. Traditionally, I should be having this conversation with your dad, but since he's not here, you're the lucky one."

Vince nods knowingly and waits for me to continue.

"Jules and I had a conversation the other day, and I want to start my forever with them as soon as possible."

"Really? How did that go?" Vince chuckles. "I'm sure she was far more intimidating than me."

"I guess weddings are in the air because Dani and Luke pulled off one hell of a surprise wedding," I start, then get to the point. "Jules asked what a fiancée was. I simply said it's someone who you want to marry. Of course, I neglected the part about the other person has to agree for it to become official. She got upset and thought I didn't want to marry your sister. But after I explained that crucial bit of information, she asked if I could be her daddy when I married Vanessa."

By the time I finish, Vince's brows are at his hairline, and his jaw dropped. "Man, she didn't pull any punches, did she?"

"Nope. But this is Julia we're talking about." I grin. "When has she ever not spoken her mind?"

Vince shakes his head. "The apple doesn't fall far from the tree—you've met my sister. Hell—all the women in my life speak their mind. Don't get me wrong, I wouldn't have it any other way, but you've been warned, and you know what you're in for."

"I take it you're okay with my plan then?"

"I've never seen my sister happier, Dame. Of course, I'm okay with it. Do you know when this might happen?"

"I bought a ring while we were in Seattle, and she doesn't have a clue," I admit. "She and Jules thought I'd stopped by a buddy's place who still lives near the U-District, while they had a girl date and saw a movie—but nope. I had another mission in mind."

"God, I'd love to see the look on her face when you ask, but I understand if you want to keep things private. I'm certainly not one to talk. I whisked Syd away and didn't think twice about it—Hell, I was supposed to wait until after graduation, but that didn't happen either. So, I can't blame you if you'd rather be alone."

I'd only thought far enough ahead to have this conversation with Vince. But as I look at Vince's eager expression, inspiration hits.

God, I just hope I can pull it off.

"I think I might need your help," I admit. Then I fill him in on my plan.

After a while, Syd stops by and to my surprise, Vince keeps everything I've just revealed between us. We finish off our beers and decide to call it an early night. As we share an Uber back to his place, my plan solidifies even further.

37

DAMIEN

SATURDAY MORNING AT THE DINER, Jack is in great spirits. Martha sits beside him, and they're a riot to watch. They didn't arrive together—as she showed up after me, but I'm fairly certain they're spending time outside the diner.

"How's that house of yours coming along?" Jack asks as he chews on a piece of bacon.

"I'm pretty close to finishing. You should come by some time and see what I've done to the place. I've still got some landscaping to do, but we could barbeque or something." Since Martha is here, I invite her to come along, too. "You're both welcome."

"I'd love to see the place," Jack says. "You've been talkin' all this time about it. I've got to see for myself if it's worth all the hype."

"It's beautiful, Jack," Vanessa interjects. "If I didn't have a place of my own, I'd buy his." Then she turns to Martha. "I've never seen a bigger tub. I could get lost in there for days. Don't even get me started on his customized closet.

"I never knew how much those mattered until you find yourself sharing half of nothing."

"What are you doing for dinner tonight?" I offer the group. "I'll pick up some steaks, and we can grill."

She just shrugs with an easy smile. "If I'm not cooking— I'm not complaining."

"What shall I bring?" Martha chimes in.

"Just yourself and this guy." I bump Jack with my shoulder.

"Gee... I'm so honored," Jack grumbles, then turns his attention to Vanessa. "I guess I'll come... as long as I get to see that beautiful girl of yours."

Rolling her eyes with the kind of smile that makes my heart constrict, Vanessa laughs. "I think that can be arranged. Do you mind if we invite my brother and his fiancée? I'd hate leaving them out."

"The more the merrier," I encourage, then turn to Jack and Martha. "You don't mind hanging out with a few of our friends, do you?"

"Only if you'll let me bring something..." Martha hedges. "I've been told I make a mean potato salad."

Jack deadpans, "Son, just let her bring somethin'. She's gonna do it anyway, so you may as well just accept it and get over it."

"Potato salad sounds great," I say a bit too enthusiastic, and Martha smirks.

"I'm so glad we both agree."

All of a sudden, Vanessa pulls out her phone from her back pocket with a panicked expression. Clearly, no one texts her at this hour unless there's an emergency. My stomach drops as she quickly reads it with a puzzled expression.

When I can no longer take the suspense, I ask, "Something wrong?"

As soon as she quickly taps out a reply, she refocuses her attention on me. "Uh... apparently Margo's in town today and wants to visit. I just invited her to the barbeque... Hope you don't mind."

"I'm looking forward to meeting her," I admit. "Of course she's welcome."

"I haven't been to a shindig in years. Are you sure you want two old birds crashing your party?" Jack clarifies.

"Watch who you're calling an old bird," Martha warns.

"Seriously, Jack. I'd like to show you my place. Besides, if you don't consider me a friend by now, you need to find another seat at the counter each day."

Jack harrumphs.

Vanessa interjects before either of us can say any more. "Jack—if you don't stop trying to get out of this, I might have to slip something into your coffee to make you more agreeable."

Holding his hands up as a defense, he surrenders, "Okay... Okay... I won't say another word—And I'll be there with bells on."

"Why don't you text Davis and invite him, too?" Vanessa says as she grabs another order to deliver.

LATER THAT EVENING, as I look around at our friends and family who've joined us, my heart feels full. Vanessa's never looked more beautiful or relaxed in her cut-off shorts and green tank as she mingles among the crowd.

Sydney's invited Chloe, and they're chatting away with Vanessa, Martha, and Margo on the patio furniture I'd recently purchased. Vince and Davis are playing cornhole with Jules and Jack.

We've already eaten our steaks with grilled asparagus. Martha's right, she does make a mean potato salad. Sydney brought her infamous cinnamon rolls for dessert that we'll have as soon as I do one last thing.

Standing in the center of the crowd, I shout, "Hey, everyone, can I get your attention?"

Slowly, everyone stops what they're doing and turns my way as my heart races with fresh adrenaline. Taking the necessary steps to stand beside Vanessa, I reach out and take her hand, pulling her beside me.

"First, I'd like to thank everyone for being here today. Each of you is an important part of my and Vanessa's life, and I'm happy you can be here to witness this."

Turning to Vanessa, her eyes practically bug out, and her chin remains dropped.

"Vanessa, you know I love you, and honesty is big for me, so... I have a confession to make."

Skeptically, she punches her hip with a fist as she cocks her head to the side and asks, "And that is?"

"This," I point around the backyard, "was orchestrated..."

Her brows knit as she looks around our friends and family. "What do you mean?"

"I mean, I wanted our close friends and family to be here tonight for a reason." Then I turn to Jules. "Jules, you should be here, too. Get over here."

In this moment, I'm on the verge of panic. Not over what I must say, but in the way I'm asking—so publicly. God, I hope I'm doing the right thing.

The minute Jules stands by my side, she reaches out her hand to mine and squeezes it tight. Then she stands by her mom and asks, "Momma, can I get a kitten?"

Shocked at the randomness, Vanessa shakes her head. "Not today, sweet girl."

Not fazed in the slightest, she looks to me and grins. "What about a daddy? Can I get one of those?"

Vanessa's head pivots so fast I'm afraid she might get whiplash. "What did you say?"

Julia just shrugs and repeats, "What about a daddy?" as I kneel and present a red leather box in my hand on her other side.

"Uh..." Vanessa stutters. "I'm afraid it doesn't work that way..."

"It does if you say yes," I interject, holding out the box in my hand.

I swear, if we weren't outside with infinite air supply, Vanessa would've sucked all the air from the room in an instant.

When she turns to me, her hand flies to cover her open mouth, and her eyes have never been bigger. "W... what?"

"Vanessa, I'm in love with both you and Jules. As you pointed out, you're kinda a package deal... So, of course, I needed to include her in this, too."

"Momma," Jules says louder than necessary, "will you marry Dame so we can be a family?"

Vanessa's shocked expression looks between me and her daughter. Her jaw may never rehinge if she doesn't close it soon. But I just point to Jules. "What she said."

Laughter can be heard throughout the crowd, but all I can focus on by bated breath is Vanessa's answer.

"Vanessa, I love you more than anything, and I need to spend the rest of my life with you. Forever won't ever be enough, but can we start with today? What do you say, will you marry me?"

Vanessa's frozen for what feels like an eternity before she drops to her knees and hugs me fiercely. Then she pulls back and kisses the fuck out of me.

Not that I'm complaining, but she still hasn't said the magic word—to make things official.

Jules beats me to asking the question, "Does that mean yes?"

Tears stream down Vanessa's cheeks as she wordlessly nods profusely.

"Words, honey!" Jack shouts out. "We all need words, or you're gonna give us a heart attack."

Through laughter and tears, the most beautiful word finally arrives, "Yes!"

EPILOGUE

Vanessa

ONCE AGAIN, we're gathered around family and friends as we take in another momentous occasion. Through the years, our family has grown in ways I've never imagined. It's hard to believe it was just Vinnie, Jules, and me against the world after my parents died.

But when I found Damien, that all changed. Instantly, his family took my motley crew in and claimed them as their own. Like Beatrice always says, the heart will always make room to love more people.

That day Damien proposed in our backyard was the first of many events to take place there. It's where we announced the genders of our twin boys, Jordan and Jasper. It's where we celebrated birthdays, anniversaries, and graduations.

Today, we have a new reason to celebrate.

Today, my baby girl's getting married. She may be twenty-six and a registered nurse like me—but she'll always be my little girl.

My sons co-escort me down the aisle to take my place near the altar we've set up at the end of the yard, where Damien will join me once he's finished with his duties. Vince reaches forward to squeeze my shoulder, and I send a secret prayer to my parents, thanking them for watching over us all these years. Yes, this is another moment they've missed—but I know in every fiber of my being, they're here with me.

Zach and his wife sit on the other side of the empty chair left for Damien. True to his word, he let Julia and I set the terms of his involvement in Julia's life. Eventually, as time went on, they got to know one another and have made up for lost time. He's still in the Navy and has two more kids with Nancy, and they sit behind us, with Vince and his crew. We may not be what you'd call a traditional family—but we're family and love each other all the same.

Jules chose Damien to walk her down the aisle on this momentous occasion. Maybe it's because he adopted her—so we could all share the same last name—maybe it's because she's always had a special bond with him. But no matter the reason, he was practically in tears over the gesture.

Those two have been two peas in a pod from the moment they concocted the plan to bring us together as a family. She's always been such a smart cookie. I never imagined the course of my entire world as I knew it was set into motion when I got pregnant with her. For years, she was my anchor, my rock, and now that she's become a woman—one of my closest friends.

When the music cues, and I stand to see my baby walk

down the aisle, I've never been more thankful for waterproof mascara. Tears flow freely as the man I love most in this world walks my sweet Julia down the aisle.

Damien's hair might be a little lighter at the temples, and his face may have a few more laugh lines, but he's still a handsome man who makes my belly flip—the way it did when he walked into the diner so many years ago.

Damien in a suit—well, that just isn't fair. My mouth dries, and my tongue sticks to the roof of my mouth. As I push back the tears, I breathe carefully to steady my emotions.

When the minister asks, "Who gives this woman away?"

Damien's voice practically chokes with emotion. "Her parents do."

He never has wanted to outshine Zach. To him, being a father isn't a competition—but just a part of him he never knew was missing—until he met Julia. He's the best father in the world to all our kids, and he wholeheartedly lives his grandma's motto. *There's always room to love more—your ticker is the one organ that expands without you even being aware.*

Boy, has my heart learned to expand. My cup runs over with joy just thinking about it. When Damien takes his seat next to me, he squeezes my hand tight as he leans in. "I'd marry you all over again—if it meant getting to join this crazy, chaotic, wonderful life you live. Little did I know, getting you to take a chance on me would be one of the best rewards imaginable. I love you, Vanessa. Crazy life and all."

The End

Want more of the Fallon Family?

Find out how Dani and Luke began in Making the Call or See what's next for Derek in The Boy Upstairs (Releasing October 28, 2021).
You can find out everything about these stories on my website.

www.amandashelley.com

ABOUT THE AUTHOR

Amanda Shelley writes romantic stories you can escape into. Some are steamy, others are sweet but all have strong characters with a little bit of sass.

When not writing, Amanda enjoys time with her family, playing chauffeur, chef and being an enthusiastic fan for her children. Keeping up with them keeps her alert and grounded in reality. She enjoys long car rides, chai lattes and popping her SUV into four-wheel drive for adventures anywhere.

Amanda loves hearing from readers. Be sure to sign up for her newsletter and follow her on social media. Join her reader's group Amanda's Army of Readers to stay up to date on her latest information.

Readers group: https://www.facebook.com/
groups/AmandasArmyofReaders/
Goodreads: https://www.goodreads.com/author/show/
19713563.Amanda_Shelley
Newsletter: https://bit.ly/3iyENe6
www.amandashelley.com

ACKNOWLEDGMENTS

First, I would like to thank you the reader, blogger, and reviewer for taking the time to read this book. There are so many stories to choose from, and I'm humbly honored you've chosen to read mine. I hope you enjoyed Damien and Vanessa's story. As I wrote about Damien's family, I realized I'm not done with them yet... There's two brothers who will get their own stories eventually—so this won't be the last you hear from them.

I'd love to hear from you and your thoughts about Damien and Vanessa. You can find me on social media, my reader's group *Amanda's Army of Readers*, or at www.amandashelley.com. If you care to share your thoughts on this book with other book lovers, please consider leaving a review at any of the retail sites or on Goodreads, BingeBooks and BookBub.

I'd like to thank Amy Queau at Q Design Covers and Premades for creating this incredible cover. You took my vision for this series and brought it to life and with those images, I'm dying to keep writing this series. Thank you so much for your brilliance!

This book wouldn't be what it is without my amazing team of support. To Renita McKinney at A Book A Day Author Services, thank you for helping me develop Damien and Vanessa's characters and make them into the best they can be.

To Susan Soares at SJS Editorial Services, thank you for working with me. This book wouldn't be what it is today without you. I appreciate your time and feedback. You are amazing to work with.

To Julie Deaton at Deaton Author Services, thanks for making my book pretty. I appreciate knowing your proof-reading is exquisite, and my worries disappear. Your eagle eyes are spectacular, and I don't know what I'd do without you. PS —you can never retire!

To Mickel Yantz, thank you for designing my chapter images. Little did you know as a graphic designer, you'd not only help me create beautiful images, but you'd be talking plots and become one of my beta readers. I appreciate your subtle reminders to stay on track more than you'll ever know.

To the people who have supported me along the way, I'm humbly grateful to have you in my life. Whether you've read my books, asked me about my progress, listened to me talk about my fictional characters as if they're a part of my family, plotted with me, or been my cheerleader, I appreciate your continued support. Please know it hasn't gone unnoticed.

Last but certainly not least, to my four beautiful girls who have had to wait patiently when I said, "Just one more minute," when I obviously meant a lot more than one. I love that you get that I have deadlines and will sometimes keep me on task with your not-so-subtle reminders that "Mom... you should be working" during my designated times. I appreciate your support more than you'll ever know. Even though you can't read these books—because that might be *weird*—for both of us, I love that you keep asking. I love you all more than words can express. You're the reason I continue to strive and reach for my goals each day.

ALSO BY AMANDA SHELLEY

Coming September 28 2021

Fix Your Crown Anthology

Everyone has been affected by cancer in some way or another. We know someone living with cancer or may even have it yourself. I recently joined the Fix Your Crown Anthology where me and 14 other amazing woman authors are taking the proceeds we make and donating to cancer research. For just 99 cents you could help fund badly needed research. Let's stop cancer in its tracks as soon as we can.

Pre-order Fix Your Crown for only 99 cents and immediately receive (7) complimentary books from the authors of the anthology! That's (22) books in total for a buck! Fix Your Crown is available on all major e-retailers!

Participating Authors: Alexi Ferreira, Amanda Shelley, Amaya Black, Angela Sanders, Barb Shuler, Brittany Tarkington, Callie Rae, E.K. Woodcock, Jade Bay, Jami Denise, Jo Richardson, Khloe Summers, Ruby Wolff, Sofia Aves and Tanya Nellestein

What you'll get from me... My story in this anthology is Hoops & Scoops. It features Chloe and DeShawn from the Perfectly Independent series. You won't want to miss their beginning.

Hoops & Scoops

When the one that got away shows up unexpectedly in my living room—I'm shocked.

When she pretends to be a stranger—I'm not having it.

There's no way she doesn't remember.

But I know her weakness—it comes in a pint and best eaten with a spoon.

I need to convince her that hoops aren't my only priority, or I won't stand a chance.

Coming October 26, 2021

The All-American Boy Series description

Welcome to Bear Creek, Colorado, an idyllic all-American mountain resort town and home of the USA Music Festival. Filled with summer love, country music and unexpected pleasures, this brand-new series of short contemporary stories will bring together a mix of summer fun and music with the backdrop of the Colorado Rocky Mountains.

The All-American Boy Series gives you a taste of 16 new books in a shared world experience. All books are standalone but may include cross-over in characters or scenes.

Series page: https://www.subscribepage.com/all-american-boy-series

The Boy Upstairs

I ran into Derek while trying to escape the neighbor from hell.

Instantly, we hit it off. Since he's only here for three months and the microbrewery leaves me little time for commitments, it's the perfect setup for a fling.

He's adventurous, challenges me, and he just gets me from the inside out.

With our expiration date quickly approaching, I'm left to wonder… Will my heart ever be the same without the boy upstairs?

https://amandashelley.com/books-by-amanda-shelley-2/

Now Available

Drew: Book One of the Perfectly Independent Series

My heart races, palms sweat and knees go weak.

I've never seen anyone like Drew in a science lab. He's made me a firm believer in chemistry existing outside a textbook.

Then his ego shows up.

Nope – No thank you. Moving on. I mean... who has an entourage in college?

When our professor announces we'll be stuck as lab partners, I nearly lose my mind – and not in a good way.

I can't afford the type of distractions Drew brings.

https://amandashelley.com/books-by-amanda-shelley-2/

Vince: Book Two of the Perfectly Independent Series

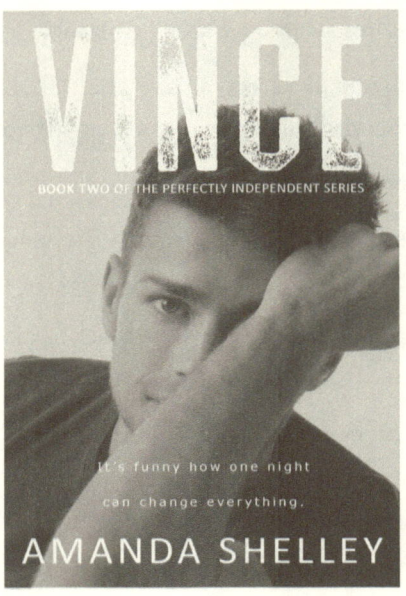

It's funny how one night can change everything.

When Sydney walks into my life she knocks my world off kilter.

She's strong, sexy, independent and possibly more than I can handle. She's everything I've ever wanted, but my reality and the secret I'm harboring, might have her running in the other direction.

Will my perfectly laid out plans go up in flames if I take a chance on her?

https://amandashelley.com/books-by-amanda-shelley-2/

Making The Call

Dani

As a bestselling romance author, most assume my life's glamorous, filled with combustible chemistry, and most of all, romance. Ha! I can only wish. With a deadline looming, I've escaped to my family's cabin on Anderson Island to free myself from distractions. My plan's great, until a man, who could pass as a cover model on one of my books, comes to my rescue. Is there chemistry? Sure. Is he everything I'd look for in a guy? Absolutely. But will my career be at risk if I give into my desire?

Luke

For a player, women line up outside the locker room. For coaches, we're lucky to get in the game. As the youngest NFL coach in the league, I live, eat, breathe, and even sleep football. To gear up for this season, I return to my home on Anderson Island for a much-needed break. When Dani literally crashes into my life, my mind's suddenly on the sexy brunette with a sailors mouth, rather than my team's next play. She has me dusting off another playbook entirely, making me wonder, did I make the right call?

https://amandashelley.com/books-by-amanda-shelley-2/

Resilience: Book One of Resilience Duet

Resolution: Book Two of Resilience Duet

Samantha never saw Enzo coming.

As the dust settles from her divorce, her life is full. She doesn't have time for distractions. She's too busy running her own company and checking off numerous items from her kids' demanding schedule to have a life of her own.

Then he walks into her kitchen with his breathtaking green eyes and a mischievous grin. He's there to surprise his father - her contractor, but his presence makes everything off kilter.

Enzo's perfectly content with his adventurous life as an elite rescue pilot, until a harmless prank turns on him. Instead of surprising his father, he finds his world thrown off course by the beautiful woman with a sexy smile, wicked sass and the mouthwatering ability to keep him on his toes.

With his limited time on leave, is she worth the risk to his heart?

https://amandashelley.com/books-by-amanda-shelley-2/

Collide: A Sweet Romance

Falling head over heels was the last thing I expected.

Literally.

Coffee is everywhere – and more than my ego is bruised.

When the handsome stranger I plowed into calls me by name, mortification sinks in.

He rushes off to class. I run home to change, hoping to forget the whole incident.

If only I could be so lucky.

I quickly find it's a small world and Gavin Wallace is completely unavoidable. Everywhere I turn he's there. In my classes. Hanging with my friends.

I've got his full attention and I have to admit, I like it a lot more than I should.

https://amandashelley.com/books-by-amanda-shelley-2/